PENGUIN BOOKS

You Float My Boat

Lulu Moore is the creator of The New York Players series, The Tuesday Club series, The New York Lions – the worst team in the MLB – and the upcoming Valentine Nook Chronicles.

Most recently she's ventured across the Atlantic to where her latest series – Oxbridge – is set, in the beautiful cities of Oxford and Cambridge, against the backdrop of the annual rowing showdown on the River Thames.

You'll find her navigating her way through Romance Land one HEA at a time, and trying to figure out the latest social media platform she needs to post to.

Also by Lulu Moore

The New York Players Series
Jasper
Cooper
Drew
Drew: The Vegas Edition (extended prologue)
Felix
Huck

The Tuesday Club Trilogy
The Secret
The Suit
The Show

The New York Lions Series
The Third Baseman
The Shake Off
The Baller

The Valentine Nook Chronicles
Once Upon a Christmas Tree

The Oxbridge Series
Oar Than Friends
You Float My Boat

You Float My Boat

The Oxbridge Series
Book Two

LULU MOORE

PENGUIN BOOKS

PENGUIN BOOKS

UK | USA | Canada | Ireland | Australia
India | New Zealand | South Africa

Penguin Books is part of the Penguin Random House group of companies whose addresses can be found at global.penguinrandomhouse.com

Penguin Random House UK,
One Embassy Gardens, 8 Viaduct Gardens, London SW11 7BW

penguin.co.uk

First published 2025

002

Copyright © Lulu Moore, 2025

The moral right of the author has been asserted

Penguin Random House values and supports copyright. Copyright fuels creativity, encourages diverse voices, promotes freedom of expression and supports a vibrant culture. Thank you for purchasing an authorized edition of this book and for respecting intellectual property laws by not reproducing, scanning or distributing any part of it by any means without permission. You are supporting authors and enabling Penguin Random House to continue to publish books for everyone. No part of this book may be used or reproduced in any manner for the purpose of training artificial intelligence technologies or systems. In accordance with Article 4(3) of the DSM Directive 2019/790, Penguin Random House expressly reserves this work from the text and data mining exception.

Set in 12.5/14.75pt Garamond MT Std
Typeset by Jouve (UK), Milton Keynes
Printed and bound in Great Britain by Clays Ltd, Elcograf S.p.A.

The authorized representative in the EEA is Penguin Random House Ireland, Morrison Chambers, 32 Nassau Street, Dublin D02 YH68

A CIP catalogue record for this book is available from the British Library

ISBN: 978–1–405–96743–3

Penguin Random House is committed to a sustainable future for our business, our readers and our planet. This book is made from Forest Stewardship Council® certified paper.

This book is for anyone who's spent time looking for something, only to find it was right in front of them the whole time.

Contents

Note to my Readers — ix

1 Charlie (Kissing with tongues: To be, or not to be?) — 1

2 Violet (And there he was just walking down the street . . .) — 17

3 Charlie (Does anyone have a JCB I could borrow?) — 33

4 Charlie (Charlie and Violet's Rules for Fake Dating) — 51

5 Violet (That Instagram Life) — 65

6 Charlie (Once more unto the breach . . . or something like that) — 79

7 Violet (There is no emoji more confusing than the winky face) — 99

8 Charlie (Who needs sleep anyway?) — 113

9 Violet (Every day's a school day. Or, Charlie Masterson learns something new) — 123

10 Charlie (Because of course I had to go and open my big mouth) — 129

11 Violet (When the day takes an unexpected turn) — 141

12 Charlie (The Violet Effect) 161

13 Violet (Maturity is overrated) 177

14 Charlie (February 14th – also known
as Valentine's Day) 191

15 Violet (Charlie doesn't share) 207

16 Charlie (Just call me Mary Berry) 219

17 Violet (Bone: verb. Slang. To have sex) 233

18 Charlie (Sex. It's like riding a bike . . .) 249

19 Violet (SHIT. Triple word score, 21 points) 265

20 Charlie (Real v crocodile = angry Charlie) 275

21 Violet (Shakespeare was right, the course
of true love never did run smooth) 287

22 Charlie (Shakespeare was an idiot.
Nothing's fair in love or war . . .) 309

23 Charlie (At this rate I could put Mary Berry
out of a job . . . but not the Poet Laureate) 325

24 Violet (Dogs > boys) 341

25 (Warning: the Boat Race may cause heart
palpitations) 355

Epilogue 379
Acknowledgements 385

Note to my Readers

Dear Readers,

Welcome back to the Oxbridge Series, it's so wonderful to have you here.

While *You Float My Boat* is set in the beautiful city of Oxford, against the background of Oxford University and the Boat Race, please remember it is a work of fiction. You may find some creative liberties because they work better for Charlie and Violet's story, so I ask your forgiveness in advance if that's the case.

Happy reading, I hope you love Charlie and Violet as much as I do. I can't wait to hear what you think, and I'll see you on the Thames riverbank in April.

Lulu xo

1. Charlie

(Kissing with tongues: To be, or not to be?)

Violet Brooks was officially late.

I'd already been warned by her brother that she would be, which is why I'd arrived a quarter of an hour after the time I'd given her, but that was forty-five minutes ago.

I checked my watch again; it didn't make the hands move any quicker. Neither had drumming my fingers against the table, or tapping my foot, or glancing at the door every two seconds. I'd have left if I wasn't so desperate for her help.

The condensation slid down the outside of my glass of soda water. Even though it was freezing outside, and snow was beginning to fall thickly, the fire I was sitting beside made the Blue Oar seem positively tropical. It was also quieter in here than usual seeing as it was technically still the Christmas holidays, but by the weekend the place would once again be heaving with students gearing up for the new term.

I glanced out of the windows, where there was still no sign of Violet. I'd already read through one of the daily newspapers left on the bar, so I picked my phone up and typed out some formulas I'd been thinking about for my physics paper – may as well not completely waste my time sitting here.

I was deep in thought about all possible solutions of

$F = -kX$, when a flurry of white snowflakes whooshed through the air as the doors flung open. The Christmas decorations, yet to be taken down from the ceiling, blew around, barely hanging on by their single silvery threads. The air cleared to reveal a girl standing on the threshold of the pub, and the doors slammed shut behind her. Her bright blue eyes scanned around, widening as they landed on me.

'Chazzle!'

The fluffy emerald-green coat, which a poor Muppet had been skinned for, had already been shucked off her shoulders by the time she arrived at the table.

The scarf came next: metres and metres of multi-coloured cashmere that looked more like a blanket big enough to keep a family of five warm. I stood as she yanked off her large, navy knitted hat with a giant pink bobble on the end of it and dropped into the chair opposite.

'Sorry, sorry, overslept.'

Overslept?

I certainly wasn't a fan of early mornings, but it was two in the afternoon.

'God, it's bloody boiling in here,' Violet exclaimed, and proceeded to remove another layer of clothing, this time a black polo neck to reveal a tight white vest, and I briefly wondered if maybe she'd been wearing it in bed, and thrown on the nearest items of clothing she could find before running here. I pushed that thought away only for her tits to squash together as her arms crossed and she pulled the neck of the jumper over her head, finally freeing herself from the confines of cashmere.

I forced myself to focus on a spot over her left shoulder until she stopped wriggling about. Staring at a girl's breasts was a big no-no, staring at my best friend's sister's tits currently snuggled into a green lace bra was *absolutely* forbidden under any circumstance.

Long caramel-blonde curls, the colour of my golden retriever, Magic, tumbled over her shoulders. Except the bottom inch looked like it had been dipped in purple paint – violet paint – contrasting with the deep azure of her eyes, ringed in navy, and the rosy flush of her cheeks.

Finally, she sat back and looked up at me, the whirlwind she'd walked in with calmed, but in less than a second she sprang up from her chair.

'Sorry, I didn't hug you hello.'

I was still yet to say a word and found myself pulled into a hot embrace as she pressed hard against me. She was raised on her tiptoes as her arms wrapped around my neck, but still managed to reach my six-feet-four height without too much effort. Her lips brushed against my cheek and the scent of dark violets and woody amber invaded my nasal passages, making my chest tighten.

'Well, Chazzle, long time no see.' She grinned, picking up my pint of sparkling water and taking a massive gulp. 'Can't wait to hear what you summoned me for. Huey wouldn't tell me. Have you been working out, you look bigger? How's training?'

I blinked, staring as I tried to make sense of the staccato firing of words, before a broad grin spread across my face.

'Violet?'

3

'Yes,' she finally paused her ramble.

'Would you like a drink?'

'Yes, please,' she replied, picking up mine again and downing the rest. 'Maybe something a little more alcoholic than water this time.'

I walked over to the bar, ordering a glass of Pinot Noir for her and a pint for me. I had planned to cut alcohol out until after the Boat Race, but in hindsight this conversation would probably need it. While I waited to pay, my eyes found themselves wandering over in her direction.

The last time I saw Violet Brooks she'd been a gangly seventeen-year-old. It was the summer after our first year had ended – Brooks, Oz and I had been at Brooks' parents' house in Somerset, where we all chilled out after the Henley Regatta, sleeping, swimming and eating for a week before we'd left for Greece with Oz.

Violet had finished her A-levels and was packing for a year abroad – she'd been a tornado spinning through the rooms, leaving chaos in her wake. That week I must have met a dozen of Violet's friends, all exactly the same as her, parading through the always open front door at the Brooks' house. Unlike her brother, who kept a tight circle of friends, Violet seemed to allow anyone entry into her world. The more the merrier.

Now, sat here, her long legs were crossed underneath her, and I peered down at her shoes – Nike high-tops. At six feet four, it was unusual to meet a girl where a hug didn't result in neck strain from them clinging onto me, but Violet had clearly inherited the Brooks' family height.

It had been eighteen months and she'd both completely changed and hardly changed at all. The chaos was still there, but the softness in her features had hardened a little, turning her from teenager to woman, and nothing short of stunning.

Tapping my bank card, I walked back to the table and placed the drinks on it before settling into my seat.

Violet's eyes reminded me of a twilight sky as she spied the wine, 'Mmm, thank you.'

'You're welcome.'

'So,' she sipped, put her glass down and leaned back in her chair. I forced my gaze straight ahead instead of at her chest where her arms were now crossed, 'what's the emergency?'

Ah, yes, the reason we were here and the reason I'd sent Violet not one but four messages, and another two to Brooks begging him to get her to reply.

'Didn't Brooks tell you anything?'

She shook her head. 'No, Hugo is incredibly annoying that way.'

I sighed.

I'd kind of hoped he would have done, then I'd have to explain as little as possible because Violet just *got it* and would agree to my request without further need for clarification. It would also save me from reliving the worst moment of my life; the day my heart had shattered so violently it couldn't be mended or glued back together.

It had imploded into dust.

The day I vowed never to love again.

'You haven't been over to the house,' I started,

hoping a little small talk would ease the anxiety ball in the pit of my stomach, the way it did whenever I thought about Evie Waters.

Violet leaned forward, the movement forcing a thick lock of hair to fall over her eye which she pushed away. Her slender wrists rested on the table and I noticed a tiny, hand-drawn stack of books on the inside of her left arm, directly above her pulse.

'I have, only you've not been there. It was very handy that the three of you were on river duty every Saturday morning. Huey's bath is wasted on him,' she smirked.

The pint glass stopped halfway to my lips, and I put it back down. 'Have you been breaking into our house when we're not there so you can have a bath?'

'No, of course not.' Violet shook her head. 'I have a key.'

I stared at her, my frown deepening. I knew that Oz would never have given anyone a key to the house we shared with Brooks, just like I knew that Brooks would never have given his sister a key without asking us.

I was also struggling to understand how the comprehensive security system I'd set up hadn't been triggered, because there was a hidden camera angled on the front door and it was supposed to alert us of anyone who approached. Not to mention the alarm we set every time we left, along with motion sensors in the garden.

Was it overkill for three students? Probably, even if one was Oz with his billions. But I'd been bored, and it had only taken me a couple of hours on a Tuesday morning after we'd moved in and finished unpacking.

Master of security systems was another skill to stick on my resumé. Or maybe not, it seemed.

'But how did you get the key?'

'I borrowed Huey's,' she shrugged, 'and copied it.'

I barked out a loud laugh. I wasn't sure what I was laughing at more, the look on Brooks' face when he discovered his sister had stolen his house key, or the idea of Violet having a bath in our house every Saturday when we were in London … no … nope … absolutely not … my brain ground to a halt for the second time … the image of Violet naked and wet in our house was not something that belonged in my head.

'You could just ask.'

'Where's the fun in that?' she winked. 'It wouldn't annoy Huey nearly as much. I don't have a bath in my room, not sure where I'll get my relaxing soak in the tub this term now you three have finished your punishments.'

'Which college are you in?'

'St Anne's.' She picked up her wine and sipped, the burgundy liquid matching the glossy paint on her fingernails. 'Come on, Charlie. Don't keep a girl waiting, *why* have I been summoned?'

I drummed my fingers against my pint glass again. Thinking about it, maybe I was being stupid. Overreacting. I could handle seeing my ex-girlfriend, I was a grown man and it had been four years, give or take. But then I remembered the anger ripping through me when I found out she'd been assigned to my philosophy tutorials, and decided otherwise.

'I need you to be my fake girlfriend until the end of

term.' I managed not to stumble over my words, even though I spat them out as quickly as possible.

Violet held my stare. To her credit she didn't flinch, nor did she burst out laughing; the only indication she'd heard me was the tiny crease in the centre of her forehead. She stared until it dawned on me that she wanted further explanation.

'My ex-girlfriend is joining my philosophy class, and I don't want her to think I'm interested in her again.'

Out loud, to someone who didn't know the history of Evie Waters, this plan sounded rather stupid. I couldn't blame Violet when the tiny crease on her forehead deepened.

'Why can't you just tell her you're not? And why do you assume that she's interested in you?'

Both very good and valid questions. If only the answer was as simple. The answer was more than I cared to admit, because Evie had been the love of my life – my first love – and I knew it wouldn't take long for her to wrap me around her little finger again. She would pull me back. It happened once before, I wouldn't let it happen again.

She was the drug of choice for my addict heart.

She was equally as toxic.

'Evie and I were together during sixth form. She cheated on me, and we broke up. When I started at Oxford, she was here too and we briefly got back together, but then she met someone else.' My fist clenched ever so tightly causing cramp to shoot along my arm. 'I've managed to avoid her for three years, but for some reason she always seems to think she can get me back. And this term she's joining my philosophy class. I figured if she knew I had a girlfriend then she wouldn't talk to me.'

There, that was enough explanation without revealing the sheer panic I felt at the thought of being in the same room as Evie again. I might be strong enough to bench press 180kg, but I was no match for Evie Waters, no matter how hard I tried.

I'd never told anyone the reason I changed my number in first year was because she wouldn't stop texting me.

Violet sat back, pulling the stem of her glass to the edge of the table, and shifted it side to side between her fingers as she looked at me.

'Charlie, do you want to make her jealous?'

I shook my head so hard my neck cracked. 'No.'

'You don't want her back?'

'Fuck, no. Never.'

'So you want me to be your bodyguard,' Violet began, a smirk cresting the corner of her plump lips, 'I'm Kevin Costner and you're my Whitney Houston?'

I wasn't sure how I felt about being called someone's Whitney Houston, but I shrugged anyway.

'Why can't you say no to her?'

'Because . . .' I sighed again, almost pathetically, 'because she has this way of making me do what she wants. It's like I'm under her spell, against my will.'

Violet's head tilted slightly, I couldn't tell if she was curious or pitying me. Either way, the silence stretched on far longer than I was comfortable with, made worse by the thoughts I imagined were playing out in her head.

I could probably guess.

'Violet, I'll pay you. Name your price.'

She grinned wide, her smile lighting up her face. The heat of the fire had deepened the flush in her cheeks, and the reflection of the flames danced in her eyes.

'I'm not going to take your money, silly. I'll do it for free. It'll be the perfect experience for *Twelfth Night*. I'm hoping to get the lead. Auditions are next week.'

'Oh,' I replied, wondering why her response felt so anti-climactic, and what *Twelfth Night* had to do with anything. 'What were you thinking about then?'

'What a girlfriend of yours would look like. I need to fit the part.'

I laughed, and the ball of anxiety stopped bouncing. 'I think you fit just as you are.'

'We'll see, I like to throw myself all in.'

'Are you studying drama?' I asked, realizing I didn't know.

'English. But I joined the Dramatic Society, and my friend Cecily is directing *Twelfth Night* at the Oxford Playhouse in May.' Her eyes widened, *dramatically*. 'And you're studying philosophy? Do you like Nietzsche?'

'I'm studying physics, actually. But I have physics and philosophy this term.'

'Oh, what's that?'

'We try to answer the complexities of the universe.'

'Good luck with that.'

'Thank you.' I grinned back, picking up my pint.

'How are we going to do this then?' She waved her hand between the two of us.

I scratched along my jaw. I'd been so fixated on

having Violet be my fake girlfriend that I hadn't actually taken any time to consider *how* she'd be my fake girlfriend.

'Um . . . well, I guess you'll have to meet me after class.'

'Yes, obviously. And . . . ?'

'And what?'

'What else?'

'What do you mean?'

'Charlie, if we're in a relationship, it's going to consist of more than me meeting you after class. What about hand-holding? Kissing? Touching? If we're going to do it, we have to do it properly.'

I coughed up the air which stuck in my throat. 'Kissing?'

Violet leaned forward, her fingers laced together and propped under her chin. 'Yes, Charlie, kissing. You need to be convincing. We're not courting in a Jane Austen novel.'

Shit.

None of this had occurred to me. Kissing or touching of any kind. I assumed that Evie would see us together and that would be enough. Maybe I needed to think this through more. I'd assured Brooks that nothing would happen between Violet and me, yet kissing didn't quite fall into that category. Maybe I could stipulate I meant no tongues.

No tongues would be acceptable. I hoped.

'Okay,' Violet slapped her palms on the table and pushed herself to standing, 'while you think on that, I'm going to the loo.'

11

The entire time we'd been talking, the Blue Oar's navy doors had been opening every couple of minutes as new patrons came in from the cold. Every time a small gust of wind had blown past causing the flames to crackle and spit in annoyance. I'd stopped getting distracted by it after Violet had sat down and I'd been sucked into her orbit.

I was still thinking about how I'd explain kissing her to Brooks when another burst of air flurried past me. The temperature dropped immediately, much more than any other gust before it.

I glanced at the offender. My heart stopped dead. My stomach curled in on itself.

Offender was too kind a word.

Evie Waters.

If I didn't know better, I'd swear she had a tracker on me. But I secured my phone enough to know that wasn't possible. She had always had a sixth sense for where I was going to be.

Like a bad smell following me wherever I went.

No, it was worse than that. It was like being summoned by a demon.

She'd once been the most beautiful girl I'd ever met. She still was.

Aside from a handful of times when I'd seen her outside my tutorials or walking my way in the library, and done a swift about-turn and sprinted through the stacks, I hadn't seen her in 562 days. But nothing had changed.

Her hair was so dark and shiny I'd once joked I could see my reflection in it. Straighter than an arrow, falling in a sharp line to her even sharper jaw, there was not a hair out of place. Even the snow falling outside didn't appear to have touched her.

I wish I didn't know she woke up like that, each strand falling perfectly where it was supposed to be, like it daren't do otherwise. Or the way her cheeks were always the same shade of pink as her lips, her ice blue eyes as cold as her heart and her eyelashes as black and thick as her soul. There had been a time when she'd only have to bat them at me and I'd fall over myself to do her bidding.

The thing I hated most of all, though, was the way my heart was now thumping and my dick twitching. Like neither of them remembered what she'd done. Or maybe my dick did, and that's why he suddenly wanted to give her his full attention. Even worse, the way she knew what was happening because the second her eyes landed on mine, I knew she was in here looking for me, and from the slow, sly curve of her lip she knew I knew.

I'd all but forgotten exactly why I was in the Blue Oar on a snowy Wednesday afternoon in January until a large unidentified lump collapsed into my lap. Unless it was the asteroid I'd just been praying for.

Except asteroids didn't kiss.

The taste of the Pinot I'd bought Violet was still fresh on her tongue as it slowly slid against mine, licking me with as much heat as the flames next to us. I was so shocked I did nothing to stop it. What's more, I didn't want to stop it, especially when she moaned softly because then all I could think about was how perfectly her arse fitted into my lap, and how I liked the way her fingers were pushing into my hair. My dick definitely liked it.

'Come on, babe. I've had enough of being out of bed, let's go back,' she whispered against my lips, and my brain short-circuited.

The diamond-bright twinkle in her eyes didn't explain what had just happened, but I found my fingers were twisting around the violet ends of her hair nonetheless, as her lips fell onto mine again.

I was beginning to question my sanity and my memory when a small, deliberate cough to my left reminded me exactly what was happening and why.

Violet's body twisted in my lap as she peered up at our intruder. 'Can I help you?'

Evie replied with a smile that didn't stretch to her eyes, 'No, you can't. I saw Charlie and came to say hello, I'm an old friend.'

Violet turned to me, a genuine smile beaming across her face, in total contrast to the mask my face had frozen into. I couldn't find the words to explain what was happening, I didn't know why Violet was smiling. Maybe she didn't realize she was in the presence of evil. But then her head turned back to Evie.

'Are you sure? He doesn't seem to know *you*.'

Evie ignored Violet, her eyes boring into me like lasers. 'Charlie?'

Violet looked at me again trying to ascertain whether I was in fact going to say hello – I wasn't – then flicked back to Evie. 'Strange, I've known Charlie a very long time, and I've never heard of you.'

But Evie wasn't paying the slightest bit of attention

to anything Violet said. 'Charlie . . . are you really going to ignore me?'

Violet shifted on my lap, and I felt her draw in a breath.

'It would seem that way, wouldn't it? Old friend or not, you should try and frown less, it won't help that line you have right there.' She reached out and prodded Evie's impeccably smooth forehead. 'I can recommend some good cream if you'd like,' Violet continued sweetly, 'but you probably need to get Botox on that before it gets worse.'

My eyes widened so much they burned. For the first time ever, Evie Waters was speechless.

Violet eased off my lap, and the air cooled along my thighs giving me some respite from her body. I was still in too much of a state of shock to find it amusing at how she towered over Evie. In the same haphazard manner as she removed them, Violet pulled on her jumper, hat, and scarf. It was the Muppet green coat contrasting with Evie's signature black which jolted me back to myself as I stood, only too happy to follow Violet's lead.

I picked up my pint and drained it, addressing Evie for the first time in over two years. 'Would you like our table? We're going home now.'

My fingers laced with Violet's as we walked out of the pub, leaving Evie in exactly the same spot. The bitter adrenaline coursing through my veins was soon replaced by a level of satisfaction I'd never felt before.

'Fuck.' It was the only word I could manage. It didn't even occur to me to ask how Violet knew who Evie was.

'I think I totally nailed the role of your girlfriend, even

if I do say so myself,' Violet giggled as we walked into the cold and the doors shut behind us, putting a much-needed barrier between Evie and me. She pushed her hand in the pocket of my jeans like it belonged there, and looked at me, 'Come on, you can walk me back to St Anne's, but you need to put your arm around me. We have to make everyone believe this if you want her to.'

I did as instructed; walking side by side with Violet whose head was now resting on my shoulder. I hadn't been entirely sure using her as my girlfriend would convince anyone, let alone Evie, but all my doubts had been melted away by her award-winning acting skills.

This would work perfectly.

Now I just needed to figure out how to tell Brooks I'd been making out with his sister. With tongues.

2. Violet

(And there he was just walking
down the street . . .)

'Violet, if we don't get a move on, we're going to be late.'

I added a final coating of mascara and turned around to find my best friend, Stella, lying on my bed, flicking through this month's *Vogue*, not in the least bit concerned about whether we were going to be late.

'You're not ready either.'

'I am, I literally have to stand up and I'm ready.'

'By that logic I'm more ready than you are.' I pushed my hands through my hair and fastened it up in a messy bun. 'Let's go.'

Vogue was flung to the end of the bed, and she jumped up. 'Do you know who else is auditioning today?'

I shook my head. 'I know what you know.'

'Ugh,' she groaned, flinging her rucksack over her shoulders. Her hand paused on the doorknob. 'I thought you might have heard whether the rumours about Leo Tavener were false.'

Grabbing my copy of *Twelfth Night*, I shoved it in my bag and pulled on my coat. 'Nope, sorry. By my calculation we still have an hour of wishful thinking before we get to the theatre, and it's confirmed he got the part without an audition.'

'Yeah. And he'll definitely be late so he can make an

entrance.' Her scoff was so thick and loud that it had her reaching for her water bottle before it turned into a coughing fit. 'Yesterday he turned up to class wearing a Victorian cape. Professor Fournier asked him where his top hat was and reminded him he was taking French, not English.'

I stifled a giggle. 'What did he say?'

'Dunno, I didn't hear over the sound of everyone rolling their eyes,' she shrugged. 'He won't have noticed anyway. That boy is entirely infuriating, I'm amazed he can fit through the doors with the size of his ego,' she continued grumbling. 'Cecily could have warned us.'

I opened the door and gently shoved her out, before locking it behind us. 'You know her feelings on keeping personal and professional lives separate.'

Stella's grunt told me exactly what she thought of Cece's stance, even though she was one of our friends. *Especially* as she was our friend. Stella was of the opinion we should be given insider secrets and preferential treatment due to the fact *our friend* was directing the summer play, but Cecily Caruthers and her ambitions to be a world-class theatre producer/director were unmatched.

'*No reason why we shouldn't behave like professionals, Stella,*' she mimicked in Cece's clipped theatrical tone as we made our way down the stairs and outside.

'If she wants professional, then someone should remind her that actors aren't exactly known for their discretion. Theatre practically runs on gossip.'

'But we're talking about *Leo Tavener*. If I knew for

sure he was getting the part of Orsino, I'd have serious second thoughts about auditioning.'

'Maybe that's why she's said nothing. You know she wants you to be in the play.'

Stella harrumphed again.

In fairness to her, she had a point.

Leo Tavener. Leo *Tavener*. Oxford University Dramatic Society's resident celebrity student. Former child actor, he began his career in a fabric conditioner advert which everyone still remembered due to his cuteness and one lisped line, *'It's thoft, Mummy,'* before he moved on to bigger and brighter things. This included several Hollywood movies, one of which earned him his first Oscar nomination. The next year he was nominated and won, making him the youngest person to receive two nominations in Oscars history.

In the unlikelihood you ever forgot about his awards, you would soon be reminded. It was something he *loved* to talk about.

Seriously, he could go on *Mastermind* with his specialist subject being himself.

Unfortunately for everyone he decided to take a break from acting, and further his education. More unfortunately for Stella and me, he'd decided to do it at the exact same time as us, which meant we had the next three years of being side by side with Leo Tavener to look forward to.

'You must always seek to expand your knowledge, Violet,' he told me last term when I asked him why he was bothering to go to university, in between telling me what

I could also be doing better. Something that had my teeth gritting together. Borderline unbearable.

Look up the definition of a person obsessed with the sound of their own voice and his face would beam out at you. And he definitely made it deeper on purpose. But I'd managed to zone it out way better than Stella had because I didn't have all my classes with him. He was reading French, just like her. I was also of the opinion that I had other things to waste my energy on than getting annoyed with him, because it would become a full-time job if I wasn't careful, and I'd burn out before the six-month marker.

'I don't know why Cece puts up with him. Or allowed him to be part of the production. It's amateur for a reason, and we all know he's not.'

'Yeah, he reminded me of that again yesterday,' I chuckled, pulling my gloves on as she pushed through the front doors and into the freezing January air. 'I'm surprised he hasn't changed his name to Leonardo di Tavener.'

She threw me an exasperated look. 'Ugh. Please. I'm sure she'll regret it once he starts telling her how to direct.'

'I'm sure you'll be first in line to say, "I told you so". But I have a feeling she didn't have much choice. Linus wanted him to add cachet to the summer schedule.'

'Ugh,' she harrumphed again, making me wonder if maybe she'd forgotten to have breakfast, because she was way grumpier this morning than she had been on any other morning since the start of term. We'd only officially been back three days; it was too early for the

20

novelty and excitement of a new year to have vanished already. 'With a name like Linus Rockwell he wasn't going to be anything other than a theatre producer was he?'

'I dunno, he could probably be a high court judge. It's got a certain *je ne sais quoi*.' I winked, and she finally smiled. 'Rockwell/Carruthers Productions . . . at least when they're both insanely rich and famous with awards lining their mantels we can say we knew them once.'

'Maybe I'll sell my story,' she snorted, pulling her beanie down lower and pushing her arm through mine, linking us together for added warmth. 'Bloody hell, it's freezing today. Can we swing by the dining hall? I want to grab a piece of toast or something.'

I knew it.

'Of course we can, my little hangry bestie,' I grinned, and we took off down the path leading to the dining hall.

'Thank you,' she replied, relaxing against me. 'Hey, have you heard any more from Charlie?'

I shook my head, trying to contain a little of the disappointment that made my belly ache any time I thought about Charlie Masterson and his proposal. Okay, a lot of it. 'Nope.'

'Do you think he's changed his mind on the whole fake girlfriend thing?'

'I dunno,' I shrugged.

It had been a week and I hadn't heard a peep.

'I'm sure you will.'

'Term has started. He would have already texted me, surely?' I kept my tone as casual as possible and not like

I'd been thinking of any and all scenarios in my head as to why I hadn't heard from him since he walked me back to St Anne's.

'He's a guy – who knows what they think?'

That was a very valid point.

'Probably for the best he hasn't. It's not really part of the whole plan I had to move on from him,' I sighed.

I'd been doing so well.

It had been eighteen months since I'd last seen Charlie Masterson, and my heart had been lulled into a false sense of security that I was over him. I'd gotten through the first term without so much as a hint of a relapse. I'd mostly avoided my brother and his friends altogether. Even on my illicit trips to use his bathtub, I never once peeked into Charlie's bedroom, no matter how much I wanted to.

But the first hurdle came crashing down around me when Hugo gave Charlie my phone number.

(Without my permission I might add, not to mention forewarning.)

I'd successfully not replied to any of his strange little messages over Christmas even though my fingers twitched every time I looked at my phone. At first I'd assumed it was some kind of weird joke or – more likely – my brother up to something. It was only when Hugo intervened and requested I reply to Charlie that I relented. I wish I'd pushed a little more on *why* Charlie wanted to see me, but I was too busy trying to ignore the way my insides were bubbling around and tying themselves in knots.

'You'll get there again. You went a whole month

in Australia without talking about Charlie when you hooked up with that surfer Brad.'

A wide smile curled my lips at the memory, and I hugged Stella tighter as a particularly cold gust of air hit us. I certainly missed the sunshine.

Surfer Brad was not to be confused with bartender Brad, who Stella spent a lot of nights with during the Gold Coast section of our gap year travelling around the Southern Hemisphere. He could have been the youngest Hemsworth brother — or at least a close cousin.

The Gold Coast was the one and only time in my life when I'd successfully got up before sunrise, because Brad would take me onto the water to watch the yolky orange sun burst through the horizon and set the ocean alight. Even though I'd yawned through most of it, I'd loved every second, and found myself completely swept away with the magic of living a life on the beach.

But, like all good things must, it came to an end when Stella and I moved on to South America, and surfer Brad morphed into polo player Gabriel.

Charlie Masterson, however, was not the same as a month-long romance with someone I'd never see again.

Charlie Masterson was my long-term crush.

Charlie Masterson had owned my heart since I was fourteen, and it would take more than a fling for it to switch allegiances.

Since I'd pushed open the doors to the pub and seen Charlie sitting by the fire, it was clear my crush had merely been dormant. The second I'd laid eyes on him my little heart fluttered in excitement at the familiarity.

I'd tried to remain nonchalant. I'd summoned all the calm I had in my arsenal, and just like Beyoncé had once done, I channelled my inner Sasha Fierce. My as-yet-unnamed alter ego. My inner award-winning actress.

If I do say so myself, I'd done a damn fine job at it. I *should* have won an award.

Eighteen months had passed yet it could have been yesterday for all that had changed about him. Unless you counted a thick coating of stubble on a previously smooth face, a broader chest, thicker shoulders and more heavily defined muscles. His hair was still the same light brown with the little cowlick at the side that never seemed to flatten, still the same bright green eyes always brimming with mischief, and a slightly crooked, bemused smile he'd never realized made my heart beat double-time.

But then his plan had been laid out, and I almost broke.

Rushing to the loo, I stood in front of the mirror with my alter-ego staring back. Even she had misgivings as to why I'd just agreed to possibly the worst idea in history. What did I think I was doing?

I went back out to tell him I'd changed my mind, only to find Evie Waters standing by our table. The panic on Charlie's face coupled with the large glass of wine on an empty stomach was all I needed to forget my own hesitations, and get him away from her as quickly as possible.

In the twenty minutes we took to walk back to St Anne's his arm didn't once drop from around my shoulder. Truth be told, I think he'd been in almost as much shock as I was – only his shock made him monosyllabic.

Mine manifested itself with verbal diarrhoea.

For twenty minutes I'd done all the talking – prattling on about Christmas, skiing over New Year, auditions and the summer play, training for the Boat Race, my brother . . . you name it, I likely mentioned it.

'Thank you, Violet,' he'd mumbled against my cheek when he'd kissed me goodbye and taken off down the path, disappearing into the darkness before I'd had a chance to respond.

I almost wondered if my exceptionally vivid imagination hadn't conjured up the entire scenario, until I remembered Stella knew about it. I'd found her sitting outside my dorm room waiting for me when I plodded my way up the stairs in a zombie-like state.

'I've really messed up this time,' I'd told her, trying to figure out if my chest might burst. Then proceeded to explain why.

'Why don't you start dating again? What about that guy from your History of English class last term? You said he was hot,' Stella continued.

I shook my head, 'Matthew Collins? Nah, he's not dating material. He's one-night-only type of fun.'

'What's wrong with that?'

'Nothing. I still have classes with him, and I don't want it to get weird. I need to get myself out of this Charlie situation first without starting another one.'

'Don't give yourself a hard time, with the play rehearsals you'll be too busy to think about him.'

My shoulders slumped. 'Yeah, I know. I just wish he'd been a terrible kisser, with bad breath or something. It would be easier to move on,' I grouched, and attempted to block out the memory of what Charlie's mouth felt like before it careered back into my brain.

Too late.

I'd spent a lot of time during my teenage years wondering what it would be like to kiss Charlie Masterson. I'd wonder whether his lips would feel as soft as they looked; if he'd cup my face or grip my hair like they did in the movies. I prayed we'd be sitting so my legs didn't give way. I knew for a fact he'd be better at kissing than Matthew Wainwright, or James Brewers, or any of the other boys that featured in my real-life formative teenage years.

He had to be. He was two years older than me. He was 'experienced'.

He was Charlie Masterson.

My number one.

Even when I started dating properly, and fell in love with my first boyfriend – Miles Garland – the flame which had burned for Charlie since the first time Hugo had brought him home one half-term never fully extinguished.

Then one week ago exactly, I'd finally discovered the answers to all my questions. They *were* that soft, and the way he curled my hair around his finger was better than having it gripped. It was enough to bring a butterfly to life in my chest. Our first kiss had lived up to the expectations and more, even if the circumstances under which it occurred were less than ideal.

'Have you ever considered that maybe you're not supposed to move on?'

My eyes flicked to Stella. 'What?'

'This could be the universe giving you a chance. Text

him, you have his number, and the perfect excuse. Just ask him what the plan is.'

'Uh uh.' I shook my head, hard. 'No. No way. It's not a good idea. If he wants to go through with this, then he'll message me.'

'Vi, this could be the role of a lifetime for you.'

The breath I huffed out clouded as it hit the cold air. 'There will be other more suitable roles.'

'Want to know what I would do?'

Even with a side eye, I could see Stella grinning mischievously. I shouldn't ask, but she'd only tell me anyway.

'What? What would you do?'

'I would use this opportunity to my advantage.'

'What? What does that mean?'

'It means be a really perfect fake girlfriend, and he'll never want to let you go,' she replied simply. 'Make him fall in love with you.'

I barked out a laugh; loud enough that a couple of St Anne's students passing us on the path stopped their own conversation and looked at me. But I was looking at Stella, trying to make it clear exactly how absurd I thought she was. Maybe it was the hunger. It hadn't just made her grouchy, it was making her delusional.

'First off, that's ridiculous. Second, I'm not his type, Stel. I'm too tall. He likes short girls if Evie is anything to go by,' I grumbled. 'And brunettes.'

'But he doesn't like her, does he. That's why he's got you faking it.'

'He hasn't got me anything. I haven't heard from him in a week,' I repeated.

27

She offered nothing but a nonchalant shrug, but that was the point where we reached the dining hall so it was likely all her brain cells were occupied with finding food, and coffee.

It was late enough that breakfast was coming to an end, and the only students still in here were ones who were more committed to sleep than a fresh coffee and first dig through the scrambled eggs. Right now all that remained on the hatch were a few slices of warming toast, and rows of cereal.

I grabbed a couple of to-go coffee cups and filled them, while Stella was working on convincing the dining staff to fetch some fresh bread for her. It didn't take her long. Stella's powers of persuasion were unmatched, and she was soon biting into a hot slice slathered with butter and orange marmalade.

She thrust a half-eaten piece out to me, 'You want a bit?'

'No thanks.'

'I can eat and walk then,' she muttered, stuffing the remainder in her mouth and starting on the next. 'Now my brain's not focused on food, I can think properly.'

We walked away from St Anne's in silence; Stella was happily munching through her toast while my mind was supposed to be thinking about the auditions, but was actually thinking about Charlie. Now term had begun, the streets were much busier. We were between the hour, so there were less students hurrying to a class they were late for, but enough that Stella and I had to step aside a couple of times to let some rush past. Some wore the dark blue colours of Oxford, mingling with those wearing the crests of the different colleges, or like us, whatever we could find in our wardrobes.

'Do you know what scenes they're going to ask us to audition?'

I shook my head. 'No, but we'll have the script with us, so it doesn't matter.'

'Are we auditioning with people?'

I shrugged, 'Stel, I know what you know, which is to say . . .'

'Nothing,' she interrupted.

'Exactly.'

'You want to rehearse some lines?' she asked as we neared the physics building.

'Yeah, go for it.'

She pulled her backpack off and found her copy of *Twelfth Night*, 'Let's start with the first scene, I'll play Olivia then we can switch.'

'Cool,' I replied, as Stella cleared her throat.

'Hey, isn't that Charlie?'

My mouth opened to respond but it wasn't a line I recognized. 'What?'

'There. Look. It's Charlie.'

My head snapped around to where she was pointing. My mouth opened another degree because twenty-five metres away Charlie was jogging across the street heading straight for us. His eyes locked onto mine, and instantly a smile spread across his face. With each long stride his smile grew.

And my heart spluttered.

The summer I was fourteen Charlie and Oz had come to spend a week at our house, along with their other friend, Olly. It was one of those heatwave weeks, and they'd spent the entire time around the pool. I was too nervous to go out and join them, so instead I stayed reading in the shade, sitting in the swing my dad had installed on our large oak tree.

One afternoon my mum had made a batch of ginger beer, and she'd asked me to take a jug out to the boys, which I'd been only too happy to do. Charlie had leapt up to help the second he spotted me. As he'd eased the tray laden with glasses, ginger beer and snacks from my fingers he'd flashed me a wide smile showing off perfect straight white teeth. The combination of sunshine and swimming had turned his eyes more blue than green, and the reflection of the water really made it seem like they were sparkling.

I'd been aware that Evie was his girlfriend at the time, but my heart never got the message because that was the point I fell hopelessly in love. I'd run back inside and called Stella, wondering when I'd ever get to see him smile at me like that again.

I had my answer.

Bloody hell. This wasn't good.

I was standing there trying to stop my mouth from dropping open, while my best friend snickered next to me. My brain and heart began arguing again about what I was doing and whether or not I should really be doing it.

The jury didn't reach its verdict before Charlie reached me.

He stopped in front of me, his smile still wide. 'I thought I recognized that coat.'

I looked down at the green faux fur.

30

It was kind of bright, but it was my favourite shade – emerald. And more importantly, it was warm.

I managed to smile, right at the moment he leaned forward. I never found out what he was leaning forward for, because I shifted my bag on my shoulder which caused me to jerk slightly and my forehead hit his with a hard thud.

'Ouch. Jesus.'

'God. Are you alright?' he asked, while I tried to stop the throbbing in my brain, especially when he reached out and touched me.

The pad of his thumb brushed against the point of collision. It helped, but only because the rest of my face immediately and uncharacteristically flushed pink and throbbed harder until it was impossible to tell what it was throbbing from more. Though the second he realized what he was doing his hand dropped and clenched at his side.

'Sorry about that.'

'My fault too,' I managed to mumble.

Next to me Stella snorted. 'God, you two really need to get better co-ordinated if you're going to be a believable couple.'

Charlie's green eyes flicked to hers with a wide blink, like he'd only just realized someone was standing next to me, then let out a soft chuckle.

'Yeah . . .' he pushed his hands into the pockets of his trackpants, and rocked back on his heels. 'Um . . . about that . . . I was going to text you, but then I saw you walking . . . are you around this afternoon? Can we talk?'

I tried not to watch his mouth move while he spoke, even though it was right at my eye level. His full, soft mouth that I couldn't stop thinking about kissing again.

'Sure. Yes. Sure,' I repeated.

Maybe the knock had loosened a few brain cells. Probably.

'Great.' He grinned, his mouth lifting a little more on the left, though I was more focused on how his dimples deepened and his wide nose crinkled in the middle. 'I'll come to you, about threeish?'

I forced myself to nod. 'Cool.'

'Cool.' His eyes never left mine, he rocked forward slightly but then stopped, like he thought better of whatever he'd been about to do, while all I could do was concentrate on not breathing him in. The air was already permeated with the scent I always associated with Charlie – warm and sweet, like honey and hot, rainy days.

The lock on our gaze was only broken by a low cough to my right, and I turned to find Stella grinning. If I wasn't so dazed, I'd have scowled at her.

'Um, we have to go, we have auditions.' I thumbed behind me, in the wrong direction.

'Oh, yeah, cool.' Charlie's eyes widened. 'Good luck. See you later.'

'Bye, Charlie.' Stella looped her arm in mine and tugged me away. I didn't dare turn around in case he caught me. 'Golly, he's definitely become more handsome than when we were at school. No wonder you're in a tizz.'

This time my scowl was on point.

3. Charlie

(Does anyone have a JCB I could borrow?)

I snatched the documents from the printer and held them side-by-side.

Was this a stupid idea? It was probably a stupid idea.

No. It was *definitely* a stupid idea.

I was supposed to have an IQ of 150 but figuring a way to get out of the situation I'd gotten myself into was beyond me. Shit-uation more like.

Perhaps I should get the keys to a JCB; it would be a far quicker way to reach the bottom of the giant hole I was digging.

Fucking Evie. This was all her fault.

As I saw it, my problem was three-fold.

If Evie hadn't been in the pub last week, I'd have never kissed Violet.

If I'd never kissed Violet, I'd still be in the realm of theory versus living the reality.

If I'd never kissed Violet then I wouldn't now be running on a combination of caffeine and Jaffa Cakes, and no sleep. I'd be able to think clearly, and I wouldn't have survived a week with an incessant guilt churning in my gut.

Guilt. That's what it was.

Guilt I'd kissed my best friend's sister.

Guilt I still hadn't told him about it.

Guilt that it would never have happened if I'd come up with a different plan in the first place.

But that wasn't the worst bit.

The worst bit? The really most heinously dreadful guilt-inducing part of kissing Violet Brooks – I *think* I liked it.

No, not think. I did definitely like kissing Violet Brooks.

I'd sworn off women after first year, when Evie cheated on me a second time with David Chamberlain. Since then, I'd had a handful of barely memorable, mostly drunken hook-ups, nothing worth repeating or talking about. I'd rarely thought about them again.

But Violet?

I'd thought about it – *her* – way too fucking much. For mine or anyone else's liking. Not that anyone else knew yet. I hadn't *completely* lost my mind.

It had occurred to me that perhaps I'd only been thinking about kissing Violet because it was months since I'd kissed anyone. Therefore, common sense would suggest it was likely the novelty of kissing someone again which was causing my brain to go into overdrive. But I couldn't be sure and didn't know how to prove it without going around campus and kissing three to six other girls – like some snogging focus group.

Except, that kind of behaviour would not only raise several questions I didn't want to answer but most certainly get back to Evie.

I was stuck with only my Violet kiss to draw conclusions from.

Violet's mouth on my mouth.

34

I'd once overheard my sister talking to her friend about some model and her pillowy lips. And I thought, *'What the fuck does that mean? How can lips be like pillows? Stupid way to describe them,'* then promptly forgot all about it. But last Wednesday in the Blue Oar, at approximately three p.m., I'd learned exactly what pillowy lips were. Soft and plump, fitting so perfectly into mine I could feel myself sink into them.

Yeah, pillowy was a perfect description.

My body had been on autopilot as it let her take the lead.

I could almost still taste the berries and wine coating her warm, silky tongue as it slid along mine; the delicate moan vibrating up her throat, the violet tips of her honey-coloured strands sliding through my fingers . . .

Arggh!

See . . . anytime I think about kissing her I drift off. It's been fucking impossible to get anything done.

I couldn't afford to lose focus. I was not in a position to get nothing done. Right now, time was very much of the essence. You get my drift?

I was heading into a long stretch consisting of the Boat Race and finals, and it was debatable what was more important.

Boat Race training was about to go from hard to brutal. To compete in it on adrenaline alone would be impossible, even for someone who didn't crave sleep more than air – unlike me.

It was the reason I'd sought out Violet in the first place – to stop me from getting sucked into Evie and her inevitable game playing again. I didn't trust myself not to. But I clearly hadn't thought through my plan properly, because kissing Violet had not been a distraction I'd foreseen and now I didn't know which was worse. Having to deal with Evie or trying not to kiss Violet again.

It was alarming how much I wanted to.

It was the reason I hadn't texted her since I'd left her outside her halls.

Yesterday, after an exhausting day of not enough sleep, too much thinking and a savage land training session in the gym I'd almost convinced myself I was panicking about Evie over nothing. I could handle her.

I'd decided to pull the plug on the entire operation, if only so I could go back to functioning like a normal human being again. I'd figure something else out.

Except Evie had been waiting for me outside the Tank.

For a split second I saw the girl I'd once hopelessly loved waiting for me, her fingers linked together in front of her. Then I remembered the time I'd spotted her waiting for Dave Chamberlain after rugby practice, right when we broke up the second time, and my heart hardened again.

'Can we talk?' she'd asked.

'Nope,' I'd replied, and jogged straight past her.

I knew she'd never attempt to catch me. Evie and cardio weren't friends.

Therefore, instead of pulling the plug, I'd gone in search of Violet first thing this morning – well, first thing after training, breakfast, and my Nuclear and Particle Physics tutorial. My first class with Evie was tomorrow, so I had until then to come up with something believable, though it was anyone's guess whether it would happen.

Swiping my beanie from my desk, I pulled it on and eased open my bedroom door, listening for any sound of my housemates, specifically the largest, noisiest one.

Do you know how hard it is to avoid someone you live and train with all day every day?

Very. It's very hard.

I'd spent most of the past week holding my breath in anticipation of any questions about Violet. But as luck would have it Brooks had been too busy with the beginning of term work chaos to have asked me anything at all, and maybe if I crossed my fingers really hard, he'd have forgotten about the matter entirely. He wasn't the most perceptive member of our household as it was, so it was possible I'd earned myself a little grace period before I had any explaining to do.

I walked into the kitchen to find Oz standing over a shepherd's pie, though standing was generous seeing as his nose was almost brushing the mashed potato.

'What are you doing?'

'What's this?' he asked without peering around.

'Shepherd's pie. What does it look like?'

'Did you make it?'

'Yes, it's for dinner . . .' I swiped the fork he'd been holding ready to dig in, and threw it into the sink, '. . . not lunch. I expect it to be here when I get back.'

He stood up, his thick black brows knitting together, and reached for the large bag of crisps he'd clearly been eating before he found something a little more appetizing. His fist was still inside the bag when he opened the fridge door and peered inside.

'Where are you going?' he asked.

'Um . . . I have to . . .' I peered down at the pieces of paper I was holding. My rucksack was still on the kitchen table, exactly where I'd dumped it earlier, and I shoved them inside to hide the evidence before Oz noticed anything. The guilt churned in my stomach again. 'Where's Brooks?'

'Lectures.'

Snatching up my body warmer, I looped my arms through it and zipped it up. I should be running out the door before I did something stupid, like confess what had happened. But also, if I didn't talk to someone soon, I might explode or have a serious mental breakdown.

Like Brooks, Oz had been one of my best friends since we were thirteen years old. He was usually good for a bit of advice, as long as he was listening.

'Actually, mate . . . can I talk to you about something?'

'Sure, what?' I think he mumbled, though his head was too far inside the fridge to decipher properly.

I should have known better. It was pointless trying to talk to Oz about anything unless he'd been fed. He was also the most inept person I'd ever met in a kitchen. He could barely butter bread. My biggest achievement in recent years had been teaching him how to successfully make our morning porridge before training, especially because it meant I got to spend an extra fifteen minutes in bed.

The rucksack was dropped back on the table. Gently

shoving him out of the way, I grabbed the remains of a chicken I'd roasted for dinner yesterday, along with salad and tomatoes.

'Get the bread. I'll make you a sandwich.'

He grinned wide and slapped me on the back. 'You turned up just in time, Charles. I'd starve without you.'

Oz removed two slices of the sourdough I'd bought this morning, placed them on the wooden cutting board, sat down at the kitchen island and waited. I'd made him enough food that he knew the drill by now. Both of them did.

We'd known each other long enough that living together was far more domesticated than it should be for three guys in their early twenties, but each of us had very specific roles.

I cooked, shopped and organized the day-to-day running of the house; Brooks managed our diary – which included everyone's whereabouts, bins and recycling; Oz managed the bills and finances.

It had been this way since we moved in together during first year. Our street was quiet, with mostly families, therefore very few parties took place keeping us awake all night like they had at Trinity College. Parents and rowers seem to follow the same early-to-bed, early-to-rise agenda.

The other reason we'd moved out of halls was Evie.

After she'd gone off with Dave Chamberlain, I'd bumped into her/them far too much for my liking. The final straw had occurred one Saturday morning: Oz and I happened to be on our way back from a jog, and spotted Evie and Dave near to Trinity, where neither of them had any reason to be, in an embrace that looked like they were trying to survive on carbon dioxide alone.

After Oz had calmed me down, he called a meeting between the three of us and announced he was taking an investment opportunity, and we promptly went house hunting.

A month later, we moved into number 5 Tolkien Lane.

It had already been modernized, and the best thing about the house was the kitchen – the people who'd lived here before obviously liked to cook. As did I.

I'd been brought up in a family who knew the value of good food. My parents own a restaurant group, the jewel in the crown of which is Petal – a three-Michelin-star establishment my dad runs just outside London, with views of the River Thames. While I'd never wanted to become a chef, my siblings and I grew up watching and learning. If you wanted a meal in our house, you earned it by chopping vegetables or making a marinade.

By the time I was twelve I could debone a chicken and fillet a fish.

I spend time in the kitchen the way other people do yoga. I can lose myself for hours on the perfect Sunday roast; and our house is usually full after a long weekend of hard training when everyone comes back here to be fed.

I spooned out a dollop of mayonnaise onto the bread and pushed it towards Oz to spread.

'Do you want tomatoes?'

He nodded, 'Yes please.'

'How's Kate?' I asked, slicing one up as thinly as I

could, while simultaneously trying to buy myself some time and figure out how to broach the subject of Violet.

While Oz was supportive of the whole 'Operation Get Rid of Evie', I couldn't see him thinking that making out with Violet was a good idea. Even *I* didn't think it was a good idea.

It wasn't.

'She's good, though I haven't seen her since New Year. I feel like I'm getting withdrawal. Spending all that time together at Christmas was amazing, but now I don't know when I'll see her again. Even though that river cleaning was a stupid pain in the arse, at least it meant I got to see her. Training is already getting more intense.'

I nodded, 'Yeah, I know. This term is going to be a lot.'

'I can't wait until the race is over so we can stop hiding,' he grumbled, tipping the bag of crisps into his mouth until the last shreds fell in, then going back to the bread he was preparing.

Oz's girlfriend Kate was studying medicine at Cambridge. He'd met her at the beginning of the school year, on a visit to the city for reasons we probably shouldn't mention. He'd been smitten at first sight, while she didn't want anything to do with him as a member of the rival boat club crew because, as he'd learned later, Kate was a member of the Cambridge women's boat club. His perseverance had paid off, however, and he and Kate soon became as inseparable as a couple could be 200 miles apart. Even though we weren't going to be racing directly against her, they'd been keeping their relationship a secret, more for Kate's sake than Oz's. Oz would shout about it from the rooftops given half a chance.

'Only two and a half months left,' I smiled in an attempt to pull him back out of the mood he'd suddenly dropped into.

'It feels so far away.' He pushed the sourdough over to me, 'That reminds me, Coach called and we have to get to the boathouse by four.'

My hand paused mid-air, half the tomato I was holding flopped on to the bread. 'What?'

'He wants to see everyone from last year's Blue Boat.'

'Why?' I asked, forcing myself to concentrate on finishing Oz's sandwich instead of panicking about meeting Violet, because if I had to be down at the boathouse I would have barely any time to discuss the much more pressing issues of Violet and me fake dating.

Oz shrugged as I pushed the sandwich back, his focus taken by food. The first half almost got swallowed in one.

'Umghawditssogoodgeniusyouare.'

Oz continued mumbling incoherently through each bite, while I cleared up and put the shepherd's pie away just in case Brooks got home early and decided to eat it, and tried to figure out what to do about my plans which had been blown up. This wasn't a conversation to rush.

'Are you not having one?'

I turned to Oz and shook my head, 'Not hungry.'

That was another thing. The guilt had robbed me of my appetite. Except for Jaffa Cakes, I could always fit them in.

With the remainder of his sandwich in his hand, Oz got up and flicked the kettle on, 'Want a cup of tea?'

'No thanks.'

I stood there silently while he pulled a mug from the cupboard. I stood and waited. I knew there was no point in talking until I had his undivided attention. Plus I was still figuring out where to start. I watched in silence as he poured the boiling water, squeezed out the teabag and dropped it on the counter. Once he'd added his milk and finished making a mess, he leaned back against the kitchen cupboard.

'Are there any biscuits?'

I sighed loudly, marched into the pantry, grabbed the chocolate digestives and placed them in front of him.

'Um . . . are you okay?' he asked. I was about to respond when he snapped his fingers. 'Shit, sorry mate, I completely forgot. How's it going with Evie? Have you seen her yet?'

I took a deep breath and nodded slowly, 'Yeah. I . . .'

'What's happening with Violet? Have you managed to get hold of her? Is she going to help you?'

Brooks hadn't been the only one swept up in beginning of term chaos, though in Oz's case he returned from the Christmas holidays later than we had so he could spend more time with Kate. In fact, as I stood there trying to figure out an answer I realized I'd managed a small miracle with it not being mentioned at all until now.

I hadn't even told them about Violet breaking into the house – though I'd probably keep that to myself.

'Yup,' I nodded, hoping I was giving off the calm, chilled vibe I was trying to summon, even though I could feel beads of sweat forming down my back, 'Yeah, yes she's going to help. I'm going to see her now, actually.'

Oz dunked a chocolate digestive into his tea, then shoved it whole into his mouth. A little puddle of brown liquid was forming under where he'd left the teabag; I picked it up and tossed it into the bin, then wiped down the counter for the second time.

'So the plan is all in place then? Get rid of Evie for good. Violet was cool with it?'

'Yeah, she said she's going to use it for acting experience.' I laughed, and the tension between my ribs loosened a fraction. One good thing about this mess was how calm Violet had remained. She didn't even blink when I asked her. And the only thing which had lessened the guilt I'd been feeling was the knowledge I might be helping her in some small way too.

'Amazing work, Charles. I'll admit I thought the plan was a little out there, but I have full faith you'll pull it off. And it's Violet . . . so it's not like you're going to be tempted to make out with her or anything. I mean, could you imagine . . .' Oz's head fell back with a loud guffaw, hard enough that he banged it on the cupboard door. 'Ouch.'

He was too distracted to notice my face had lost all colour. I knew it had. I'd felt the warmth drain from my cheeks the second he mentioned kissing her.

Oz was still laughing as I took a step back, followed by another. Making a big show of looking at my watch,

I grabbed my backpack from the table and hurried to the door.

'Shit, is that the time? Must dash. Don't eat the pie. Meet you at the Tank later.'

I was on my bike and down the road before he had a chance to reply, peddling away like my life depended on it. Oz was far more perceptive than Brooks, and he'd be able to suss out any secret I was keeping within a matter of minutes. And if Oz thought kissing Violet was a bad idea, then it definitely was.

I needed a solution, and fast.

With each turn of my wheels the cold January air invigorated my lungs. By the time I arrived at St Anne's and chained my bike up, I hadn't exactly come up with a better plan, but the fresh oxygen had given me a renewed optimism that perhaps it wasn't as bad as I'd been thinking it was.

I was just reaching for my phone to let her know I was there when a flash of green caught the corner of my eye and a smile spread across my face before my brain registered why it was doing so.

'Charlie?'

'Hey, Violet.'

'You're very prompt, aren't you?' she said, stopping in front of me.

'Not usually,' I chuckled, and just like this morning I leaned in to kiss her cheek. I don't know why I did it, but there was something about her smooth rosy skin, cold from the air, that I wanted to feel against my lips. Her blue eyes wide and sparkling, like sunshine in a cloudless sky. 'How was your audition?'

'It was good . . .' her smile was followed by a loud sigh, 'although . . . ugh, God . . . do you know the actor, Leo Tavener?'

'Um . . .' I nodded. 'Yeah, maybe. I don't think I've seen him in anything though. Why?'

'You know he's at Oxford?'

'No.' I shook my head, and my eyes opened wider, especially at the annoyance crossing Violet's face, because I'm not sure I'd ever seen her annoyed. As far as I was concerned, Violet was eternally happy and full of sunshine, but I kind of liked the scowl she was wearing.

'He is, and he's an insufferable know-it-all. He got the part of Orsino without even auditioning.'

'Oh,' I replied, trying to hold in the grin at how annoyed she clearly was. I also wasn't entirely sure what she was talking about, because Shakespeare was not my strong point. 'But, did you get the part you wanted?'

Biting the end of one of her striped gloves, she eased it off and brushed a loose violet strand of hair away from her face, 'I don't know yet. Hopefully – we'll find out next week – but the part I want is opposite him, and it means I'll have to spend the next few months with him. Ugh.'

'When's the play?'

'The beginning of next term. Rehearsals start in two weeks.'

'I'd offer to step in, but I'm not sure my skills stretch to Shakespeare.' I finally let out the laugh I'd been holding onto. In turn it made her laugh – a deep, throaty sound that set off a flutter in my chest that made me

46

wonder if I was having an aneurism or something. Not that I knew what that felt like, but it was probably similar.

'No, I can't exactly see you on stage, Chazzle. Though you'd certainly fill out the tights and doublet nicely, if your rowing singlet is anything to go by.'

As soon as she said it, her eyes popped wide and her cheeks turned from light pink to deep fuchsia. The Violet I'd always known said whatever popped into her brain and did it with zero shame or embarrassment, so I wasn't entirely sure why she was now staring at me. I stood there, waiting to see if she was going to add anything else, or maybe blink, while also trying my hardest to bite down on the smile threatening to break out.

'I'd hope so. Otherwise all that training would have gone to waste,' I replied eventually.

'Yes, well . . . quite,' she spluttered when she finally recovered, though didn't quite meet my eye. 'Anyway, what was it you had for me?'

I eased my backpack off, and pulled out the two pieces of paper I'd printed off earlier. Violet took them from me, and after thirty seconds of studying the coloured grids on each page, she looked up.

'What is this?'

I peered at the one in her right hand, 'This is your timetable, the other one is mine. We can overlap them, and see where we can meet up.'

'Mine is purple?'

I glanced down at the page again, 'Yes . . . violet, actually. To match you.'

Her eyes shot to mine, and I kind of wished I hadn't

pointed that out, or done it in the first place. Why did I make them violet?

'Charlie, how did you get my schedule?'

'Um . . .' I cleared my throat, 'I can access the university servers.'

Her eyebrows shot up, almost disappearing under her navy beanie. 'Huey always says you're freakishly scary with computers.'

I grinned. 'I'll take that as a compliment, and I don't do it for anything underhand. I don't change grades or anything.'

'You can change grades?' she whispered.

'Probably. I've never tried though.' I tapped the pages again hoping to move the subject away from anything which would likely get me kicked out of Oxford, and probably invited to do some prison time. 'Anyway, you can see on the grids where we both have study periods and where our classes overlap. And this one here is the class which Evie is attending, thankfully you have free time here.'

'Wow, you've really thought this through,' she muttered under her breath.

I just about stopped myself from telling her that I definitely hadn't thought it through at all.

'This Evie class is tomorrow.'

I nodded. 'Yeah.'

'And you want me to come and meet you afterwards?'

'Yeah, if that's still okay.' I pushed my hands deep into my jogging bottoms suddenly feeling so awkward it was all I could do to drop my head with a pitiful shake. 'Sorry, I know it's short notice. I should have texted you

48

this week. I was trying to figure out how this is going to work, especially with your brother.'

'Huey?' Her perfectly shaped brows dropped in a frown. 'What's he got to do with this?'

'Um . . . well, you're his little sister.'

I'd hoped she'd catch my drift, but her frown only deepened. 'And?'

'I haven't told him we kissed.' I winced, and checked my watch, cursing Coach. I definitely wasn't going to have enough time. 'Look, are you around tonight? I'm so sorry, Coach called us in early and I wanted to have more time to talk. Can you meet me in the Blue Oar, we can go over all the rules of how we're going to do this?'

'Rules?'

'Yeah. Fake Dating Rules.' I replied, remembering once more about the way she'd slipped her hand in my back pocket. 'You seemed much more adept last week at how we should behave, but I have a few thoughts we can discuss. Also, it'll help things with Brooks. I'm sure he won't care that much about us kissing, because it's not real or anything, but I still feel like I should have told him. I just can't figure out how to broach it. Maybe I just need to take a leaf out of your book and use it as an opportunity to brush up on my acting skills. You know, for when I'm filling out my tights.'

I grinned, but it wasn't a smile which flashed across her face.

'Of course.' She nodded slowly. 'We're acting. It's not real. Rules are a great idea. We can make it believable, and I promise you, my brother won't care.'

'Great. Thank you, Violet, seriously. I really appreciate

49

you giving up your time for me. And if there's anything I can do . . . I can't get on stage, but I can definitely help learn lines with you.'

She chuckled, 'You might regret saying that.'

I shook my head, 'Nope. You can hold me to it. I promise. See you at eight?'

'Yep, I'll see you, and let's not sit so close to the fire this time.' She grinned.

I bent down to unlock my bike. 'Deal.'

Sister or not. Real or not. Something about the way Violet was looking at me as I cycled off had my heart beating faster than usual.

4. Charlie

(Charlie and Violet's Rules for Fake Dating)

Glass of wine for Violet. Check.

Sparkling water for me (plus another for Violet). Check.

Far away from the fire. Check.

I lined up the edges of my notebook so they were perpendicular to the edges of the table, placed my pen on top and sat back to watch the door.

I'd never left training quite so fast. I'd showered, dressed and cycled to the Blue Oar in less than twenty minutes, and still managed to get here before Violet. It wasn't quite eight yet, however, so she wasn't technically late but I wasn't holding onto the belief that she'd be on time.

Truth be told I kind of liked that I'd arrived first. I wasn't quite as on edge as I'd been last week waiting for her, and this time I'd get to enjoy seeing her hurry in, remove 90 per cent of her clothing and drop down into the seat I'd moved so it was next to mine, instead of across the table.

I'd made the reasoning that couples sit next to each other, but really I just wanted to be close to her. There was something about being in her presence that made my entire nervous system relax.

Opening my notebook again, I looked at the top line.

51

Rules.

1. No kissing
2.

Christ I was bad at this. I'd come up with one lousy rule. And the only reason I'd added *no kissing* in the first place was because it was the only rule I needed to have.

It was the only one I wanted to break.

'Hello.'

My eyes shot up and a split second later I sprang to my feet. I'd been so engrossed in my list I missed Violet walking in. I slammed the notebook shut.

'Hey.' I leaned in, just as she did. This time I narrowly avoided bashing her head with mine, and instead planted my lips on the edges of her open, smiling mouth. 'Sorry.'

But she was too busy laughing as she removed her coat and sat down. It wasn't her big Muppet coat from this afternoon; this one was a cream, fluffy number that made her look like a cloud, and I had a sudden desire to float away with her on it.

'Stella was right. We do need to get better at this,' I grumbled and sat back in my chair.

'This for me?' Violet asked, picking up the wine in front of her and taking a large sip before I had time to answer. 'We will. Don't worry. Evie will believe we're a couple.'

I smiled over to her with more gratitude than I'd possibly ever felt. 'Thanks.'

'How was training?' she asked, tucking her legs underneath herself and shifting her body to lean forward so that she was almost entirely in my space, like she'd done it a thousand times before.

It took me a second to blink through the closeness, to stop myself from focusing on the freckles sprinkled across her nose and the onyx flare of her pupils in their sea of azure, and realize what she was doing.

Being my fake girlfriend.

Anyone walking past would never question us not being a real couple, and I spent too long wondering if I should brush the strand of hair away from her forehead.

'It was good,' I replied eventually, clearing my throat. 'Coach wanted to remind us that our spots on Blue Boat weren't guaranteed.'

Her face screwed up in confusion. 'Does that mean you might not be racing this year?'

'No, we're all going to be on Blue Boat. The only change we have this year is Marshy, because last year he'd broken his leg and couldn't compete.' Fuck it. I reached out and swept the strand away with my fingers before I could think any more about it. Except now she was rolling her lips and I caught a flash of her teeth as she worried them. I leaned back in my chair to create some space. That was better. Now I could focus. 'How was the rest of your afternoon?'

'Oh you know . . . essays, essays and more essays. I should probably make a start on learning lines, but I don't want to jinx anything.'

'Who else is up for the part?' I asked, picking up my water to quench my suddenly dry mouth.

She shrugged, 'I don't know for certain. There were

a couple of other girls I saw going into the auditions but that could have been for any of the parts. Cecily and Linus kept it all under wraps.'

'Cecily and Linus?'

'The producer/directors. They're putting on the production. Cecily is one of my friends, but she likes to keep things professional, so she won't tell me.' She laughed.

'Guess that means she won't give you the part outright either.'

She shook her head with a giggle, forcing the ends of her ponytail to flick over her shoulder. 'God, no! Are you kidding? Otherwise Stella would have confirmed her part yonks ago.'

She picked up her wine again and for the first time I noticed she'd changed the colour of her nail polish. Last week it had been dark red, today it was pale pink. I couldn't decide which I liked more.

A sharp breeze of cold air had my eyes flicking to the door and the large group which entered before returning to Violet and the reason she was here in the first place.

Rules.

'Anyway, I know you have tons to do. I won't keep you too long.' My hand moved to the notebook.

'What's that?'

'I started to write out some rules . . .' I began before the notebook was snatched up, and Violet flicked through the pages until she found what she was looking for.

'There's only one rule.' Her forehead creased deeply, 'No kissing? But Charlie . . . we did already.'

54

My mouth held in a firm line. 'Yeah, I know. But I think maybe we shouldn't.'

'Oh —'

'Just because I don't think Brooks would be too happy,' I blurted before I could change my mind, especially given the look on Violet's face, which kind of resembled disappointment. Or maybe it was just wishful thinking. Because no one was more disappointed than me. 'You're his little sister.'

Violet rolled her eyes.

'My brother needs to get over himself. No kissing isn't exactly realistic,' she replied, grabbing the pen and scribbling something on the page, though from the angle I couldn't see what she'd written. 'Okay, next rule. What have you been thinking about?'

I was *not* going to answer that question.

Instead, I went with, 'How often we see each other?'

She took a deep breath. 'If we're talking realistically, we should probably do at least one more than just the class with Evie in it, and you ought to come and meet me at mine too otherwise it's a little weird. If I was your actual girlfriend I wouldn't be happy always meeting you if you didn't come to meet me.' Her eyes briefly flicked to mine, 'And we need to be seen together outside of that too, like for coffee or something. What else can you think of?'

'Um . . .' my eyes widened, 'what about coming to my races? That's a girlfriend thing to do, right?'

She nodded, and I could tell she was trying not to laugh. 'Yeah, that's a girlfriend thing to do. When are they?'

'Saturdays.'

'Ah,' she winced, 'we'll definitely have rehearsals on Saturdays, but I'll try and make it when I can.'

'That's okay,' I replied, hoping to keep the disappointment from my voice at losing a fleeting vision of having Violet cheer me on from the riverbank.

Another point was recorded in the notebook.

'I could meet you after training sometimes.'

My heartbeat kicked up again. 'That sounds good.'

'Now what about touching?'

'Touching?'

'Yeah. We talked about it last week. Touching in public. We're going to be seen out and about, so if we're together we should be holding hands or something.'

She tapped the pen against her plump bottom lip, and it took all my energy to force my gaze away.

'Holding hands is good,' I managed eventually, 'and that back pocket thing you did.'

Her eyes shot up, capturing my gaze so intently that I had to grip my fist around my glass to stop myself from pulling her into me and kissing her until we needed to come up for air.

What was wrong with me?

'Yeah, I can do that again,' she answered finally.

Down it went in the notepad.

'Next one. Instagram.'

'My Instagram's private, and I never use it,' I frowned.

I wasn't sure whether it was wise to admit that the only reason I'd been on it recently was to check on what Violet was doing, because that sounded weird at best and voyeuristic at worst. But Violet's Instagram was always filled with images of her on nights out with friends, or in the theatre, the Brooks family dog, or her gap year around the Southern Hemisphere with Stella.

What was more weird, scrolling through her pictures last week made me realize how many of them I'd already liked – except ones of her and other guys. None of those had been hearted, and they would stay that way.

'But people still follow you, and pictures still get out. You'll have to start using it,' she replied simply. 'There's no way we wouldn't be all over each other's social media if we were together.'

I sighed. This was becoming way more real than anything I'd been expecting and I was once again reminded of how a) incredibly naïve I was to think I could keep Violet as my fake girlfriend under wraps, and b) this was absolutely not the best idea I'd ever had, but I was in far too deep to be able to do anything about it.

'Okay,' I conceded.

Maybe I could just leave it up to Instagram to remind Brooks about what was going on.

'And you have to like and comment on every single picture of mine,' she pinned me with a determined glare, 'and they need to be good comments, none of that *Y R U SO HOT?* shit. Use proper words, not letters.'

I laughed loudly, because I didn't think I'd ever heard a more girlfriend-style comment. 'I can do that. Words not letters, only the best for an English student.'

'Great.' She grinned, pushing the notebook over to me, and tapping the bottom. 'Sign next to my name, I'm just popping to the loo.'

57

She jumped up, her hand draping along my shoulder as she walked off, sending goosebumps flurrying down my spine. The kind of goosebumps I hadn't had in a very long time. It was only when I lost her in the crowds by the bar that I looked down.

1. ~~No kissing.~~ Kissing only when appropriate.
2. Violet to meet Charlie after a minimum of two classes (inc. Evie's).
3. Charlie to meet Violet after a minimum of two classes on different days.
4. Violet to attend rowing meets when she can or after training.
5. Violet and Charlie to meet for coffee/lunch a minimum of twice a week.
6. Touching in public always. This includes hand-holding, hugging, hands in pockets, etc.
7. Instagram posts must be liked and commented on properly. One post a week featuring Violet and Charlie together on either Instagram.

My eyes scanned down the lines, and I debated hard on whether to add 'no tongues' next to the first point Violet had amended. I probably should, but if we were only kissing when appropriate then maybe that also included tongues when appropriate.

The pen hovered over the first line as my brain whirred and whirred with inappropriate thoughts of kissing her, *how* I would kiss her, *when* I would kiss her ... until I ignored the hammering of my heart against my ribs, picked up the pen and signed my name next to Violet's, just as she returned to the table.

Instead of sitting back in her chair, she pulled her phone from her pocket. Before I had a chance to ask what she was doing, she dropped into my lap. I wasn't any more prepared for it this time than I'd been the first time, nor was my dick, providing me with the unwanted reminder that Violet Brooks fitted perfectly against me.

'Wh . . . what are you doing?'

Slinging her arm over my shoulder, she replied, 'Photo for Insta.'

My entire body tensed as she wriggled around, leaning back into my chest until she was comfortable. Another five seconds of holding her before my dick joined in the action.

Finally, she stopped moving and opened up her camera. 'Okay. Now, kiss my cheek.'

'What?'

'Kiss my cheek, we need to look cute.'

I'd long passed the point of questioning Violet. It was clear she was the expert when it came to this sort of shit, so again I did as I was told. Moving the ends of her ponytail away from her shoulder, I wrapped my arms around her and leaned in. Her scent still lingered on her skin from earlier in the day, and I breathed in as deeply as I could without making it weird.

Her cheeks were warm and soft against my lips. Holding still, I was unsure of how long I was supposed to stay in this position and whether my eyes should be open or closed. Or if I should tilt my head to where the camera was raised, but she was done before I could think any more about it.

'Oh, it's cute. Look.' She held the screen in front of me. 'Yeah, I like that one.'

Reluctantly I loosened my hold on her and turned to see what she'd snapped. I had to admit, it was cute. She'd managed to capture us perfectly.

Her broad smile, her cheek slightly squashed from my lips pressing into it, her freckles and the amusement sparkling in her eyes. Even the smile curving my mouth was visible. The happiness was there for all to see.

It looked real. Too real.

I didn't need to worry about fooling everyone else, when I could almost fool myself.

'I'll post it later, and don't forget to write something underneath it.'

'I won't,' I chuckled, again. 'I'll make it good, just for you.'

'Are you going to tell anyone about this?' asked Violet, placing her phone back down and making no move to stand up. Not that I wanted her to. I could stay like this all day, even though I was acutely aware of my hand spread along the curve of her waist, almost spanning her stomach. Inches away from the swell of her boob.

'About us fake dating?'

She nodded.

I shrugged. 'Not if I can help it. Your brother and Oz know, obviously. Though seeing as he's not mentioned it once, I think your brother's forgotten.'

'Not for long once he sees this.' Violet tapped her phone.

'No. And if we're all over Instagram I'm probably going to have to tell some of the guys at the boathouse, and swear them to secrecy. But the fewer who know the better. Evie can't find out.'

'She won't.'

'Are you telling anyone? Apart from Stella, that is?'

'Nope. No reason to.' She shook her head. 'It can stay our secret.'

'Okay,' I replied, reaching for the ends of her pony-tail because it counted towards rule 6 – always touching in public – the one I'd already memorized, and had nothing to do with the fact I wanted to see what it would feel like twisting between my fingers. Good, it turns out. 'Thank you, Violet. I know I've said it before, but I really appreciate you helping me out.'

She opened her mouth to answer, but instead of her usual dulcet tones a much *much* deeper voice sounded out.

'Hi, mate.'

I glanced up to find Bitters – one of my nosier crewmates – peering down at me with an ill-concealed grin. In fact, it wasn't ill-concealed. He hadn't made the slightest effort to conceal it at all. It was right there out in the open for everyone to see exactly why he was grinning like the Cheshire Cat. Of all my crewmates to discover me in the pub with Violet on my lap, it had to be him. Of course it bloody did. Though on the plus side I wouldn't have to break it to anyone else – including Brooks – because they'd all know I was dating someone before Violet had gotten off my lap.

Bitters moved faster than a rocket at take-off when it came to gossip.

'What's going on here, then?'

In an ideal situation I would have preferred a little more notice before going public. Especially as the ink hadn't yet dried on our agreement, but at least the notebook was shut.

'Just taking a study break.'

Bitters raised one thick eyebrow. 'A study break?'

I waited a beat, not daring to look at Violet in case I bottled it, and I could sense she was waiting to see what I would do. Here goes nothing.

'Yes, a study break. With my girlfriend, Violet.' Before Bitters could jump in with one of his trademark borderline inappropriate comments I added, 'Violet, meet Otis Bitterson, one of my crewmates. Bitters, Violet.'

'Only my grandmother calls me Otis. Call me Bitters.' He thrust his hand out for Violet to shake, and she took it.

'Hello.'

He turned to me, though I didn't fail to notice he was yet to release Violet's hand. 'Now I understand why you rushed off from training.'

'I didn't want to be late,' I answered truthfully.

I glanced from him to Violet and back, expecting Bitters to realize she was Brooks' sister any second. But we were now two minutes in, and it didn't appear he was going to recognize her any time soon. I couldn't decide if that was a good thing. It probably was.

'Anyway,' he thumbed behind him, 'I should go and join my friends. Nice to meet you, Violet. Charlie, see you bright and early.'

'See you, mate,' I replied, watching him walk off,

62

slowly taking one backward step after another. The second Violet looked away his two thumbs shot up and he mouthed 'NICE!' before disappearing out of sight.

'So *that's* Bitters.'

'Yes. Do you know him?'

Violet shook her head. 'No, just heard Huey talking about him.'

'I thought he might have known you, but I guarantee he'll have texted everyone before he's even sat down.'

In fact, I thought I could already feel my phone vibrating with messages.

'Oh well, like my granny used to say, "better to rip it off all at once than do it slowly".'

'Is that what we've done? Ripped it all off.'

'Yes,' she laughed, her deep gravelly tone warming my skin until I questioned whether we were still too close to the fire. 'Do you need me to kiss it better for you?'

I stayed quiet. I figured it was better all round if I didn't answer that.

5. Violet

(That Instagram life)

'This pic is cute. You make a great fake couple, plus you look hot. Both of you.'

I spun around, almost garrotting myself on the cord for my curling irons in the process, to find Stella standing in my doorway, scrolling through her Instagram with a grin you could have seen from space. Or . . . you know . . . a significant distance.

'Or as the French would say *"tu as l'air magnifique"*.' Her fingers burst open against her lips.

'Oh, shut up.'

'What? I'm telling the truth,' she shrugged, 'and Charlie's liked it. He wrote "best study partner" underneath. He put a little heart next to it. What's not cute about that? I liked it too, by the way. Wanted to add some authenticity to it.'

I freed my hair from the grip of the iron before I singed it entirely. It was too hard to concentrate on curling my hair while my heart was flip flopping about at the thought of Charlie liking the Instagram I'd posted last night. Even though I'd told him he had to.

'You're being a menace.'

She let the door close with a bang, dropped her bag on the floor and flopped onto my bed – rather the pile of clothes hiding my bed. 'I'm not. I promise.'

I knew better. 'Hmm.'

She wriggled around, yanking a pale blue cardigan from underneath her hip, then tossed it over on the chair. 'Vi, why does your room look like your wardrobe threw up in it?'

'Couldn't decide what to wear,' I muttered, trying to keep my face as still as possible while I mastered the perfect flick of eyeliner.

'Wear to what?'

'I've got to go and meet Charlie after his tutorial, as the good fake girlfriend I am.'

And because he hadn't ventured far from my thoughts since this entire escapade started, or the past five years, my phone buzzed on the dresser with his name flashing up.

Charlie: *Meet you by the fountain?*

I put down the eye pencil and let the little buzz of nervous excitement work its way through my system. At least it gave me enough time to pause before I responded, so it didn't look like I was hanging around waiting for him to message me.

I wasn't doing that. Nope.

Violet: *Yes, I'll be waiting.*

I typed out an x then deleted it. Should a fake girlfriend put a kiss on their message? I typed another, then deleted it *again* before deciding against it entirely. Too soon for the x.

Hopefully he wasn't watching the *dot dot dots* of indecisiveness.

Shit, I really needed to get a better hang of this. I was yet to decide if it helped that Charlie seemed way more nervous than me, although thinking about it he was probably just distracted by Evie.

'Violet, what are you staring at?'

I glanced back up at the mirror, my gaze cutting to the reflection of Stella now tidying up the clothes explosion behind me.

'Nothing, just replying to Charlie.'

She thumbed through a copy of *Emma* which she'd found under a pair of jeans, and tossed it onto my desk. 'How are you feeling about it? Calmed your racing pulse yet?'

I sighed. 'I think so. I dunno. It's hard to tell.'

'What d'you mean?'

'When I'm with him, and it's just us two, it's like I'm a different person. I'm playing this role he wants, and it's all good. I can forget he's the guy I've fancied for years. But the second we part ways, and I'm alone, I panic all over again that I'm going to fuck up or he'll somehow see right through me and have to let me down gently that we're just friends. I don't need the reminder.'

'Hmm, quite the conundrum,' she replied, without offering up any kind of solution. 'Where do you have to meet him?'

'At Radcliffe.'

'Oh great!' She placed a now folded t-shirt on top of another one. 'That's on the way, I'll come too, I can assess how believable you are as a couple. And then it also doesn't look like you're trying too hard . . . you know, like you're passing and thought you'd wait quickly.'

67

'You're right,' I nodded, more from habit than anything, because she probably was.

I, on the other hand, hadn't really thought about the granular details of the situation because my brain was too focused on seeing Charlie. Out of the two of us she was the one who was right more often than not.

It was how we rolled, and one reason we rarely argued despite the fact we were almost polar opposites.

'And after we can swing by the theatre and see if they've made any early decisions.'

'They won't have. Cece said they'd let us know next week.'

Stella shrugged as she re-hung a cute, polka-dot mini skirt I'd immediately dismissed as not 'Charlie girlfriend-wear' back in the wardrobe. 'No harm checking. Then we can go for lunch before my three hours of French conversation. *Très bon.* Or it would be if Tavener wasn't in it too. Maybe I can have a glass of *vin* at lunch, that would make him less insufferable.'

'Is he any good at French?' I asked, running my fingers through my thick curls to make them more of a casual wave instead of the eighties bouffant I was currently sporting.

Based on Evie's sleek, glossy hair I couldn't see Charlie being with someone who looked like they'd stepped out of one of those retro shampoo ads.

'Unfortunately, yes, annoyingly so. Probably why he took it, because he knew he'd ace it.'

'You never know, he might put in a good word with Cecily, and you'll get the part of Olivia.'

'I'd rather get it on my own merit.' She moved over

to my dresser, twisting the lid off a pot of lip balm and swiping her finger through the top. She held it out to me. 'Here, you better use this, get your lips all nice and kissable for your new fake boyfriend.'

Dropping onto the chair next to me, I waited until she'd stopped laughing like it was the funniest joke she'd ever told, but her throaty cackle was too infectious not to get caught up in it.

'You're an idiot,' I grinned, snatching it from her and, against my better judgement, lightly coating my lips in the rose-scented balm.

After all, rule one did state kissing where appropriate. Perhaps there would be appropriate kissing today. Wishful thinking and all that.

I stood up and turned to Stella, waving my hand along the length of my body.

'This okay?'

She sat forward, giving it proper consideration, and reached for my glasses which I'd left on the desk, tapping the end of one arm against her lip. Slowly, her eyes travelled up from the bottom of my high-waisted jeans to the pale-grey cable-knit jumper. I probably shouldn't admit I'd been thinking about this ensemble since last night, including the freshly vibrant violet ends of my hair.

'Hmm. What are you going for?'

'I need to look like I haven't really bothered trying to look good. But just look good anyway.'

'And *'ow long 'as it taken you to achieve zis?'* She peered over my face and the barely-there make-up I'd spent an hour trying to perfect.

'Way too long, I don't know how anyone has the time every day.'

She sighed softly, but smiled, 'Vi, you don't need to try. You always look good. I told you that you looked *magnifique* when I walked in.'

'I know, but this isn't about me. It's about the part of Charlie's girlfriend.'

'Well, I say lucky Charlie you're going to so much effort, but you still need to be yourself.'

I shook my head, 'Uh-uh. Not a good idea.'

From now until the end of time, my alter-ego would be required whenever Charlie Masterson was present. It was the only way I could protect my heart, I'd decided.

'Let's get coffee on the way,' I glanced quickly at the time on my phone screen, 'if we leave now, we can treat ourselves to that cute place near the theatre.'

Stella put down the brush she was running through her hair, and pushed out of the chair. 'Good idea.'

Carefully pulling on my cute navy beanie with the pink bobble so my waves weren't crushed, I grabbed my thick bodywarmer, fanned my waves around my shoulders and followed Stella out.

'We don't have plans tonight, do we?' she asked, jogging to the main door being held open for us by another St Anne's first year.

'Thanks,' I called out, except she walked off before I reached the door.

'Do we have plans tonight?' Stella repeated, pulling a pair of aviators out of her backpack.

I squinted hard, cursing myself for forgetting my sunglasses. It might be nearly freezing, but it was one of those cloudless, crisp January days and the sun was blinding.

'No, I don't think so. Unless you want to learn lines again?'

She shook her head, 'I think we should go out. We can get a couple of the girls together, Cecily will be up for it, she's always keen for a party.'

'Yeah, okay, I don't have to be up early tomorrow.'

One good thing about my English course — 75 per cent of my classes were after ten a.m. It wasn't why I'd picked it, but I'd be lying if I said I didn't check out the timetable when I was applying.

'Excellent.'

Stella jumped into action and pulled her phone out to make arrangements. By the time we'd arrived at Rupert Pump's Coffee Emporium and joined the queue, she'd organized five of our girlfriends into meeting for cocktails in her room first so she could break in the new cocktail shaker she'd been given for Christmas. I wasn't surprised. In fact, Stella McAdams was one of the most organized and efficient people I knew; there was very little she couldn't accomplish when she put her mind to it.

'Cece's not answering,' she tutted. 'I think I'll go and find her while you go and meet Charlie. Do you mind?'

'No, of course not.' I shook my head, waiting until she'd slipped her phone back into her bag. 'Are you having your usual?'

'Extra shot coconut latte with chocolate foam? Yes please,' she grinned, right as her eyes opened wide. 'Hey, you know what? You should take Charlie one. That would be a girlfriend thing to do.'

'You don't think that's too keen?'

'Nope. It's exactly the right amount of keenness. Especially if that ex of his sees. Shows you know his coffee order.'

I nodded, once again she was correct.

'You know, between the two of us, we make a pretty decent whole girlfriend.'

She slung her arm over my shoulder and leaned in. 'You mean whole fake girlfriend.'

The twinge in my chest flickered again. 'What do you think he drinks?'

'Probably something boring like black filter. What does your brother drink?'

I shrugged, 'Dunno, but I saw him put butter in his coffee at Christmas, and I'm not ordering that.'

'Butter?' Stella's face said exactly what I was thinking. Disgusting. Or *A total waste of butter,'* as my mum told him.

'Yeah, apparently helps with body fat or something. Boat Race training, I guess.'

We moved forward in the queue another foot, as three customers walked out carrying steaming cups.

'Do you think they'll win this year?'

'I hope so. They've been training hard enough. It would be nice if the boys won for their final year. Shame we won't get to see many of the races before though.'

'Yeah, there's no way Cece will let us out of rehearsals.'

The people in front of us turned around as Stella let out a loud snort, and I almost dreaded what was about to come out of her mouth given the mischievous look on her face.

'Do you think Charlie will want you to be waiting with a warm towel by Chiswick Bridge?'

I shook my head, 'No, don't be silly. That's two and a half months away, and term will have finished. We'll be done by the Boat Race. This is a one-term thing.'

She forced her mouth down so it drooped at the edges. 'Sorry to hear you guys are breaking up. I'll make sure we go out and commiserate.'

'Thanks,' I grinned back, just as we reached the front of the queue and the impatient-looking server waiting for our order. 'One flat white, please. And one . . .' I pointed at Stella to give her order because I'd probably get it wrong and annoy this gentleman even more than he clearly already was.

I should have known she'd add a black filter coffee.

'For Charlie,' she winked.

Five minutes later we were making our way towards Radcliffe. All my concentration was going on not spilling coffee down myself, while also ignoring the nervous knots which were beginning to make their presence known the nearer we got, so I didn't hear the booming of my name until it was close enough to deafen me.

'VIOLET. Vi . . . Violet. VIOLET.'

Stella and I spun around to find my brother running towards me, completely oblivious to the scene he was causing. I was tall, but Hugo was Goliath, and several people stopped to move out of his way or watch him jog past.

'My god! Is that the result of butter in his coffee? Or has he been eating little children too?' mumbled Stella.

'I dunno . . .' I muttered to her, as Hugo stopped in front of us, looking more annoyed than I'd seen him in a while. Two girls walking past nearly collided with a lamppost because they were too busy craning their necks to look at him.

'Hello, what are you doing over this side of town?'

'What?' he frowned. 'What does that mean?'

'Nothing, I've just never seen you around here before,' I replied, with a shrug. 'Shouldn't you be in the gym or something? Wouldn't want your muscles to shrink.'

Next to me, Stella snorted loudly enough that it earned her a deep scowl, but that was it. He knew better than to retort. Because Stella and I had grown up together, she had also been present for Hugo's transformation from a gangly beanpole with a mop of curly hair once his obsession with the gym hit, before the even bigger obsession with rowing.

The summer we'd turned thirteen had coincided with another Marvel film being released in the cinema. Hugo had shot up three inches and expanded approximately four feet wide in a matter of months, and promptly decided that he could be the next superhero if he worked hard enough.

Since then, there'd been too many occasions to count when I'd caught him checking himself out in the mirror, therefore it was my job as a younger sister to keep his head a size which could fit through doorways. Stella was only too happy to lend a hand.

Shooting one last scowl in her direction, he focused on me, holding his phone so close to my face I needed to step back. 'Care to explain this?'

'Um . . .' I blinked as my eyes focused on the screen and the Instagram picture of Charlie and me. 'Which bit do you need explaining, exactly?'

'All of it.'

'Honestly, Huey, how did you get into Oxford?' Stella drawled, pointing at the screen. 'It's clearly a picture of Charlie and Violet. See, this is Violet, your sister, and this is Charlie kissing Violet's cheek.'

This time she earned herself a snarl.

'Why is my best friend kissing you?' he gritted out.

Taking another step back I crossed my arms. Or would have if I wasn't holding two steaming cups of coffee. My scowl would have to do. 'Are you serious?'

'What?'

'You were the one who gave him my number in the first place. If you didn't want him kissing me, then you should have thought about that.'

'Violet, what are you talking about?'

'Helping Charlie with Evie,' I replied, slowly, because he was clearly struggling today.

It took a second before realization dawned. Charlie was right, he'd forgotten. Hugo's eyes widened as quickly as his mouth formed an oval. 'Ohhhh. Evie. The fake girlfriend thing.'

'Yeah.'

His gaze narrowed like he was still trying to wrap his head around the concept. 'And this picture is part of that?'

75

'Yes.'

'So you're not going around making out with my friends?'

I rolled my eyes, mostly because I refused to dignify that with a response but also because I didn't have an answer. Not a black and white one anyway.

'Is checking up on my dating life the only reason you've graced this side of the city?'

'No,' he scoffed, too quickly. Quickly enough that it made it clear my dating life was *exactly* why he was over this side. 'Where are you two going anyway?'

My head tilted toward Stella. 'We're popping into the theatre to see if the roles have been put up.'

'For your play?'

'Yup.' I nodded.

'Okay, well, good luck with that.' He glanced at Stella, then back down at the two cups in my hand. 'Who's the spare coffee for?'

'It's mine,' answered Stella before I could. 'I just really love a big coffee and these take-away cups are simply too small.'

My brother stood there, peering between the pair of us, like he was trying to figure us out. I wasn't about to hold my breath; it had been eight years already and he still wasn't any closer. I think we'd finally got to the point where he'd stopped questioning, and just simply thought we were eccentric.

I could live with being eccentric.

'Okay,' he replied finally, before adding, 'call Mum. She asked me to tell you.'

'She never answers when I call,' I grumbled. 'Only bloody you.'

'That's because I'm her favourite.' He grinned, before his expression became serious again. 'I mean it Violet, you better not be going around snogging my mates. They're off-limits.'

'Haven't you got some weights to lift?' I snapped back.

His eyes narrowed before he finally moved away. 'See you around, weirdos.'

'Technically, you're not going around playing tonsil hockey with his mates. Plural,' whispered Stella, leaning in, once he'd jogged far enough away to hear.

I rubbed away the tickle she'd caused on my ear. 'No.'

'Just the one.'

'Yep. Looks that way.'

6. Charlie

(Once more unto the breach . . . or something like that)

Brooks: *Why is there a picture of you on my sister's Instagram?*
Brooks: *Why are you kissing her?*
Brooks: *Is this the hot girl Bitters was talking about seeing you with last night?*
Brooks: *My sister?*
Brooks: *You've got some explaining to do.*

I ignored the messages coming thick and fast, slipping my phone back into my pocket as the church bells chimed the quarter hour, ringing like an albatross around my neck.

Each step I took towards the entrance of Radcliffe became heavier and heavier.

By the time I reached the fountain – throwing out a silent prayer that in an hour Violet would be waiting – I was convinced I was squelching through mud. Everyone else was rushing past me, yet I was having difficulty putting one foot in front of the other.

I stopped and sat down on the edge of the fountain without thinking, only to immediately shoot back up when I realized it was wet. Even the temporary distraction of drying off the damp patch from my jeans didn't help the dread which had been festering since I'd woken up.

The cloudless blue skies were doing nothing for me.

I was also trying not to be overly dramatic, but as I stared up at the pale cream brick of the building I may as well have been clipping in the starting blocks of the longest, hardest gauntlet.

I didn't even want to get it over with.

I was quite content standing here, waiting for my jeans to dry. Or better yet, going home and back to bed so I could squeeze in a nap before training later.

The devil on my shoulder was telling me to do exactly that.

The guy on the other side was saying it wouldn't be as bad as I expected.

At least that raised a smile. It would absolutely be as bad as I expected. Worse most likely.

Either way, at some point I would be walking through the doors I was currently staring at, and I would be in a room with Evie Waters.

The only thing which had me moving again was the realization that I was eating into the early start I'd had. There was a reason I was arriving fifteen minutes before class began, and it would all be for nothing if I didn't get inside in the next sixty seconds.

One foot in front of the other and all that.

I was still so deep in my thoughts that I didn't notice the person exiting as I reached the doors, only seeing the glum outline of my reflection. The next thing I knew, I'd succeeded in knocking them plus all their books to the floor.

'Sorry mate,' I muttered, grabbing the books as quickly as I possibly could, and pulling the guy to his feet. Though looking at him, skinny arms now laden with the pile I'd stacked in them, it was debatable whether I'd knocked him over or if he'd just toppled.

Whatever happened, it seemed to have ignited the sense of urgency I'd been missing all morning.

'Sorry again,' I called behind me and sprinted for the staircase, taking the steps to the first floor two at a time.

For the next eight weeks, ten of us would spend an hour every Thursday discussing themes within the Philosophy of Physics, and writing up summary papers. I already knew Professor Rivers was going to split us into groups, but there was absolutely no way any group I was in would also include Evie.

No way. None.

Therefore, I'd spent last night devising a strategy to ensure it didn't happen under any circumstances.

I'd taken Rivers' classes before, and I knew he held a more *laissez-faire* attitude to the way he taught. Students took responsibility for themselves. While he might tell the room to divide into two, the actual organization of each group would be down to us. I couldn't risk leaving it to chance which would no doubt descend into a jumbled rush of deciding on the spot so I took the initiative to do it ahead of time.

It was brilliant, if I do say so myself.

The only downside was the way I'd had to split the group so Rivers wouldn't suspect an ulterior motive. Rivers or anyone else. I hadn't reached the top step of the first floor before Gordon Cherriot spotted me. His hand shot in the air with a wide wave.

'Charlie. Charlie. Over here.'

I stopped walking for a fraction of a second, reminding myself I had bigger things at stake, and they'd come with a cost. Gordon was the price I had to pay.

Oxford University was teeming with nerds. There was one around every corner. Hell, I was one – or would be if I didn't have a life outside the physics department. But Gordon Cherriot was in a nerd league of his own. Easily the biggest in the entire university.

He had no competition.

I didn't even know where his IQ stood, somewhere in the 170s probably. He'd be walking away with a first come the summer, no doubt about it. And that wasn't the most impressive thing about him – because Gordon Cherriot was only sixteen.

A child prodigy, a chess Grand Master – he'd taken his A-levels before his thirteenth birthday and arrived at Oxford the following September. There was a rumour on the grapevine that if Oxford hadn't insisted he kept to his academic schedule he'd have taken both his first- and second-year courses concurrently.

But the downside to Gordon – he didn't play well with others.

I'd known him since the first term at Oxford when we'd been in the same quantum mechanics class. I personally found him harmless, and kind of amusing. But I'd also learned to tune out most of what he said. I tried to remember he was a kid who'd never really had the chance to be a kid, and as someone who knew what it

82

was like to have their intellectual capacity make them stand out, I mostly cut him some slack.

To nearly everyone else, he was self-important, smug and borderline intolerable. It was hard to see him as a sixteen-year-old when he was constantly telling you why you were wrong. And how wrong you were. He excelled at it almost as much as he excelled at Einstein's Theory of Relativity. And it wasn't exclusive to students. More than once he'd told our professors they were wrong, although that did usually raise a smile from everyone else in the class.

Luckily, even in our small group, I'd managed to weed out enough people who Gordon hadn't completely alienated, and therefore found him tolerable enough to be around; or at least tolerable enough for me to plead to their sensibility and desire for an overall first grade. Plus, I knew Evie well enough that she would take one look at Gordon and dismiss him as not worth her time.

I eased off my backpack and dropped it on the ground near his feet. 'Hi mate. How are you today? Rivers here yet?'

He frowned and pushed his glasses up. The ones forever sliding off his nose. 'Yes, of course he's here.'

'Did you talk to him?'

'He's in a class, Charlie. I'm not interrupting.'

I nodded, stupid question. 'Anyone else from our group here?'

'Laura will be here in five minutes, but she's always late. David went to check on his timetable. It's fine, it gives me a minute to talk to you.'

83

My eyes glanced up and down the hallway before focusing back on Gordon. 'Talk to me? About what?'

He took a step towards me, just veering outside of my personal boundary but enough to make me realize he meant business.

He pushed his glasses up again, 'About our class, Charlie. I've been thinking, we should probably meet three times a week. I have outside study sessions, but none with a group like this where we're all responsible for everyone's grade. So, I'm willing to focus on this group, because while I don't have any doubt you'll work as hard as me, I do worry about the others so we may need to carry them.'

I stopped concentrating on who might be approaching from either end of the corridors and looked at him. This was one of those times when I'd tuned him out without realizing. 'Sorry what?'

'I checked everyone's grades from last term and Laura didn't come away with an overall first, so she'll need some help . . .' he continued like I was following every word, but I was still wondering if I'd heard correctly that he wanted to meet three times a week.

'We should set up Monday, Wednesday, and Friday revision sessions.'

Yep. I definitely heard correctly.

'Gordy . . .' I stopped. He hated being called Gordy. He'd told me many *many* times. But honestly it suited him way better than Gordon. No one likes a Gordon . . . anyway. 'Gordon, mate, I think it's a good idea, I really do. But I can't commit to three days a week with Boat Race training on top.'

Gordon's eyes widened for a nanosecond before his nostrils flared from a deep breath, but he was not to be deterred. It was one of the reasons people found him so insufferable. I'd decided it was an effective strategy to get you what you wanted. 'What about Mondays? Can you commit to Mondays?'

'It would depend on the time.' I dropped a hand on his shoulder, my eyes once more quickly flicking around us, before shooting back to Gordon again. 'You should hold the session, I'll come when I can.'

His mouth opened to say something when Laura Foster, a student from Oriel College, appeared at the top of the stairs.

'Hey guys,' she smiled, dropping her bag next to mine with a much louder thud. 'Where is everyone?'

'Miraculously, you're one of the first to arrive,' replied Gordon with absolutely no hesitation or embarrassment.

'Must have been the seventeen thousand alerts you sent me not to be late.' Her grin widened, and even though Gordon harrumphed, it was impossible for him to argue when Laura was looking at him with genuine amusement, her freckles crinkling along her nose as it scrunched.

I was too distracted to find it amusing. According to my watch and the way the corridor was beginning to fill with students waiting for their next class, we had five minutes to go. Curls of anxiety twisted around my veins, and I was almost tempted to go and hide in the loo.

'I have to say, Charlie, this was a great idea of yours. It'll save on so much time with everyone faffing about during class.'

Once again I dragged my nervously darting eyes to the person in front of me: Laura. 'Huh?'

'I was just saying I think this is a good idea.'

'Oh, thank you.' I managed a smile. 'Yeah, I thought it would be a good time saver too. Need to get ahead of the timetable.'

'Laura,' Gordon interrupted, 'I suggested to Charlie that we meet three times a week to go through the coursework. We all know how Professor Rivers likes to leave it up to our interpretation, so I suggest we spend the time getting it right.'

I didn't get a chance to hear Laura's response, and hopefully second my view that meeting three times a week would not be happening, because that was the moment my mouth dried up and a high-pitched ringing sounded in my ear.

In the next second, Evie appeared at the top of the stairs, walking normally. Not floating up on a cloud of brimstone or flying in on a broomstick like I'd expected her to.

I stood frozen on the spot.

I was still pretending to listen to what Laura and Gordon were talking about, watching their mouths form words I couldn't hear because I was too busy not looking at Evie, or counting every step she made towards our little group.

Gordon and Laura halted their conversation as Evie stopped in front of them.

'Hello.' Laura smiled at her, showing her the same amount of kindness she showed everyone, whether

86

they deserved it or not. Evie didn't. 'Are you here for Professor Rivers' class on Physics and Philosophy?'

'Yes,' she replied, her stare moving to Laura from where it had been boring a hole right through me. 'I'm Evie.'

'It's great to meet you! I don't think I've seen you in any of our classes before? Which college are you?'

'I'm in Pembroke.' Evie smiled back, her pale blue eyes shining in a way that made her seem more human than devil spawn, but I knew better. 'This is my first class here actually. I've read Philosophy, and Professor Rivers suggested I take Philosophy and Physics as an extra class this term.'

Gordon's mouth dropped open. 'You've never taken physics?'

Evie shrugged, 'Does A-level count?'

It was only when his mouth still hadn't closed, and his eyes looked like they might fall out of their sockets that Laura jammed an elbow into his ribs. 'Gordon, don't be rude.'

Gordon was too speechless at the thought of someone not caring about physics the way he did to retort. Instead, he dropped his head, turning closer to me, and mumbled something which sounded a lot like, 'Good job our group is sorted.'

'Sorry,' Laura cringed, gesturing her hand around the three of us. 'This is Gordon by the way, and Charlie.'

Evie's gaze moved slowly from Laura and across Gordon until it landed on me again, and she casually tucked a lone strand of hair behind her ear, but I didn't miss the sly curve of her lip. The others might not understand what it meant, but I knew exactly.

'Oh, Charlie and I go way back. Don't we, Charlie?'

I didn't reply, but Laura's eyes lit up the only way one's could when they didn't realize they were in the presence of evil. 'That's great, oh you should join our . . . OWWW!' She squealed loud enough to cancel out the ringing in my ears. Huh. 'Gordon! That was my foot.'

I summoned every single drop of discipline I had not to laugh as Gordon stepped back. Because if he hadn't just stomped on Laura's foot, she'd have been crying from the kick to the shins I'd have given her. My plans to avoid Evie weren't about to get shelved at the first hurdle by Laura being far too nice for her own good.

'Sorry,' Gordon replied, not seeming sorry in the slightest.

Laura looked like she was about to argue but thankfully that was the moment the classroom door in front of us swung open, providing a much-needed distraction. Out swarmed a large-ish group of first years, from the looks of their deer-in-the-headlights expressions, all clamouring for the exit, and sprinting down the stairs in their break for freedom.

It was the same expression I imagined I'd had after my first class with Professor Rivers – someone I'd once heard described as the Marmite of the physics department. In what I'd found was atypical of a physics professor, he didn't like the sound of his own voice. More so, he pushed you to think. As a result, his classes were some of my favourites. On the flip side, students who liked the structure of physics weren't so keen on him, but in the end couldn't argue with the grades he always seemed to coax out.

By the time the man himself arrived at the threshold of the classroom to summon us inside, the corridor had started to empty once more. Younger than most other faculty members, Professor Rivers still had the youthful exuberance of someone who remembered what it was like to be a student, even if the bushy handlebar moustache was more reminiscent of an American railroad owner, than of a man who realized that facial hair was actually a trend.

'Ah, my final year students. Come in, come in,' he boomed, waving us forward.

Gordon shot forward with a quick 'Good morning, Professor,' rushing to get the seat he wanted before anyone else sat there. Though if they had, he'd only have made them move.

I was tempted to run in after him, but instead I stayed where I was, knowing Evie would do exactly the same.

I turned and blocked her way. Any other person would have been startled at someone stopping directly in front of them, but not Evie, standing there with her arms crossed over her chest. She'd been watching every move I'd made since she arrived.

'Charlie . . .' she began, her big blue eyes widening. Her skin was absolutely flawless; not one single line or crease or divot formed as she looked up at me.

'Evie,' I cut her off before she wasted both our time, 'we have to get through the next eight weeks of being in the same room as each other. Please don't make it harder. We have nothing to talk about, but I will be civil when required within these four walls. Outside of it I will go back to pretending you don't exist.'

I could have predicted she'd huff a little in indignation, and it only hardened me further. 'God, Charlie, come on. You're so dramatic.'

'Listen to my words. I do not want to talk to you.'

I left her standing in the doorway and I stalked inside, making my way to the spot near to where the others were sitting.

'Well done, mate,' I muttered to Gordon as I sat down next to him.

'Close call, Charlie. We definitely wouldn't get a first having someone who's only taken A-level physics in our group . . .' I could almost see the scorn forming a puddle on the floor underneath him for how thickly it was dripping, and once again I stopped myself from laughing.

I didn't look at Evie again, though I knew she'd sat down when Professor Rivers closed the door behind her.

> **Brooks:** *I just saw Violet. She told me about the fake relationship thing.*
>
> **Brooks:** *Sorry mate, I forgot.*
>
> **Brooks:** *Just as long as it stays fake though.*
>
> **Brooks:** *Too fucking weird to see you two together.*
>
> **Brooks:** *I told Violet in certain terms that no way was she to go around snogging my friends.*

One down. Only seven more to go.

Just as the class before ours had, we rushed to the doors the second the big hand hit the hour.

I was likely outside before Gordon had finished telling Rivers what he could do better. The cold air hit me just as I spotted Violet, and I wasn't sure which jolted me more.

I don't know why, but I waited for a second before I ran over to her. I watched as she scoured through the hordes of undergrads coming and going, knowing she was searching for me. A rush of adrenaline spiked my blood; the same one I'd had yesterday when I'd met her at St Anne's, along with the same giddy kick of excitement powering against my ribcage.

I had an exceptional memory, but even for the brief couple of seconds I stood there watching her, I couldn't recall a time my chest had felt like it might pop.

When she finally spotted me ten metres away a smile spread across her face matching the one I knew I was wearing. Just like when I'd met her last week in the pub, her hair was tumbling over her shoulders, only today it had my fists clenching before I reached out to run my fingers through it. Then I remembered I could and these rules might actually be the best idea I've ever had. I could find out for myself if it was as soft as it looked, with that indescribable violet shade – reminiscent of twilight, right before the skies turn navy and the stars begin their night-time twinkling.

Had she always been this pretty? No, pretty was too pedestrian. Beautiful. Violet Brooks was beautiful.

Unfortunately my thoughts about Violet were rudely interrupted by the unmistakable sound of my name being called, followed by the wheezing of someone who probably shouldn't be running.

'Charlie . . .'

I picked up my pace.

'Charlie . . .'

Throwing Violet what I hoped was an apologetic expression right before I reached her, I turned to find Gordon gesticulating wildly while also trying to stop his backpack from falling to the ground. Only the force of the books inside seemed to be propelling him forward at a faster pace than his legs were carrying him.

'Charlie, we didn't come to a decision about Mondays,' he puffed out.

I rocked back on my heels, 'Hmm. Didn't we? I thought you were going to hold the session and I'd come along when I could. You know I'm good for the work. I just have to schedule it around other commitments.'

'We need to agree a time you can make it,' Gordon replied, his eyes darting to Violet who wasn't bothering to hide her amusement, and back at me. 'I spoke to the others and they said two p.m. works.'

I side-eyed Violet, who was still watching Gordon, 'Um . . . two p.m. . . . Monday. Monnndaaaay. Um, I feel like something happens at two p.m. on Mondays . . .' Gordon in turn was hanging onto my every word, while I was trying to stop what was about to happen from happening . . . but I couldn't. 'Oh, sorry mate, how rude of me, let me introduce my girlfriend, Violet.'

I shouldn't have done it.

I knew I shouldn't have done it as soon as her eyes widened. I should have kept my big mouth shut. There was no need for me to introduce her at all. But we clearly hadn't set any parameters for how widely this lie should be spread.

On the flip side . . . no harm in giving this fake relationship a real test drive.

It was impressive how quickly she recovered herself.

'Hello,' she waved with a smile.

'Hello,' Gordon replied, though it was more of an impatient snap, before he looked back up at me. 'Well?'

I sighed so deeply it almost rattled my bones.

I should be using Violet as an excuse to get out of Gordon's study session. It would have provided me with a legitimate reason for introducing her as my girlfriend. But the annoyingly much less selfish side of my brain was reminding me that Gordon had also saved my ass from Evie. Even if he hadn't realized it.

'Sure, mate. Count me in. Email me the invite.'

'Excellent news. Thank you, Charlie.' He grinned, widely, to the point I don't think I'd ever seen him so excited, evident given the little hop he made while hitching up his backpack. 'Bye Violet. I like your hair.'

The pair of us watched in silence as Gordon scurried off through the gates of the square.

'Interesting guy,' Violet chuckled.

'I'm so sorry about that. He's decent, just super intense. But working with him is the only way I could ensure I wouldn't be stuck in a group with Evie.'

I didn't like the way Violet's smile dropped into a straight line. 'Ah. Seems like you made the right choice though.'

'I hope so,' I grimaced, 'though he wanted study sessions three times a week, and if you hadn't been here, I'd definitely have caved.'

Thankfully, the face I'd pulled at the thought of three Gordon sessions a week was enough to make her laugh.

93

'Happy to help.'

'Yeah, if I'd known having a fake girlfriend would provide the perfect excuse to get out of doing anything I didn't want to, I'd have called you years ago . . .' I stopped talking and held her gaze. I wasn't sure if she was going to respond, or if there even was anything to respond to, but the longer we stared at each other the faster my pulse thudded, until I realized I wasn't quite smiling any more. It's hard to smile when you're concentrating on counting the flecks in the eyes of the girl standing in front of you, along with the freckles on her nose. I cleared my throat before it got awkward.

My attention was drawn to the two coffee cups in her hand as she thrust one at me. 'Sorry. It's probably cold now.'

A weird little flip happened in my belly. Or maybe it was my chest. Somewhere, anyway. No one had ever brought me coffee.

'Did you get me a coffee?'

'Yup. Black,' she nodded.

'Did you know I take it black?'

'No, just guessed. Thought it was the easiest. I didn't add butter . . .' she grinned.

I frowned. 'Butter?' Yuck. The only person I knew who added butter to their coffee was Brooks. 'Oh . . . way to ruin good coffee I say.'

'Yeah, exactly.'

Amazingly the coffee was still warm as I sipped it and watched her soft *pillowy* mouth rest around the cardboard lid as she sipped her own, reminding me of why we were here in the first place.

94

'Thank you, Violet. For the coffee and coming here . . . and saving me from extra study sessions.'

She paused, like she was about to say something, but then her gaze flicked over my shoulder. From the way her pupils flared, almost blending into the green of her irises, and her features tensed for a split second, I didn't need any guesses to figure out what had caught her attention.

'Um . . . Evie's over by the main doors,' she whispered.

Before I registered what I was doing, I stepped in towards Violet, my free hand snaking around her neck until it cupped the back of her head.

Rule one was no kissing unless appropriate. Did this constitute appropriate? Or would this be crossing a line?

Brooks had already lost his shit over a simple kiss on her cheek, and I still needed to break the news of the one last week. The one I couldn't stop thinking about.

How hard could not kissing be?

While I pondered on that I pulled her in, until my lips were a hair's breadth from hers and paused. Everything else silenced around us. If I wasn't holding my breath, we'd have been sharing oxygen. To anyone passing, we were in an intimate embrace, my lips on hers. But, in reality, we could have been a chasm apart for how they never touched. Yet *somehow* this was way more intimate.

Somehow this was worse than kissing. Like when you take away a sense and all the others are heightened. Because not kissing meant I could feel the way her heart was hammering under my fingertips.

Not kissing meant I could see the way her eyelashes were fluttering against her cheek like a butterfly wing.

And not kissing meant I'd never smell the rich dark floral and cedar scent she drenched herself in without thinking of this exact moment.

Every cell in my body screamed at me to close the distance. Instead, I inched back.

'Is she still there?' I asked, reluctantly loosening my grip in her hair, though not fully. I wasn't ready to let go.

Her eyes flicked to where she'd spotted Evie, but shook her head. 'No.'

I should have moved farther away, I should have dropped my hand, but as the opportunity had presented itself, I raked my fingers through her violet strands. They really were as soft as they looked.

I looked up to find her watching me twist the ends around my index finger, because I didn't seem to ever be able to stop myself. 'I like this colour. It suits you.'

'Thank you,' she replied softly, and I couldn't help but notice it got me a bigger smile than the one she'd shot Gordon's way when he'd said the same thing.

My dick noticed too, and this time I stepped back.

'No, thank *you*, Violet. I really appreciate you helping me, I don't know how I'd manage without you.' I paused, my eyes catching the time on the church clock. Bollocks. I was soooo late, yet I didn't want to leave. I wanted to stay. 'Um . . . I need to hustle to my next class, but I owe you massively. You saved me twice in five minutes. We need to add rehearsing lines to the rules. Quid pro quo. I'll text you about it later, okay?'

I swear I caught a tiny hesitation, but it disappeared into a smile before I could think more about it. 'Sure.'

'Great.' I took one quick look around.

I couldn't see Evie, but I'd learned long ago she could be lurking around any corner.

But this time when I leaned in to kiss Violet's cheek, I wasn't sure whether that was in case Evie was watching or because I couldn't not.

And if I really wanted to know the answer.

7. Violet

(There is no emoji more confusing than the winky face)

Charlie: *Well?*

Violet: *Well, what?*

Charlie: *Did you get the part?*

Violet: *I'm there now. Just waiting to hear.*

Charlie: *You'll get it. My fake girlfriend is born for the stage.*

Violet: *I appreciate your support.*

Charlie: *I'm already on my way to the bookstore for a copy of Shakespeare's Complete Works.*

Violet: *You really don't have to help me. Stella will run through them with me. It's cool.*

I eased my feet off the chair in front of me and sat forward.

Scrolling to the top of Charlie's messages I read through them again. Just like I had yesterday and just like I had the day before that. Four times he'd mentioned rehearsing lines with me. Five if you counted this last one, *and* he was going to the bookstore for a copy of *Shakespeare's Complete Works*.

Maybe he was joking about that last bit.

I couldn't tell. I couldn't tell a lot of things about Charlie Masterson, it seemed.

I also wasn't sure why I was so insistent on him not

99

helping me, because there in equal parts black and white were my responses every time. I'd kept them lukewarm at best.

First off, it was pointless having him help. I'd never be able to concentrate. My chest was already thudding erratically at the thought, so to sit across from him while he recited lines for me? Yeah, nope.

And really, there's no way he had time. His finals were in less than six months, *and* he had the Boat Race. Which, according to my brother, was far more important.

So really, me declining his help was the best solution all around – he'd have more time for training, and I wouldn't be distracted by the way his mouth moved as he spoke to me.

But I'd yet to deter him.

The tell-tale buzz of a new message only proved my point, and I scrolled back down to the bottom.

> **Charlie:** *I'm not taking no for an answer, plus Shakespeare's one subject I don't know much about. You can teach me* 😊

That. That winky face. Who puts a winky face? What did it even mean? I was intelligent enough to get into Oxford, but understanding that winky face was beyond my skills of interpretation.

'Stel . . .' I leaned into her and whispered as quietly as I could. 'Stel . . .'

'What?' she replied, not bothering to look at me.

In fact, she barely moved from the eager, upright position she'd been sitting in since we'd arrived.

She was doing what I should be doing – namely

paying attention to Cecily and Linus on the stage in front of us, discussing the forthcoming production of *Twelfth Night* before they announced who'd been awarded the coveted main roles. I'd paid attention for as long as I could, but they lost me when a debate started over official poster design, and whose name should go above the credits.

I didn't need to look around to know I wasn't the only one not giving them their full attention. Half the heads of people on the six rows in front of me were dipped down, clearly scrolling through their phones for something much more interesting. I wasn't even sure why Cecily and Linus were going into such minute details, considering half of everyone in here didn't know what job they were about to be given. Not to mention half of that half would then up and leave once they didn't get the job they'd wanted.

I hadn't expected it to be quite so popular, but there had to be enough people in here to fill the role of every single Shakespeare character in every play he'd written and still have some left over to read the Sonnets. Even Stella was finding it way more interesting than I expected her to. I glanced up to see if I'd missed something, but now they were going on about lighting, so for the life of me I couldn't figure it out.

It was only when the doors at the back of the theatre flung open, hitting the wall behind with a loud clatter, that I realized why they'd been stalling.

'Damn,' she grumbled, sinking back into the crushed velvet of the theatre chair. 'For a second I genuinely thought he wasn't coming, and they were going to announce someone else.'

I glanced at the time on my phone. 'Wow, fifteen minutes late is pushing it, even for him.'

Leo Tavener's arms spread wide in the air as he marched purposefully towards the stage, his strategically placed dark blond hair flopping over one eye.

'Sorry. So sorry everyone. I apologize profusely for my tardiness, my agent loves to talk and sometimes it's nearly impossible to get off the phone.' His laugh boomed over the wave of giggles and not very well disguised sighs.

Plus, the loud scoff directly to my right. 'Gimme a break.'

Of course, Leo Tavener was why more people had auditioned for this play in the history of all plays held at the Oxford Playhouse, and why there was a waiting list to volunteer.

'Bloody hell, look at Cece. She practically has cartoon hearts floating around her.'

My eyes flicked over to where Cecily Caruthers was indeed looking a little flushed as she beamed down at Leo, who was now making a great production of removing his thick scarf and winter coat, while simultaneously bowing.

'I can't watch this.' Stella shrunk down in her seat by another degree. 'Anyway, what were you saying before?'

'When?'

'Just then. Before Marlon Brando walked in,' she replied. 'You nudged me.'

My forehead creased a little as I tried to figure out

what she was talking about, then wondered how I'd ever forgotten.

'Oh. Oh! Yeah.' I opened up my messages and passed the phone to her. 'Read these.'

Her eyes scanned through the texts. A funny little gurgling started up in my belly, wondering if she would maybe, possibly, come to the same conclusion I had. Because I wasn't entirely sure, but it was something that had struck me during a middle of the night insomnia session.

'Stel, do you think . . . Is Charlie flirting with me?'

I was well acquainted with a guy who flirts. Without sounding like my ego needed knocking down a few rungs, I knew what it was like when a guy flirted with me. It happened on a regular, if not fairly regular, basis. In fact, there was a guy on my English course who flirted with me every week in our Historical Prose lecture, and I let him because it was fun.

But this . . . in no world I lived had Charlie Masterson ever flirted with me. It was something I'd never even been able to conceive within my imagination, and I could imagine a lot. Therefore, I didn't want to jump to conclusions because I hadn't spent enough time with him to have knowledge of his flirting skills. Yet I'd also spent enough time with him to know for sure he didn't seem like the winky face type of guy.

'I've been going over and over it,' I muttered, filling the silence between us as she continued reading, while the rest of the theatre was yet to settle from the excitement of Leo being in their midst. 'We've never spent time together before, I can't tell. But he seems to really want to rehearse lines with me. It's not just being polite right, or do you think it is? I mean even if he is flirting it doesn't mean anything, but I can't tell . . .'

'Vi, shut up,' she hissed, stopping me in my semi-conscious brain dump. 'I'm trying to think.'

I held my mouth in a hard line as she scrolled to the top again and read from the beginning. I waited. And waited.

'Stel . . .' I almost whined.

She held the phone out for me to take. 'Look, you could say he's just being friendly, which he is. And if these came from anyone else you probably wouldn't think about it, but also you guys are doing your thing publicly and these are private . . .'

I turned to her, my eyes wide in anticipation of the verdict, 'And?'

'I think he's flirting.'

'Shit.'

'Yeah, but I don't know what it means outside that.'

I slumped down in my chair, just like she had.

'You guys definitely have chemistry, even if it is weirdly awkward. I'm assuming you haven't knocked heads again.'

A little chuckle popped through my lips. 'No. No more collisions.'

'Have there been any more non-kisses?'

'Not really. Nothing that counts anyway.' I shook my head.

There was really very little to report. Charlie had met me after class twice in the last week, as well as for coffee, and we'd walked through the streets to his class, taking the long route. Every time we'd held hands, or his arm had been over my shoulder as per rule 6. But he hadn't so much as kissed my cheek. There'd been no kissing or non-kissing much to my dismay, because that non-kiss had been the hottest thing I'd ever done, or hadn't done. Whatever it was or wasn't, I'd told Stella about it the second my legs had been able to move again, which had been a good five minutes after Charlie jogged off to his next class.

It had taken me that long to recover. Not that I really had recovered. But seriously how could something which barely involved any touching be so insanely hot?

My entire body had felt like it had been dipped in paraffin and set alight. By the time he'd finally dropped his hands and run his fingers through my hair I could feel my heartbeat in every cell of my body. The vest under the grey jumper I'd so carefully selected had been completely soaked through.

'Nope, nothing. I bet my bloody brother threatened him or something,' I grumbled. 'But even so the non-kiss was only for Evie's benefit. If I hadn't spotted her, he'd have stayed where he was.'

Evie.

All of it was for the benefit of Evie and Evie alone, and I'd actively reminded myself of the fact every day. I could still see the faint blue biro markings where I'd written THIS IS NOT REAL on my hand as a panicked reminder two days ago, when he'd come to meet me after my Victorian Poets class and all I'd been able to think about was how good he looked in jeans and a cable knit. Like he'd just stepped out of a magazine.

Goosebumps erupted over my skin at the memory and I turned my palm over again to check. I should probably go over the letters with permanent marker.

'Maybe, but I stand by my assessment. I think he's flirting. But it could mean nothing, Vi. Guys flirt.'

My belly gave another little flippy gurgle thing. 'Yeah?'

'Yeah. You should totally have him rehearse lines with you,' she hissed. 'I thought you put it in your rules anyway.'

'But that's in public.'

'So do it in private.'

It was as I took my phone back that I realized the incessant chatter in the theatre had dropped to almost silent, and I looked up to find Linus glaring at us.

'If you two have finished your own meeting, can we get on with the one the rest of us have come here for?'

'Sorry, Linus,' mumbled Stella, and the pair of us immediately sat up straighter, a feat in itself considering Linus' glare was usually considered withering at the very least. Every single person on the rows in front of us turned around to see who he was talking to, and it would have been hard to tell if Leo hadn't stood up from the front and waved.

'Ah there you are, Stella, hello. Glad I could persuade you to come and join in our merry show. Let's chat after, okay?'

'I hate him,' she hissed.

I had to bite down on a loud laugh at the look of fury on Stella's face, especially because even Linus seemed to take it as a warning not to call us out again. One loud clap of his hands and the attention of everyone in here was back on him.

'Welcome. Welcome. Thank you all for joining us, and thank you for being part of the journey for Oxford University's summer production of *Twelfth Night*. This year promises to be a very exciting time for all of us, and it goes without saying that we are ecstatic to welcome award-winning actor, Leo Tavener, as Duke Orsino. It's the first time in the history of Oxford productions that we've had an Oscar winner perform here *after* they've won their award.'

Linus' simpering grin was only made worse by the girlish giggle he let out as he looked down at the front row. Stella groaned as Leo jumped up again, turned and waved to everyone in the rows behind him, which only increased the already deafening cheering and whistles piercing the air.

'You're too kind, too kind. It's my honour, and I'm so happy to be here. Don't forget my door's always open if you need advice of any kind. I was once a beginner too,' he crowed before sitting down.

Cecily, who up until this point had been mostly quiet, while also staring at Leo, cleared her throat and removed the microphone from Linus' hand.

'Hello, everyone. I concur with Linus, this year is going to be the most exciting year yet. You're all on the brink of something very special.' She grinned, though I couldn't tell if she was smiling because she was genuinely excited about the play or because she had a very obvious crush on Leo. 'Now, without further ado, we will announce the roles. Following this session, notices will be posted in the artists' vestibule including back of house teams, rehearsal schedules and important dates for you to be aware of. Please do check it, and any changes we make will be emailed also.'

Everyone on the first three rows sat up straighter, the anticipation of finding out their parts buzzed like electricity throughout the theatre, especially when Leo jumped onto the stage to join Linus and Cecily.

'Oh, hell no. If I get called, I'm not going up there.'

'Good luck telling them that,' I hissed back to Stella.

Cecily cleared her throat once more and looked down at her clipboard, then straight at the pair of us. A mischievous smirk quivered on her lip.

'Starting with the supporting roles . . .'

Stella groaned loud enough that the group on the row two in front of us turned around.

'The Sea Captain will be played by Simon Lamb, understudy James Barrell . . .'

'Let's save applause until the end, please. Otherwise, we'll be here all day,' cried Linus over a round of loud whooping and cheering.

My head fell back against the seat rest. By my calculation there would be at least ten minutes of Cecily talking, and Linus asking everyone to be quiet. The part of Hannah Smith as Washer Woman Three got an even bigger cheer.

Linus would combust at this rate. Somehow he managed to keep the excitement on a steady simmer until finally . . . *finally* we were at the role I'd been crossing my fingers about for weeks.

108

'The part of Viola will be played by Violet Brooks, understudy Sarah Josephs.'

'Yes, Vi. I knew you would,' Stella nudged me in the ribs, 'well fucking done.'

Thankfully he made no indication for me to join the three of them on stage so I stayed put.

'Olivia will be played by Stella McAdams, understudy Aditi Patel.'

I reached over and squeezed Stella's hand, 'Eeek. We did it Stel. This is going to be such an awesome summer.'

It took another thirty minutes for the rest of the production names to be read out, which included fifteen of Leo addressing the team again to assure everyone that he would be available twenty-four/seven for any and all acting advice people wanted, before excusing himself for another meeting. Following further congratulations, and after Cecily handed all the principal characters a thick folder containing the official schedule of rehearsal times for the next month, we finally escaped only to find it raining heavily outside.

'Let's go and get a drink and celebrate,' Stella said, stopping under the canopy of the theatre so we could both pull our hoods up, while cursing our lack of umbrellas.

The Blue Oar was around the corner and would provide some shelter while we waited for the downpour to stop.

'Okay, a quick one. I have class after lunch and I have to go back to St Anne's before.'

'Let's go.'

We sprinted down the street as fast as we could. And I found a new use for Cece's giant folder, as I held it over my head for extra protection. We'd only been in the theatre a little over an hour, yet it was enough time for huge puddles to form on the road. Stella let out a loud screech as a car came around the corner, only to hit a puddle – the people five metres in front of her were showered with a wall of water. Completely soaked.

'Bloody hell,' she cried, shaking off the excess of puddle which had caught her, 'hope they've got a change of clothes.'

As usual, the Blue Oar was busy, though mostly with people who had the exact same idea as us. Shelter.

'Go by the fire,' I called to Stella as she charged in, pushing through the heavy doors. 'I think I spotted a spare table.'

I was so focused on getting out of the rain, and dry, I didn't notice anyone in my path as I shook my folder free of water while simultaneously trying to remove my coat without getting anything else wet.

'Hey, watch it,' snapped a voice to my left.

'God, I'm so sor—' I spun around to find who I'd accidentally soaked, the apology already forming on my lips. But it died just as quickly.

I just caught her pale blue eyes flaring in recognition at who'd inadvertently bumped into her, before they narrowed to barely more than a slit. Even with the ferocious clench of her jaw and hard purse of her lips Evie was incredibly beautiful. I ignored the way my stomach churned as a reminder that this woman in front of me was the woman Charlie once loved. This small, dark-haired person who was my exact opposite looked like she was trying to melt me with her glare.

I cleared my throat, while Evie didn't move a muscle, 'I'm sorry. I didn't see you there.'

Stella was calling me from the table she'd secured, and it soon became obvious Evie wasn't going to say anything, but as I turned to walk away her voice cut through the noise.

'I'm going to get him back.'

I spun around, slowly, using the time to figure if I'd heard what I thought I'd heard. 'Excuse me?'

Her arms crossed over her chest as her chin jutted up defiantly. It was a wholly unnecessary move, because everything about her screamed defiance. It struck me that this was a girl who was used to getting exactly what she wanted when she wanted it, and I was merely a pawn in her way.

'I've asked around about the two of you. You haven't been together long.'

I stood there, staring, waiting to see if she was done making her statement or if she had more to add. I did my best not to let the panic flush over me at the thought of Evie asking any questions about me or us period, because at this stage it probably wouldn't take much for her to make assumptions which would be too close to the truth. It became clear why Charlie seemed so genuinely terrified of her.

'Charlie and I have history, and we *always* find our way back to each other.'

'Not this time,' I found myself saying.

Evie's smile didn't reach her eyes. 'Always, Violet.'

'I don't think so.' I stepped in closer, kind of enjoying the way her neck had to crane back, because it was that or step away, but I already knew she'd never give up her ground. I doubted that anything intimidated her, even though I was giving it my best effort. 'Charlie's not a game to be played with, only for you to get bored again.'

'Who says I'm going to get bored this time?'

I shrugged, 'It doesn't matter, because there's not going to be a *this* time.'

'We'll see.'

I stood there staring down at her, trying my hardest not to blink. My ribcage was rattling so hard from the force my heart was pumping adrenaline through me that by the time Evie eventually turned around and walked away I realized I'd been holding my breath.

'Vi . . . hurry up, what are you drinking?' Stella shouted over from the table she'd secured but it was the buzz of my phone that jolted me into moving.

> **Charlie:** *Now the proud owner of one copy of Shakespeare's Complete Works. It's massive! This could double as my workout.*
>
> **Charlie:** *When's our first session?*

Underneath he'd sent a picture of himself, his face so impossibly happy at what he'd accomplished that I could only laugh.

I couldn't be certain that I wouldn't have made one last attempt to dissuade him from wanting to help me if I hadn't bumped into Evie. But I didn't give it a second thought as I typed out my response.

> **Violet:** *I'm free this evening.*

8. Charlie

(Who needs sleep anyway?)

I tapped my card against the reader, grabbed the sandwich and the bottle of water from the counter, shoved them in my bag and moved to the side to wait for my coffee.

Every muscle in my body ached this morning. I wasn't sure if it was the lack of sleep I was running on currently or the way training had stepped up, or just the general fact that my mind didn't want to stop whirring with thoughts I had no business having. Probably all three.

I did what I always did, and squeezed along my shoulder, hoping it might ease the tightness building, though it didn't seem to help. I needed a massage. I needed something . . .

'Charlie?' called the barista, waving around my Americano far too haphazardly considering it was boiling water. 'Char—'

I was also far too precious about my third coffee of the day to risk him spilling it. I snatched it away before he could finish calling me again, and turned around to find Gordon standing behind me.

'Oh, Charlie, hello.'

'Hey, mate. How's it going? How long have you been standing there?'

He looked at his watch, 'Twenty-three seconds.'

'You waiting for a coffee?'

He shook his head. 'No, I don't drink caffeine. I've ordered a hot chocolate.'

Mmm, hot chocolate. Even the thought of thick hot chocolate warmed my insides, unfortunately it wouldn't even touch the sides of my tiredness, especially as I was stifling a yawn, 'Good choice.'

'Are you tired?'

'You could say that.'

Maybe it *was* the lack of sleep that had my body dragging itself through the motions of the morning. Truthfully, I was still trying to catch up on all the sleep I lost by kissing Violet, though the not kissing her didn't help with that either. Not one bit.

In fact, the not kissing her had made things worse.

And then there'd been the meeting after class, the hand-holding, everything in the rules, including the rehearsing.

Since Violet had been awarded her role, we'd only managed one session together, where I'd played all the parts opposite her character. I still wasn't entirely sure what the play was about – secret identities, secret crushes and secret something else, she'd said, but I wasn't sure what that meant. If I was being honest, I hadn't exactly given it my full attention because every time Violet spoke I was too captivated by watching her mouth move. Then I'd lose my spot on the page when it was my turn to speak and it kind of broke the momentum of her concentration.

I'd had to hold the spot on the page with my finger, like a fumbling idiot.

I'd never been fumbling in my life, but Violet Brooks seemed to bring out that side of me.

'How's training going?'

'Good, tiring.' Tiring was the soundtrack of the day. 'But it's worth it, because we're going to win.'

Gordon's head bobbed, 'Good, glad to hear it.'

'You coming to watch?'

'Yes, I shall be there.' His eyes lit up enthusiastically, 'My parents come to watch too, and we spend a long weekend in London with my sister.'

'That sounds fun. I didn't know you had siblings,' I replied, realizing I actually didn't know a huge amount about Gordon's life outside university, mostly because he was usually talking so much about his own achievements, they kind of all merged into one. Plus, the zoning out was an issue.

'Hot chocolate for Gordon,' shouted the barista and I reached between the two guys in front to grab it for him.

'Thanks. Are you on your way to our tutorial?'

'Sure am.'

'Great, we can walk together, and I can pick your brain on a few ideas I've had,' he said, taking a long gulp of his drink before wiping away the chocolate sprinkled milk moustache which had been left.

'Cool. Sounds good. How's chess club?' I asked, weaving my way through the small group of students all waiting for coffee.

'Oh great,' he piped up behind me, his excited voice breaking through the chatter. 'We won the tournament last weekend, it was a really nail-biting final. You should come down and watch next time.'

A nail-biting chess final. I'd played chess at school, but only because it got me out of a series of detentions that I had no interest in completing. My headmaster had said if I played on the team for one term, my punishment would be null and void. Therefore chess club was a no brainer.

I didn't mind it, and we won more than we lost. Not sure I'd ever describe chess as nail-biting, however. But I probably hadn't played the way Gordon played.

'Sounds good. As long as I don't have a race, count me in.'

'Excellent. I shall,' he replied, as we stepped back onto the street side by side. 'Hey, Charlie, isn't that your girlfriend?'

I frowned, 'What?' I didn't have a . . . 'Wait, what?'

'Yes, I'm sure it's her. In the bright green jacket.'

My eyes snapped up, following the direction Gordon was pointing. Sure enough there was Violet, walking along the opposite pavement, her arms laden with books. She was wearing her muppet green coat, but in lieu of the navy hat with the pink bobble, she had on an enormous pair of noise-cancelling headphones. Even from this distance I could see the soft glow of her cheek from the cold air, and her face was lit up with a smile that made me want to know what she was listening to.

She was also not paying the slightest bit of attention to where she was going, but luckily that coat was warning enough to anyone walking towards her that they moved out of the way.

'It is her, isn't it? Her coat's very bright.'

I grinned, it certainly was.

Anything else Gordon said fell on deaf ears, as I was already jogging halfway across the road and narrowly missed a couple of cyclists who made their annoyance known.

I stopped in front of her. I knew she hadn't been looking where she was going when she almost walked into me.

'Hello.'

Her blue eyes flared wide, and her nose crinkled the way it always did when she was a little confused or annoyed, though I hadn't quite got it down which was which. She pulled off her headphones to rest around her neck. 'Hey. What are you doing here?'

'I just grabbed a coffee and spotted you.'

There was something about her smile that I felt deep in my chest. A twinge . . . a heavy thump . . . I dunno. But it was there.

I tried to rub it away, but it wasn't budging. In fact, the longer we stood here staring at each other, the more pronounced it got.

'Hello, Violet,' puffed a voice to the side of us, thankfully breaking whatever moment had been going on between us.

'Oh, hey Gordon.' She turned her smile to him, 'Where did you come from?'

'I was talking to Charlie but he ran off the second he spotted you,' he tutted, and I had to drop my head to hide my amusement. 'He does that a lot.'

Violet turned to me, one perfectly arched eyebrow raised in question. 'Does he now?'

My shoulders jerked up in response because there wasn't much more to say. Plus, I was trying to ignore the way my cheeks suddenly warmed.

'Where are you going with all these books?' I nodded to her hands, and peered at the spines. The biggest one looked like it weighed a minimum of five kilos. '*Wilson's Guide to Every Literary Character Ever.*'

'Returning them to the library, need to swap them out.'

'Oh yeah? For what? A guide to all the books ever written?' I grinned.

Her teeth might have sunk into her bottom lip to stop herself from laughing, but it couldn't disguise the amusement in her eyes. 'Something like that.'

I couldn't tell you where it came from but the second the idea popped into my head, there was no stopping me.

'Great, we're walking that way.'

'No, we weren't,' added Gordon before I could stop him too.

'We are now.'

'Charlie, we have tutorial,' he pressed.

I looked at my watch. 'In half an hour.' Though I knew it could say we were running late and I'd still be walking in whatever direction Violet was going.

As if to illustrate the point to myself, I reached out and took all her books from her – I was wrong, that literary guide had to be nearer ten kilos, and Violet Brooks was freakishly strong.

Her entire face screwed up, and the little line that creased her nose deepened, 'What are you doing?'

118

'Carrying your books for you.'

'Why?'

'Because you have a lot, and they look heavy.'

'We're not in the nineteen-fifties, I can carry my own books.' She reached to take them back, but I shifted around so she couldn't, only to grin wide when she huffed a little.

I liked that little huff more than I wanted to admit.

'I'd just let him Violet, Charlie seems to do what he wants,' grumbled Gordon.

I refrained from pointing out that he was perfectly free to go to class, and I'd meet him there.

'He does, doesn't he?' she replied, though I didn't miss the little curve of her lip as she side-eyed me.

'Are you reading English?' he asked, as the three of us made our way in the direction Violet had been heading.

'Yes.'

'I enjoy English. In my first year I took it alongside Physics, to help me balance my coursework. I very much enjoyed Shakespeare, although I wasn't a fan of Professor Simpson. A bit subpar, in my opinion.'

Violet's eyes widened, 'You took English for one year as an extra credit?'

'Gordon's a genius, more so than me,' I winked as she turned to me, her mouth slightly open. 'I'm just of the regular variety, therefore can only do one subject at a time.'

'Well, I'm impressed.'

'Have you been to the Globe?' he continued, 'I go every summer with my parents, we saw *Twelfth Night* last year.'

119

I peered around Violet to look at him, 'That's what Violet's studying. She just got the part of Viola in the summer production. I've been helping her learn lines.'

'You?'

'Yes.'

'Actually, I have a Shakespeare class, but the play is separate,' Violet added.

I'd never been on the end of one of Gordon's withering looks before, and now I had I could safely say I'd been put in my place. Even *he* knew Shakespeare wasn't my forte.

I decided to stay silent after that, and the three of us walked along the pavement towards the library. Me carrying Violet's books, while the two of them compared their favourite characters, and while I had nothing much to add to this conversation, it was almost enough that I could witness it. Violet was quite simply mesmerizing.

I couldn't tear my eyes away from the way her entire face lit up as she debated with Gordon. I couldn't even remember a time I'd seen Gordon talk so excitedly about something that didn't involve an equation.

But Violet had this way of bringing everyone under her spell, and it seemed even Gordon wasn't immune.

By the time we arrived – far too quickly in my opinion – my heart was pounding out a beat I didn't recognize.

She stopped right before we reached the steps and turned around. 'Well, here we are.'

'Yes,' I replied.

'Can I have my books back now?' she asked, her tone filled with amusement.

I placed them gently into her outstretched arms. I don't know what came over me – maybe it was Gordon, maybe it was the lack of sleep – but this moment, I'd decided, constituted an appropriate kissing moment. I leaned in as she gripped onto her books, and softly pressed my lips against hers. She stilled against me, and I couldn't stop myself from breathing her in, not even a little bit.

It seemed I had absolutely no self-control this morning, though I did manage to keep my tongue to myself which I was counting as a win.

She moved back with a smile, 'Thank you.'

'You're welcome.'

'See you later. Bye Gordon.'

'Bye Violet.' Gordon waved, and we watched her walk towards the revolving doors. 'Can we go now?'

'Sure,' I replied, though my eyes stayed trained on the girl in the green coat until she'd totally disappeared from sight. Now we could go. I turned to him with a sigh, patting his shoulder. 'Lead the way, my friend.'

He was silent for a second as we walked off, then, 'I like Violet, she seems very nice.'

'Me too, mate. Me too.'

9. Violet

(Every day's a school day. Or, Charlie Masterson learns something new)

Charlie: *Did you know Shakespeare wrote 39 plays?* 🎭
Violet: *I did.*
Charlie: *Did you know Twelfth Night has two titles? It's also called What You Will . . .*
Violet: *I did.*
Charlie: *Did you know Twelfth Night was written in 1601?*
Violet: *Are you reading Wikipedia or something?*
Charlie: *Might be.*
Charlie: *Gordon can't be the only Shakespeare know-it-all in the physics department* 😊
Charlie: *Anyway, Shakespeare also wrote 154 Sonnets. What's the difference between a sonnet and a poem?*
Violet: *Charlie what are you doing?*
Charlie: *Just trying to get a full grasp on the role I'm helping with, plus – you know – as you theatre people like to call it, gain an immersive experience.*
Violet: *Do we call it that?*
Charlie: *Pretty sure you do. I think you said it to me the other day 'Charlie, Shakespeare's an immersive experience'.*
Violet: *idntswqythat*
Charlie: *What?*
Violet: *Sorry, I was typing one-handed and brushing my teeth with the other. Didn't mean to press send.*

123

Violet: *I didn't say it was an immersive experience.*

Charlie: *I think you did. But we'll agree to disagree. Although it could be our first fake relationship fight.*

Violet: *You want a fight?*

Charlie: *No, not with you.*

Charlie: *It says here Twelfth Night is in the First Folio (looks up what is first folio).*

Charlie: *Oooh! There's a first folio in The Bodleian. We should go and see it.* 🎭

Violet: *You want to go to the library with me?*

Charlie: *I do!*

Charlie: *Did you know Shakespeare died on his birthday?*

Violet: *Yes. Did you know his dad was a glove maker and they lived above a glove shop?*

Charlie: *No, I haven't got to that bit in Wikipedia yet.*

Violet: *Did I ruin the ending?*

Charlie: *Maybe. We'll see.*

Violet: *I'm sure you'll get over it.*

Charlie: *I dunno, I'm quite sensitive.*

Charlie: *Violet?*

Charlie: *?*

Charlie: *Says here a sonnet is a poem of 14 lines . . .*

Charlie: *Have I bored you with my Shakespeare facts already.*

Violet: *No, sorry I jumped in the shower quickly. Still enjoying the facts.*

Charlie: *Oh. Shower before bed? Me too.*

Violet: *I went to the gym earlier.*

Charlie: *Good workout?*

Violet: *It was thanks, Stella and I had a HIIT class. Then we ate our bodyweight in noodles.*

Charlie: *So, you're noodled out?* 😊

Violet: *Hey, I didn't know you and my brother shared a joke book . . .*

Charlie: *Everything he knows he learned from me.*

Violet: *Oh dear.*

Violet: *How was your day? Aside from all the Shakespeare reading?*

Charlie: *It was good. Tuesdays are a light day class wise. I took a nap.*

Violet: *A nap?*

Charlie: *It was accidental, but yeah. Training was exhausting this morning and more so tonight. I'm already in bed with my bedtime reading.*

Violet: *I'm also in bed with my bedtime reading.*

Charlie: *Shakespeare reading?*

Violet: *No, Victorian Women.*

Charlie: *Oh. I draw the line there, I'm afraid. I'm not Wikipediaing Victorian Women. You might actually have to rely on Gordon for that.* ☹

Charlie: *But out of interest, what are you reading?*

Violet: *The Mill on The Floss by George Eliot.*

Charlie: *Um . . .*

Violet: *George Eliot was a woman.*

Charlie: *Really?*

Violet: *It was her pen name.*

Charlie: *Wow, every day really is a school day.*

Violet: *Don't tell me I'm teaching you something. Mr *I can change my grades*.*

Charlie: *I'm only clever when it comes to totally useless things, unfortunately.*

Violet: *Hmm. Not sure changing grades is useless. I'd love a First in astrophysics.*

Charlie: *I'll see what I can do, then.*

Violet: *That's all I'm asking. I kind of need it if I want to become an astronaut.*

Charlie: *You want to become an astronaut?*

Violet: *I'd like the option at least.*

Charlie: *Did you know there are more stars in the Milky Way than there are humans that have ever been born?*

Violet: *Are you back on Wikipedia again?*

Charlie: *Nope. I just know that. Told you I'm pretty useless.*

Violet: *I wouldn't go that far.*

Charlie: *No?*

Violet: *No.*

Charlie: *Well, that's good. A not totally useless fake-boyfriend* 😎

Violet: *I think it has a nice ring to it, if I'm honest. I can write it in your references for the next time you need a fake girlfriend.*

Charlie: *No need. You're the only fake girl for me.*

Violet: *Awww. Shucks.*

Charlie: *I should probably let you get on with your floss book. I'll let you know the rest of Shakespeare's interesting facts tomorrow.*

Violet: *I'll look forward to it.*

Charlie: *Good night, Violet Brooks x*

Violet: *Good night, Charlie.*

Carefully, I placed my phone on the nightstand.

Tucking my hand underneath my head, I lay there and watched to see if the screen would light up with one more message. Just one more. *Skippity skippity skip*, went my heart as we waited.

The screen stayed dark long enough for me to know another message wasn't coming, so I picked it back up again and scrolled to the beginning. There was something about the way he used my full name with the x on the end, and as I reached it, I went right back to the top again.

After the fifth time, my cheeks were aching so much from the width of my smile, that I had to put it down and go fetch a glass of water. Slipping back into bed, I put the screen face down and turned off the bedside lamp. George Eliot would have to wait, a new author had taken my attention tonight, and if I was lucky I would meet him in my dreams. The only place Charlie Masterson had ever been.

It didn't occur to me that perhaps my dreams were starting to become reality.

10. Charlie

(Because of course I had to go
and open my big mouth)

Charlie: *I'll be done at training by 7pm. Meet you in the library at 8?*

Violet: *Stella and I rehearsed earlier, I have an essay I have to write instead. So, you're off the hook tonight. You can do your own work instead of mine* 😊

'Who are you texting?'

I ignored the question and dropped down on the bench by my locker. My fingers hovered over the letters on my screen, trying to figure out how to reply and whether telling her I'd still meet her in the library was a good idea. I rarely went to the library, I usually preferred to work alone.

But . . . I wanted to be working with Violet.

I didn't want to be off the hook, I'd prefer to be very much on it. Especially as I was becoming somewhat of a Shakespeare expert. Sort of.

As much as a couple of weeks of reading would allow, anyway. I mean, reading Shakespeare was what you'd find Oz doing outside of training.

But since that day we'd walked to the library, or rather the first day I'd rehearsed with her, I'd spent every evening reading up. I'd also memorized every line in *Twelfth Night*, because after the first time of watching Violet recite her lines, I realized if I knew *my* lines I wouldn't have to keep looking at the page.

I could simply look at her, and once I did it was almost impossible to look away.

I was beginning to wonder if Violet could capture my attention away from even the most complex equations.

There was a uniqueness about her I'd never noticed before. Never had the opportunity to notice before because, I realized, there had always been something in the way. Whether that was Brooks refusing to let her join in with anything we did, because he said, *'her enthusiasm is far too annoying'*.

Or, worse, Evie.

Every time I saw Violet she seemed that little bit different; a priceless oil painting created from a palette of a thousand shades – the longer you stared, the more your eyes picked up. Something like that anyway. This is why I stuck to formulas, Shakespeare would be able to come up with a much better analogy. But my point is that I was starting to see Violet in a way I never had before, and I wanted to find out what else I'd been missing.

I wanted to know what she'd be like as a study partner, what she looked like when she was concentrating. Whether, for once, she was silent. If she wrote out revision cards, or used memory tests like Brooks which he forced us to help him with as part of his history degree, and at this point I knew more about Japanese Imperialism than I'd ever expected to.

I wondered how quickly she typed, or if she went

old-school and wrote out long-hand first, scribbling across a lined pad. I could imagine her doing that, there was something of a traditionalist about her. Though she'd call it something else – romantic, probably . . . *'Charlie, Shakespeare wrote long-hand. There's something to be said for the romance of penmanship.'*

I'd never cared about a girl's handwriting before, but I pictured Violet's from our list of rules. Her brother's needed to come with an Enigma code – that's how indecipherable it was – but Violet's was clear and neat, with rounded vowels and loopy lettering.

'Charlie?'

I was still smiling to myself as my head flicked up and I found Oz staring at me. 'Yeah?'

'Who are you texting?' he repeated.

I shut the phone off and slipped it into my pocket. The sole problem with Violet that I'd figured out was her ability to be entirely distracting even when she wasn't there. My brain seemed to be on hiatus.

'Um . . . no one.'

'That expression on your face says otherwise.'

I schooled my features to be as passive as possible. 'I don't have an expression.'

Oz's eyes narrowed, and he added a head tilt that said he wasn't sure if he was buying my flavour of bullshit today. 'Are you being weird?'

That was debatable.

I pulled off my hoodie and threw it into the back of the locker. 'Nope.'

'Then tell me who you were texting. You're being secretive.'

131

'I'm not. I wasn't texting anyone,' I replied, immediately regretting it. I should have told him I was replying to Gordon. Why didn't I tell him that?

Oh, right, because my mind only had room for Violet.

Oz dropped down onto the bench next to me. I could tell he was on the verge of asking something else I didn't want to answer, but thankfully the door to the locker room flung open and in walked Marshy, our coxswain. Actually, it was more of a stomp, his heavy feet thudding with each step as he failed to acknowledge either of us sitting there watching him pass by, and he pushed through the set of doors leading into the gym with such force they clattered back against the wall.

I clearly wasn't the only one with something on my mind. Though thankfully it provided me with the decent excuse to change the subject I'd desperately been hoping for.

'What's up with Marshy?'

Oz shook his head, 'I dunno. He's been in a bad mood for a while now.'

'Huh,' I muttered, switching out my trackpants for running shorts.

It might be freezing cold outside, but it was about to get very sweaty in the gym. My muscles were still feeling the burn from water training this morning, and I still hadn't had nearly enough sleep for my liking.

The doors were still swinging when in walked Bitters, Joshi, Drake and Frank, followed by several of the junior crew all looking far too cheery. The smiles would soon be wiped off their faces once our training session began.

There was no time for smiling.

It would take all our concentration to keep our breathing steady and in sync through each tug on the rowing machines. We might not be out on the water, but we would still be pushing our bodies through the motions of being in the shell. Pushing them to their limits.

Twice a day, seven days a week until the Boat Race was over, and we'd be victorious again.

If I wasn't such an overachiever, I'd wonder how I found time to think about Violet.

'Where's Brooks?' asked Joshi, sitting down to switch out his trainers.

'On the way, his lecture ran over,' replied Oz just as the doors opened again and in ran the man himself, his face red from a combination of the cold and the exertion he'd clearly used to get here.

'Thank fuck,' he puffed, slumping against the wall, 'I'm not late.'

We could all feel his sigh of relief. Late was not something you ever wanted to be.

Late meant you had to complete an extra five minutes of flat-out sprints, and after an already intense and fully loaded training session, you didn't want to do anything you didn't have to. Late came with zero excuses – no matter whether lectures ran over or you were hit by a bus – you did those sprints.

'No, mate,' Oz slapped him on the shoulder as Brooks fell onto the bench next to him, 'I don't even think you're the last here. I've not seen Fellows yet.'

I looked around; a couple of the guys were already in the gym, everyone else was just finishing up getting dressed, or undressed. Drake was fiddling with the heart monitor he'd strapped around his chest, Bitters was chugging a protein shake and Frank was searching through Spotify to find the playlist he'd made for all of us – he swore it was the perfect mix of tracks to get us through an hour of hard work.

I grabbed my own heart monitor, along with my headphones, and shoved the rest of my stuff into my bag before throwing it into the locker.

'Let's go, boys.'

We all headed in, Oz holding the door open for as long as he could be bothered.

Rows and rows of rowing machines lined the middle of the room. We'd had new ones installed at the beginning of this year, ergonomically designed which made them better for our bodies and promised to feel like the closest thing to rowing on water.

I had to admit, they were pretty good.

Out of habit the first thing anyone did on entering the gym was to check the board for the *Workout of the Day*. I couldn't see it through the wall of crewmates, but several groans told me that it wasn't good.

'Round Robin,' someone grumbled, though not loud enough for our coach to hear from the back of the room where he was in a huddle with the other coaches.

My own groan dragged through my chest. If there was anything I wanted to do less it was a session of Round Robin sprinting – a relentless pursuit chasing your teammates on an imaginary river, which we could all see projected onto the wall at the front. Every thirty seconds five of us were picked at random and had to double our speed to overtake the rest of the crew, while also trying to take the overall lead.

'No one puke this time,' added someone else, who sounded a lot like Bitters. 'Frank, that includes you.'

'I didn't puke,' Frank muttered, 'I nearly died though.'

Oz clapped his hands together, summoning attention, though not enough for everyone to stop grumbling about the torture we were being subjected to. 'Okay boys, let's go in ascending order of birthdays for who goes first. We started with December last time, we'll go with June today.'

There was silence for a couple of seconds before one of the juniors shouted, 'June 30th.'

'June 10th,' added Fellows, as he walked in and slunk to the side trying to hide the fact he was late.

Brooks turned to Fellows, 'Your birthday's June 10th?'

'Yeah, why?'

He shrugged. 'No reason, just didn't know that's all. It's the same day as my sister's.'

My head shot up just as Bitters asked, 'You have a sister?'

'Yeah.'

'Why have we never seen her?'

Brooks shrugged again as he clipped into his rower. 'She's just started in first year.'

'Has she got a boyfriend?'

From the look on Brooks' face, it was obvious he wished he'd never brought up the subject of Violet. I was kind of wishing the same thing. Especially when he looked at me and replied, 'Not a real one.'

Fuck.

135

And then it came out of nowhere. The thought of Violet with someone else pulsed under my skin as unwelcome as sewage, powered by a churning in my stomach.

'She hasn't got a boyfriend,' I snapped, before I could stop myself and ten sets of eyes shot to me. Some filled with amusement, some confused, and one set outright annoyed.

Yeah, I definitely wished Brooks had never mentioned Violet.

'Wait, you know her?'

I rolled my eyes and looked up at Bitters. I knew I'd never get away with not telling them. It was a miracle I'd made it a few weeks without it being brought up.

'Yeah, Violet. You met her . . . remember?'

His brows dropped deeply a split second before his entire face widened with . . . surprise? Shock? I dunno.

'That insanely hot chick was Brooks' sister?'

I tried to keep my face as passive as possible, and nodded. 'Yes.'

'What the fuck? You're dating Brooks' sister? She's so hot.'

Brooks got there before I did.

'Stop fucking calling my sister hot. And they're only fake dating.'

This time it wasn't just Bitters who looked confused. Everyone did, and I couldn't blame them.

'Violet is helping me with a problem I'm having with my ex-girlfriend. And she's helping me by pretending to be my current girlfriend.'

'Wait . . .' said Bitters, his tone, not to mention the

broad grin spreading across his face, reminding me exactly why we called him the shit-stirrer of the group. 'Charlie, are you telling me that the girl on your lap in the pub was just for show? You guys aren't really banging?'

'No, they're absolutely fucking not,' snapped Brooks before I could reply, and I was certain his glare was still laser-trained on me. It was likely if I looked down, I'd see a red dot dead centre in my chest.

'No,' I reiterated.

'Sure about that? You guys looked pretty cosy.'

I swear I heard Brooks growl.

'I'm sure. It's not real, she's helping me out. We have rules,' I forced out.

'Great. So I can ask her out then?'

'Don't be a dick,' I snapped. 'You're not asking her out. To the outside world, she's my girlfriend.'

There, that should buy some time and save me from this conversation I didn't mean to enter or want to be in. But unfortunately it wasn't enough to deter Bitters.

'So I can ask her out when you're done with this thing you need her for?'

'No!' Brooks and I snapped in unison.

'No,' he reiterated. 'No one is asking out my sister.'

'Charming,' grumbled Bitters, still through a grin he was sporting. 'I'll have you know I'd make a great real boyfriend.'

Brooks rolled his eyes and dropped down into the seat of his rower, hopefully ending the conversation. *Please let it be the end of the conversation.* It should have been, there was really nothing else to say on the subject,

137

but the deep breath I'd been holding onto stuck in my throat when he added, 'No one is dating my sister for real.'

My chest squeezed tighter. I could already predict the next question given the look on Bitters' face. Predict it, but unfortunately not stop it.

'Even Charlie?'

I didn't glance at Brooks. I was too busy trying to act as nonchalant as possible while ignoring the spiral of jealousy I was spinning down into at the thought of Violet in any kind of anything with another guy – especially Bitters. I clipped into the rower and adjusted my headphones, but the tilt of Brooks' chin told me he was once more looking straight at me. 'Even Charlie.'

Fuck fuck *FUCK*. Why did I have to open my mouth? Why did I have to bring Violet into it?

I tugged hard on the rowing strap, shooting back in my seat to fire up my muscles while simultaneously trying my best not to think about the way my stomach had curled in on itself.

I knew Evie had messed me up enough that I'd spent the best part of the past few years avoiding girls. Maybe that was the problem. That I'd avoided girls for so long, it had never occurred to me that I might like Violet.

Or maybe I liked Violet because I'd been avoiding girls for so long.

No, that wasn't it. I liked Violet because she was incredible.

I liked Violet because she made me laugh.

And I liked Violet because somehow, whenever

I was with her, she made me forget about absolutely everything except being in that moment.

Everyone flinched as a whistle pierced the air.

'Are we here to talk about girls or to win the Boat Race?' called Coach.

'Boat Race,' came back the unanimous response.

'Good, and Fellows, don't think I didn't notice you were late.'

A loud groan sounded out followed by a chorus of whoops and cheers. I joined in, but only in body, my mind was miles away. Back with Violet.

For a genius it might have taken me longer than it should have to figure out I *like* liked her. I just hoped it didn't take me quite so long to figure out what to do about it.

11. Violet

(When the day takes an unexpected turn)

'Class, I'm expecting your papers in by next Thursday. If you have any questions, please remember my office hours are not twenty-four/seven. As much as I love teaching you, I also love having a life outside these four walls.'

There was a chorus of groans though I couldn't tell whether it was to do with the paper we had to hand in or the lack of help we'd have with it because Professor Simpson's office hours were only between eleven a.m. and two p.m. Otherwise known as lunchtime.

Right on cue my stomach rumbled, its Pavlovian response to any class ending. Stella was stuck in French all day, which meant I'd be grabbing a sandwich on the way to the library for a couple of hours before my next class. And given Professor Simpson's classes always tended to run over, I was thankful I could take a more leisurely approach compared to most of my classmates now sprinting to their next lectures.

Shoving everything into my backpack, I heaved it up and just about managed not to topple over as I looped my arms through it. I could probably try out for the army considering the weight of it and pass with flying colours.

141

'There needs to be a one-way system here,' I grumbled to no one, rubbing my shoulder after being knocked hard by someone rushing too quickly to notice me as I pulled my big woolly hat down over my ears and walked outside.

I was not suited for the cold. And January seemed to be getting colder and colder.

'Violet . . . Violet . . . wait up.'

By the time I'd turned around at the familiar voice, my face was already sporting a wide smile, coupled with a little confusion, because there's no way I'd have forgotten any plans I had with Charlie. But there he was, running towards me.

Even after all the time we'd spent together recently, my heart still hadn't got the message and predictably it stuttered against my ribcage for a couple of seconds, like I'd somehow trapped a butterfly in my chest. If my focus hadn't been so intently trained on him, I'd have noticed the group of girls walking by, all of them nudging each other and turning around as he jogged past.

He stopped a metre away from me; the green of his eyes seemed more emerald today, even under the peak of his navy baseball cap I could see them glinting.

'Hey, what are you doing here?' I asked, ignoring the kick in my pulse. 'Did I forget that you were meeting me?'

Even as I said it out loud, I knew it seemed unlikely.

'I was passing by and remembered you had a class today.'

'Oh,' I replied, and watched as his smile turned into almost a wince. A grimace even.

'Actually . . .' he scratched through his thick stubble, and his perfect white teeth caught his bottom lip, 'that's a lie. I wanted to see you.'

My brows knitted together, and it took me a moment to figure out what he'd said, but as it sounded exactly like he'd come to meet me, specifically, all I could manage once more was, 'Oh.'

Jesus. All my words seemed to have fallen out of my head this morning.

'Shit. I'm fucking this up.'

I watched him. A version of Charlie I'd never seen before; kind of nervous, kind of bumbling and very awkward. All of which bolstered me, and I found myself laughing. 'Charlie, are you okay?'

'Yes. Yes, I'm good.' For a second he kicked the ground, shuffling the gravel under his feet. But then he looked up, and his grin, the self-assured Charlie grin I knew so well, spread across his face, and my chest, once more, was on the verge of giving out. 'I came on purpose. I wanted to see you. Is that weird?' His grin widened, while I just stood there trying to figure out what was going on and what alternate universe it was I seemed to be in. 'Yup, I'm making it weird.'

'Weird that you wanted to see me?'

He nodded deeply. Earnestly. 'Yeah. I just . . . we haven't seen each other for a few days, as you've been rehearsing with Stella. I know we've been texting, but it's not the same thing.'

His gaze searched my face; I did my best to hide my amusement that he felt he needed to explain the difference between texting and seeing each other, while also

143

trying very hard not to leap in the air at his declaration that he wanted to see me.

'No, Charlie, of course it's not weird.'

I wasn't exactly sure what it was. Weird wasn't the right word, confusing maybe. Unexpected, definitely, but not weird. It had been a couple of weeks since we started our fake relationship and I still didn't know what to make of it. I wasn't a fake relationship aficionado or anything, I'd never been in one before, but I was pretty certain you didn't spend time together outside of when was pre-arranged, or necessary. Or as agreed in the rules.

But here my fake boyfriend was, standing in front of me, declaring he wanted to see me.

I was starting to wonder if maybe I didn't understand how a fake relationship worked. Or maybe he didn't.

My fist curled in; the words I'd written on it had long washed off but I could clearly do with another reminder. THIS IS NOT REAL.

'So, do you have time for lunch? Please tell me you don't have to rush off to something we forgot to add to the schedule. Did I miss a rehearsal?' He grinned, like I wasn't struggling with some kind of internal turmoil, and I wasn't second guessing everything. No, he was just standing there, perfectly Charlie Masterson-esque looking as handsome as I'd ever seen him, asking me if I had time for lunch.

'You want to go for lunch?'

'Yes, I do,' he laughed, holding his hand out for me to take. 'Come on, there's somewhere I have in mind.'

'Okay then, lead the way.'

His long fingers wrapped around my hand, his fingertips brushing across my knuckles ever so slightly, before he led me off down the narrow cobblestone street, away from the English faculty, toward the Bodleian.

'There's a great place I want to take you to,' Charlie nodded, guiding me through an alleyway at the top of which there seemed to be a crowd gathered.

It was large enough to assume there was a busker present. The lunchtime rush was always a coveted time, and especially when it wasn't raining they could earn quite a bit of money. The crowd, however, turned out to be a long queue, all waiting outside a small store front over which a dark wooden, slightly tattered sign swung slowly in the wind.

Flanagan's: Purveyors of Bespoke Sandwiches

To the side of the door was a small hole in the wall, where a red-headed woman was handing out brown, wax-paper bags to whomever was at the front. As we got closer, I realized there was an entirely separate line for anyone trying to get into the shop.

'What is this place?' I whispered, my brows knitting together in confusion, looking back up at the sign, because for the life of me I couldn't ever remember seeing a queue like this for a sandwich. Especially in the freezing cold.

'I thought Brooks might have told you about it.' Charlie's hand squeezed mine tightly and he leaned into me, his face lighting up with a broad smile. 'But I'm so glad I get to be the one to introduce you. This is Flanagan's. It opened when we were in first year, and became legendary. It's kind of a secret, not that you'd know from the queue, but anyone who does know about it keeps it on the D/L because there's a limit on orders every day and no one wants to get here only for them all to go.'

I'd been holding his gaze the entire time, and not once did he look like he was joking about this secret sandwich shop. Even when his story became more preposterous.

'The line used to start forming at eight a.m. on Fridays, until they put the rule in you couldn't queue for someone else, or hold a place in it.' He pointed to a sign by the hatch saying exactly that. 'Some of the third years used it as initiation for the first years.'

'For a sandwich?!' My eyes widened in disbelief. 'What happens on Fridays?'

'Roast beef,' he replied with all the solemnity of a high court judge.

'Charlie . . . come on.' My head dropped with a loud laugh. He could tell a tale, I'd give him that. 'There's no way people were getting out of bed to queue for a sandwich.'

Charlie held his hands up. 'Hey, I love sleep too. But you need to try it before you pass judgement.'

'No. There's no way.' I shook my head, firm.

'Come on. Follow me.' He squeezed my hand again and pulled me past the line. I had no idea what he was planning, but we may as well have been walking to the velvet rope at the front of a club, given the death stares being shot my way as I followed him.

'Charlie,' I hissed, 'the back of the queue is over there.'

146

He replied with one of his knowing smiles, just as a man – an enormous man, no less – with two full sleeves of tattoos, a burly-looking beard and an apron wrapped around his waist, stepped out through the shop door.

'Charlie,' he boomed, his hand outstretched, 'I wondered when I'd see you. We're already two weeks into term are we not?'

'Sorry Jamie, been busy. Better late than never, though, eh?'

'S'pose.'

I came from a family of tall people. Charlie was tall, but this guy looked like he recited 'Fee-fi-fo-fum' every night, and I swear I heard a crunch of bones as his thick, meaty hand wrapped around Charlie's and pumped hard. Not that Charlie seemed to notice, even though telling him to be careful was on the tip of my tongue.

Jamie let go, then slapped him on the back with enough force to knock most people over, but again Charlie seemed unfazed, 'Come, hope you're hungry.'

'I worked extra hard at training this morning in preparation.'

'That's what I like to hear. How's your dad?'

'He's good. Been looking at a new site. He's hoping to lure you back –'

The rest of Charlie's sentence was drowned out by Jamie's booming laugh, but I stopped listening the moment I stepped inside after them.

It wasn't quite a restaurant, it wasn't quite a store. If I was being kind I'd call it a type of cobbled-together pop-up food spot, though if we hadn't walked past several empty small tables all far too close to each other, we

147

could just as easily be in a butcher's. White metro tiles, cement floor and random posters of cuts of meat only added to the aesthetic and something told me it wasn't ironic. Maybe they'd moved in and never changed the décor.

Jamie stopped in front of a wooden table and chairs rimmed in aluminium; reminiscent of a desk-set I'd had at school. 'Sit. I'll be back with water.'

I did as I was told, taking one more look around before glancing at Charlie, hoping he was about to provide me with an explanation, only to find him staring at me with more enthusiasm than I'd ever seen in anyone before.

'Okay, we have some ground rules to cover. One. I don't share my sandwich . . .'

'What?'

'Two . . .' he continued like he hadn't just made the most bizarre statement ever, 'you need to get a side of gravy because in my opinion it doesn't come with enough.'

I glanced over my shoulder, still unconvinced this wasn't some kind of practical joke. This had to be the weirdest place ever. We were the only ones in here, even though there were at least two dozen people waiting outside. If the air wasn't filled with the distinct scent of meat cooking, I'd think it was a prank – although I wasn't sure what sort of prank. Not a funny one, anyway. I turned back to Charlie to find him still talking.

'Three . . . it's Wednesday which means it's Pork and Apple Pie day. It's not my favourite, but it's still good.'

'Charlie, seriously? What? Where are we? I thought we were getting a sandwich.'

'Shit, you're not vegetarian are you?'

'No.'

'Good. Jamie's not a fan.'

'Of what?'

'Vegetarians.'

'Charlie! I'm going to need you to start from the beginning. What is this place? Where are all the people? I was kind of expecting Pret.'

We certainly weren't in Pret.

'Yeah, this is not Pret.' Charlie looked at his watch, picked up the water which had been placed on our table and sat back with a grin. 'They'll all be let in in fifteen minutes. I called Jamie on my way to meet you and asked if we could come in early. It gets really busy and I wanted a little time on our own.'

I opened my mouth to speak, but I had no words; the last hour had taken an unexpected turn. In fact the whole of this month so far was unexpected.

'I've known Jamie a long time, he trained under my dad, who's a chef . . . my parents own a restaurant group, primarily in London. What . . . why are you looking at me like that?'

This time, I closed my mouth before I did something stupid like reel off the names of all of Charlie's dad's restaurants, which I worried might come across a little odd. But honestly, there's not much a teenage girl with access to the internet can't find out.

'Um . . . sorry. Do you cook?' I asked, scraping the

barrel of logical questions I could ask without a) arousing suspicion and b) lying.

He nodded, his grin widening, 'Yup. If I didn't, we'd all starve in the house. Your brother's not bad, when I let him in the kitchen. But everything he knows, I've taught him. And don't let him tell you otherwise.'

My eyes widened because that was, in fact, news to me. I tried to tamp down the smile though, 'I didn't know you liked cooking.'

'Brooks has been hiding it . . . clearly. You'll have to come over for our Sunday lunch one weekend.'

'I'd like that,' I chuckled, trying to suppress the giggle which really wanted to let itself out because sixteen-year-old Violet would have died if she'd known one day Charlie Masterson would take her for lunch then invite her round to his place so he could cook for her.

It would have taken weeks to plan her outfit.

'What's so funny?'

I rolled my lips, 'Nothing really, I was just thinking . . . I like getting to know things about you . . .'

He was silent for a moment, his finger running around the edge of the water glass, 'Yeah, me too. Even though I've known you for years, I've never properly *known you*, known you.'

I nodded, 'Same.'

'Though,' he grinned, 'I bet I still know more about you.'

My eyebrow arched. I wasn't about to tell him he'd lose that bet spectacularly. 'Oh yeah? What?'

'I know you like books. I remember a couple of summers ago I was at your place, and you spent most of it in the swing reading. You wouldn't even come and swim.'

I hoped the blush on my cheeks wasn't as obvious as it felt. I remembered that summer very well, and my memories weren't of me not swimming or wanting to read, but rather from my vantage point in the swing I could get away with staring at Charlie wearing his swim trunks and nothing else. Reading provided my perfect alibi.

But the fact he noticed I'd stayed in the swing, more so *remembered* I'd stayed, had my heart fluttering.

'I do like books.'

'And you have your tattoo.' He glanced down at my wrist resting on the table, and the little hand-drawn stack I'd had done on my seventeenth birthday. It was filled with the classic love stories – *Pride and Prejudice*, *Emma*, *Romeo and Juliet*, *Little Women*, *Wuthering Heights* – because one day I wanted a love worthy of the greats.

'Very observant, Mr Masterson,' I smiled at him.

'Is that your only one?'

'No. I have another. Right here.' Charlie's eyes dropped to my finger, rubbing the bottom of my ribcage. 'What about you? Any tattoos?'

He shook his head with a grin. 'Nope. I'm scared of needles.'

The thought of this man sitting in front of me, almost too big for the tiny school-style chairs, being scared of anything had me giggling hard. 'It's just a tiny scratch.'

'Maybe, but I'm not willing to find out.' His laugh boomed out, before he quietened and looked me. His green eyes held mine for long enough that a tiny heartbeat kicked up between my thighs.

I found myself reaching for my glass of water to gulp down, just to break the tension, right as two enormous sandwiches were placed in front of us, and from the look on Charlie's face he'd completely forgotten about anything that had happened up to this very moment.

Layers and layers of dark pink meat overspilled from the softest-looking bread, smothered with a gooey sauce dripping down the sides. From the size of it, I wasn't even sure how I would fit it in my mouth. There was no way of eating this and maintaining a pretence of being ladylike – it was worse than spaghetti bolognese and I already knew most of it would end up around my face.

'Sorry, I should have warned you it can get messy,' Charlie laughed as he pulled one of the plates towards him, sunk his knife into the bread and somehow managed to cut it in four. He pushed it back over to me. 'Here, this makes it easier.'

'Thank you . . .' I reached over, examined it for longer than I should have and picked up the one that looked least like it would fall apart. 'Here goes.'

Charlie was watching me so intently, with so much childlike anticipation brimming in his eyes, that even if this sandwich was only worthy of being thrown straight into the bin, I'd have told him it was the most perfect thing I'd ever tasted.

Luckily for me, I didn't have to stretch my acting skills.

'OMIGAWD.'

His smile spread from ear to ear, and given my mouth was still full, it took all my energy not to smile back.

'It's good right?' he said, before picking up his sandwich *whole,* and taking a massive bite.

I nodded and for a good two minutes, the pair of us watched each other eat in silence.

It wasn't as weird as it sounds, because that's when the rest of the queue had been allowed entry and the tiny space was now bustling and loud with chatter.

'Why did you want to study English?' he asked, after another giant mouthful.

Wiping my fingers with a paper napkin, I sat back in the chair. I wasn't quite at the jeans unbuttoning stage yet, but I was close. 'I love words. I love books. Books have been around in one form or another for thousands of years, and the thought of being able to read something written that long ago . . .' I shrugged, for some reason downplaying my love for reading in case Charlie thought less of me, because that's exactly what Hugo did. Well, not less of me but you know, like reading was a waste of time when you could be doing something else. Rowing, for example. 'It's kind of silly, but I feel like there's a magic to it. Anyway, that's why.'

'That's how I feel about physics,' he grinned.

'Really?'

'Yeah, there's something so pure about it,' he nodded. 'I guess Brooks missed out on the reading gene, huh? In fact, I'm not sure I've seen him with a book that's not mandated by his class.'

'Yeah. We're so different. He's smart, but his life has revolved around sport since he was little. Just like I was

153

never very sporty, he's never read for pleasure. Therefore, he thinks I live in my head,' I chuckled, throwing out an eye roll for added effect, 'and that I'm a drama queen.'

'Then I'm in good company, he thinks I am too.'

'Why are you a drama queen?'

He hesitated for a split second, and sipped his water. 'Probably a story for another day.'

'Well, at least you still have sport going for you too. Are you excited about the World Championships this summer?'

He nodded, his mouth too full of pork and apple to properly answer. Charlie was part of Team GB Rowing, alongside Oz, and the most important competition for them after the Boat Race this summer was the Rowing World Championships.

'Mmm hmm,' he answered, swallowing his mouthful. 'Yes, the crew's not been announced yet, but I should be selected if all goes well. There are a couple of guys from last year's Team GB who are injured so the spaces have opened up. I'm feeling quietly confident that it might lend itself to a decent crew. We have some good juniors moving up.'

As he continued talking, I picked up another piece of my sandwich, realizing how totally relaxed I was in Charlie's company. Even when we'd been rehearsing, there was always a tiny part of my brain reminding me of how close I was to him. But right now, sitting here with the world's messiest lunch between us – it was almost like spending time with Stella.

Point being, it was easy. Charlie was easy. The only

not-easy thing was coming to terms with the fact that spending time together like this – even without the first-date-style line of questioning – was doing nothing to help my crush.

Quite the opposite in fact.

It took another twenty minutes before we finally finished eating – or Charlie finished his, along with the rest of mine after I'd waved a white flag and admitted defeat. I drew the line at unbuttoning in front of Charlie and rolling to my next class.

I was almost tempted to go back to St Anne's and change into leggings.

'That was truly the best sandwich I've ever had,' I told him.

'Good enough to get out of bed for?'

'Oooh,' I grimaced, my nose scrunching up, 'not sure I'd go that far.'

'Tough crowd.'

I glanced down at our empty plates, only to find his fingers millimetres from mine, lined up middle to middle, index to index. I couldn't tear my eyes away as his hand closed what little gap there was until the tips were brushing together. It was so soft that if I hadn't witnessed it happening, I might not have known.

Stealth almost.

'We should probably go. You don't want to be late for class, and I have my session with Gordon I can't miss.'

I managed to tear my eyes away from where our fingers were touching, to find him pulling a face, and whatever moment we'd had was over.

155

'No. You mustn't miss that. Not sure I want to know what happens when Gordon's pissed off.'

The screech of Charlie's chair along the tiled floor muffled the chuckle he let out as he stood up, 'Oh he'd probably recite equations at me until I relented and apologized. And . . . I hate to say it, but I do think it's been helpful. We've only had three sessions, but he runs them with an iron fist, as you can imagine, so there's no way we're not getting a first.'

'Let's get you there, then. Mustn't be late.'

Jamie was nowhere to be seen when we looked around to say goodbye, so we stepped outside and into the cold. If possible it was even colder than when we'd entered. Charlie pulled on his baseball cap, zipped up his thick bodywarmer and once more held out his hand for me to take.

This time I didn't question it, except as I took it something caught in my periphery. I don't know why, out of everyone on this busy street, this particular movement was what had me turning around, but it did. Five metres away, standing halfway down the queue, was Evie with a friend, and I finally understood the term 'if looks could kill'.

Just from the way her eyes hardened as she peered down to where Charlie and I were joined, she could probably be found guilty of grievous bodily harm.

If I wasn't already shivering from the cold, her glare would have frozen me.

'What are you . . .' Charlie's gaze shot over to where I was staring to find out why I'd stopped walking, and groaned. 'Just ignore her, Violet. Come on.'

He dragged me off before I could argue or think any more about her, and his hand tightly wrapped around mine.

'So, what's the class this afternoon?'

'Victorian England.'

'Fascinating,' he drawled, making it clear he absolutely didn't find it fascinating, as his hand teasingly squeezed mine. 'More *Mill on the Floss*, is it?'

'*Mill on the Floss* is no less fascinating than x equals y plus whatever it is . . .' I shot back. 'At least mine has some romance in it.'

'Hey . . . there's romance in physics.'

Whatever the look I gave him had him throwing his head back with laughter. His perfect smile on full display, deepening the dimples which only came out when he was really happy.

'Come on. We can't have you late for all the romance.'

We left the way we came, down the narrow, cobbled passageway – Charlie stepping back to let me go ahead of him, while somehow at the same time never letting go of my hand – until we reached the main road.

My palm cooled as his hand dropped, and I turned to find him easing a hand along the back of his neck.

'Charlie, are you okay?'

He nodded, though it was clear he wasn't quite sure. I waited, and waited some more. By my count, it was at least fifteen seconds of watching him have a conversation with himself. I was about to ask if he was going to share when . . .

It was so quick I didn't see it happening. It was probably because all the confusion whirring through my brain had dulled my reflexes. But before my heart had time to beat again, my face was held between his huge hands, and my lips had been surrounded.

This was nothing like the kiss in the Blue Oar a couple of weeks ago. Nothing at all.

This was the first kiss I'd dreamed about as a teenager.

Strong and forceful, yet so gentle and delicate it was causing my eyes to water. Insistent, needy almost. Lips, Charlie's lips that I'd been thinking about on a near-hourly basis since the first time I'd experienced them were once again on mine. Soft and firm, giving me no chance to escape. Not that I would have.

Nah uh. No way.

Somewhere between leaving the sandwich place and here, in the most perfect spot which existed in Oxford, he'd slipped in a stick of gum. Peppermint burst against my tongue as his roamed around my mouth, making me wonder if perhaps this kiss was something he'd been thinking about.

Thinking about it the way I had – and that perhaps this kiss wasn't quite as impulsive as it initially seemed to be.

I didn't know how long we were there, but the noise of the street and the bustle of people walking past – along with what might have been a cry of *'get a room'* – came back into my consciousness as Charlie eased away.

His eyes scoured my face, but he'd find nothing but a flushed, thoroughly starry-eyed nineteen-year-old . . .

'Sorry . . .' was the first thing he said. And his hands

dropped from my face, but only to my neck where his fingers were twisting into my hair.

'Sorry for kissing me?'

'Yeah.'

'Why did you then?'

'Because it was becoming impossible for me not to.'

Well . . . bloody hell. I didn't see that coming.

12. Charlie

(The Violet Effect)

I lied to Violet.

I wasn't the least bit sorry I kissed her.

I'd tried to be. I'd tried really hard. Most of yesterday afternoon, in fact, when I should have been listening to Gordon and the rest of my team. Instead, I was trying to be sorry. But it was nowhere to be found.

Eventually I gave up.

What's more, it appeared my sorries had vanished along with any feelings of guilt I'd been carrying around – even though I really *really* did have something to feel guilty about now. But weirdly, this morning was the first time since term started I'd woken up feeling fresh and successfully managed to stretch out of my sleep without the all-consuming, churning sensation which threatened to choke me for the first minute of every day.

I was calling it the Violet Effect.

I slammed my hand down on the alarm, killing it before it fully pierced my brain, but even the shrill beeping couldn't stop the smile splitting my face in half. I couldn't remember the last time I'd woken up before it.

Yeah. I felt good. Better than I had in a long time. My muscles didn't ache, even though they should after last night's land training, featuring heavy weights and more burpees than anyone should ever have to do. I'd powered through them with a renewed energy and strength which had me adding another 25 kg to the bars.

It hadn't gone unnoticed, but I'd shrugged off the raised eyebrows enough that no questions were asked, because there was only one answer.

The Violet Effect.

I could no longer deny it.

I liked Violet Brooks.

I liked how tall she was; the perfect height for me to sling my arm around her shoulder and pull her into me, so her temple was ripe for dropping a kiss onto.

I liked the way her hand fitted into mine.

I liked the way the bright blue of her eyes seemed to darken and sparkle at something amusing, or how she always worried the left side of her top lip whenever she was nervous.

The gruff timbre of her giggle, the way she was genuinely interested in what I had to say, her kindness, her sense of humour. The way she kissed me back.

I liked how her lips moved ever so slightly as she followed the lines on the page with her finger, because I could watch the little dent in her top lip purse and fall all day.

But most of all, I liked the way she looked at me whenever she saw me for the first time. It only lasted for a second or two, but in that brief moment where our eyes met, she made me feel as though I could accomplish anything.

She made me feel something I'd never felt before. And it appeared my conscience was okay with that. I just hoped my conscience would also come up with a good way to break the news to Brooks that I no longer wanted to fake date his sister. I wanted to *real* date her.

Picking up my phone I opened Instagram, going straight to Violet's page out of habit. There was one new image – of her at the theatre holding a script to cover the lower half of her face so only her eyes peeked out. It was all you could see – those bright blue eyes of hers – but she was nothing short of stunning.

Without giving it a second thought, I typed Y R U so HOT ♦ ♥

Throwing off the duvet, I was too busy laughing at picturing her reaction to grumble at the cold blast of air the way I normally did before pulling on my training gear, thick hoodie and beanie. I was still brushing my teeth as I flung open the bedroom door and jogged down the stairs two at a time with more energy and enthusiasm than I'd ever had before six a.m.

Or before nine, if truth be told.

The Violet Effect.

Brooks was standing over the stove stirring a pan with one hand, holding his phone in the other when I walked into the kitchen. If I wasn't already running on my supercharged energy, seeing him standing there and not Oz would have been enough to wake me up. The three of us were creatures of habit, and Brooks did not make breakfast.

His head snapped up to me, 'Can you stop writing shit like this on my sister's Instagram?'

Ignoring him, I rinsed my mouth in the sink and turned to him, 'What are you doing?'

163

'The porridge. Are you supposed to stir it this much?'

'No,' I replied, easing the spoon from his hand, 'where's Oz?'

'He's not up yet.'

'Seriously?'

Brooks shook his head. 'Nope. Did something happen last night? I thought Oz was staying at Kate's, but his car's outside.'

'Um . . .' I frowned, trying to get my brain to kick into gear. 'Yeah, he came home when I was making dinner for us, but he went upstairs. I had work to finish, and assumed he was working too. I didn't see him again. Didn't hear you either.'

Brooks walked over to the coffee machine and flicked it on. 'When I got home you were asleep on the sofa, snoring like a little baby. I put a blanket on you.'

I stared down at the porridge as it bubbled and thickened. Last night I'd cleaned the kitchen, left dinner out for the boys and sat down to do some work, but I'd woken at midnight on the sofa with a book in my hand. I must have been more tired than I thought, if Brooks crashing about the kitchen hadn't woken me up – because he was not quiet, and crashing about was kind of his thing. But when I'd eventually made it to bed, the house had been silent.

I opened up the fridge. It was emptier than it had been when I'd gone upstairs. 'I left dinner out . . .'

'Yeah . . . I ate it.' Brooks' eyes widened sheepishly.

'I left it for you both.'

'Yeah . . . I ate that as well.'

'The whole thing?'

164

He shrugged, 'I was starving, and it was late. I didn't get in until ten, so I figured it was fair game. Delicious, mate. One of your better ones, for sure.'

I rolled my eyes. 'Is Oz really still in bed?'

Brooks nodded, 'Yeah.'

I turned the stove off and set the porridge to one side. Something wasn't right, I couldn't remember the last time I was up before Oz. 'Come on, we need to find him.'

Brooks rubbed his hands together with a glee that had no place while it was still dark out. 'Ooh. House mystery.'

The pair of us walked back up the stairs to the top floor of the house where Oz's room was situated. I glanced at Brooks; it didn't look like he had the same ominous feeling I did, but something definitely wasn't right. Just like I never woke before the alarm and usually needed four to five strong coffees to get me talking, Oz never failed to get up.

He was just one of those inexplicable people who liked mornings.

Number 5 Tolkien Lane seemed to be playing a game of Freaky Friday.

'You definitely didn't hear anything last night?' I whispered, but Brooks shook his head.

'No, everyone was asleep.'

We stood outside the door. I was just about to press my ear against it when Brooks stopped me.

'Wait. You don't think Kate's in there do you?' he hissed in my ear, enough that I needed to rub away the ringing it left.

I stepped back just in case. Kate and Oz in his bed-room was not something I could unhear.

Instead, I knocked. Loudly. 'Oz?'

Nothing.

I tried again. *Rap rap rap.* Reminiscent of the way our old school housemaster used to.

'Oz . . .'

'I don't hear anything.' This time, Brooks pressed his ear to the door. 'If they're both in there then they're both asleep. I'm going in.'

Twisting the handle with surprising delicacy, he eased the door open enough so the pair of us could peer around.

It only took a second for it to hit us.

'Jesus, it smells like a distillery in here.' I wafted my hand through the air and opened the door wide.

It was still early enough that the sun hadn't yet emerged, and we stood in the entranceway waiting for our eyes to adjust to the darkness in Oz's room, and the lump underneath the navy duvet in the middle of his huge bed. Brooks cracked open the window, and imme-diately the cold outside air flowed in.

Flicking on the study lamp on Oz's desk, I turned to spot one arm hanging listlessly down the side of the mattress, though his fingers still gripped the neck of an almost empty whisky bottle.

One that had been full yesterday.

'Holy shit.' I picked it up, my socks immediately soak-ing into a dark, wet patch I hadn't noticed and breathed a sigh of relief we probably wouldn't have to make a trip to accident and emergency. 'Doesn't look like he's drunk it all.'

Brooks pulled back the cover to find Oz appropriately snoring like a drunken sailor, and eased out the phone stuck under his cheek.

'What time is it?' whispered Brooks, though whispering was pointless. Based on Oz's current position it would probably be easier to wake the dead.

Flicking my wrist around to check my watch, I replied, 'Five forty-five.'

'Shit. We can't leave him here, but we also don't have enough time to get him ready for training.'

'Mate . . . he's not going anywhere. Even if he only had half that bottle, he's still going to be drunk. Do you think he needs to go to hospital?'

Brooks' eyes flicked to Oz and back to me. 'What for?'

'Getting his stomach pumped?'

'Nah,' he scoffed, with all the ambivalence of someone weighing in at 100 kilos, and whose food and drink intake had very little effect on his day-to-day. Though I don't think I'd ever seen Brooks drink quite this much in one go. 'We have bigger issues, namely what are we going to tell Coach? He's already worried about Oz given everything happening with Kate – he might drop him from the crew.'

Glancing down at a snoring Oz, I attempted to ease away the tension building in my temples. Brooks was right. In the past few weeks, the tabloid media had discovered Oz and Kate's relationship, and as Oz was deemed a person of interest – whether he wanted to be or not (he did *not*) they'd unwittingly been pulled into the spotlight. While Oz was used to it, Kate wasn't, and after an incident involving a speedboat and the

Cambridge rowing crew training on the Tideway, Oz had been understandably upset.

Actually, upset was an understatement. Apoplectic was more like it. On the warpath was better, and after he'd smashed up most of the lockers in the locker room, Coach had asked if he wanted to step down as president.

I had a feeling Coach wouldn't be quite so lenient the second time around, and Oz wouldn't be given the choice. He'd simply be removed.

We needed a plan.

The snap of Brooks' fingers pulled my attention, 'What if we all call in sick? A twenty-four-hour stomach bug or something. We can say we've all got food poisoning from that pie last night.'

'From my cooking?'

'Have you got a better idea?' he hissed.

I didn't.

We were still staring at each other when a low rumbling noise sounding more animal than human croaked from the lump on the bed. 'I can hear you, you know?'

The pair of us stared down at Oz, still not moving. The snoring was continuing at its steady rate and there was absolutely no indication he was awake, or even semi-conscious.

Brooks leaned into me, 'You heard that too, right?'

'Oz?' I tried, 'Osbourne, what happened?'

I was beginning to think we had both imagined him speaking when his lips opened a fraction.

'You're right. That's what happened.'

'What?' Brooks' eyes sliced to mine holding just as

168

much confusion, and let out a loud snort. 'Yeah, he's definitely still drunk if he thinks you're right.'

'Shut up.' I shoved him, focusing back on the lump. 'Oz, mate, what happened?'

'Girls are the worst.'

'Did something happen with Kate?'

He opened his mouth a little wider – Brooks and I held our breath, waiting to discover the cause of our inebriated housemate and also maybe a little from the smell, because it was very likely we could get drunk off his breath. But then his eyes flew open along with the distinct, and unmistakeable sound of a gag.

'Move,' Oz managed to grunt, and sprinted to the bathroom faster than I knew a human could move.

'Ugh.' Brooks' hands flew up to cover his ears from the sound of violent retching, and I caught his chest heaving.

'Go and get him some water,' I ordered, before I had two housemates puking on me.

The speed he left rivalled Oz.

'And message Coach to tell him we're not coming.'

I slowly made my way to the bathroom while also praying Oz had managed to throw up in the toilet and not all over the floor. Best friend or not, it was far too early to be dealing with his puke. Thankfully, he'd taken that into account.

I found him slumped against the wall, his entire body limp with his cheek pressed into the cold wall tiles. His eyes might have been closed, but his face was so ashen that the pain etched on it couldn't have only been from his hangover. No matter how head-splitting it was.

He looked like someone had died.

'Mate, what happened?'

It took him a moment to answer. I realized I hadn't seen his eyes properly before he ran to the bathroom, because there's no way I'd have forgotten the state of them. Red, bloodshot, brimming with tears spilling down his cheeks, too fast for him to brush away.

'Kate and I broke up,' he choked out.

'Oh mate . . .' I eased down on the floor next to him, leaning against the side of the bath, 'I'm so sorry. Is this all because of the Boat Race?'

'Because of my fucking life, and the baggage I come with. She doesn't want another six years of having to deal with me,' he snapped out through loud sniffs while clutching his head, 'instead she decided to rip my fucking heart out.'

I inched closer and put my arm around him. 'I'm so sorry, Oz.'

His reply was too incoherent to make out. His head dropped down onto my shoulder just as Brooks finally reappeared with a large bottle of water and his eyebrows raised in question.

'Kate broke up with him.'

'Oh mate. I'm sorry,' he replied, putting down the bottle of water and dropping onto the floor next to us. 'I've told Coach by the way, I think he bought it. But we cannot leave this house today.'

I nodded in agreement. Thankfully it was a Tuesday, a light day for classes. I might get a chance to catch up on all the work I'd not been doing.

170

'So, what happened with Kate? Breaking up's a bit extreme.'

Oz gave another big sniff, drawing his hand under his soggy nose. I got up and found a fresh facecloth for him to use instead.

'Aren't you going to say I told you so?'

I glanced over to Brooks to see if he knew what Oz was talking about, but he looked as baffled as I felt. 'What?'

'You told me love sucks. I should have listened to you, Charlie. Relationships are the worst. How long until this feeling goes away?' he blurted out, before taking a glug of water so huge that I was expecting him to throw up again.

From the corner of my eye, I saw Brooks' eyes flare.

I took a deep breath, and made another attempt at rubbing away the impending headache which seemed to have appeared from nowhere, though more likely the whisky fumes emanating from Oz.

For the first time I wished I hadn't been so vocal about my stance on love, or relationships, or girls period for that matter. Because even though I was staring directly at clear-cut evidence of the adverse effects of love, somehow I couldn't quite bring myself to agree with him.

That maybe love, or relationships, or girls weren't quite as awful as I'd once thought.

The Violet Effect.

'Oz . . .' I began, only to be interrupted.

'Charlie, how long until it feels like my chest isn't haemorrhaging?' he snapped, and once more slumped onto my shoulder.

It had been a long time since I'd thought about the day Evie and I had broken up, the first time. My seventeen-year-old self had never known pain like it. The days that followed were like I had to learn everything again from scratch – how to breathe, how to think, how to move hour by hour while my heart slowly bled out. Weeks passed. I trudged through. If Oz and Brooks hadn't been with me, I would have failed all my end-of-term exams because I simply wouldn't have turned up. I lost the will to care.

The two of them were solely responsible for me finishing the last month of the summer term and passing my A-Levels.

They distracted me. They forced me to concentrate on rowing.

The fact I'd medalled in the Under-23s World Championships was all credit to them.

Eventually my heart healed, we rowed more, we recuperated in Greece at Oz's family home, and once our gap year was over we made our way up the M40 to Oxford. Where Evie also was.

The inevitable happened.

It wasn't quite so bad the second time around, but it was enough that I knew I never wanted to go through it ever again. I thought I'd never heal.

It took meeting Violet in the pub to realize that I'd healed a long time ago.

'I don't know, Oz. I think it's unique to everyone.'

172

'But you never got over Evie,' he sniffed, pressing his palms so hard into his eyes they turned even redder.

'I . . . I did. I have. I just . . .'

What? What had I just?

I'd been thinking about it over the past few weeks. That panic fight or flight mode I'd fallen into the second I'd heard she'd be joining my class, terrified I'd revert to the teenager wrapped around her finger. But it was nothing more than a knee-jerk response. My body remembering the way it used to react whenever Evie was concerned. When the reality was I couldn't recall the last time I'd thought about her.

Even having her in class with me had been less anxiety inducing than I'd expected. I still ignored her, but more because she didn't have much to say rather than using silence as its own response. Plus Gordon talked enough for everyone.

What's more, I'd realized that the effect she used to have on me had vanished. I didn't love her, I hadn't in a long time. But I didn't *hate* her.

And that was new.

I didn't hate her. I didn't feel anything for her now. I was indifferent.

She no longer had the power to fuck with me.

'I did get over Evie. I *am* over her,' I finally said, quietly. Quieter than I should have given the weight of the statement. 'But this isn't the same thing. Kate hasn't cheated on you, she's been going through a lot, and things got too much for her, but she hasn't stopped loving you. You're older than I was back then. I didn't know any better.'

Oz lifted his head, pinning me with a look which

would have had most people stepping back. It was intense to say the least. 'What are you saying? You think I can get her back?'

I sighed. 'I'm saying I was seventeen, and what the fuck did I know? I don't even know if it was really love. What does love even mean?'

From the way Oz frowned, he didn't seem all that satisfied with my answer, especially when he turned to Brooks. 'What do you think?'

Brooks scratched through his thick beard, while he pondered so long, even I was waiting on tenterhooks. 'I'm no relationship expert but . . . I think you can do anything you put your mind to. If you want Kate back, you can get her back.'

I rolled my eyes so hard my brain hurt, but it seemed to have done the trick given Oz resumed his position with his head back against the wall and his eyes closed. Brooks followed his lead, and five minutes later none of us had spoken. It was only the sound of a stomach rumbling which brought me back to the present, and realization that none of us had eaten yet.

'What time is it?'

'Just gone seven,' I replied. 'Oz, how are you feeling?'

'Like I sank half a bottle of whisky, and there's a hole in my chest.'

'Okay, well I think you need to eat something, so I'm going to make eggs for all of us and get you some electrolytes.' I pushed up off the floor. 'Brooks?'

'Yeah. And bacon if there's any going.' He rubbed his stomach and grinned. 'I might have finished the porridge already.'

My head dropped with a shake, though I couldn't hide the amusement. 'Fine, can you make sure Oz can stand up? And maybe get him in the shower too.'

'I'm right here,' Oz grumbled from where his head was now slumped onto his arms, giving no indication he was capable of moving by himself.

'It'll be ready in twenty minutes,' I waved behind me.

I didn't rush down the stairs. Oz's words echoed around as I made my way towards the kitchen, *'love sucks'* and *'you never got over Evie'* alternating with each slow step.

Witnessing the pain Oz was going through should have had me reconfirming all my initial instincts. Love did suck. But somewhere in the distance, I could hear Violet's voice shouting over Oz and everything I'd ever declared about love. Maybe it was all this play rehearsal we'd been doing, or her telling me about the books she loved, or simply her . . . whatever it was had me reaching for my phone as soon as I stepped back into the kitchen.

I opened the fridge and removed the box of eggs with one hand. With the other my finger pressed down on the name that had recently moved to the top of my contacts list. It rang so long, I thought I was going to have to leave a message.

'Charlie?' Violet croaked, right as I realized my mistake. 'It's the middle of the night. What's wrong?'

I bit down my smile, and stopped myself from correcting her that it was seven-fifteen a.m. 'Shit, I'm sorry. Go back to sleep. I totally lost track.'

'Why are you calling me?'

175

'I wanted to hear your voice.'

We'd agreed not to leave the house all day, but the soft hum she let out in response had me wondering how I could escape.

The Violet Effect.

13. Violet

(Maturity is overrated)

Oh, bollocks.

'Stel, I'll call you back.'

I hung up before she had a chance to say anything else and stared at the heap of books I'd just dropped. My *Twelfth Night* manuscript, along with three other books I needed to mark up for an English assignment were spread at my feet, and the small white box I'd been so carefully balancing was at the bottom of the pile underneath.

Please don't be crushed, please don't be crushed, please don't be crushed.

Gingerly squinting through one eye, I bent to pick it up. Eased off the slightly wonky elastic ribbon and breathed a sigh of relief.

The contents were somehow still intact.

Gathering everything as quickly as possible, I swore to myself, plus whoever was listening, that I would no longer try and break a world record for carrying everything at once, while also talking on the phone and not paying the slightest bit of attention to where I was going.

'Do you need help with those?'

I glanced up to find an eager face smiling down at

177

me, though most of it was covered in a large bobble hat sliding too far down her forehead.

'Oh, no thanks. I got it. Just clumsy,' I replied, slipping my almost empty backpack off my shoulders to load up.

Yes, I know. I should have been using it.

'Okay.' The girl stepped over my mess and headed into the library without another word.

This time, I shoved my books into my backpack, and held the box – and only the box – secure in my hands.

Amazingly, I wasn't more flustered as I walked into the library and around the stacks, spotting Charlie over at the table in the far corner where we'd agreed to meet in ten minutes. I couldn't even find it in myself to get annoyed because, of course, he was early. In all the times we'd met in the past few weeks, I'd never once got there before him.

Even today, when I'd made a special effort to arrive first – hence not using up precious seconds to load my backpack – there he was, rocking back on his chair while his fingers typed away on his phone like he had all the time in the world. Science students were not known to have a lot of spare time, but Charlie seemed to have more spare time than me – a first-year English student. In fact, coupled with the Boat Race it should be next to impossible to find a space in his calendar, yet he'd never once cancelled on our times together.

The only bonus about arriving second was that I had the luxury of seeing him in his space without any interruptions. We'd spent so much time together over the past few weeks, but I'd never properly had a chance to really look at him – not without him asking whether I'd forgotten how to blink, anyway. Plus, I was usually too busy rushing. But now, this morning, I could take my time to see who I was becoming so familiar with, in a way I'd never been.

Thankfully, I'd reached the point where I no longer stared at his mouth whenever he spoke. Whereas before I'd always been a little too nervous in his presence, this Charlie was so easy to spend time with, as though we'd known each other for years instead of him just being my brother's best friend. He teased me like it was his job to make me smile. I was learning his habits – the way he slowly ran his knuckles along the stubble coating his jaw whenever he was thinking hard, just as he was doing right now. Or how he always wore a baseball cap to study, and curled the rim like it was a stress ball.

My hardest lesson was that there was no way I wasn't going to fall hard, because I was already plummeting. The last few weeks of spending time together, holding hands and touching whenever we could, it had become clear that any rules we'd put in place to appear like we were in a relationship were merely superficial. Because after that kiss – the one where he couldn't not kiss me – it didn't feel like there was anything fake about us at all.

It was part of the reason I'd wanted to arrive early. Part of the reason I'd brought a box filled with freshly baked sugary goodness. Because as much as I was desperate for it to happen again, I needed to get some answers before it did. Because that was the mature thing to do.

That's right, I, Violet Brooks, was being mature.

Any concerns I was having about kissing or not kissing disappeared the second he spotted me. Whatever he'd been typing on his phone was forgotten as he stood up with a grin so wide it rivalled hot chocolate on a cold day for how warm and inviting it was. I might have stopped staring at his lips, but I would never get over that smile. The one that lit up his face and charged the sparkle in his eyes like he'd been plugged into the mains.

Oh boy. He could kiss me all he wanted if he kept looking at me like that.

Focus, Violet.

Answers first. Then kissing.

'Hey . . .' he breathed out, the deep timbre of his tone ghosting over my skin until every cell tingled.

How was it possible for one person to have such an effect?

'Good morning,' I smiled back, amidst the adrenaline and excitement rushing through me as I leaned in and kissed his cheek, because that was the polite thing to do. 'I'm late again, I see.'

'Nope. I'm just early. I had a study session cancelled so I thought I'd save our spot. Didn't want anyone else to get it.'

'Good idea,' I replied, while subtly inching around to the other side of the table so I could concentrate, because that distinct Charlie freshly showered smell of postrowing exertions, oaky and clean which always heightened my senses, made it virtually impossible to do so.

I placed the box down and eased off my backpack. His eyes tracked the movement, 'What's in there?'

'A present.'

'Seriously? I love presents,' he replied, with that same enthusiasm I'd seen at the sandwich shop.

'You'd best open it then.'

He leaned across the table, reaching out long fingers to pull the box closer. Carefully, he eased off the red and white elastic ribbon, and wrapped it around his wrist.

'Cupcakes, brownies, jam doughnuts? And are those chocolate chip cookies?' he gasped as he peered inside, breathing in that sweet sugar hit. 'You really brought these for me?'

'Yup, you took me to your favourite sandwich shop, I thought I'd bring you a selection of my favourite studying snacks from my favourite bakery.'

'How did you know cupcakes were the way to my heart?'

'They're the way to everyone's heart.'

His laugh was loud enough that an echo of *'shhhh'* sounded out from somewhere nearby. He bit down on his lip with a chuckle. 'Whoops. Forgot we're in a library.'

'Don't get us in trouble and kicked out,' I scolded, though there was only jest in my tone.

'So, what flavour are we talking about here?'

'Double chocolate chip, with vanilla frosting for the cupcakes, salted caramel brownies, raspberry doughnuts.'

Using his finger, he swiped it through the thickly swirled buttercream on the top of a cupcake and stuck it in his mouth. I really wish he hadn't. I just about stopped my jaw from dropping, even though my chest nearly caved in from the sight of his pink tongue darting out to catch a stray blob from the corner of his lip. I would never unsee that.

Dear god.

I was still trying to regain my composure when I noticed him chuckling.

'What's so funny?'

'Nothing. I just figured you'd have picked violet frosting or something.'

I dropped into the seat opposite him, determined not to smile at his teasing, 'Not everything is violet you know.'

My forehead creased a fraction as he stood up, only for him to walk around the table, and assault me with that scent. My heart was already thudding double time, but by the time he'd pulled out the chair next to me and sat down it had kicked up to triple.

'It should be.' His lip quivered with a smirk as he picked up a loose strand of hair from my shoulder and wound it between his fingers. 'What's your favourite colour?'

'Actually, it's blue.'

'Really?' he replied, gently tugging me closer to him. And I put up absolutely no resistance. None. Pathetic. I could see my plans already floating out of the window. 'Mine too. Though right now I think it's coming in a close second to something else . . .'

He was close. Too close almost. I tried to lean back, but I honestly couldn't tell whether it was his grip stopping me, or my brain. 'Wh . . . why did you move seats?'

'Because I can't kiss you hello from across the table, can I?'

'You're going to kiss me?'

'Yes. I think it's the *appropriate* thing to do right now,' he winked.

No. Not the wink. I was not strong enough to hold off against *the wink*.

Snapping around in my chair, I glanced left and right before realizing I only had a wall behind me on one side and a stack of books on the other. I couldn't spot anyone over his shoulder either, and come to think of it, when I walked in there were only a couple of students on the far side, and that girl who'd stopped to pick up my books.

Charlie turned around to see what I'd been looking at, but only found exactly what I had – an empty space. There was no one here.

His eyes locked onto mine, and I swear Mature Violet, *stupid* Violet – damn her – was trying to ruin my life because she almost pulled away before doing something like kiss him back, or worse drag him under the table.

Fuck it. A girl only lives once.

My hand snaked around his neck, my fingers spearing through the thick hair at the nape of his neck as my lips snapped onto his. They fitted perfectly, two magnets joining together. Compared to the other day, it was chaste, barely enough to taste the sweetness left from the vanilla frosting as my tongue slipped into his mouth. But, it was plenty to get my insides curling and my heart crashing around on a rush that definitely wasn't caused by sugar.

I could kiss Charlie Masterson all day and still never

183

get enough. I was kind of glad I'd only just discovered how good at kissing he was, because if I'd known earlier I'm not sure I could be held responsible for my actions.

As a little moan escaped from one of us, Mature Violet made her presence known and this time succeeded in pulling me away.

'Charlie . . .'

'Yes, Violet.'

I eased back a little more. Charlie's elbow was leaning on the table, fist propping up the side of his face making him seem even more amused with me than usual. It was only when I took a deep breath that the smile dropped a little. 'Is everything okay?'

'Yes . . . I just . . . can we talk about something?'

'Of course,' he replied, his eyes filled with enough concern that it was making me feel like I was blowing this out of all proportion.

No. Focus, Violet.

He was still staring at me as I rubbed my clammy palms over my jeans. 'Um . . . Evie's not here.'

In the space of a split second, his entire body tensed, his eyes flared and he snapped around again to double check I was telling truth before finally relaxing back into the position he'd been, except with a small frown on his face.

'No, she's not here.'

'And the other day when you kissed me, I don't think she was around either.'

'She wasn't,' he replied simply, matter-of-factly,

184

ignoring the confusion that was definitely present on my face.

'Well . . . then I guess my question is about rule one. Kissing when appropriate. And don't get me wrong, I'm not complaining because . . . you know . . . I just . . . um . . . you'd originally said no kissing, and I'd said it wasn't realistic and now you're kissing me . . . so . . . I'm kind of confused.'

He nodded slowly, understanding flashing across his face, and then, just as I had, he took a breath. 'She wasn't around, you're right. I'm sorry. It crossed a line. I would have talked to you about it yesterday, but then Oz was drunk and I wanted to do it in person, but I couldn't leave . . .'

My eyes opened wider the longer he rambled, 'Oz was drunk?'

He nodded slowly. 'Yeah . . . he broke up with his girlfriend. It's messy . . .' He pushed his hat off, scratching through his thick hair with a soft sigh before replacing it and sitting up straighter. Sitting up like he meant business; firm, direct, a look in his eyes that was equal combinations intimidating and possibly the sexiest thing I'd ever seen. I didn't know what he was about to say but I was all ears. 'Anyway, the kiss. Our kiss.'

It was the way he said *our* kiss, like it was a complete story with a beginning, middle and end that had my entire body thrumming.

'I'm sorry, Violet, I've been doing this all wrong. Or maybe right . . . I dunno . . . maybe there's no other way it could have happened.'

I was trying to focus on him, but as he sat up, his hand inched forward and now his thumb was swiping over my knee – back and forth like a metronome and just as hypnotizing. So much, in fact, it took me a second to realize he'd stopped talking, and from the look of it he was expecting me to say something.

But God, if this is how I rambled no wonder people got annoyed with me.

'Charlie, I'm not following.'

'Yeah . . . I'm not very good at this. What I'm trying to say is, Violet, I like you.'

'You like me?'

'I do.' He smiled.

I opened my mouth to speak, but honestly my brain could not compute what was happening. I was working at the speed of sound when everyone else was zooming past on light. Charlie Masterson was sitting in front of me, in a situation I'd literally dreamed about since I was fourteen, telling me he liked me, yet I'd never got as far as imagining how I would answer.

Was this shock? Was I in shock?

Possibly, seeing as the only response I could come up with was, 'What do you mean you've done it all wrong.'

'Well,' he grimaced, 'just because of the way we started spending time together.'

'You mean because of Evie?'

He nodded, 'Yes. And I really wish it hadn't been the case, but I also know that if I hadn't asked you to be my fake girlfriend, then I'd have never spent this time with you . . . I'd have never realized how much I enjoy spending time with you.'

186

'Um . . .'

'But,' he continued, like I didn't have my mouth open to speak. 'I know you only agreed to help me because it would be good practice for your acting. In which case, let's just pretend I never said anything, and normal behaviour will resume.'

I was still staring at him, slightly open mouthed, when two thoughts occurred to me.

One. Stella had been correct. I'd managed to fake-relationship my way to Charlie liking me.

Two. I must be really good at acting if Charlie never realized *I* liked *him*.

'Sorry,' he started again, 'I should have got it all out there before I kissed you and started making things awkward. Can you tell I've never done this before? Okay, I'll shut up now. You go.'

Wow. This was not how I expected this morning to go.

I'd gotten so used to my love/crush being unre-quited that now it seemed to be very much requited, I wasn't entirely sure what to do with it.

How long had I waited for Charlie to say those words to me? It felt like forever. Even in the weeks since the beginning of term I'd been secretly hoping that one day I'd hear them. I'd resigned myself to the fact this wasn't real. It could never be real, and yet here he was sitting in front of me, saying exactly that. Kind of.

'Are you going to say something?' he asked finally. 'It's not normally me who's the chatty one?'

I stifled a giggle, which seemed to unstick me from the mental block I was having. I really needed to start practising the second halves of conversations I had with myself. It would certainly be more helpful in situations like this.

'You really like me?'

He nodded, 'Yeah.'

'*Like me* like me?'

'Yes. I *like you* like you. Since the moment you kissed me in the Blue Oar, I haven't been able to stop thinking about you. Or thinking about kissing you again. When we're apart, I want to see you. When I see you all I want to do is kiss you, touch you, hold your hand, breathe you in. I like you, Violet, and I haven't liked anyone in a long time.'

Whoa.

'But I guess I should be asking you the same question,' he added, lifting one hand off my knee so he could release my lower lip from the grip of my teeth. 'Because if we're kissing for real, it kind of changes the rules.'

I nodded, deeply. 'Yeah. Our fake relationship seems to have changed, doesn't it?'

'It does. And do you like me enough to see where things could go?'

I'd been holding back the smile for what felt like forever, and it finally let itself free. 'Yes, I like you enough to see where things could go.'

Charlie let out a deep breath I didn't realize he'd been holding. 'Thank god for that.'

I glanced down to where his hand had inched towards mine, lacing our fingers together. 'But . . .'

'Not sure I like the sound of that.'

'What about Evie?'

Out of nowhere the conversation I'd had with Evie a few weeks ago flashed into my brain, along with the death stare she'd given me outside the sandwich shop the other day. I could just about cope with Charlie and Evie if I kept myself at arm's length, but if she was telling the truth, and Charlie and I became what I'd always wanted, then I wasn't sure how I'd manage. I had the feeling she wasn't going down without a fight, and I wasn't even fighting.

'What, Violet?' he asked, his brows almost touching for how deeply they'd dropped. 'What is it?'

'I should tell you something . . .'

'Okay.'

'I bumped into Evie a few weeks ago and she said you two always find your way back to one another. She's determined to get you back.'

Concern brimmed in his big green eyes as they searched my face until he dipped down to make sure that I could see him properly. His hands cupped my cheeks, holding firm enough that I couldn't look away, so I could see how sincere he was.

'I'm sorry that happened. Or that I wasn't there to refute her, but believe me when I say that I will never get back together with Evie. Never.'

I looked at him, holding his gaze while on the precipice of something I'd wanted for so long. 'Okay.'

'Okay? As in . . .'

'Yeah. Let's see where things go.'

A brilliant smile split his face; my favourite smile. The ginger beer smile that I could almost feel reaching into my chest and squeezing it gently.

'I like the sound of that. Now, can I kiss you officially? Not as an appropriate rule but because I can't not. Then I promise we can start rehearsing.'

I was barely able to nod my head before his lips fell to mine.

Best Charlie Masterson kiss yet. *Officially.*

14. Charlie

(February 14th – also known as Valentine's Day)

'Okay, oars up.'

The eight of us followed Marshy's command and for the final 25 metres we glided down the river towards the dry dock, stretching out our legs.

We needed it. My muscles had been screaming for the last fifteen minutes, and based on the groaning coming from Brooks in six seat behind me so were his.

It was safe to say that since the beginning of the year, our training sessions had ramped up.

At the beginning of January, they'd been hard. But we'd powered into February and with less than two months to race day, the training was pushing us to the brink of collapse because *'you'll be near death on race day, no reason why you shouldn't get used to it now'*, Coach had reminded us last week.

Every day he'd spouted one of his little missives about how we likely wouldn't survive, or how many ambulances would be waiting for us by Chiswick Bridge. Some iteration of it, anyway. Even this morning while I was trying to concentrate on how to breathe he'd been yelling foreboding warnings down his megaphone from the support boat behind us.

It didn't help that Oz seemed to have taken it upon

himself to become a one-man rowing machine. As stroke it was his job to set the pace, but if I didn't know better I'd swear he was trying to kill us – given I was still sucking fresh air into my lungs – or at least take seriously Coach's instructions to drive us to collapse. Even over the many years I'd rowed with Oz, through school and for Great Britain, I couldn't recall ever seeing him more determined to win a race than he appeared this week.

In fact, it was possible I'd blanked on last year's training because I don't remember pushing ourselves quite so hard, *ever*. Which, in hindsight, may have contributed to why we'd lost.

At the rate we were going, not even the Olympic squad could beat us. Not this year. Every single drop of sweat we had was being poured into this race. It was one of the reasons the main OUBC crew was leaner. The weak links had been cut weeks ago, and we were now down to the final numbers our crews would be selected from.

Blue Boat and Isis. Two boats. Two coxes. Sixteen rowers.

It hadn't been announced yet, but we all knew who would be racing in the number one spot – Marshy, Bitters, Joshi, Fellows, Drake, Frank, Brooks, Oz and me.

We were the crew to beat.

We were the crew to take Oxford over the finish line first. We would be crowned champions.

We could feel it. All of us. We *knew.*

There was no way we'd lose this year. None.

'Nice pace today, fellas. Fast, very fast,' added Marshy from the confines of his thick winter parka and wool beanie, huddled at the front of the shell.

'Jesus . . . Christ,' puffed out Brooks behind me. 'How was this a Friday session? We're out on the river all weekend, when am I supposed to recover?'

'When we're dead?' I turned around to find his bright-red face dripping in sweat. 'Poor little Brooksy, d'you need me to run you a hot bath when we get home?'

'Thanks, mate. I do actually,' he grinned, before dropping his voice. 'Take it this session was about Kate?'

My head flicked up to where Oz was talking to Marshy. Call it a coincidence, but since Kate and Oz had broken up the punishing durations of our training regimens seemed to have increased. While all the boys had noticed, only Brooks and I had put two and two together, to equal an Oz who seemed to be trying to exorcise himself into forgetting Kate, seeing as drinking himself into forgetfulness hadn't worked.

It wasn't just in training either. On Wednesday I'd gotten home to find Oz revising, an occurrence rarer than a solar eclipse. At least he hadn't attempted to cook anything, because then I'd really start worrying.

I turned back to Brooks. 'That's a fair assumption.'

'Maybe we can get them back together before he kills us all then.'

'Hmm.'

'Everyone out and packed up,' boomed Coach over the megaphone. 'Shells away.'

'Why does he repeat it every morning like we don't

know what we're doing?' snapped Oz, pushing his oar out to one of the junior crew members waiting on the dry dock ready to pull us in.

It sounded like a rhetorical question to me, and Brooks' single raise of one eyebrow was all the response I needed, especially when Oz stormed into the changing rooms after we'd safely placed the boat back on the pipes. Marshy wasn't far behind him, slipping through the swing door Oz had flung open.

'Has Marshy been dumped too?' mumbled Brooks, standing far too close to me. 'I didn't even know he was seeing anyone.'

I stepped back and shrugged. 'No clue.'

'Well, thank fuck we're single.'

I jerked forward slightly as he slapped me on the back with a guffaw, and ignored my eye roll. Not a day had passed that Brooks hadn't failed to make some kind of little jab about Violet and me, or the daily query into how much longer was left of our 'arrangement'. I could almost believe that he thought he needed to mention it just so I wouldn't forget.

As a result, I was yet to break it to him that Violet and I were no longer fake dating.

I knew I had to do it, I just hadn't found the right moment. It was hard when Brooks was being more of a pain in the arse than usual.

Plus the kissing with Violet was taking up all my spare time, and any precious minutes left over were dedicated to training, studying, training and more training. Then sleep.

Not that I was complaining in the slightest. In fact, if

all I could do for the rest of my life was sleep and kiss Violet I'd die happy.

Something that might come sooner than expected the way our training sessions were going.

Brooks was also on a diet of training, studying and sleeping, so really it had been virtually impossible to speak to him. But that wasn't a good enough excuse either.

We didn't just stand around doing nothing, like we were just now.

Shit. I pulled on the red and white cupcake band I still wore around my wrist, and it snapped back with enough of a sting to kick me into gear.

'Mate . . . have you got a second to talk?' I started, right as the doors from the changing room were flung open and Oz stormed out.

'Are you two ready to leave or are you standing around gossiping?'

'We're ready,' replied Brooks, who definitely wasn't ready given he was in the same state of rowing undress as I was, and I wasn't ready. 'Two minutes, let me grab our things. Charlie, I'll get yours.'

'Thanks,' I called after him, glancing at Oz. 'You okay? Hard session today.'

'We have a race to win,' he grumbled, and I didn't fail to notice he wouldn't meet my eye.

'Yeah, we do. Let's try and make sure we're still alive come race day though. Eh?'

'Don't be stupid, Charlie. Of course, we will be.'

I didn't bother to argue or point out that there was a high possibility if he pushed every session as hard as he had this morning, he would exhaust himself before the end of March. Luckily he didn't seem to be waiting for a response and that was the moment Brooks reappeared carrying bags, while also trying to pull his hoodie on.

'Good, let's go home,' Oz said, marching off towards the car so fast we were jogging to keep up with him.

'I'll take that, thanks.' I saved my backpack before Brooks dropped it.

'I'm absolutely famished. What's for second breakfast?'

'You need to fend for yourself, I have to go to the library. But there are fresh breakfast muffins in the pantry that I made last night.'

'Ooh, my favourite.' He clapped a big hand on my shoulder and opened the car door for me to hop in – the back door. 'You're a good boy, Charles, especially as you're letting me ride shotgun.'

I'd agreed to no such thing. But it was an argument I never won. I also had a feeling Oz may have banned me from the passenger seat for some stupid reason, like he didn't care for my music selection, but I couldn't quite remember. Normally I'd have put up a fight, but right now I was more than content to stay in the back seat for the journey home, because it meant I could sneak in a twenty-minute power nap.

The wheels spun on the gravel with a loud crunch, as Oz reversed and sped out of the car park without a word.

Leaning my head on the seat rest, I closed my eyes expecting exhaustion to overwhelm me as it usually did but a minute later and I was still wide awake. My muscles were sore, yes. My body was kind of tired, but my brain was wide awake.

Glancing out of the window, the sun was fully emerging on the horizon, the orange glow illuminating the inky skies, turning them a perfect shade of violet.

Violet.

She was the reason I felt so recharged. Like I'd been mainlining caffeine since I'd woken up.

I might not love sitting in the back but at least neither Oz nor Brooks could see me smiling to myself as I pulled my phone out.

> **Charlie:** *How's my no-longer-fake girlfriend doing today? Enjoying a lie in?*
>
> **Violet:** *No! She's rushing around.*
>
> **Charlie:** *Rushing this early already . . .*
>
> **Violet:** *Tell me about it. I have rehearsals all morning, lectures all afternoon. And we're in the theatre today, which adds another twenty minutes to my journey time.* ☹

I checked the clock.

My first class didn't start until after lunch, but I had to return a couple of books and I'd promised Gordon I'd meet him before our Friday physics tutorial. If I really hurried I could swing by the theatre and see how all Violet's hard work was paying off.

It was on my way.

At least, it was on my way if I took a huge detour across the city.

I eased open the doors of the theatre as carefully as I could, hoping to catch a glimpse of Violet in her natural habitat because as she was perpetually late, it wasn't often I got to see her without her noticing me.

'Bollocks,' I hissed to myself as the hinge stuck and shoved me forward with a clattered close. So much for being careful.

Thankfully no one on stage seemed to notice, so I slipped in undetected and sank into one of the plush velvet seats on the back row. I'd even managed to remove my very wet coat, and put down my umbrella without causing too much of a commotion. Or any commotion.

The commotion seemed to be happening on stage.

'No. No. No. It's stage left. Stage *LEFT,* Matthew. It says right here in the script, supporting cast come in stage LEFT,' bellowed a voice from the front.

Clearly size didn't equal volume because right then a very small red-headed girl stormed up the steps in front of the stage brandishing what looked like a script, still bellowing. I was amazed her voice hadn't given way as she strode across the stage, short legs powering her towards a group of people, one of which I assumed was the errant Matthew. It was hard to believe she was capable of producing such a loud volume, and where in fact she had room for the vocal chords needed to produce it. If she ever gave up studying whatever it was she was studying, she could apply to be a foghorn in the navy.

One thing for sure, based on half the people who shrank back and the others who half rolled their eyes and turned away, this girl was in charge. Either way, I did not want to be on the receiving end of her wrath and had a feeling she wouldn't be quite so happy with a stranger being present, so I sank further down in my seat, praying I wouldn't get caught.

Even if I was here to see one of the stars.

'Ah . . . Cecily,' crowed a voice, equally as booming but much deeper, 'that's my fault. I told them to come on from stage right. From an audience perspective, it's much more helpful for the scene I have with Stella, and really brings her to the forefront for Olivia's entrance.'

I watched as a guy, dressed head to toe in what looked like dark-green velvet, sidled up next to the redhead and put his arm around her. Points for bravery, I'd give him that. Not sure I'd be getting so close seeing as she looked capable of breathing fire and reducing him to a pile of ashes.

'You see?' he said, turning them around so their backs were to the audience. 'Stella, come out. Show Cecily.'

I had to hold back the laugh rumbling fast up my throat at the sight of Stella shuffling onto the stage looking like she'd rather be anywhere else. Her jaw was clenched so tight I could see it popping from here, along with her arms crossed tight over her chest. It should have been a warning to this guy, but he didn't seem to have noticed.

Plus, you know, he was brave.

'Come on, Stella, come here.' He gestured her over, ignoring the impatient look she shot at him.

Stella took a deep breath, glaring to her left, before looking back to Cecily. 'Leo's correct. It's better,' she said through gritted teeth.

Ohhh. So this was the famous Leo Tavener. Maybe if I squinted a little he did look kind of familiar, but if

I was being honest he wasn't in the kind of films I ever watched. Or we watched in the house.

But this guy had me paying attention because he was the one who Violet complained about more than anything. Actually, thinking about it, I don't think I ever heard her complain about anything else, period. She wasn't that type of girl. Violet was easy, happy and nearly always smiling.

More important, she made *me* smile.

Glancing around, however, I couldn't see her.

She wasn't on stage. She wasn't with Stella. I sat up in my chair, hoping I'd missed her sitting on the front rows, but none of the backs of heads I could see belonged to Violet. It was only on my second sweep of the theatre that a flash of caramel-blonde caught my eye.

There she was.

Maybe if I'd come to the theatre weeks ago, I would have realized sooner that this girl was one of a kind. Absolutely stunning. It wouldn't have taken me most of January to figure out that I liked her. And I wouldn't have been surprised by the realization that I did.

In fact, right now, watching her wander across the stage to join in with whatever discussion they were having, the violet ends of her blonde hair bouncing across her shoulders as happily and carefree as she was, I was surprised how I hadn't liked Violet Brooks for far longer than a month. I pulled out my phone, taking a quick snap I could add to Instagram later.

'Cece, I agree too.'

'I'm the director, Violet. I say what's happening.'

Leo had stepped away nearer to Stella, so the space was clear for Violet to be next, and once more Cecily had an arm slung over her shoulders. 'I know you are, Cecily, but come and watch from down here. You'll see. And when Linus gets back we can show him too.'

Somehow, Violet managed to coax Cecily off the stage, taking her down the stairs and back to her seat.

'Do-over,' Violet called, and everyone jumped into action, resuming their positions until only Leo was left in the centre. 'Stella?'

Stella walked onto the stage from the right and stopped, looking down at Cecily.

'Well?'

It was faint, but I heard a huffed 'fine', from the front row, before standing to resume with the foghorn. 'Okay, ten-minute break. Ten minutes people.'

I eased up from the chair just as Stella ran down the steps to Violet and spotted me. Her face split with a wide, knowing grin and ten seconds later Violet shot up and spun around.

Rushing across the city in the pouring rain, clocking up a library fine because my pile of books was definitely going back late, not to mention almost dying in training this morning, was all totally worth it from the look on her face when her eyes locked with mine.

If I'd had any doubt at all about liking this girl, it melted away from the warmth of her smile until I swear it was only her and me in the entire theatre. Especially when she made her way over to me, breaking into a little jog for the last few metres.

'What are you doing here?'

'Thought I'd come to see if all our rehearsal time's paying off.'

Her giggle hit me square in the chest, and I knew my smile matched the size of hers. Taking a step forward, I was just about to kiss her when I realized we had an audience. An audience of one. I managed to tear my eyes away from Violet to see who it was.

Up close, Leo looked much more familiar than he had on the stage, and much taller. The velvet suit was still velvet, but somehow he managed to pull it off. In an Austin Powers kind of way, or in the way a velvet suit should never look good on anybody. Maybe it was the shiny brogues he'd paired it with, shinier than I'd ever known shoes could be.

I found myself wondering what he did on rainy days like this because shiny shoes, velvet and rain were not friends.

'Hi?'

'What's up, Leo?' asked Violet, from her tone clearly annoyed at the interruption. Though I noticed she didn't frown at Stella who'd also joined us.

'Well, I came to see if you wanted a coffee, but now I want to know who this dishy chap is. Your boyfriend I presume, given how you're looking at each other.'

My eyes shot to Violet, who looked utterly mortified, or perhaps that was the face she made when she was trying to bite her tongue. Because I think she was trying to do that too. Whatever it was, I was still learning. I'd got most of her faces down, but this was new.

Stella's, however, needed no translation. The clenched fists raised to her temples did all the talking.

'God, Leo. Who speaks like that. You're twenty years old. No one says "dishy chap" under the age of seventy-five, and Charlie isn't . . .'

'I dunno,' I interrupted and grinned at Leo. 'I kind of like it. It has an old-world charm to it. I should thank you, my good sir.'

Leo looked like he might burst with happiness, in contrast to Stella who appeared to be trying to melt him with her glare. But he was impervious. And I liked him all the more for it. Violet, however, was still twisting her lip and it took no guesses for me to figure it was down to the boyfriend comment, not that I could have cared less.

We might be seeing how things were going, but that didn't stop me from looking at her the way I always looked at her – like she was lit with a spotlight only I could see. If that's what a boyfriend did, then so be it.

'You're very welcome.' He thrust a hand out to me, 'Leo Tavener.'

I took it, momentarily surprised at the firmness of his shake. 'Charlie Masterson.'

'Oh, bravo, Violet. I'm glad you've met someone worthy, and just in time for Valentine's Day too.'

Valentine's Day? Shit, when was that?

I both heard and felt Violet groan next to me, and I'd imagine the wince I was wearing now mirrored hers.

Leo leaned forward in what I assume he'd call a stage whisper and said, 'February fourteenth.'

'Thanks, mate.' I saluted.

'You're very welcome,' he winked, and turned to Stella. 'Tell me, do you have plans for Valentine's Day?'

For the first time I'd ever seen, Stella was completely speechless. Her mouth opened and closed like a goldfish as she stared at him, almost to the point I was starting to feel sorry for her, especially as Violet just looked confused.

'Um . . . I . . . Yes. I do,' she spluttered finally, making it obvious to anyone with eyes and ears that she was lying. 'Anyway, I have to go. Vi, see you later.'

She hurried off through the doors before the three of us could stop her or call after her to remember her umbrella.

Leo was the first to break the silence with a low chuckle. 'She certainly is a feisty one, that one. Keeps me on my toes every day.'

Violet and I both turned to him. She paused with her mouth open like she was about to ask him a question then thought better.

'Anyway, coffee,' he smiled, thumbing behind him. 'Charlie, good to meet you.'

'Bye, mate,' I waved, before I realized what I was doing and put my arm down. I watched him jog after Stella and turned to Violet. 'I don't know why you're always complaining about him. I like him.'

She rolled her eyes, letting out a loud groan. 'Of course you do.'

Stepping as far into her personal space as I could, I reached around and gripped a handful of hair, gently tugging it until her head tipped for me to kiss.

'Alone, finally. Hello.'

'Hello.' She smiled against my lips, then arched back looking at me with a raised brow. 'My good sir?'

'What?' I chuckled, wrapping my arms around her waist, relishing how perfectly she fitted next to me and once more thinking how nice it was to be similar heights. 'It's always fun to wind up Stella. I'd forgotten how much Brooks used to do it whenever we were at your parents' place. I give it until the end of term before they're together.'

'Who?'

'Stella and Laurence Olivier.' I nodded to the door where they'd both disappeared.

'What? Don't be stupid.'

'I'm telling you. Those two are getting it on.' There was something about the way Leo looked at her, even when she was being incredibly rude. And I'd seen Stella get annoyed with people before – mostly Brooks – and I'd not once thought she'd rather be in bed with him. But Leo on the other hand was a good-looking guy, even if he did wear velvet suits and say things like 'dishy chap'.

'Are you feeling alright?' She lifted her hand to my forehead. 'Or is a fever making you delusional?'

'You're the only one giving me a fever.' I shook my head with a smirk, catching her hand and holding the palm to my lips, 'Come on, Shakespeare, let's go and get a coffee. By my timing we've only got five minutes left, and for four of those I want to be kissing you.'

She grinned up at me, 'Are you sure you shouldn't be taking English? You're awfully romantic for a physicist.'

Throwing my head back with a laugh, I pulled her in and tucked her under my arm. And if I really wanted to step up and show her romance, the pink hearts in all the windows we passed told me I should probably do it soon.

15. Violet

(Charlie doesn't share)

I was undecided as to whether this was a good idea or not, but the longer I waited, the longer it would be too late to run away.

Due to my rehearsal schedule, I hadn't had the opportunity to wait for Charlie after training yet, but as luck would have it, tonight's was cancelled.

Worst comes to worst I'd blag it, and say I was waiting for Hugo.

I mean, I could be waiting for him. Even though I've never waited for my brother a day in my life, but there's always a first time for everything, right?

It wasn't that Charlie wouldn't be happy to see me, or that he didn't know I'd be waiting. Neither of those – this would be the first time we were around his friends. The two of us, together, with friends including my brother, none of whom knew the fake part of our relationship had been removed.

The second thoughts didn't have a chance to take hold, or give me the opportunity to make a swift getaway because the doors to the gym opened and out walked my brother. It could have been any number of people, still providing me with enough head start not to get caught, but no.

His head was down, doing his usual texting and

walking, and not paying the slightest bit of attention to where he was going. It must be a family trait.

A slow grin spread across his face, one I wish I didn't know the meaning of, before he slipped his phone into his pocket and jogged down the steps. The grin died, however, the second he lifted his head and spotted me.

'Violet? What're you doing? What's wrong? Is Buddy okay?'

'Buddy?' I replied, wondering what our family Labrador had to do with anything. Or why I'd be standing outside his training facility if something had happened to him. No way. I'd be on the first train home. Or I'd steal a car.

'Why are you here, Violet?'

'I came to meet Charlie.'

'Charlie?' Hugo's thick brows, the ones he inherited from my dad, the ones I get waxed on the regular, dropped low. 'Why are you waiting for . . . oh, is this part of the whole fake dating thing?'

'Yes, exactly.'

'Ugh, look, I'm trying to pretend this doesn't exist, and you doing it in front of me doesn't help with that.'

I wasn't exactly sure what the *it* he was referring to was, especially as all I was doing was standing against the railings. I also wasn't entirely sure I wanted to ask either. I still couldn't figure out why my brother cared so much, or if he was more annoyed about me dating Charlie or Charlie dating me, because up to this point in my life my brother had shown exactly zero interest in anyone I dated. Even when I brought Miles Garland home to meet my family, Hugo couldn't have cared less.

But seeing as he was still scowling at the thought of a *fake* relationship, it was clear we needed to devise a suitable plan to broach telling my brother the truth.

'Huey, I'm just standing here.'

'So, nothing's wrong with Buddy?'

'No, there's not. At least, not that I know of,' I shrugged, which only made his eyes narrow.

'See, *I* would know if there was something wrong with him. This is why he loves me more than you.'

'He does not –'

'Does too,' he shot back, and honestly if the loud throat clearing to our left hadn't interrupted us we'd have continued this all night. It wouldn't have been the first time either.

The pair of us turned in sync to the interruption, though not before Hugo shot another glare my way. The interruption turned out to be Bitters, and if I could only use one word to describe him it would be trouble. The lopsided smile, the glint in the eye, the insolent way his arms were crossed over his chest. All trouble.

'Well, well, well. We meet again, fake girlfriend. And how I never realized you are Brooks' little sister is beyond me. You mustn't have come to any races, there's no way I'd forget you.'

I rolled my eyes, letting out a scoff, though not as loud as Hugo's.

Bitters' grin spread across his face, making it very clear exactly why my brother had scoffed. It didn't help when Bitters lifted my hand and kissed it.

I wasn't sure whose eyes widened more. Mine or Hugo's. And as much as I didn't want this guy kissing my hand, it was almost worth it to see the annoyance on my brother's face. I snatched it back.

'Knock it off, will you? For fuck's sake.' Hugo shoved him in the shoulder.

Bitters' grin became distinctly more devilish as he turned to me. 'Did you know your brother's put a moratorium out on any of us dating you? I mean, for real dating. Not whatever it is you're helping Charlie with. When's that over by the way?'

I take it back. It wasn't devilish, it was thoroughly shit stirring.

'What?' This time the annoyance and the glare were all mine, so much so I barely noticed when the heavy arm was draped over my shoulder. 'Hugo. What is he talking about?'

'See, Brooks. Don't think Violet's too happy about you making decisions for her. Even less than I am at the news I couldn't ask you on a date.'

I was too busy glaring at Hugo to tell Bitters I had no intention of dating him. 'Hugo. What is he talking about?'

'Come on, Violet. What d'you say?'

Ignoring Bitters again, my eyes narrowed on my brother, though I knew it wouldn't make the slightest bit of difference, just like I knew he had no intention of answering me. My brother was more stubborn than a mule. Sometimes it was like playing a game of chicken – who'd give in first – especially when he raised my glare with pursed lips and a clenched jaw.

'Not sure she's too happy you're dictating her dating life, mate,' Bitters added with a deep chuckle.

'Will you shut up.' I shrugged his arm off me, just as the doors to the gym opened and out walked a small group of the boys, including the one I'd been waiting for. The only one I wanted to see.

The one whose face was becoming more thunderous the closer he got.

'What's going on?'

'Nothing,' I snapped, hoping the deep frown and the large step away from my brother and his idiot crewmate would get the message across to them and Charlie, that I was not happy about whatever was happening right now. Not to mention, it was far too cold to be standing outside arguing.

'Just trying to convince Brooks to let me take Violet on a date once you two are done with your project.'

I'd never been tempted to punch someone in the face before, but Bitters was veering dangerously close to that line. I'd never seen Charlie in a bad mood, there was always a smile nearby. But from the expression he was currently wearing it was clear that if I told him I wanted to punch Bitters, he'd hold him still for me.

'What?' Charlie growled, the lines on his forehead deepening.

'To be clear, I date who I want and my brother has no say in it,' I snapped, daring Hugo to reply.

'Great. How about Valentine's Day then?' Bitters barked out a loud laugh, enormously pleased with this super fun game he'd just invented, and a couple of guys in the audience we seemed to have acquired chuckled along with him.

On any other day, and if he'd found something else

to annoy my brother with, I'd have captained the team. But seeing as I was the subject, and now couldn't tell who was more annoyed – Charlie or me – I couldn't shut it down quick enough. I'd barely glanced at Charlie since he'd arrived, but that didn't mean I couldn't feel his eyes on me. And it wasn't in a good way. The way I was getting used to. The way he managed to make me feel like I was the only girl he'd ever seen.

I spun around to Bitters, 'No!'

He clearly wasn't the type of guy who liked to take no for an answer, however, because I could see him on the verge of replying when Charlie interrupted.

'Shut the fuck up, will you? She said no. Stop being a dick.'

Wisely, for a guy who seemed to have limited brain cells, Bitters stayed silent. Though I still wanted to punch that smirk right off his stupid face. No one said anything for a good ten seconds, which thankfully lost the attention of ninety-five per cent of our audience who presumably had left to find warmth. Sensible.

'Violet, let's go,' ordered Charlie, and stormed off so quickly, he was down the path before I even realized.

'Violet –'

'We'll talk about this tomorrow,' I snarled at Hugo, jogging off to catch up with Charlie, but not before I noticed Oz standing to the side, witness to the entire interaction. Or the way his eyes flicked from a rapidly distant Charlie to mine with a frown that had nervous knots twisting in my belly.

He'd covered a surprising amount of ground by the time the moon reappeared from behind a cloud and I spotted him in the distance, turning down an alleyway. Must be those long legs, good job mine were too.

'Charlie . . . Charlie, slow down.' I jogged a little further, grabbing his arm. 'Charlie.'

He stopped dead and turned. For a split second the rage shadowing his face had me stepping back, but it vanished just as quickly. When he refocused on me, his expression held confusion. It was almost as though he hadn't realized I was there.

'Didn't you hear me calling?'

He dropped his head with a shake.

'Are you okay?'

'Yes, I'm fine . . .' he started, then paused. 'No . . . yes . . . no. No, I'm not.'

My fist was still gripping on to his sleeve, and I dropped it as I stepped in. 'What's wrong?'

He was about to answer, but the flare of his pupils did all the talking, and for the first time I noticed the green had turned to a dark forest colour. It was three degrees out, and yet the fire burning in his eye licked across every inch of my skin as he stared, long enough for beads of sweat to trickle down my back.

Within the space of a heartbeat he stepped towards me, moving us until my back hit the wall. Warm fingers brushed along the edge of my jaw, right before his lips crashed into mine. Not even the cobbled brick could cool my skin as his tongue plunged into my mouth.

I couldn't move. I couldn't do anything except surrender to the way this man was taking full control, staking claim. It was ownership, plain and simple. Even when he softened against me, his tongue roaming against mine, there was still a need and insistence I'd never experienced before. Ever. I'd never experienced a kiss like this, period.

Hot. Needy. Consuming.

I'd been taken hostage by his mouth. My entire body was vibrating on a frequency I didn't know I had, heavy pulses buzzing over my skin, and by the time he pulled away the only reason I was standing was because of the grip he still had on me.

'Fuuuck,' he breathed out, one long word, as his head dropped on my shoulder.

My sentiments exactly.

I waited to see if he had any more to add, while also catching my own breath. He was so quiet, resting his head on my shoulder, he could have fallen asleep. It became clear he wasn't going to add anything else.

It was only when I shifted my shoulder slightly that he finally lifted his head. The fire no longer burned in his eyes; instead what looked like sadness had replaced it, though for the life of me I couldn't figure out why. Because all I wanted to do after that kiss was take a cold shower.

Cupping his cheek, I moved his face until he couldn't look away. It wasn't quite the grip he had me in, but it was good enough. 'Charlie, what's going on?'

A thousand thoughts flickered through my brain as his gaze held mine, and when he eventually spoke his voice had dropped an octave: rumbly, gravelly and doing nothing to help the electricity coursing through me.

'I didn't like that.'

'Like what?'

'The boys . . .' he sighed deeply, 'my friends. I did not like seeing Bitters with his arm around you. Fuck,' he added, again, though this time it was less needy and more frustrated. Sharper.

I could feel the frustration radiating from him, though why was harder to figure out.

Bitters and my brother were two idiots that I probably wouldn't think about again for a very long time. Bitters at least; unfortunately I had to see my brother at family functions and weekends at home, and he really wasn't too bad most of the time.

But either way, it didn't seem to warrant the anguish on Charlie's face, which he seemed to realize I was having a hard time understanding.

'Bitters with his arm around you . . . I can feel the jealousy clawing right here,' he placed my hand on the centre of his chest above the distinct thump of his heart, 'I've just found you. I can't lose you already.'

'Why would you lose me?'

He let out another of those deep sighs and as his head dropped back onto my shoulder it all clicked. I was such a dummy, an angry dummy. And I now had a new target for the punch I'd wanted to send Bitters' way.

I was becoming quite violent, it seemed.

'Is this about Evie?'

He nodded, though his head was still resting on my shoulder. 'She's the only person I've ever been in a relationship with, twice technically. Both times she cheated on me, and seeing Bitters all over you . . .' His eyes were watery when he eventually lifted his head. 'I'm sorry.

I'm so sorry, Violet. I knew Evie fucked me up . . . I always said, I'd never be in another relationship. Stupid, I know, and it's the reason why your brother thinks I'm a drama queen, but now I've met you . . .'

I stood there absorbing his words, realizing the magnitude of what he was going through and the profound sadness I felt at the damage Evie had caused. If I could go a little way to fixing it, then it would be totally worth it.

Or it could drastically backfire.

But he'd been honest with me, so I could be a little more honest with him.

'Do you trust me?' I asked.

He answered with no hesitation. 'Yes.'

My hand rested back on his cheek, 'It's going to take a lot more than Bitters hitting on me to drag my attention away from you.'

'Thank you,' he smiled softly.

'I'm serious, Charlie. My feelings for you aren't new.'

'What do you mean?'

This time it was my turn to look away, but I'd said it now and I couldn't back out.

'Violet, what do you mean?'

'It's only ever been you.'

'Been me what?' he asked, still so confused, and for a genius he really wasn't that quick. Maybe his genius only spread to things like physics.

'I've had a crush on you since I was fourteen. Since the first time Hugo brought you home during half-term.'

He wasn't very good at hiding the shock. I don't think I saw him blink for ten seconds.

I craned up to kiss his cheek. 'So when I say it'll take more than Bitters putting his arm around me, and my brother banning anyone from asking me on a date, I mean it.'

'Violet . . .'

The way he said my name . . . reverential, like he was trying it on for size and found it to be the perfect fit. I'd never loved being called Violet more than I did right in this moment.

'I didn't know . . .'

'I'm a good actress,' I shrugged.

This time when he kissed me there was a tenderness present. He was slow, taking his time to discover me, his tongue sliding against mine with no urgency. My bones had barely solidified from the previous kiss, but here they were melting all over again.

I wasn't ready for him to ease away, his mouth leaving mine with a soft pop and a chuckle which had my heart skipping.

'Christ, Violet. How have I been so thick? Be patient with me, please.'

'Hey,' I laughed. 'Patience is my middle name.'

Dropping his lips, they barely brushed against mine before he let out a groan. Not the good kind.

'We need to figure out what to do with Brooks.'

'Tomorrow,' I replied, bringing his mouth back to mine.

We had more important things to do right now.

16. Charlie

(Just call me Mary Berry)

I've said it before, and I'll say it again. I could totally win *The Great British Bake Off*.

Peering through the glass on the oven, the cupcakes were rising nicely. There was still another ten minutes on the timer, but I reckoned they'd be done before that. Any longer and the chocolate in the centre wouldn't stay gooey.

And they needed to be gooey. Perfect, fluffy, gooey.

Yeah, I could totally win. These cupcakes would be my showstopper.

I opened the cupboard under the sink and got to work on cleaning up the kitchen. Since I was young, Dad had drilled it into me that a kitchen should be cleaned on the go. It was a cardinal rule in all his kitchens, and I'd witnessed more than once what happened when it wasn't followed. I tried to run the kitchen in this place with the same regimental style, but it hadn't worked.

The only person who paid any attention was, ironically, our cleaner, who was happy she had one less room to clean, mostly because Brooks' room took her most of the day.

By the time the alarm beeped on the oven, I'd soaped and rinsed the counter and stove, reorganized the fridge, piled up the dishwasher with all the mixing bowls, along with the stove tops, and taken the bin bags out. The chocolate chips were back in the cupboard, and the frosting was set on the side ready to be piped out once the cupcakes had cooled enough.

I was in the process of laying them on the cooling rack when I heard the click of the front door. I thought I'd timed it so that both Oz and Brooks were out of the house while I'd been baking, because it would raise fewer questions. Plus, they usually argued over who got to lick the bowl and I didn't have time for that today.

'Oh my god, something smells amazing Charles,' Brooks announced as he appeared in the kitchen archway, followed closely by Oz. 'What culinary delights have you baked today?'

'Cupcakes,' I replied, slapping Brooks' hand away as he reached for one. 'They're still hot. Just wait.'

His bottom lip protruded so dramatically I decided it wasn't just Violet who'd inherited the theatrical gene in their family.

Oz slipped onto one of the large kitchen stools surrounding the island, and frowned. 'Why've you made so many?'

This was exactly the type of question I didn't want asked. Because I'd never made thirty cupcakes before. I'd never made cupcakes, period. But I *did* know that whatever I baked would have to include enough for the boys. They would get their portion, but two thirds of these babies – the best two thirds – were going elsewhere.

'Because I need to take some for a project.'

'What project?'

'A work project.'

'A work project that involves three dozen cupcakes?'

'Mmm hmm.' I turned away to find Brooks standing by the kettle as he peered into the bowl of frosting. I snatched it right before he stuck his finger in. 'For fuck's sake. Make the tea, I'll make you a cupcake.'

He grinned wide. 'You have yourself a deal.'

I glanced back to Oz who was rolling his eyes enough for the both of us. Standard Brooks behaviour.

I picked two of the worst looking cupcakes from the tray, though worst was the wrong word because they were all amazing. This frosting was going to slide right off without letting them cool properly, although knowing Brooks he'd probably inhale it before it got the chance.

Ripping off a sheet of baking parchment, I folded it into a cone, cut the end off and scooped in a dollop of the frosting. By the time Brooks had finishing making us all a cup of tea and taken a seat next to Oz, said frosting was neatly piped onto the top of the cupcakes like a little Mr Whippy.

I placed one in front of each of them, and I leaned back. Five seconds later and neither of them were touched. Brooks, in fact, was looking at his in a way that could only be described as suspicious.

'What's wrong?'

His mouth crooked as he looked at it. 'The frosting, it's purple.'

My chest tightened. 'Yes?'

'These aren't vegetable cupcakes or some shit, are they? This isn't beetroot frosting, is it? Because honestly,

221

Charlie, beetroot tastes like dirt. I don't want a dirt-tasting cupcake.'

I looked at Oz who was trying to hold in a smile, 'First, no one's forcing you to eat it. Second, no it's not beetroot.'

'Excellent.' He lifted the cupcake to his mouth then stopped. 'Wait, it's not lavender is it? Because I'm not on board with that either.'

'No, just plain old vanilla with some —'

Half the cupcake had been inhaled before I'd finished the end of the sentence.

'Idsreallygoob.'

I picked up my tea and sipped it, hiding the smirk. 'Thank you. And thank you for the tea.'

The second half of the cupcake disappeared, and Brooks washed it all down with a glug of tea, then peered longingly at the as yet untouched one sitting in front of Oz.

'Are you going to eat that?'

'Not right now,' Oz replied.

'Great.' Brooks snatched up the cupcake then looked at me with a shake of his head. 'Purple frosting. You really are hanging out with my sister too much, and now it's affecting my snack times. Remind me when this thing is going to be over between you two?'

'Um . . .'

'At least can we have brown frosting next time?' He held his hand up. 'It's all I'm asking.'

'I'll see what I can do,' I replied, trying to ignore the squeezing in my chest, for the first time thankful that Brooks' stomach always led the conversation.

Oz and I watched as the second cupcake vanished in less time than the first. Sometimes I wondered if Brooks even tasted his food or if it just got swallowed without touching the sides.

'We should definitely have cupcakes more often in this house.'

I moved the remainder of the cooling tray out of his reach.

'Hey, did you know it's Valentine's Day tomorrow?'

I nodded. Oz looked as startled as I had when Leo Tavener had announced it.

'Shit. Tomorrow? Shit. I should send something to Kate. Do you think? I should. Shouldn't I? That would be the right thing to do. So she knows I still love her. I'm still thinking about her, right?' Oz's head flicked from me to Brooks and back again. 'Right? Yes?'

I nodded, one deep nod. Over the past few weeks Oz had been moving through the five stages of grief. I think we were currently in bargaining, and that was based on nothing but the fact that our morning training sessions on the river had been getting easier. The anger Oz had used to power us through the week before last seemed to have lessened.

I didn't know whether sending her a Valentine's gift would get her back, but I *did* know that if he kept pushing us at the rate he had been, we'd all collapse. Therefore, I would be encouraging anything that involved him doing something else.

'Yes, mate. That's a good idea.'

'What d'you think would be good. What would work? What do girls like for Valentine's?'

223

'Can't go wrong with flowers,' answered Brooks, like he was an expert. Which he wasn't seeing as he clearly hadn't known Valentine's Day was tomorrow, not to mention the fact that when we were sixteen he broke up with Annabel Caterham two days before Valentine's so he could be single. And to my knowledge he's never had a girlfriend on Valentine's since.

Oz raked a hand through his hair. 'Yeah. I could do flowers. Roses? Yeah, roses.'

Reaching for his phone currently plugged in on the counter, he hit speed dial. It only rang twice before it was picked up by a voice we all knew well.

'Osbourne,' answered Oliver Greenwood, also known as Olly, and the unofficial fourth member of this household. 'What's up?'

The four of us had all attended school together. Being in the same boarding house meant we were rarely apart but while Brooks, Oz and I had all taken the rowing path, Olly was a natural at rugby – something he'd only taken up to help him get girls. And it did, far too well.

Unfortunately, just like the three of us were destined to attend Oxford, Olly was fated to go to Cambridge, follow in his family's footsteps studying law and less so, but just like his older brother, cause havoc among the first-year girls. Most likely second, third and fourth years too.

'Ol, I need you to do me a favour.'

'I'm still doing the last favour you asked me.'

Oz frowned. 'What was that?'

'Keep an eye on Kate.'

'Oh, well, it's the same thing then. I'm going to order some flowers, but please can you deliver them to her?'

'Florists deliver, Oz. They can do it,' he drawled.

'I need to make sure they've arrived safely. Please.' He stretched out his pleading so long that I'd have said yes just to stop it.

The grunt down the phone said Olly was of the same opinion. 'Fine. What about a card?'

'A card?'

'Yeah, Valentine's card?'

Oz's panicked face shot up to Brooks and me. 'Shit. I didn't think about that. A card . . .'

'The florist will drop a note in,' piped up Brooks, only to be shot down with a scowl from Oz.

'I'm not having the florist write my note to Kate,' he snapped, 'Ol, I'll call you back. Okay, I need to find a florist, find a card, and drive it over to Olly.'

It was hard to tell whose eyebrows had shot higher, mine or Brooks'. Oz didn't notice because he was too busy scrolling through his phone, but the way Brooks was still staring at me made it clear he thought Oz was losing his mind. Or maybe he'd lost it already, seeing as driving two hours across the country to deliver a Valentine's Day card when we both knew for a fact he had classes this afternoon, not to mention cutting it fine for training this evening was something only a crazy person would attempt.

Instead, Brooks pushed out of the stool and dropped his empty mug in the sink. 'Those cupcakes were just what I needed. Now if you'll excuse me, chaps, I have work to do.'

Shifting around Oz to pick up the bag he'd dropped on the floor, he walked out with a backward wave and jogged up the stairs.

Typical.

I flicked on the kettle again and turned around. 'Mate. Are you sure you want to be driving to Cambridge? It's a four-hour round trip and that's with light traffic. You'll miss your classes. The florist can print the note, it's not a big deal.'

He didn't reply, just kept scrolling through his phone, and I wasn't about to push the point. Instead, I checked the cupcakes, because I was also running on a time limit. But, they'd cooled enough, so I picked the best twenty-one and got to work.

'That's not purple frosting, is it Charlie?' Oz said quietly as he watched me scoop it into the piping bag.

'It looks purple to me,' I frowned, 'Are you colourblind?'

'Nope,' he replied, picking up his phone. 'But that's violet.'

I stayed silent for long enough that we both knew exactly what he meant.

'Exactly.' Oz turned at the door before leaving the kitchen, 'If you want me to keep up the pretence that this relationship of yours is fake, then I suggest you mind your own business where Kate and I are concerned.'

Fuck.

I was still thinking about Oz's comment as I rushed over to St Anne's. Not *rushed* rushed, because I had a box of perfectly frosted cupcakes in my hands, but I'd been walking with enough speed so as not to be drastically late, but not so much that I'd risk violet frosting getting everywhere.

But turns out that the payoff for being careful didn't pertain to other things.

If I hadn't been carrying cupcakes, I'd have cycled. But because I was, therefore didn't, I ended up getting caught in something much worse than a frosting mishap.

Though I told myself if she hadn't found me now, she would have found me another time. She'd find me wherever I was.

'Charlie?'

I spun around and braced myself for the panic I knew was about to rush through me, filling my nervous system with a toxic combination of adrenaline and cortisol. I stood there and waited. Waited some more.

Nothing.

It was pure annoyance making my heart pump harder.

I was already running late. I didn't want to be later.

It dawned on me as Evie got up from the bench she'd been sitting on and closed the ten feet between us, that I hadn't thought about her at all this week. In fact, I was certain that Evie had barely crossed my mind since I'd walked out of the class last Thursday to find Violet waiting for me. Because the Violet Effect had kicked in and she'd become my sole focus.

Even as Evie stopped in front of me, wrapped up head to toe in her standard black, which I knew she wore so her blue eyes appeared bluer, I felt nothing.

Well, except for the annoyance.

'What are you doing here?' I asked, my tone harsher than I meant it to be. Actually on second thoughts it was exactly the right amount of harsh.

St Anne's was around the corner, Pembroke – Evie's college – was twenty minutes in the opposite direction. There was absolutely no reason for her to be here.

'Waiting for a friend,' she replied.

I held back the shoulder shrug, because I honestly couldn't be bothered to waste the energy. 'Okay, cool. Well, see you.'

'You're avoiding me, Charlie,' she called after me.

I spun back around, 'I'm not avoiding you, Evie. I'm not doing anything.'

'You don't speak to me during class. Even when I've asked a question and I can see you know the answer, you don't respond.'

'Other people get there first,' I replied, which was totally true. Gordon. Gordon always got there first. I might not have any intention of responding to Evie's question, but I'd never had the chance anyway. 'Beyond that I have nothing to say to you.'

Evie's hands were wedged into her pockets but even from where I was standing I could tell her fists were clenching from the movement through her jacket. It used to be that not many people said no to Evie, maybe that was still the case.

'You haven't replied to any of my messages.'

My brows dropped as I wracked my brains. Pretty sure I hadn't erased the memory of receiving a message from her, though it wasn't out of the realm of possibility.

'I've not had any me—' I stopped talking.

Based on the expression she was wearing, she knew exactly why I'd not replied, she just wanted me to admit it. I'd not received any messages because I'd blocked her years ago, not to mention changed my phone number, and clearly forgotten all about it.

I could almost feel the sting of that news through the sharp twitching in her eye.

Probably a new experience for her.

Oh well.

Her lips rolled into a hard line, 'Okay. I deserve that. But if you want to know what they said . . . I miss you.'

She never gave me the chance to tell her I wasn't interested in what some old, blocked text message said. Or that I'd been standing here for five minutes now, and I was really cutting it fine. Evie was eating into my Violet time, and it was beginning to piss me off.

'You miss me?' I snapped, though one could say it bordered on a snarl.

She nodded. 'I do, a lot.'

I could have handled the *I do,* and left it at that. It was the *a lot* which really pushed me over the edge. This girl didn't know the meaning of what it felt like to miss someone. All she cared about was the attention, the game.

'What is the matter with you? You are so full of shit. How can you not see that?'

It was stupid of me to think she might back down. She was Evie Waters. She never took no for an answer. It didn't even look like she'd heard me.

'Charlie —'

'Enough. I'm so sick of this. You don't miss me. You miss someone to control, and tell you how pretty you are. You didn't miss me when you went off with Hector Bygraves. You didn't miss me when you went off with Dave Chamberlain. This is all just another one of your games, and I'm not playing this time. I'm done, Evie. Please get that through your head and leave me alone.'

'Can we not even talk about it?' she continued, because she clearly hadn't heard a word I'd said. 'Be reasonable.'

Reasonable?

'I feel sorry for you. I really do. I hope one day you can find someone that will give you what you need, but it's not me. Maybe it never was,' I added with a long shake of my head, suddenly weary of all the time I'd wasted because of this girl standing in front of me.

All the connection I'd blocked myself off from, all the love I'd built a wall against.

Until one person knocked it down.

The one I was late for.

I thumbed behind me, 'I'm going. I'm late to meet my girlfriend.'

I didn't bother looking behind me as I walked/jogged down the path still trying to be as careful as possible. I knew well enough that Evie would stay on her spot until I was out of sight.

Thankfully I made it, though given Violet was locking the door to her room, I only *just* made it. Any thoughts I was having about strangling Evie vanished the second Violet spotted me. Her face lit up with so much happiness I forgot why I'd been running late entirely.

'Hey, what are you doing here? Don't you have class?' She smiled against my lips, a smile sweeter than anything in this box.

Wrapping my spare arm around her waist, I said, 'Yeah, I do. But I wanted to drop these off first, because I won't get to see you before tomorrow.'

'Tomorrow?' she frowned, right before her eyes opened as they focused on the box still carefully gripped in my other hand.

'Is that for me?'

'Yup.'

Stepping back, she took the box and eased off the cardboard lid.

Her gasp was enough to let me know I'd done a good job. Mary Berry eat your heart out.

She peered down, her hand flying to her mouth as she read the words. One pink-iced biscuit letter had been placed on each of the twenty-one chocolate chip cupcakes, heaving with violet frosting.

WILL YOU BE MY VALENTINE?

17. Violet

(Bone: verb. Slang. To have sex)

'We should have cupcakes for breakfast more often,' Stella declared, staring longingly at the cupcake in her hand like she wanted to get a room with it.

To be fair, they were *that* good.

I looked up at the darkening skies and reached for my umbrella, 'You better eat that quickly, it looks like it's about to chuck it down. And that cupcake deserves more than to be rained on.'

'You're right,' she replied, sinking her teeth into the frosting, then stopped walking. 'God, it's good.'

She was still licking her lips as I tugged her jacket, 'Come on, we don't have time to stop and appreciate cupcakes. We need to meet Charlie and also . . .' I looked up again, 'rain.'

It was definitely going to rain.

'Wait!' She took another bite. 'Now we can walk. Seriously, these are really good. There'd better be more left.'

There were more, but not *that* many. Yes, I'd shared.

I wouldn't have, but no one in their right mind could eat twenty-one full-sized cupcakes without being sick. No matter how much they wanted to.

And I did want to. I'd tried. The T, B and one of the Ls had all been eaten before yesterday was out.

233

But thinking of my poor dentist, I decided sharing them while they were still fresh was the best answer, because it would have been criminal not to. A couple of girls on my floor in St Anne's were the recipients of the W, A, E, N and the rest of the Ls. I'd taken a few more to my English and the Romantic Period tutorial first thing this morning – something I thought was wholly appropriate, given it was Valentine's Day and what was more romantic than sharing a batch of fresh Valentine's cupcakes made especially for you? Nothing.

But the question mark I'd saved for Stella, and the little shortbread symbol was the first thing to have been demolished. She bit into it like it was the head on a gingerbread man. My V was still sitting on top of my dresser, resting against the mirror. The cupcake underneath it, however, was digesting nicely in my tummy.

And the sugar rush? Yeah, that was pretty good too.

'No one's ever baked cupcakes for me,' she grumbled, taking another bite that resulted in a blob of frosting wedging into her nose. 'These are so good too. And chocolate chip. Your favourite. And they have violet frosting.'

'I know.' I could barely contain the smile; to be honest I didn't want to. I hadn't been able to for a few weeks now.

A boy I liked had asked me to be his Valentine on cupcakes he'd made in my favourite flavour.

It didn't get better than that. It was the type of thing Taylor would write a song about.

'I think I might cry from the cuteness,' she wailed. 'Or maybe throw up.'

'Don't throw up on me.' Side-eyeing her as she threw the last piece in her mouth, she genuinely looked on the verge of tears. Unless she was acting. Or trying her 'fake cry' face. Either way, I couldn't blame her, I knew how she felt. I could cry from the cuteness too.

'Who even knew that Charlie Masterson could be swoony. Like, this is pretty swoony.'

'I know.'

I looked back up at the sky, I shouldn't have worn my green coat. It was going to get totally ruined if I got rained on.

'Do you think he was this swoony with Evie?' she asked, sucking the remaining frosting off her fingers and pulling them out with a loud pop. 'Nah, there's no way. You don't cheat on someone this swoony.'

I didn't answer, Stella seemed quite content having a conversation with herself while I prayed to make it to shelter before the clouds burst.

I also didn't really want to think about whether Charlie may or may not have been swoony with Evie, because it wouldn't be the first time I'd wondered. It was hard not to. It was bad enough I could still remember the period of time when they dated, or worse when they ended and he came to visit with his little broken heart.

I wasn't trying to compare myself with Evie, but – knowing everything I now knew about Charlie – like the way he always held the back of my head when he kissed me, and never pulled away from my lips without leaving another quick smack or three. Or how he always wrapped his hand around mine to walk, unless the street was crowded and he needed to walk behind, *then* he'd thread our fingers together, so he didn't have to let go. Because he never let go.

But, it was hard. Hard not to wonder what they'd been like together. If he'd done all those things with her.

Before, when it had been fake, I hadn't cared enough to overthink it, because not caring about Evie protected my heart. Now though, now it was no longer fake, I'd found myself going back to the day I'd bumped into her along with the words which loved to echo around my head at the most inappropriate times.

She was like one of those dark clouds hovering over me, ready to burst and completely ruin my day.

Thankfully, a swift nudge in the ribs brought me back to the present.

I frowned at Stella. 'Eh? What d'you do that for?'

'I was asking about tonight.' Her eyes had lit up with a grin spread across her face. Must be the sugar rush. 'What's going to happen? Do we need to put a sign on your door that says "*If this room's rocking, don't come knocking*"? Or a sock? Do some people put socks on their door?'

Socks. Something else I'd been trying not to think about too much, but this one was virtually impossible.

I groaned quietly, the girl made a very valid point. At some point, Charlie and I would be moving the kissing portion of our relationship to the next level. And I loved the kissing portion. LOVED it. Like, sitting in a tree all day next to Charlie and kissing, *loved it.*

But let's face it, we were both young and full of hormones. And all the kissing had been doing was making me hungry for the next course – like the perfect appetizer.

'Do you think that's what the cupcakes were for?' Stella continued, because my mind was wandering too much to keep up with her one-way conversation.

'What d'you mean?'

'You know . . . to move you to the next level. So you think he's sweet and cute and wants to take off your knickers?'

I rolled my eyes. 'I thought he was sweet and cute before the cupcakes.'

'But maybe he wanted to reaffirm that, just to really make sure.'

'I dunno. It doesn't seem like his style. He seems too much of a gentleman,' I replied, because that's exactly what Charlie was.

A door-holding-open, chair-pulling-out, carrying-your-books type of guy.

Respectful. Courteous.

'Huh. Didn't expect that.'

I shook my head, 'Yeah, me neither. I just assumed he'd be like Hugo, but a little more refined.'

'Yeah.'

It had been a very pleasant surprise to discover that the Charlie Masterson I'd crushed on for years was actually more wonderful than I'd ever imagined. Kind, thoughtful, considerate. He was interested in my days. He wanted to hear about rehearsals. He insisted on practising with me. And in the past week instead of texting me to say good night, he'd call me for thirty seconds just to hear my voice.

Every day I discovered something new.

For example, he always sneezed in threes. He always liked to walk on the left-hand side. And if I checked his pockets, I could guarantee I'd find a pack of gum – no particular flavour preference – could be mint, could be cinnamon. Last week I'd found a packet of cola Hubba Bubba. *Cola*. We had to have a serious talk after that.

Cola aside, all these little unique Charlie details I was learning only made him easier to fall for – hard.

But apart from the one time he pushed me up against the wall and turned my bones to mush as he almost kissed the life out of me, I'd found very little evidence to suggest we'd be moving to the next level soon.

And thinking about it, I realized that we'd never spent time together in private. We'd kissed and kissed and kissed, but it had always been in places where other people were – the library, the theatre, the street. The natural progression had never happened because we'd never given it the opportunity.

'Maybe he's nervous, you know, because you're you.'

'What does that mean?'

She shrugged, unhelpful. 'Just that you told him you'd crushed on him. And then obviously he's best friends with your brother, and he's not exactly going to go and talk to him about boning his sister, is he.'

'God, why d'you have to say bone,' I groaned, giving her a big shove, which almost pushed her into the nearby hedge, though all it did was make her laugh louder.

'What?' She lifted a shoulder, far too innocently, especially when she added the little flutter of eyelashes. Stella and innocent were not usually found together. Stella and trouble, or Stella and menace. Now those worked perfectly. '. . . All I'm saying is you might need to give the guy a little push in the bed-rocking department if you want your bed rocked tonight . . . ya know what I'm sayin'?'

I nodded. One deep nod. I knew exactly what she was saying.

'Do you want your bed rocked tonight? I mean, I know you've wanted to bone Charlie since the dawn of time . . .'

'Stop saying bone!' I hissed, and she jumped out of the way before I could shove her again.

Her giggle turned into more of a cackle. 'Well, do you?'

'Of course I want to. I mean . . . look at him. Ugh . . . do you really think I'll have to make the first move?'

'I dunno. You might just need to show him that you're interested in more than kissing.' She stepped to the other side of the path to let a group of runners pass between us.

'How do I do that?' I asked, once she was next to me again. This was not a conversation to have at a loud volume.

'What are your plans tonight?'

'We're going for dinner somewhere.' When Charlie had brought the cupcakes over yesterday, along with asking me to be his Valentine, he'd also asked me on a date. And again, that was the thing, yesterday he'd only just caught me as I left. It was the first time he'd ever been up to my room.

Technically, it would be our first official proper date, because while the library and the theatre and the sandwich shop were all amazing, they weren't *date* dates. Not like this one.

I just prayed it wouldn't be as messy as the sandwich shop.

'Great, I have the perfect dress you can wear.'

'Stel, I can't fit in your clothes.'

'Don't worry, you'll fit in this, and it'll hug you perfectly,' she cackled, 'he'll want to eat you up.'

I groaned again, but didn't reply. I had plenty in my wardrobe suitable for a date with Charlie and obviously I'd been mentally plotting it out since last night.

'It's like when I hooked up with bartender Brad —'

'What's like when you hooked up with bartender Brad?'

'The little push you need to give Charlie, just do that.'

My eyes popped, right as my hand shot out to stop her talking. 'No way. First off where am I going to find a —'

'I didn't mean *literally*. Just use your imagination. You still have the key to his place, right?'

'Yes.'

'There you go then,' she added, with no further explanation. 'This conversation might all be moot anyway. Charlie Masterson might pleasantly surprise you,' she paused, throwing me a side eye I just caught the end of, 'and bone you like you deserve.'

I reached to grab her, but she jogged the last few

steps through the gates of Radcliffe, letting out a loud laugh. Tugging on her arm, I pulled her towards the fountain. 'Come on, we wait over here and for god's sake please don't mention socks or beds or rocking of any kind. *Or boning.*'

'Promise.' Swiping a finger across her lips she threw away an invisible key, and moved to sit on the edge of the fountain wall.

'Don't sit there, you'll get a wet arse.'

She shot back up. 'So, we just wait here then?'

I nodded, and looked up at the big clock on the old stone building across the road. 'Yep. Won't be long, it's nearly eleven and he's usually the first out.'

'Rushing out to you,' she added, clasping her hands to her chest as the corner of her lip tugged upward.

I didn't reply, because even though she was joking, that's exactly what he did. Instead, I let the butterflies fluttering in my belly warm me from the inside.

'So how far behind is Evie usually?'

I held in the groan, 'To be honest, I'm not sure. I'm usually paying attention to Charlie instead of watching for her, I think I've only seen her twice.'

'How many more classes do you have to wait now?'

'Only four more. Then it's Easter break,' I replied.

This term was starting to snowball. It would be March in two weeks and we'd be in the final stretch of rehearsals for *Twelfth Night* and from what I remembered of previous Boat Races, Charlie's training would become even more intense.

I was on the verge of asking Stella what she was planning for Easter when the clock chimed the hour. Ten seconds later the first flood of students burst through the doors, narrowly avoiding the clash with everyone rushing inside to get to their next class.

By the time Charlie appeared, my heart had already kicked up in anticipation of seeing him, like it did every week. He stopped at the entrance for the briefest second while his gaze searched until he spotted me.

'Shiiit,' muttered Stella as we both watched a grin spread across his face while he strode purposefully toward us swinging a big rolled umbrella like a walking stick. The sharp line of his jaw, the pop of his dimple, the way his long lashes almost batted as his smile grew. Even under the padding of his body warmer you could see the heaviness of his muscles, thick wide thighs clad in jeans stretching out with each of his long strides.

Wrap a ribbon around him and he'd be nothing short of the best present ever.

'I know.'

'If you don't bone him tonight, I think I might have to.'

She was still moaning from the sharp elbow I'd rammed into her side when Charlie stopped in front of us. He reached around and tugged on my ponytail, bringing my mouth close enough for a quick smack of his lips on mine.

'Hi.'

'Hi,' I smiled back.

He turned to Stella who was groaning and rubbing her side, far too dramatically. 'You alright there?'

'She's fine,' I replied, glancing over his shoulder to spot Gordon rushing towards us, backpack far too full, as usual.

'Charlie, I wish you wouldn't rush off every time. You never told me if you can make Tuesday next week.'

'Hi Gordon,' I smiled, because as usual he didn't seem to notice when I was standing next to Charlie.

His head flicked between Stella and me, and I swear he didn't know which one of us had spoken. Though seeing as I was the only one he'd met, he replied to me as the safe bet. 'Oh, yes, hi Violet. How are you?'

'I'm very well, thank you. How's physics life?'

'Oh, you know,' he pushed his glasses up his nose, 'full of Energy.'

I assumed that was some kind of physics joke given there was now a broad smile spread across his face, and Charlie started laughing. I was still trying to figure out what exactly he'd said, especially when Stella threw her head back with a loud guffaw, and clasped her chest.

'Full of Energy. You're funny. That was funny.'

Granted I didn't know Gordon well, but I'm not sure I'd ever seen someone look so pleased with themselves. It was short lived, however, because his attention went back to Charlie.

'Don't pretend you understood that,' I hissed, while the two of them discussed whatever it was Gordon had rushed over here for.

'I'm an actor,' she replied, flicking her hair over her shoulder. 'But it *was* funny.'

I rolled my eyes. 'Whatever.'

Maybe it was because I didn't laugh at his joke that he said goodbye to Charlie and scurried off without giving me a backward glance.

'Interesting guy,' said Stella, pulling on a thick strand

of hair and looping it around her fingers as she watched him leave.

'That's Gordon,' Charlie and I replied in unison, like that explained everything. Though it kind of did.

'Alright then,' she grinned, and her eyes flicked up to Charlie. 'Oh, hey, Happy Valentine's Day, Chuckles.'

'Happy Valentine's Day, Stella.'

'And may I congratulate you on some very nice cupcakes? Great touch. Delicious,' she nodded, solemnly. '*Great British Bake Off* worthy, I'd say.'

If it was possible for a person to explode with happiness, I'd say Charlie was on the verge, 'Thank you! That's what I said. Yes! They are.'

'You told someone your cupcakes were *Great British Bake Off* worthy?'

'I told myself.' His grin was wide and toothy.

'Of course you did.'

'What? I always make it a point to agree with myself.' He chuckled as he leaned in, planting a kiss on my cheek.

'You know something?' Stella began, and we both turned to find her staring at us intently. 'You two are actually quite cute. I wasn't quite so sure about this,' her finger flicked between Charlie and me, 'you know given that morning you banged heads, but I see it now. I like it.'

Charlie cocked his head, 'Thanks Stella. I appreciate the approval, not that I asked for it.'

'Well, you know, I like to give it anyway.' She smiled sweetly, too sweetly. 'You might not have asked for it, but you do need it.'

I bit down on my lip before I started laughing.

'Does Big Bad Brooksy still think this is fake?'

Charlie and I nodded our heads in sync, while Stella's face lit up with an unparalleled level of glee. Or mischief. It was hard to tell. Probably both.

'Oh pleeeeease let me be there when you break the news.'

Beyond saying we needed to tell my brother we hadn't discussed it. I was still pissed off about the incident outside the gym. But I knew it was starting to weigh on Charlie, more than I realized, seeing as his face suddenly lost all colour and his smile vanished.

I slipped my hand into his and squeezed it, 'Hey, it's not going to be that bad.'

He nodded, but there was no conviction in it.

'Charlie, it won't be.'

'I think it might be,' he replied quietly. 'But I'll deal with it.'

'*We'll* deal with it.'

He glanced at me, a small smile curving his lips. 'Yeah.'

'Hey, if you need me to be back up when you tell him, I'm always happy to take on Hugo,' declared Stella, letting out a bark of laughter. 'Unless you change your mind, in which case I'll have to take back everything I said about the cupcakes.'

Thankfully, that seemed to raise a smile, even though my insides were now doing somersaults at the thought of him changing his mind about the two of us. He must have noticed my body tensing, because this time it was him squeezing my hand.

245

'I'm not changing my mind. I also realized I liked you way before he decided no one can date you. He will have to deal with it.'

My teeth, my jaw, my fists, *everything* clenched. Were we living in the Dark Ages? Or Tudor England? Or even the 1950s? If Charlie wasn't around I'd date every single one of his crew mates just to piss him off. Yes. I was *that* petty.

'Hey,' Charlie nudged me, totally misreading the annoyance on my face, 'it'll be okay. We're all adults.'

'*We* are. The jury's out on my brother.'

Charlie snorted a laugh, which seemed to do the trick in smoothing out the worry on his face. He turned to Stella. 'So, what are your big Valentine's plans?'

Stella's brows knitted together tightly as her eyes darted between Charlie and me. Quickly. Suspiciously quickly. 'What? What does that mean?'

I could see Charlie biting down the smile; he wasn't doing a very good job of it, but he was trying. I'd not mentioned his theory to Stella, even though he brought it up nearly every time I saw him. Instead, I'd been on the lookout, not that I'd noticed a single thing going on between them beyond the usual sniping from Stella, but Charlie was adamant – Leo and Stella were hooking up.

I swear to God if he was right, I'd never hear the end of it.

'I just remember you saying you had plans tonight. Remember, we were all in the theatre and Leo asked you.'

'Oh . . . um . . .' she spluttered, her eyes darting to

mine and back so quickly I wasn't sure if I'd imagined it. 'Oh yeah, that was just to get him to shut up. No plans tonight, just me, Ben and Jerry. Plus *The Holiday*, I think.'

'*The Holiday*?' A small crease formed on Charlie's forehead as he looked at me, 'That's a Christmas movie, isn't it?'

I nodded, 'Yes. But it's the only one acceptable to watch any time of year. Plus, it's Stella's favourite.'

'Oh.' His mouth held in a straight line while he tried to understand, but clearly didn't. 'Cool, well, enjoy it. What's Leo doing then?'

'I dunno. Why d'you keep asking me about Leo. Why would I know what he's doing on Valentine's? Probably annoying some poor girl by talking about himself all night,' she snapped.

'I only asked once,' replied Charlie calmly, and there was no disguising the amusement in his voice.

'Well, I don't know what he's doing.'

Charlie's head bobbed and he looked up to the skies. 'Come on, I'll walk you two to rehearsals.' He opened his umbrella, big enough to shelter the three of us. 'Maybe Leo will be there, and we can ask him.'

If I'd been paying attention to more than Stella grumbling about Leo, or the feel of Charlie's hand sliding into the back pocket of my jeans, or the way his lips softened as they pressed into my cheek, I'd have noticed Evie storming past with enough fury to open the Gates of Hell.

And I would have known exactly why the rain clouds chose that moment to break.

18. Charlie

(Sex. It's like riding a bike . . .)

Bloody Valentine's Day. I did not think this through.

Scuffing my shoe along the dirt path, I cursed every decision I'd made tonight. Or at least the last one. The one where I'd left Violet at her door.

I wasn't sure it was possible to be an idiot and a genius at the same time, but I was definitely giving it a good try. I, Charlie Masterson, was definitely an idiot.

Yup. You are. The voices in my head agreed. *You really ballsed this one up.*

I couldn't deny it. Up to approximately twenty minutes ago, everything had been perfect.

The whole day had; from the moment I'd left Violet at the theatre, and kissed her goodbye with a promise to see her later. Even training hadn't been too hard. And we'd just returned from dinner.

In hindsight, the second she opened her door, I should have known I'd choke. Sweet, lovely, funny Violet had been replaced by a fifties sex bomb. The smile she greeted me with wrapped around my heart and whispered, 'You're totally fucked.'

I was.

Violet had looked nothing short of spectacular. I mean, every time I saw her she looked beautiful, but tonight my mouth had dried up.

249

Just like the day she'd walked into the pub, I hadn't known where to look. I was also seriously considering making an eye appointment because I couldn't understand how I'd possibly missed her and *that body*. Her dark-green dress had wrapped around her like a bandage, stretching across every curve she had and ones I didn't even know existed, with heels so high they almost brought her up to my height. Her thick blonde, violet-tipped curls tumbled across her shoulders and down her back, and all I'd wanted to do was wrap them around my fist.

I mean, I'd had my hands on her. I wasn't a complete stranger to how perfect Violet's body was, but that dress . . . it should have been illegal.

I'd taken her to The Snail – a minuscule French bistro just outside the city centre, owned by a friend of my father's. Only six tables, I figured it was unlikely we'd bump into anyone we knew. I knew we could still get away with the pretence of fake dating, but until I told Brooks, a date on the most romantic night of the year with his sister was probably best kept on the D/L.

Which brings me to my problem.

The most romantic night of the year. The one day of the year dedicated to love. Or sex. Or both.

It had been a while since I'd celebrated Valentine's Day. The only other time had been with Evie, and because that particular year the day had fallen on a Tuesday we'd celebrated the weekend after, when all the hearts and flowers had been taken down. And the Valentine's cards had been replaced by Easter ones.

The point . . . on that Saturday after Valentine's Day,

when I'd been sixteen, I'd completely bypassed the pressure. There had been none where now I wish I'd had some. Some idea of what I was doing, that Valentine's Day is *the* day. *The Day*.

Because the pressure … my god. The pressure is monumental. I'd competed in the last three Boat Races, the rowing world championships, Henley Regatta to name a few, yet the pressure of Valentine's Day is unmatched.

Like I said, I did not think this through.

It's what happens when you swear off love and refuse to have anything to do with girls. And it's been … let's just say … some time since you last had sex.

You forget.

Up to twenty minutes ago, I had never choked in my life. But now I could add it to my list of things I'd overachieved in.

Because I'd forgotten about *the pressure*. I'd had no expectations of tonight, not a single one. Until she opened the door.

Now, I'm not going to lie and say I haven't thought about sex and Violet. Sex *with* Violet.

Of course I have. I'm a red-blooded twenty-one-year-old man.

But the second I laid eyes on her, all I wanted to do was drag her straight back in, lock the door behind me, and only come up for air and snacks.

Instead, we'd gone for dinner. With that dress. The Valentine's Day dress that left absolutely nothing to the imagination, and no doubt as to why it was being worn. It was possible that Violet had been thinking about sex as much as I had.

You know when you really don't want to think about something then it becomes all you think about?

Well, that's where I was up to.

That dress and sex with Violet. That dress and her expectations.

In hindsight, we should have talked about it sooner. But I'd wanted to be respectful. Because Violet is special. I wanted to let us develop at a pace she was comfortable with, that *we* were comfortable with. But based on her wardrobe choices tonight, she was right there waving the chequered flag. She was very comfortable.

And I'd *choked*. Full on in-need-of-a-Heimlich choked.

I'd stopped talking five minutes before we reached St Anne's. With all the voices going round in my head, shouting over each other, it was virtually impossible to form a coherent sentence. By the time we reached Violet's room, I hadn't heard a word she'd said.

I became so paranoid about what I'd missed that I figured it was best to cut my losses and leave with what little dignity I had left, and hopes of salvaging it in the morning. As she'd gazed at me, her blue eyes filled with expectation, the scent of her hot, excited body shot an arrow directly into my frontal cortex. She'd been given nothing more than a quick peck on the lips before I'd taken off.

I'd been mentally plotting my apology before I'd even left the building. Violet was too special to have been left on the doorstep. Maybe I needed to take a page out of Oz's book and send her some apology flowers, or whatever it was he'd done.

The thoughts were still going round and round in

my head when I turned down Tolkien Lane, and up the path to number 5. The house was eerily quiet when I opened the front door. Quiet and dark. Too dark for anyone to be here, given they usually lit the place up like it was a football pitch. I guess it was still only nine, but I figured one of the boys would be home, especially as we had to be awake for training in seven hours.

'Brooks? Oz?'

No reply.

'Anyone?' I shouted louder.

Of the two of them, I assumed Oz would be home. I'd *hoped* he'd be home, because I really needed to talk to someone. Not that he'd been in the talking mood since he stormed off yesterday.

The kitchen was tidy when I walked in, like the type of tidy I left it, so maybe neither of them had been home at all. Dropping my bag on the table, I grabbed a bottle of water from the fridge and trudged up the stairs while the voices in my head shouted at me.

Idiot.

Scaredy cat.

Shouldn't have left her.

Idiot.

You would have choked anyway.

Idiot.

She's perfect.

Idiot.

'God, shut up!' I snapped, kicking open the door as I pulled my jumper off. The quicker I got in a hot shower and rinsed away the evening, the quicker I could go to sleep and forget this day ever happened.

253

Actually, I just wanted to rinse away the part where I'd left her standing, slightly open mouthed and definitely confused. Everything leading up to that moment could stay.

My head was still in the confines of my jumper when I heard a small but purposeful throat clearing. The jumper was yanked off and tossed to the floor, along with quite a few brain cells.

'I've never been in your room before. And I wanted to see for myself.' Picking up the bottle of aftershave I'd left on my desk, she sniffed it. 'I like it. It feels like you.'

Well, this was new. I'd never hallucinated a person before.

Bollocks. Maybe it was the voices. It had to be their work.

I squeezed my eyes tight, then opened them.

Nope. It was still there. Maybe I didn't squeeze them hard enough. Next I tried jamming my fists into my eye sockets and giving them a good rub, but that didn't make a difference either. Unless you counted the stars I was seeing along with the hallucination of Violet.

This Violet, dressed in trackpants and a hoodie, was *my* Violet. Not the Violet I'd left at her door, the one who looked like she could break me.

'Charlie, what are you doing?' the hallucination asked, while I stood there having some kind of blinking fit in case that might jumpstart my brain into working again. 'Charlie?'

'Look.' I said to hallucination Violet, 'I just left you at your door. There's no way you got here before me.'

'I got an Uber and I have a key.' She held her fist

out and uncurled it. Indeed there was a key lying in the centre.

'But –'

'I'm not an hallucination.'

Did I say that out loud?

I sat down on the bed, 'Okay, if you're real, what did I give you for Valentine's Day?'

She smiled softly, so softly it made my chest ache. It made me want to sprint back to St Anne's, take back the peck on the lips and go with my original plan of dragging her inside her room, locking the door and only surfacing for air and snacks. 'Twenty-one cupcakes asking me to be your Valentine.'

Not snacks. We'd live on the cupcakes.

It had been a stupid question, anyway. The voices would know. But okay . . . I'd play their game.

'Violet, what are you doing here?'

She bit down on the corner of her lip, 'Because you kind of left me standing in my doorway, and I wasn't ready to end Valentine's Day with you just yet.'

'So you came over?' I asked quietly, though she might not be able to hear me over the hammering in my chest.

'Yup. And I know you have rowing in the morning, so I can totally leave if you need a good night's sleep. Or . . .' she paused, biting into her lip again, and I wanted to pull it free. 'I could stay.'

'Stay?'

'We don't have to do anything, but I just wanted you to know that if you did want to do something, I'm okay with that. More than okay.'

'You are?'

255

With every word she spoke, she was stepping closer to me, slowly like she was afraid she might scare me off if she went any quicker.

'Yes. I am,' she replied, taking position between my legs.

If there was any part of me which thought this was a bad idea, it was silenced the second my hands touched the backs of her legs. Running up and down her firm hamstrings. No, there were no bad ideas here. Every cell in my body was thinking Violet in my room was the best thing that ever happened.

If my body was cheering, my dick was holding the megaphone.

It was as she ran her warm palms along my shoulder and up my neck, pushing fingers through my hair, that I realized I was half naked. The t-shirt I'd removed along with my jumper was currently lying in a heap on the floor. And my door was still wide open.

'Hold that thought.' I leapt up and slammed the door shut as quickly as I'd opened it, turning the lock behind me.

She looked so beautiful standing where I'd left her at the foot of my bed.

I had a girl in my room. A girl I really liked, and one I couldn't get caught with. I may as well have been fifteen again.

And I knew that fifteen-year-old would be yelling at me to stop being such a pussy.

I made my way slowly back to where she was standing, her eyes raking over me until I sat down and pulled her into my thighs. The sigh that escaped as I dropped my head on her stomach went part way to releasing some of the tension knotting between my shoulder blades.

'I'm so sorry I left you, Violet,' I whispered, before leaning back to peer up into her beautiful face. 'I shouldn't have . . . I . . .'

Fuck. God, I was lame. I swallowed down the thick ball building at the back of my throat.

'You what, Charlie?'

It was hard to think with Violet's fingers twining through the ends of my hair. I reached up and stilled them. 'I shouldn't have left you. You looked so beautiful tonight, and you deserve everything to be perfect, and truthfully I panicked.'

'Charlie –'

'No, hang on. I know this is new and we're figuring it all out, and even though we've known each other forever, we're actually just getting to know each other . . . shit. I mean, what I mean is . . .'

I was stopped mid-sentence, silenced by Violet's lips, and her tongue sliding into my open mouth. She was an elixir, relaxing every muscle in my body with her calm. Her touch was so soft that I barely felt her hands leave my grip and ghost their way back to my neck, pushing into my hair.

By the time she pulled away from me, my breath was shaking. Me a semi-professional athlete shaken from a kiss.

'You talk too much, Charlie Masterson. Did anyone ever tell you that?'

'No,' I chuckled. 'Not with you around. The queen of talking too much.'

'Ah yes, true. But I also know when to shut up.' She shifted away and I almost asked where she was going, but then she straddled my lap, fitting as perfectly now as she did that afternoon in the Blue Oar. 'As I was saying, I just didn't want tonight to end, and you looked too freaked out to leave alone. Plus, I didn't get a proper goodnight kiss. And I want one.'

'That's all you came for? A kiss?'

'Yup.'

But as I leaned forward to oblige her request, she arched back. 'Why did you panic?'

I sighed. 'Because . . . I'm nervous. I've never done this before, Violet.'

The freckles splattered across her nose almost disappeared as her face scrunched. 'You've never had sex?'

'What? No. I've had loads of sex . . .' I scoffed and, taking in her arched brow which had shot up, immediately wished I hadn't. 'Shit. I mean, I've never done the dating and the relationship and leading to this bit. The feelings bit, and I don't want to fuck up.'

One hand moved from the back of my neck and cupped my cheek, soft skin against my scratchy stubble. 'Charlie, you're not going to fuck up. We're good, this is good. I like what we're doing.'

'Yeah?'

'Yeah, it's us, we're just figuring things out along the way. I'm not going to break, if that's what you're worried about.' I hadn't been, but her smile was so bright and warm that it pushed away the last pieces of worry and anxiety that had been rolling around in my belly, and no new ones took their place. 'Plus, sex is like riding a bike.'

258

Riding a bike . . .

Before I could think any more about it, I flipped her over and onto the bed, bracketing her under my body. In hindsight, I probably should have given her forewarning because then she wouldn't have squealed loudly enough to alert the entire street. If there was anyone in the house, they'd have heard.

We both stilled, waiting for one of the boys to bang on the door and demand to know what was going on.

'Violet, we have to be quiet,' I whispered. 'No one can know you're here.'

She nodded, silently. Her eyes portraying exactly what I felt, that we were about to cross a line.

My head dipped down, and the second my lips made contact with hers, I forgot about everything else. There was no rush as our tongues tangled together, their own little dance of happiness, as Violet's fingertips ran up and down my spine. We'd done so much kissing over the past few weeks, I could safely say I knew what she liked. I knew how to tease her until a little moan escaped, like just now. I knew that she loved it when I held her face, so she could surrender control to me. Let me decide the rhythm.

I didn't break contact as I moved away from her lips, travelling across her jaw down her neck until the barrier of her hoodie stopped me. Her gaze never left mine as my hands slid inside and pushed the thick fleecy fabric up, revealing a slice of smooth creamy skin I was desperate to run my tongue along. So I did.

When my fingers brushed over her pelvis, her belly convulsed, her hand shooting to her mouth to cover her giggles. I hated she had to do that, her giggle was perfect and I wanted to hear it on repeat.

I don't know if she'd done it on purpose, but as I pushed higher, the green lace bra – the one she'd worn to the Blue Oar – came into sight, along with the boobs I'd been dreaming about since that day. Then I spotted something else, nestled on her left side, right below her ribcage.

A tiny handwritten tattoo: *one must have chaos within oneself to give birth to a dancing star.*

That day. The Blue Oar. More memories flashed as I remembered her asking about Nietzsche. I remember thinking about the chaos which came with Violet, the whirlwind she rode on . . . but really a dancing star was much more accurate.

That's exactly what she was.

I reached out and ran my thumb along the letters.

'Charlie . . .'

My eyes refocused back on hers, with a grin. 'You have amazing breasts.'

'Thank you,' she replied and sat up.

In the next moment, her arms were crossed over her chest and her hoodie had been chucked across the room. I never realized how hypnotizing boobs could be, or maybe it was just Violet's sending me into a trance as they bounced from the movement.

I stilled her hands as they eased under the elastic of her track pants. 'We're not in a rush. Plus,' I grinned wide, 'I want to do it.'

'Go on then.'

And just like that Violet Brooks was naked in my bed.

Her gaze was soft as she peered up at me, but it was the crook of her mouth that had me grinning down at her. She broke through the intensity of the moment, creating an ease that I hadn't otherwise felt. But that was exactly Violet. Easy and thoughtful. She had an awareness about her I'd never seen in anyone else.

Barely-there tan lines accented her smooth skin, and I couldn't stop myself from dragging my lips across her stomach, and up to the words I'd forever associate with her. The gasp she let out as my tongue flicked across her peaked nipple hit my groin dead centre.

'Did you like that?'

'Mmm hmm.'

The attention I gave to her other nipple earned me a deep groan. Shifting forward to steal a kiss, at the same time my hands reaching between her thighs, trailing slowly up her warm skin and slipping inside her, I was rewarded with a deep arch of her back. One of her fists bunching the sheets flew to her mouth, smothering a low rumble.

Just that small action made me want to take her to the middle of a field or lock us in a padded room, so she could let rip. I wanted to hear every sound which fell from her lips.

This entire time my own body was beginning to resemble a nuclear reactor. The pressure inside me was nearing combustible levels. Beads of sweat appeared at my temples. One more muffled groan from Violet and I couldn't wait any longer. Tugging off my jeans and boxers, a rip of foil, and a much needed thirty seconds for me to regain composure later, I was once again bracketing her under my arms.

'Are you ready?'

'Oh yeah,' she giggled, breaking through the thick tension which had built around us. 'Show me what you've got, Mr Masterson.'

Burying my face in her neck, I muffled my laugh, 'Jesus, Violet . . .'

I wish I could have captured it; the way her jaw dropped and her long black eyelashes fluttered. It was so perfect I would watch it over and over. As for me, the composure I'd regained flew right out of the window, especially when her legs wrapped around my hips. My teeth clenched, my jaw hardened, the pressure in my spine became almost unbearable.

I'd never felt anything like it. Nothing. I didn't know if it was the way she pulsed against me, or how the blue of her eyes had somehow darkened to almost navy – the little flecks dancing like stars in a night sky.

I just knew I'd found a perfect moment, and I would never be the same.

We became a tangle of limbs, trying our hardest to stay quiet, though it only served to increase the intensity we both felt. To speed up the combustion we'd been trying to keep at bay.

'Are you okay? Is this okay?' I asked, between peppered kisses, pinning her fists above her head and holding her gaze for as long as I could.

She replied between long quiet moans, where her mouth would drop and her eyes would roll back. 'Yes, Charlie.'

I'd never heard my name spoken like that before. Like it was the answer to all her questions.

The end came too quickly, too intensely. Black spots blurred my vision, until it narrowed so much that her face was the only thing I could see. We lay there, catching our breath, silently, slowly, letting the reality sink in.

She turned to me on the pillow, her blonde hair splayed out behind her, except for one violet strand resting on my shoulder. 'Hi.'

'Hi,' I replied, kissing her nose.

'Told you, it's like riding a bike.'

Later, I looked down at Violet, asleep on my chest, and I couldn't remember a time I'd felt more content. We were miles away from the snowy afternoon at the beginning of January when I'd asked for her help. Miles.

And it hit me. I was falling for this girl.

But then, as it always did at the moment you least wanted it to, reality slapped me hard in the face. The floorboards creaked above my bed. Brooks had returned from wherever he'd been.

I was acutely aware of the magnitude of having sex with Violet. The potential cost it came with.

I was not going to fuck it up.

19. Violet

(SHIT. Triple word score, 21 points)

Having sex with a genius really pays off.

I don't say this lightly, but I think it might be the best I've ever had. Of my life.

All nineteen years of it anyway. Or, if you want to be technical, three years, four months and . . . twenty-three days. Which is how long ago I lost my virginity to Miles Garland, and then all the sex which followed, including the five guys I dated after Miles. None of whom matched up to what I'd been experiencing.

I knew it would be good because, you know . . . it was Charlie, but I wasn't expecting it to be quite this good, just yet. I figured it would take some time to get to know each other properly.

To figure it out.

But Charlie is Charlie, who I only needed to tell once and he'd get it. A moan here, a gasp there and he'd move heaven and earth to make sure he heard it again.

And he did move heaven and earth.

But hey, like I said. Genius.

The proverbial band-aid had been ripped off so to speak. The lines had been crossed. There was no going back, and it seemed we were definitely making the most of it.

Over the last week, we'd had sex every single day. I'd briefly wondered how we'd found the time, but it turns out two people who'd recently discovered their mutual lust, attraction and feelings for each other are very clever at scheduling when they put their minds to it. Between my college room, the upper stalls of the theatre, and the library – from which I still had carpet burn on my arse – we'd covered quite a bit of ground.

The only place we hadn't returned to was Charlie's bedroom. For obvious reasons.

Namely, the fact my brother still thought we were fake dating, but mostly because even I didn't want to be having sex, with him in the room above us. Therefore, my advice was to hold off telling him until after the Boat Race, to which Charlie had responded, 'That's still a month away. I can't lie for another month, Violet.' But then I'd dragged him off to the stacks in the library and we didn't talk about it again.

I was rushing down the street and still deep in thought when a large wheezing lump appeared to my right, careering towards me like a bowling ball. Due to the fact it was still getting dark at 5 p.m., I didn't see her in time, therefore didn't move quickly enough to avoid her.

'There you are,' Stella puffed, doubling over to rest her hands on her knees, while I righted myself. 'I've been looking everywhere for you.'

'Why? I told you I was picking up the dry cleaning.'

'Dry cleaning. You never go to the dry cleaners.'

'You do, though. It's that dress you lent me.'

Stella stood up, a knowing smile breaking across her

mouth as her hands crossed behind her head so she could inhale more air. 'Oh. That dress. The one that broke Charlie's brain.'

I rolled my eyes. 'Yup.'

'Poor Charlie,' she cackled.

'I'll pass on your concern,' I replied, stopping in front of the dry cleaners, with a sigh of relief. It was still open. 'Why were you looking for me, anyway? And why were you running?'

The little electronic bell rang out as we stepped into the shop, joining the queue of everyone else who'd rushed to get here before closing time. 'My class finished early, thought we could go for a drink.'

'Oh, yeah,' I replied, handing my ticket over as we got to the front of the counter. 'Okay. I don't have anything else to do.'

'Gee. Thanks.' She rolled her eyes.

I nudged her. 'Shut up, you know what I mean. I'm done with classes, and just handed an essay in. Which means the next one I have to start can wait until tomorrow. Unless you want to practise some lines.'

'Ugh, no,' she groaned, her tongue lolling to the side as she threw her head back. 'Let's take the night off from work and stay in the pub until closing time.'

I really didn't have anything else to do. Not that it made a difference; between classes, rehearsals and now seeing Charlie, it had been a while since we'd drunk until the bell rang.

I took the dress, wrapped in clear plastic, and passed it over to Stella. 'Here, thank you very much. You were right, this dress was perfect.'

267

'My work here is done,' she grinned. 'You can buy the drinks.'

'Sounds good.' I looped my arm through hers and we walked back out into the street. 'Let's see if the other girls are around. I don't think we've seen Cecily outside of the theatre since the beginning of term.'

'She lives for the stage,' Stella grinned and led the way to the pub.

Less than forty-five minutes later we were ensconced in one of the leather booths at the Feather and Farthing next to a roaring fire, a giant bowl of chips between us along with two large glasses of merlot, the plastic-wrapped dress carefully draped over the empty seat next to her.

Stella leaned back against the leather, the stem of her wine glass spinning between her fingers. 'Mmm. This is what student life is about.'

'It is,' I nodded, dipping a fat chip into the bowl of ketchup.

'Actually,' she said, putting her glass down and sliding out of the seat, 'hang on.'

I watched her rush off to the bookshelf across the bar, ease the box of Scrabble out from under the boxes of other board games and rush back.

'Now it's proper student life.'

She shook the lid off the box, laid out the board and placed a tile holder in front of me.

'Okay,' I threw all the letters into the drawstring bag, 'but we're playing English scrabble this time. I never win at French, I don't know enough words.'

268

'*Très bon*,' she replied, and reached into the bag for seven tiles. 'So, how's Charlie and his broken brain?'

'Good, I fixed it up nicely,' I winked.

'Honestly, you looked so hot in that dress. I'm not surprised it broke, to be honest. We should rename it the brain breaker. I'll try it out next.'

'Like a science experiment?' I chuckled.

'Exactly,' she replied, reaching into the bag for a tile which she held up. 'M'.

I did the same and pulled out the letter D. 'Me first.'

I laid down five tiles. 'Phone. Double word, twenty-six points.'

Stella pulled up her phone and typed it into the notepad we always used to keep score. By my calculations she'd recorded four years' worth of games. She'd won our last two, because we'd played in French, but that had only brought her up to my tally.

We were currently even for the win/lose percentage.

'God, Vi, did you ever in a million years imagine you'd be with Charlie, having sex all over campus? Remember when we joined your names together? Violie. I think we should bring it back.'

'Let's not,' I laughed, watching her place five tiles down so they interconnected where the H lay. She added twenty-six points to the note.

'I dunno. I think it's got a good ring to it.'

'Maybe, but I'm not sure it's something Charlie needs to know about me just yet,' I replied, peering over my letters as I sipped my wine. Using the Y from where she'd placed down HAPPY, I spelt out PYLON.

'Ooh, double letter and double word. Another twenty-three points.'

'Are you afraid he'll take away all the orgasms he's been giving you?'

'What? No.'

'Okay —'

'I'm not,' I protested, though I wasn't exactly sure what I was protesting against or why Stella was trying to wind me up. 'Sounds like you need to start finding some orgasms of your own, though.'

It was only when Stella didn't respond, or place any tiles on the board, that I looked up to find her sipping wine. None of that was unusual, it was the prolonged silence and the fact she was clearly avoiding meeting my eye which told me something was afoot.

'Is there something you want to tell me?'

'No, just thinking about which of my letters to play.'

'Because —'

'ACROBAT. Ugh, it's only eleven points. Bollocks.' She reached into the bag to pull out more letters and I couldn't help noticing that she still didn't meet my eye. 'Oh hey, did I see the Boat Club has a race at home next weekend?'

I nodded, biting down my smile at the very obvious subject change. 'Yeah, against Bath. Shall we go and watch? Charlie said it should be a good race. It's the last one before the Boat Race.'

'Yes, that'll be fun, especially as it's the start of the Easter holidays. Everyone will be out to support.'

I glanced down at my tiles as a familiar voice called

our names. The pair of us spun around to find Cecily dodging a waitress clearing away dirty glasses, and she rushed towards us. Her long red ponytail was swinging behind with as much force, because the girl didn't know how to take things slow.

'Whoa. This place got busy.'

'Hi girls, sorry I'm late.'

'You're not late, we're planning to be here all night so you arrived just in time,' grinned Stella, standing up to wrap Cece in a hug. 'You want some wine?'

'God, yes,' she replied, 'today's been so tedious. Linus is quickly becoming the bane of my life.'

'Oh dear, is this going to be the one and only Rock-well/Carruthers production?' I patted a space on the booth and held my arm out. 'Come on, sit down and tell us all the gossip.'

It was as Cecily dropped her backpack on the spare chair and moved to take a seat next to me that a group of girls walked past, the last one passing so quickly she knocked Cecily with her shoulder. Letting out a shriek, Cecily was shoved forward and would have face planted into the booth if Stella hadn't caught hold of her arm.

It was possible the girl hadn't noticed Cece, given she was small enough to fit in my pocket, but she'd have definitely felt the force of the impact. Yet she had not bothered to stop and apologize.

'Are you okay?'

Cecily composed herself far quicker than I would have done and nodded. All three of us tracked the route the girl had taken, trying to figure out what sort of person bodychecks into someone like she was in the middle of a rugby match and walks off.

The glossy black hair was unmistakeable.

Stella turned back to me, her eyes wide.

'Where did she come from? Shit, was she sitting next to us?' she whispered, though it was probably still loud enough for Evie to hear. 'Did you see her sit down?'

I shook my head. 'No, did you?'

'No.'

'Golly, what's her problem?' Cecily rubbed her shoulder where Evie had knocked her. 'She looks like someone murdered her cat.'

'She always looks like that,' Stella and I replied in unison, which had Stella grinning wide, while I was trying to ignore the nervous knots going around in my tummy.

'Do you know her? Who is she?'

'Charlie's ex-girlfriend.'

Cecily's mouth dropped open. 'And he dumped her for you?'

I scoffed, pulling my gaze away from the direction Evie had gone and focusing back on Cecily. 'God no. They broke up years ago, she's been in a relationship since then, she just seems to think she has a claim on him.'

'You know, I'm beginning to understand why Charlie wanted you to help him in the first place. She's actually quite scary.'

'I know. Wonder when she'll get the hint.'

Cecily leaned back in her chair and watched as Evie

finally stalked out of the pub. 'Doesn't appear to be any time soon.'

I glanced back down at the Scrabble board where Stella had rearranged the letters to spell out UNDERSTATEMENT.

'Sixteen points,' she smirked, picking up her glass of wine.

20. Charlie

(Real v crocodile = angry Charlie)

Charlie: *Mate, are you around later? Need to chat.*
Brooks: *Is this about how weird Oz is being? I think he might be losing it.*
Charlie: *No, but we should probably talk about that too.*

Violet: *Say hi to Gordon for me. I think he likes me.*
Charlie: *Everyone likes you.*
Violet: *Awww. <3*
Charlie: *Don't forget I like you the most.*
Violet: *Never.*

Brooks: *Cool, yeah see you later.*
Charlie: *You better not. Or else.*
Brooks: *Huh?*
Charlie: *Sorry, wrong thread.*

Fuck.

My heart gave a nervous thump, while my belly flipped in relief that I hadn't sent something less easily explainable to Brooks, and I slipped my phone into my pocket before I did it again.

Thankfully, it had been innocuous enough that he'd likely have forgotten about it the second he shut his phone. It wasn't like I'd asked him to send a picture of

275

boobs nestled in the green bra to get me through the next few hours.

Because that would have had disaster written all over it.

I'd have fallen at the final hurdle, before I'd even managed to tell him about Violet.

It was today's plan. Tell Brooks. It was literally all I had on my list.

If I left it any longer I'd be mainlining Alka Seltzer for breakfast, lunch and dinner.

My mind was still flipping between thoughts of Violet's boobs and how I was going to break the news to Brooks when I almost tripped over a large pile of books. A pile of books along with a girl in a giant beanie who appeared to be crying, based on the volume of the sobbing.

'Shit, are you okay?' I bent down to help, only to stand back up when I saw who exactly was crying.

What were the goddamn chances? I mean, seriously. What were they?

Looking around, I'd never seen it so quiet on the path leading along the side of the physics building. I'm sure it was usually much busier. Nearly everyone used it as a cut through between buildings. Surely there was someone else around who could help.

There had to be.

Of all the people who attended Oxford, lived in Oxford, walked down the streets *in Oxford*, why did I have to be the one to stumble upon her, and crying of all things.

Another loud sob and I tried hard not to roll my eyes. *Tried.*

I'd had experience with this particular brand of crying. It was usually of the crocodile variety, though from this close up and the angle I was standing, they did look kind of real. Which was unusual.

'Charlie?' Evie wailed. 'Are you just going to stand there?'

I sighed, though I stopped myself from telling her I'd rather walk off, because my mother had always drilled it into me to behave like a gentleman, and she did genuinely look in some kind of pain, so I bent down.

'What happened?'

'I don't know,' she sniffed. 'I was walking and then I must have rolled on something and my ankle gave way. I think it's broken.'

I glanced to where her ankle was stuck under her other leg. It didn't look broken, and I'd broken bones before. She'd be in *way* more pain.

'You've probably just twisted it.'

'It hurts so much.'

Again, I tried hard not to roll my eyes because one thing I remembered about Evie was her flare for the dramatic. Spider – *scream* – any type of creepy crawly – *scream* – one time I'd suggested we go camping by a lake near to my parents' house. I never made that mistake again.

'Can you feel and check?' she sniffed *again*, uncurling her leg and sticking it out to me.

I didn't need to feel it to know it wasn't broken. It didn't even look swollen in the short black socks and those thin flat shoes girls wore.

'It's just twisted, Evie. Get some ice and compression on it, tomorrow you'll be right as rain.'

'Can you help me up at least?' Her hand shot in the air for me to grab.

I briefly wondered what I'd do if I'd actually been given the choice in the matter. I mean, I wasn't a total dick but I also really didn't want to see, speak to, or touch Evie. I definitely debated it long enough that Evie started waving her arm at me, and eventually the better part of my conscience won.

'Thank you,' she smiled, her tears drying as she wobbled about on her other foot before she found her balance. Then I realized she was waiting for me to collect all her books.

'Why weren't they in your backpack?' I asked, gathering them together, and piling them back into her bag. Her *zipped* bag.

'I was in a rush.'

I stood back up and held the bag out to her, at which point I realized we were not about to part ways.

'I can't carry that, silly. I need you to help me.' She grabbed my arm again as if to illustrate the point.

My eyes snapped to the clock as it struck the hour. Ugh, I know it was only a study session but I'd definitely hear it from Gordon if I was late. I mean, I *was* late. I was going to hear it.

'Come on,' I slung the bag over my shoulder. 'Let's go, there's a first-aid nurse in the building, I'll take you to her.'

'Oh, thank you,' she replied, this time wrapping her arm around my waist. I could feel her fingernails digging into me. 'I know I don't deserve you being nice to me, but honestly thank you.'

Her words came out in a stutter as her breath caught, and I let out a deep sigh.

'You're welcome. You'll be fine.'

'Do you remember how clumsy I always was? Remember that time I walked into the doorframe at home, and had a bump on my head for a week.'

'Um –'

'I went to the summer ball with a purple eye . . .' she pressed, leaning into me as we walked/hopped down the path. At least it wasn't that far, though far enough considering Evie now seemed to be wrapped around me.

'Oh, sure. Yes,' I replied, though I actually had no idea what she was talking about.

'You were always saving me from some mishap or another. And now here you are again. We're quite the pair, don't you think?'

'Mmm,' I mumbled, as she moved her hand up to grip my shoulder so she could hop up a step.

'So, how's your philosophy group going?'

'Good. Gordon's cracking the whip. But we've got a great, hardworking group. We'll come away with a first. I'm actually on the way there now.'

'Oh, right. You meet today. We meet on Tuesdays. I'm so sorry I'm keeping you,' she replied, her tone almost martyr-like, and very un-Evie. 'You can leave me here if you like. I'm sure I can manage to hop the rest of the way.'

'It's fine, we're nearly there.'

'Bet your group is so fun. We always had fun revising together, didn't we?'

Again, for the life of me I didn't know what she was talking about. I couldn't recall any time we'd ever done work together. We went to different schools for one, so we could have only revised during the holidays, but I couldn't remember that either.

Maybe I'd blocked out the memory.

'Do you have any plans for Easter?' she asked, while I was trying to hurry her along. It would be much quicker if I carried her, and I was seriously debating picking her up, but the thought of my face being that close to hers was enough to stop me.

Maybe I could give her a piggy back.

'No, the Boat Race is the weekend after, so I'll be here. Might go home for the day if Coach lets us.'

'How are your mum and dad? Say hi to them for me.'

'Sure.'

'And a hug for Magic. He was so cute as a puppy.'

'Okay.'

God. I wished she'd stop talking. I was also pretty sure she'd never found Magic cute, especially after he'd chewed a pair of her favourite shoes.

'I think I'll be staying over the holidays too, my parents are away and I need to revise. I can take you out for a drink to thank you for helping me.'

The side door to the building was less than twenty-five metres away. My eyes had been trained on it ever since we'd turned the corner but if I didn't know better I'd swear we were slowing down.

'Can you hop a bit faster?'

'Sorry,' she puffed out, appeared to take a giant leap, though I think she'd just landed back on the same spot.

The clock struck the quarter hour. It had taken us fifteen minutes to walk less than a hundred metres. Up to this point, Evie had only been clinging onto me as I'd carried both her and my backpack, but fifteen minutes was ridiculously slow under any circumstances, and roping my arm around her waist and hoisting her the rest of the way was the price to pay for not having to spend the rest of the hour listening to Gordon complain about timekeeping.

'We're here,' I announced as we crossed the threshold, and I almost dragged her halfway down the corridor to the first-aid room and knocked on the door. Dropping her bag on the floor, I managed a smile, ignored the fresh tears brimming in her eyes, and thumbed behind me. 'I have to dash. Hope it heals quickly.'

'Oh, Charlie, thank you. I'm so glad you were there to help. I don't know what I'd do without you,' she called after me, just as the nurse answered the door.

She would no doubt be thrilled at having to deal with the mundanity of a twisted ankle instead of electrocutions, or singed body parts, and whatever else usually went on in physics labs.

It was safer than the chemistry building though, that's for sure.

I sprinted up the stairs, managing three at a time, and powered down the corridor fast enough that I was out of breath by the time I reached our study room.

I burst through the doors. 'Sorry, I'm so sorry I'm late.'

All six of them turned to look at me. Gordon's mouth opened, I knew I was about to get the telling off I'd been expecting since I'd found Evie. This guy was going to make a formidable professor one day.

I held my hand out before he could speak. 'I wasn't

late because I forgot. I was helping Evie, she'd fallen over,' I explained, hoping it might cut down his lecture from ten to maybe two minutes. Three if I was lucky.

'No she didn't.'

'Didn't what?' I asked dropping down in the nearest empty seat and removing my laptop.

'Fall.'

'What?'

'Evie didn't fall over.'

My eyes flicked away from my screen to find him staring at me intently, 'What d'you mean? I just helped her up and took her to the nurse. It's why I was late.'

'But she didn't fall. I was looking out of the window, and saw her sit down and scatter her books around on the ground. I thought it was a bit odd, but I don't know girls very well.' He shrugged. 'Anyway, now you're here can we get on with this session? It's the final one and we have to hand our paper in to Professor Rivers tomorrow. We were just talking about –'

'Hang on. Go back. What did you say about Evie?'

'She didn't fall over.' He tutted loudly, pushing his glasses up his nose, and glanced out of the window. 'Look, there she is.'

I stood up so quickly my chair fell over. But there, walking normally without any sign of a twisted ankle or the need for someone to cling on to, was Evie.

'Now where are you going?' cried Gordon as I threw open the door and sprinted back outside just as quickly as I'd arrived.

I ran quick enough to stand in front of her and block her path. 'That healed quickly.'

282

Her eyes flared in surprise, but only for a second and to give her credit she didn't even try to pretend she'd faked it.

'What d'you expect me to do? You won't talk to me.'

'I HAVE NOTHING TO SAY TO YOU. WHY CAN'T YOU GET IT INTO YOUR HEAD?'

'Don't shout at me.'

'You need help. You really do. What the fuck is it going to take to get you to leave me alone?'

The black gloss on her fingernails shone as she tapped her forefinger against her cheek. 'Hmm. What about . . . you've got a race this weekend, haven't you?'

'Yeah, and? What's that got to do with anything?'

'Win it, and I'll leave you alone.'

I blinked, checking to see if I'd heard her properly. 'What?'

'Win the race at the weekend and I'll leave you alone. We don't have any more classes together after the end of term, so you don't have to see me again if you don't want to. I'm sure we'll bump into each other though.'

'Evie, what are you talking about?'

'Win the race and I'll leave you alone.'

'What game are you trying to play? I'm not interested.'

'No game, Charlie. I promise.' She smiled, so saccharinely sweetly it set my teeth on edge. She was every Disney villain rolled into one and I'd never seen it before now. I couldn't even remember why or how I'd ever liked her. The Evie tinted glasses I used to wear had been well and truly smashed.

I'd always known she was manipulative, but I could

finally see her for what else she was – nasty, spiteful, vindictive.

Yet it had taken her for me to find Violet.

Violet who was nothing but sweet, kind, thoughtful – she wasn't just the antithesis to Evie, she wasn't even in the same stratosphere. There was no comparison.

Violet, who I had a sudden overwhelming urge to see.

'We win the race on Saturday and you'll leave me alone *forever*?'

She nodded.

'Fine, done.'

'But . . .' my stomach sank, I should have known. There was always a fucking *but* with Evie. 'If you lose then you take me on a date, and we try again.'

'Why if I lose? Because you think you're my consolation prize? You aren't,' I scoffed.

'Because you can't throw a win,' she said simply. 'Just putting myself back in the game, and you've lost the last two races, so odds are in my favour I'd say.'

I stared at her; none of this was a coincidence. She didn't just know the race results off the top of her head, and she knew exactly that I'd have figured out her fake ankle and run out after her. It was true, we had lost, but we'd lost because Coach had switched the teams around – he'd been trialling a couple of alternative Blue Boat options. We hadn't rowed with a full-strength crew and this weekend we would be.

We'd win. No doubt about it.

'There's no game, Evie. At least not one anyone else is playing. But you have yourself a deal. We win, you leave me, Violet and anyone else alone.'

She held her hand out for me to shake, only for her smirk to grow when I stared at it instead. 'Deal. Just like that.'

'Yeah. Just like that. We're not losing.'

I didn't bother to wait for her response, just turned on my heel and marched back to my class, though I'd missed most of it. I owed Gordon a massive apology.

The familiar buzz of a message vibrated in my pocket and I pulled my phone out.

Brooks: *Hey, get home will you? We need to call a house intervention.*

21. Violet

(Shakespeare was right, the course of true love never did run smooth)

I'm not sure I would ever get used to waking up early, even with Charlie as my alarm clock.

I cracked one eye. Christ, it was barely light.

'What time is it?' I croaked.

'Just gone six,' he grinned as his mouth continued its trail over my shoulder.

On the other hand, I could probably get on board with kisses as an alarm clock. And whatever he was doing with his tongue right now.

'We're going to need to discuss this insistence you have with waking up before the sun. In case you hadn't noticed, I'm not a morning person.'

'Funny you should say that,' he murmured, reaching my neck, 'I'm not either. Or I never used to be, but since I met you I kind of like the idea of being awake early if it means I get to see you for more minutes of the day.'

'God,' I groaned, 'why d'you have to say stuff like that. Makes it so much harder to be mad at you for waking me up.'

He rolled on top of me, his mouth breaking contact with my skin for the first time, smiling down, making me think I was looking at a Colgate advert.

'You can still be mad at me. In fact, why don't you show me how mad you are before I have to leave for training.'

My thighs flopped to the side.

I couldn't even stop them, I was so pathetic. I only had to feel the nudge of his dick at the apex of my core, and I'd give in. I didn't try to put up any kind of fight. No protest, no objection, and barely any complaint even at the crack of dawn.

Charlie Masterson had all of me.

'Why couldn't you play a more sociable sport. One that meets at a more reasonable hour?' I managed to breathe out, my neck craning back as he slid inside me. 'Like rugby.'

The rumbling of a groan rolling through his chest set a wave of goosebumps shooting over my skin. On instinct my body arched into him for more.

'You want me to play rugby?'

'Yeah, they don't get up so early.'

'I could play rugby,' he muttered, his tongue tracing the outline of my mouth, 'I definitely could. But . . .' he rolled his hips slowly against mine, too slowly almost. Frustratingly slowly, barely ghosting over the spot where I really needed the pressure, 'the thing about rowers . . .' one more roll, 'they have stamina . . .' roll, 'they have endurance . . .'

The last rock of his hips ground so deep into my pelvis that I prayed these walls at St Anne's were sound-proofed, because the groan I just let out could have been heard across the city. In my next breath I found myself flipped over so quickly, it was only his fingertips digging into my hips that stopped me from toppling off him, and the bed.

I stilled for a second, adjusting to the new position and the feel of him inside me. The soft smirk, green eyes twinkling, the way his hair always curled around the left side of his face, even at this disgusting time in the morning, he still looked insanely good.

The calluses on his palms, as he ran them over my skin, sent another cascade of goosebumps across my body to join the rest now pooling at the base of my spine. The delicious twisting of pressure was kicking up further with each swipe of his thumb against my pebbled nipples.

'You're so beautiful, Violet. I could look at you all day.'

His hands slipped to my thighs, gripping into my arse so he could control the movement – slow, deliberate thrusts with each steady rock of my hips until he needed more. *We* needed more. It didn't take long for the tell-tale sign of an impending orgasm to make itself known.

My thighs gripped tighter, and his fingers dug harder. What started as slow and steady descended into two chaotic rhythmless writhing bodies, desperately chasing a release. Only when his thumb brushed against my clit with the pressure I'd been craving did my body give in and push me over the edge.

He followed less than a second later.

Just like every time before, we stayed glued together until our breathing synced and settled. Until he pushed the sweaty strands of hair away from my face and kissed me like he had no intention to ever stop.

He dropped a final kiss to my lips, 'I have to go. I need to get back before the boys wake up, we have training at eight.'

He made no signs of moving away from under me, his arms wrapping me up while I listened to his heartbeat settle.

Eventually, I tipped my head up, 'Charlie?'

'Yeah?'

'No pressure, but seeing as you've spent nearly every night here this week, we probably should tell my brother . . .' Glancing away, my bottom lip caught in my teeth, 'I know I said wait until the Boat Race, but you know, if this is a proper thing between us . . .'

'Violet . . . Violet, look at me.'

My eyes flicked up again.

'It's a proper thing.' He snuggled back down under the duvet with a long sigh, curling a strand of my hair around his finger, but all I could stare at was the red and white pastry box band still around his wrist like the most precious friendship bracelet. 'You're right, we need to tell him. *I* need to tell him. There's so much drama going on in the house right now with Oz, and every time I try to talk to him something else happens. I haven't wanted to add to the chaos, but I know I owe it to him, and you. I'm going to do it today. I wasn't planning on waiting until the Boat Race.'

'So you weren't going to listen to me?'

'I always listen to you.' He smiled as he dropped one last kiss on my mouth, making me laugh.

'Fine, but if he gives you a hard time, tell him he has me to deal with.'

He flung back the covers and stood up with a laugh. 'Don't worry, I will.'

Pushing myself up against the pillows, I took the opportunity to gaze at his fine *fine* arse before he pulled on his boxers.

Well done, Violet. Bloody well done.

'Hey . . .' I began, as he picked up the rest of his clothes, 'can you leave me your hoodie?'

'Yeah, why?' he asked, tossing it onto the bed.

'I want to wear it today, you know how girls wear their . . .' I stopped talking, seeing as we hadn't actually had that particular discussion. Were we still seeing how it was going? Because I think I already knew.

I glanced up to find Charlie peering at me in amusement. 'You can finish that sentence.'

'You know what I was going to say?'

'I do. Even though I also like watching the conversation going on in your head, and reading it all over your face, I want to hear you say it.'

I shuffled up the bed, staying wrapped in the duvet just like they did in the movies, though I definitely wasn't as graceful. Charlie sat down, his hands pushing through my hair until he caught a violet strand between his fingers and ran it under his nose.

'Say it.'

'I was asking if you'd leave your jumper with me, so I can be one of those girls who wear their boyfriend's clothes to their games, or races . . .' I shrugged, ignoring the grin plastered on his face. 'Whatever.'

'You want me to be your boyfriend?'

My shoulder jerked up again, even though there had

to be a thousand worms squirming in my belly. It was only what I'd wanted for the past five years.

'Yeah, if *you* want.'

Charlie shook his head, a smirk curving the side of his lip. 'I want. A real one, that your entire family knows about. But . . . would you rather I was a rugby player?'

Sucking in the side of my mouth, my head crooked as I looked at him. 'Nah. I'll keep you as a rower. It's okay. Hmm, my boyfriend's a rower . . .' I drummed my fingers against my cheek, 'yeah, I like the sound of it.'

'Well, thank fuck for that.' He smacked a kiss to my lips, except he didn't pull away like I expected him to.

Instead, it deepened. His big hands held tight onto my face as he became more insistent. Needy almost. And by the time he pulled away, if I hadn't already been sitting in bed, I'd have needed something to cushion my fall because there's no way my legs would have held me up. 'I'm so glad I found you, Violet. You've no idea. I can't believe you were under my nose the whole time.'

When I glanced up, there was an expression I couldn't read swimming behind his big green eyes. 'Are you okay?'

'Yeah, never better.'

He turned and winked, right before he closed the door behind him. The second I heard the click of the latch I fell back against the pillows with a smile you could have seen from space, before falling back to sleep. I was so tired it didn't dawn on me until later that he never called *me* his girlfriend.

*

'God, where have all these people come from? I swear there aren't this many students at Oxford. Why is it so busy?' Stella grumbled.

'It's the final weekend before Easter and everyone's stayed instead of going home, plus it's sunny.'

Sunny was putting it mildly. According to the weatherman this morning, the southern parts of England would experience one of those freak early heatwaves with temperatures expected to reach 30 degrees. Therefore, in true British fashion the pub doors had been flung open and beer tents had been erected along the banks of the river. While I was all for the warmer weather, it did mean I couldn't wear Charlie's jumper unless I wanted to die from heat exhaustion. So, I'd tied it around my waist, but I could already feel the sweat pooling at my back where it was resting.

I'd predicted it would be busy, but I hadn't guessed it would be *this* busy and I kind of wished I'd dragged Stella out a little earlier. Even with my post-sex nap I'd been fully awake and raring to go by nine a.m., but Stella had insisted we eat breakfast at the table instead of on the go, so by the time we finally left to walk down to the river we'd found ourselves among the crowds of Oxford students who'd had exactly the same idea.

We were walking among a sea of navy flags, carried by an army of pastel-shorts-wearing guys; a rainbow of pinks, yellows, pale blues and greens because the first sunny day meant the summer wardrobe had been raided.

'Okay, we need a plan for where we're going to watch. I say we go to the finish line.'

'You don't think it'll be too busy?'

'It will, but last year they set up a drinks tent so it'll be easier for us to drink and watch.'

'What about if I go to the riverbank and secure our spot, and you go to the bar?'

'Good idea.' She grabbed my arm and pulled me quickly past a group of approximately twenty guys, until I was almost jogging alongside her. 'What are you doing?'

'We're not getting to the bar after them,' she hissed, 'we'll be waiting all day.'

Her plan seemed to work because there was only a very small queue by the time we made it, deciding to abandon our original plan of splitting up, small enough that I waited with her as she ordered, and we took our drinks to an open space beside the Isis, between two of the college boathouses.

Across the banks, on the other side of the river, University of Bath supporters were out in full force, distinguishable by their royal blue and yellow colours.

'Can't believe this is the first race we've managed to get to.'

'I know. I'm sure someone intervened to get Cecily to let us have this weekend off.'

'Leo did,' muttered Stella, and looked away.

I waited to see if she had anything else to add to her announcement, like he was the biggest pain in the arse she'd ever met, how annoying he'd been in rehearsals the other day, or French, or life in general. But now I came to think about it, I hadn't heard her complain about Leo for a while.

'Anyway,' she continued before I could think any more of it, 'what's the run of the day?'

I turned around, looking for the notice board which usually listed the times of the races, 'I'm not sure. It'll get announced soon.'

Oxford had four main crewed eights – the men's and women's Blue Boats were the number one boats for each club followed by Isis and Osiris, the men's and women's second boats.

The women's crews went first: Osiris followed by Blue Boat. While Osiris won by a photo finish, Blue unfortunately was nearly a full length behind.

Isis, the men's reserve boat, fared a little better. Winning by a healthy enough margin that it spurred the crowds on to cheer even louder than normal.

By the time the men's Blue Boat was set to get under way, sufficient amounts of beer had been drunk by the spectators that everyone was gearing up for a showdown. Rowdy chants were now providing the backing track for the day, and you could say what you wanted about Oxford, but there was nothing like it when the supporters were out in full force.

The sound of an airhorn ripped through the air, signalling the beginning of the race.

'OXFORD! OXFORD! OXFORD! OXFORD!' came the chants down the banks again.

'Where are they? I can't see,' croaked Stella, whose voice had almost given up from all the shouting.

Squinting up the river, I could just make out the ripple of water where the two shells cut through, followed by the judges' motorboat. This was the problem with rowing – you were either at the beginning, middle or end. You only truly got to relish in the excitement of the race up close, once the section next to you had passed on the baton of cheering.

'They're there, you'll see them in a minute.'

'Who's winning?'

'I can't tell.'

I squinted again. It looked neck and neck, but it wasn't. The closer they got, the more obvious it was that Bath was in the lead by half a length.

'Shit,' screeched Stella, pointing to the shells, just in case anyone didn't know where they were. 'They're losing. Come on, Charlie! Pull your finger out!'

'Come on, Charlie,' I screamed next to her as they neared. 'Come on, Hugo.'

'DARK BLUES! DARK BLUES! DARK BLUES!' sounded out another wave of chants.

'CHARLIE! MOVE! OXFORD! MOVE!' Stella screamed louder. 'COME ON! MOVE!'

There's no way any of the boys in the boat could have heard us. But fifty yards out it was like they hit a second wind of energy because out of nowhere Oxford picked up speed. Even from this distance I could see Oz powering through each stroke, setting a punishing rhythm.

Eight oars sliced through the water.

I could see the red face of my brother in six seat, rowing like his life depended on it. They all were. But my eyes barely flickered over the other boys before focusing back on Charlie, in seven. Even behind the sunglasses I could tell he was putting every last drop of strength he had into moving past Bath. His jaw popped with each formidable stroke, biceps and triceps piston-ing and so in sync with Oz's that you'd think they were attached by an invisible string.

I winced as Stella grabbed my arm so hard I swear she'd drawn blood. 'Shit. They're moving.'

I couldn't breathe, even if I'd wanted to. Air stuck in my lungs, and by the time the two boats passed us they were neck and neck. One final gruelling pull on the oars, and Blue Boat slipped over the finish line first.

The sound was deafening. Almost as deafening as when Oxford won the Boat Race, and if they repeated today's performance in two weeks' time, you'd hear the chanting from the northern tip of Scotland.

Stella was still jumping up and down. 'That was amazing!' she screamed.

'I know!' I screamed back, because neither of us seemed to be able to stop, as we clasped onto each other, until it became clear I really needed to pee. 'Come on, let's get out of here. I need the loo, then we can go and find the boys.'

Holding out my hand, she grabbed it. The pair of us wove through the crowds thick with Oxford stu-dents. Several times we narrowly dodged a group of boys armed with several pints of beer each. Too many for them to safely hold without the risk of one being knocked, as the girl in front of us discovered. But she looked too drunk to care. We also dodged flying empty pint glasses, several Oxford University paper flags which had been waved around during the race, along with a couple of scarfs and one hat.

'This is the problem with nice days, we can't control

ourselves,' grumbled Stella as a rugby ball flew past her face, only to be caught by a guy on the other side of the crowds. 'I mean, why do they need to be playing with a ball here? There's a perfectly good field nearby.'

'You tell 'em, Stella,' I laughed. 'Hey, shall we go to the bar on the way? The boys will need to get back to the club house anyway, we can meet them there.'

'Yeah, good shout. Is there anywhere along the way that won't be rammed?'

I shook my head. 'Nope.'

'Wishful thinking. Let's just go to the last pub before we get there, then there's less chance of us spilling, and more opportunity to drink.'

I slung my arm over her shoulder as we finally made it through the first throng of people, 'I knew I was friends with you for a reason.'

'Yeah. My ability to find suitable drinking establishments is unmatched.'

It took us nearly half an hour but we made it, virtually unscathed. The same could not be said for another rugby ball which this time, unfortunately, came into contact with Stella, and promptly found itself launched into the nearest hedge. The pub was quiet in comparison to those further up the river, and I managed to pee quick enough that our drinks hadn't arrived by the time I got to the bar.

'I'm going now. You wait here,' Stella called as she ran off.

'Hello.'

I turned to my right, and the owner of the voice I'd come to recognize. She really was like a bad smell.

298

'What do you want, Evie?'

'Just came to offer my sympathy.' She jerked up a delicate little shoulder, the straps on her black sun dress barely moving.

I was too busy watching the barman pour out the two glasses of wine to really pay attention to anything Evie was saying. Plus, I wasn't interested.

'You know, about you and Charlie breaking up.'

My attention flicked to her, and back to the barman as he put two glasses down. I handed my bank card over to him.

'What?'

'Well, I assumed you'd broken up seeing as he asked me to meet him if they lost today. You know, to commiserate, I s'pose.'

'You're full of shit. Please go and bother someone else.'

At least I expected to be totally ignored, and she was still standing there when Stella returned.

'What's going on? Why are you here? Honestly don't you have anything better to do with your time except torment people?'

'No, not really.'

Even when Stella stepped in, towering over her, Evie didn't flinch. 'Were you following us?'

'No,' she shrugged, 'just a lucky coincidence I guess.'

'I don't believe in coincidences.'

'Oh well.'

I wasn't sure who was going to win this staring competition. Stella had the height, but Evie had the deadness behind her eyes that made her seem invincible.

299

'I'll make it your problem unless you fuck off right now. Seriously, just fuck off. Leave Violet alone, leave me alone and leave Charlie alone.'

I tugged on Stella's arm, 'Come on, she's not worth it. Let's get our drinks and go.'

'Why is she here?' she hissed, spinning back around to Evie who hadn't moved. 'Why are you here?'

'I was just congratulating Violet on the boys' win.'

'What?'

I tugged again, waving Stella's drink in her face, hoping she'd get the message. 'Stella, let's go. She's full of shit.'

'But I specifically wanted to let Violet know that in class this week Charlie had asked if I'd meet him for a drink if they lost today. You know . . . to console him.'

Stella's head twisted around to mine, but I held my mouth in a straight line and said nothing. She turned back to Evie. 'You're a filthy stinkin' liar.'

I wasn't sure Stella needed to add the 1920s American Gangster accent onto it, but it did add a little something. Evie was unfazed by it, however. Merely offered up a shrug and one of those smarmy smiles I really wanted to smack off her face.

Her ability to get under someone's skin really was unmatched.

'Ask him. I'm sure you're on the way to the boat-house now. I did tell you, Violet, we always find our way back to one another.'

Stella finally snatched the glass of wine I was holding out to her, 'Come on, let's get out of here. Evie, go back to your coven.'

I left her standing at the bar, no doubt watching us leave, as Stella dragged me through a fresh swarm of students who'd descended on the pub, probably with the same idea we'd had.

'That girl . . .' Stella spluttered, 'she's genuinely got something wrong with her. How did Charlie ever like her?'

I shrugged, with a slow headshake, 'Honestly, I think about it every day.'

'You don't think there was any truth to what she said?'

She'd asked the question right as I brought the glass to my lips, which resulted in me snorting a laugh and the wine shooting straight up my nose. At least wearing Charlie's hoodie hadn't been a total bust. It was a very handy face wipe.

'No, I don't. I can't imagine a truthful sentence has ever passed her lips.'

The pair of us were still huffing and grumbling about Evie by the time we arrived at the boathouse five minutes later. And because luck seemed to be – mostly – on our side today, it was the exact moment Charlie pushed through the doors.

In less than a second, my mouth dried up. I almost slapped a hand over Stella's eyes, because I wanted to be the only one to appreciate the work of art that was Charlie Masterson in all his post-race, sweaty glory. He'd pulled down the straps of his rowing singlet and was walking down the ramp, muscle upon heavily stacked muscle on full display. Even his abs seemed to have grown since this morning.

'Holy crap,' muttered Stella.

'Hello, fancy seeing you here,' he grinned, though stopped short of giving me the kiss I was expecting – the kiss he usually gave me – and instead I received a quick peck on the corner of my mouth and I realized why when he glanced behind him.

My brother was inside somewhere, and he still hadn't told him.

Instead, the quick brush of his fingers against mine was enough to push away the minuscule shard of disappointment I knew was only popping up because of what had just happened with Evie.

'Congratulations.'

'Thank you, I won for you,' he winked.

I smiled up at him right as Stella nudged Charlie's shoulder with her own, 'Nice win, Chuckles.'

'Thanks,' if it was possible his grin got wider, 'it was a hard-fought race.'

'You clearly fought the hardest,' she croaked, and let out a little cough, 'I've screamed myself hoarse.'

'We appreciate it. That glass of wine seems to have helped though.' He nodded to the plastic cup in her hand.

'Yeah, never doubt the power of a glass of wine.' She took a large sip as if to illustrate the point. 'It was amazing, and well done Oxford for claiming overall victory.'

'We've got some work to do over the next two weeks. But if today was any indication, the crew is in place for Blue.'

'We'll be there cheering you across the finish line at Chiswick Bridge.'

'You'd better,' he replied, looking directly at me, and

this time a little spark of electricity shot between us as he touched my hand again.

'Oh my god,' Stella continued, not noticing she was completely interrupting a moment, 'you'll never guess. We bumped into that psychotic ex-girlfriend of yours.'

Charlie's hand left mine and all the happiness dropped from his face, only to be replaced by deep frown lines marring his otherwise smooth forehead. 'Evie? What? Where?'

'In the pub. Honestly she's so full of shit, she tried to convince us you'd made her promise to meet you if you lost, so she could make you feel better, or whatever.'

'Yeah,' I laughed, 'I think Stella was ready to burn her at the stake if I hadn't pulled her away.'

'Evie told you I was going out with her if we lost the race?' Charlie repeated.

'Yeah, that girl is absolutely Coco-Pops,' Stella snorted. 'One day you're going to end up with a rabbit boiling away on your stove.'

'Ugh, Stel. Don't say that. Don't even think it,' I frowned, and looked back up at Charlie.

For the first time I noticed how still he'd gone, the smile had completely vanished and the pinkish sheen of exertion was now kind of greyish. If his fists hadn't clenched, I might not have questioned it any further. But, coupled with the panicked way his eyes narrowed, twisting knots kicked up from nowhere and stirred deep in my belly.

'Charlie?'

Stella's eyes shot to mine and back to Charlie. 'She was lying, right? Evie was lying?'

303

'Yes.' He nodded, 'Of course. I mean, I didn't ask her to meet me, there's no way . . . Of course, she was lying.'

His words should have made me feel better, but they didn't. There was something about his tone. Why is it you can always sense the *but*?

His hand reached around to the back of his neck, 'Um . . . *but* she just made me say I'd take her out if we lost today.'

'What?' Stella and I blurted in unison.

I replayed it. I needed to make sure I'd heard correctly. Stella was of the same opinion given the way she was now looking at me.

'What do you mean? Made you?'

His eyes were filled with sincerity, 'No, it's not a big deal, it's not like how it sounds. She said she'd finally leave me alone if I went out with her. It was only if we lost though, and we didn't so it's okay.'

Yep. I'd heard, my eyes flicking to Stella again, who looked as confused as I did.

'But you agreed to go on a date with her?'

'Yes,' he nodded. 'To get her off my case.'

'Sorry . . . what?' interrupted Stella, because it was clear we needed a lot of clarification. 'Say again? You were going to go on a date with that psychotic lunatic?'

'No, of course not. No. Don't be stupid. I was never going to go,' he scoffed, like he couldn't understand why we were having difficulty grasping what he was saying.

'But you told her you would,' I repeated, because I was also having difficulty. A lot of it, to be exact. 'You told Evie you'd go on a date? Charlie, a date with someone who's been terrorizing you so much that you asked me to be your fake girlfriend. Which I did. But you were going to go on a date with her anyway.'

'It wasn't a date. I just said I'd meet her if we lost. Lost,' he repeated slowly, like I was remedial, or hard of hearing. I was definitely hard of something.

'But you didn't know what the outcome of this race was going to be.'

'No, but –'

'You could have lost.'

'But we didn't –'

'But you could have. Which meant you'd be voluntarily meeting Evie.'

'I guess. But I wasn't going to go.'

'Right, but you still agreed. And did you think for a second how I might feel about it?'

'No,' he replied so quickly he may as well have slapped me in the face. 'I mean, no because I never thought we'd lose. We didn't lose, so it's irrelevant. I don't know why you're so upset. She agreed to leave me alone if I won. Leave *us* alone. Job done.'

'But she clearly isn't leaving you alone, *or* me alone,' I snapped, 'she just accosted us in the pub!'

'Violet –'

My brother had never had the best timing in the world. Therefore, I never got to hear Charlie's response because that was the moment Hugo decided to make an appearance.

He walked down the ramp, his arms held wide open while he tunelessly sang, *'We are the Champions'* at the top of his lungs, followed by Oz, Bitters and two more from the crew whose names I couldn't remember.

''Ello 'ello 'ello, what's goin' on 'ere then, ladies and gents?' he smirked, before throwing his arm around me. I promptly threw it off before he could pull me into a headlock or worse, kiss my cheek.

It didn't seem to deter him, however.

''Ello, Stelly Belly,' he tried again, though he wisely didn't touch her.

He stepped back, and just stood there with Oz, Bitters and the other two. It didn't take long for them to notice the tension running through the three of us; Stella and me standing with our arms crossed, and the clench of Charlie's jaw. Five sets of eyes widened as realization dawned that we were in some kind of stand-off.

The humour on my brother's face was quickly replaced by confusion, and a little concern.

'Seriously, what's going on?'

'Nothing,' I snapped, my eyes still fixed on Charlie though he was no longer looking at me. He'd shuffled back and was looking at his feet.

It hadn't bothered me up to this very second that he was yet to tell my brother about us, but right then as he shrank away it became clear that he had very little intention of doing so, even after our conversation this morning. I'd been blind to the fact that the boys lived together, trained together. He had had plenty of chances, and if he was serious about the two of us, then he would have said something already.

If he was serious about the two of us, he would have

given me some consideration before agreeing to go on a date with his ex-girlfriend. I'd even have settled for him telling me about their run-in as soon as it had happened, but he hadn't done that either.

It hadn't occurred to him, because he hadn't thought about me at all.

Either way you looked at it, it was fucked up.

'Nothing is going on at all,' I repeated, as I tried to swallow down the hot ball of tears creeping up my throat. 'In fact, Stella and I were leaving. We just came to offer our congratulations.'

'Yeah. Congratulations boys. So glad you don't have to go through the ordeal of losing. Even if some of you deserve to.' It was clear the snarl in her parting comment was only aimed at one person.

'What?'

It didn't surprise me that my brother's face showed nothing but confusion. It did surprise me, however, that Charlie was yet to look at me, though given Stella was now trying to incinerate him with her stare it was unlikely he would.

'See you around,' she said, linking her arm with mine.

Before the two of us had even fully left the boat-house, the comments started up.

'God, my sister is so weird.'

'Mate, please let me ask her on a date? I beg you.'

'Violet . . . Violet, come back!' called the only voice I'd wanted to hear, but it was the one I was ignoring the most. 'For fuck's sake, Violet . . .'

At least I made it around the corner before I burst into tears.

22. Charlie

*(Shakespeare was an idiot. Nothing's
fair in love or war . . .)*

'What the fuck did I just walk in on?' Brooks asked, all of us staring at Violet's rapidly retreating back. Or maybe it was just me staring.

Anything else he said was drowned out by the ringing in my ears.

Fuck. Fuck. Fuck. How could I have done this? How could I have been so stupid.

'Charlie?'

I turned to find Brooks glaring at me, Bitters looking confused, Oz leaning against the railings and staring at his feet, while Fellows and Joshi were both on their phones doing their best to look like they weren't the slightest bit interested in what was going on in front of them. They were.

Based on the direction she'd headed, I had about thirty seconds to make a decision before she reached the path, and I wouldn't know which fork she'd taken. I only needed five. I stood in front of Brooks.

'Stay here. Please. Stay here and wait for me to come back. I need to talk to you. It's important.' My eyes flicked to Oz, who was no longer staring at his feet, imploring him to understand what I was talking about. 'Keep him here.'

309

I didn't wait for his or Brooks' reply, before I took off after Violet.

She hadn't got as far as I'd expected; walking with Stella's arm wrapped around her while her head was dropped onto her shoulder must have slowed them down.

'Violet . . . Violet wait.' I picked up the pace, 'Violet!'

Stella turned around first, dropping her arm as Violet ran a hand under her nose. Even from fifty metres away I could tell she'd been crying; each tear streaming down her cheek may as well have been an arrow straight in my chest.

I'd really screwed this up.

'What do you want, Charlie?' she sniffed when I stopped in front of her.

'I want to talk to you. To explain.'

'There's nothing to explain, Charlie. I understood perfectly clearly.'

I frowned, that made one of us then, because I *didn't*. 'What do you understand?'

'That I wasn't important enough for you to consider when you agreed to go on a date with Evie.'

I sighed so deeply it made my brain throb.

'I didn't agree to go on a date with her,' I started, except that's exactly what I'd done, so I raised my hand before Violet jumped in to point it out. 'I don't mean a *date* date. It wasn't a romantic date. I asked her what it would take for her to leave me alone. *Us* alone – me and you. And her reply was she'd leave me alone if we won today. But if we lost the race, then I needed to take her out for a single drink. Just one. One.'

310

'And you agreed.'

'Of course I agreed. I never thought we'd lose. I wasn't going to bet against myself. And I should point out, I was right, we didn't lose. So I don't really understand why you're so mad at me,' I snapped as the tension and stress from weeks . . . months, even years of dealing with Evie's bullshit hit again.

That she was on the verge of ruining another good thing in my life was almost too much to contain.

Except, given the way both Stella's and Violet's eyes narrowed, I immediately wished I hadn't snapped quite so loudly. 'I'm sorry . . .' God this was hard enough without having an audience too. 'Stella, d'you think you can go and find something else to do, please?'

I didn't miss the way she glanced at Violet for permission before stepping to the side. 'Sure, I was about to call my parents anyway.'

I reached out and took Violet's hand, giving a small thanks that she allowed me to do so, because it felt like it could have gone either way.

'I'm mad, because you didn't tell me about it, Charlie. I had to find out through Evie. Now I understand why she was looking so smug. I feel so foolish.'

'I'm so sorry, it really was a stupid, thoughtless thing to do. I'm sorry about Evie, I really am, and that you've been dragged into this whole mess. I should have told you, but it meant so little to me that it didn't occur to me to do so. And because I never would have gone on a date with her anyway, I forgot until you mentioned it.'

She gave a loud sniff, running her hand under her

nose again before pressing her palms deep into her eye sockets to stop the tears.

'Look, I understand how awful she is, I really do,' she sniffed again, 'but put yourself in my position. When Bitters had his arm around me, you almost punched him before storming off. Yet you just expect me to be okay with the fact that you agreed to go on a date with the love of your life.'

'What?' I scrubbed both hands through my hair, linking my fingers behind my head, hoping to relieve the pressure that seemed to be building in my brain. 'Violet . . . no.'

How did I begin to explain to her that wasn't the case?

Evie might have been the love of my life once, but that ended the day Violet walked into the Blue Oar two and a half months ago. Though in reality it ended long before that, *years* before. Maybe she'd never been the love of my life, because I'd never felt about Evie the way I felt about Violet.

It had just taken my brain a little longer to catch up.

'I loved her once, when I was sixteen. But since you came into my life for real, it's like I had a reset. My life began again.'

'Charlie . . .' the sniffs got heavier, 'don't you see? It's exactly what she said to me – you always find your way back to one another. I thought *I* was naïve,' she added with a huff that was so laced in sarcasm and totally un-Violet I had to take a step back.

I was not naïve. I knew full well what Evie Waters was capable of, probably more than anyone – she could be awarded a gold star for causing chaos. Which is why this entire conversation was all the more frustrating.

I took a deep breath before the anger bubbling through my veins turned into full-on rage. I was close though, especially when Violet was standing in front of me questioning my loyalty to her. Loyalty and feelings.

'No, Violet. You're wrong. That day I nearly punched Bitters, do you remember what else happened? We walked back and you asked me to trust you. Do you remember that?'

There was a tiny hesitation before she nodded.

'Well, I do. I trust you. I've never not trusted you. Now you need to trust me.'

'I do, I just . . . you loved her so much. I remember. I remember you loving her, and I remember when she broke your heart.' One fat tear slid down her cheek but I managed to brush it away before it fell.

'Loved,' I repeated, wondering how many times I needed to before the message got through. 'Loved. Past tense. I don't love her now and haven't for a long time. Years, in fact. Evie is so irrelevant to me now, unless she's causing a problem for you, because you showed me that Evie Waters is nothing to me. That's all this was about. Getting her to leave you alone. You're the one I want, Violet Brooks. Please don't let Evie ruin things between us,' I begged, and I could sense the desperation in my tone. 'It was less than twelve hours ago that I sat in bed with you and asked you to be my girlfriend.'

I thought I had her then. I thought I saw her eyes brighten, and maybe they did for a fraction of a second before she shook her head slowly. 'You didn't actually. I brought it up, and then you asked me to repeat it. The word girlfriend was never mentioned.'

'Violet, come on. Of course I want you to be my girlfriend. You are my girlfriend for fuck's sake.'

'By default.'

'What?'

'I'm your girlfriend by default, because we decided we were going to see how it went. But we've never talked about it.'

My nostrils flared wide as I took another deep breath. 'Violet, of course you're my girlfriend.'

'Actually, I'm a secret –'

'You're not a secret. Everyone knows,' I snapped.

'No, they don't. Everyone who knew we were fake, still thinks we're fake. Except Stella,' she snapped back. 'My brother doesn't know.'

Never in a million years could I have predicted today would go so drastically wrong.

Not after this morning.

I also didn't know Violet moonlighted for the debating team, because it was clear this wasn't an argument I was going to win. She had a response for everything I said, and the fact that they were all valid made it all the more annoying.

But the only thing she was really *truly* correct about was Brooks. And there was a very simple fix to that problem, I just prayed she'd step in before he punched me.

'Come on.' I held my hand out.

'Where are we going?'

'To tell him. Let's go.'

All this time Stella had been on the phone, and I

314

wasn't sure if it was a coincidence that she hung up the exact same time I suggested we leave. But I wasn't about to question it.

Instead of taking my hand, Violet walked next to me, Stella on her other side, and we made our way silently back down the path to the boathouse. I didn't point out that Stella was about to get her wish of being present when Brooks was told, though the thought did ease my nerves a little.

On second thoughts, the nerves had simply been replaced by the gurgling nausea I had at the thought of losing Violet through my own stupidity.

I wasn't going to lose her when I'd only just found her.

I don't know how the three of us looked as we rounded the corner, but from the way Brooks' arms were crossed over his chest, I'd say not great. Oz was standing next to him, the pair of them waiting for us like the parents of errant teenagers. I'd had enough of that when I was *actually* a teenager. The only plus side I could find was that the rest of the boys were nowhere to be seen, no doubt lured away with the promise of a cold pint to celebrate our win.

'Care to explain what's going on?'

I reached for Violet's hand only for her to snatch it away. Okay . . . guess I deserved that. Unfortunately, everyone else caught it too. Brooks' eyes narrowed a further degree, and I think Oz shook his head, but I was concentrating too hard on steadying my heart rate so I could get this out in one go.

'Someone speak.'

Here goes nothing. 'I'm in love with your sister.'

There was silence for only a split second before a combination of thunderous shouting and a croaky screech broke it.

'WHAT?'

It was hard to tell whose *what* was the loudest: Brooks' or Stella's. It wasn't Violet's because she was just standing there staring at me with her mouth open. This time, thankfully, she let me take her hand.

'I love you,' I repeated, hopefully at a volume only she could hear. I wasn't sure whether it was a good sign her tears started again. I held her gaze as her beautiful blue eyes overflowed with a combination of confusion and – the real kick in the nuts because I'd caused it – hurt, but also a little happiness I think from the way her mouth turned up. I *hoped.* Taking her face in my hands, I wanted her to see me and only me along with all the sincerity and truth I could dig from the depths of my soul. 'I love you, Violet.'

I kind of wished her brother wasn't witnessing it, however.

'Hang on,' interrupted Brooks. 'Back the fuck up, right to the beginning. I thought this was fake. I *agreed* to fake.'

I pulled down on Violet's hand before she started shouting and/or punched Brooks, because I was well aware of her opinion about her brother and his ban on her dating life, having been on the listening end of many a rant. I also happened to agree with her.

'Yes, it was fake.' I tried not to choke over the word. 'You're right. It was. But we started spending time together. And the more time we spent together, the more I realized that I liked Violet. Liked her a lot. And somewhere along the line it stopped feeling so fake.'

I gave Violet's hand a gentle squeeze, but from a quick side-eye I could see she was looking at her feet. Shit.

'How long's this been going on?'

I glanced to Violet, still looking down, guess I was answering all the questions. 'About six weeks, maybe a little longer?'

Someone, probably Stella the shit stirrer, let out a low whistle.

'Six weeks? Six weeks?! Oh my god, are you . . .' he stopped talking and I really prayed he wasn't going to finish the sentence, because I *knew* what he was going to ask. 'Nope, no. Not asking that.'

I had no doubt Violet felt my sigh of relief. I think everyone did, until he focused on her.

'Violet, have you been in our house recently?'

Her chin jutted as she nodded defiantly at him, leaving absolutely no room for interpretation as to why she'd been in the house. Maybe now was the time to share she'd copied his key and had broken in to use his bath.

Or maybe not.

'And you . . .' he pointed at me, just in case anyone was unaware whom he was addressing. 'I knew I heard you come in the other morning, I hadn't just imagined it.'

I groaned. On Wednesday morning I'd woken up next to Violet, a small sliver of light was sneaking through a crack in the blinds and sliced across her bare back, traversing the ridges of her spine. She'd been fast asleep, and instead of getting out of bed, I'd stayed there watching it move over her smooth skin as the sun made an appearance.

It was then that I knew, right that second, that I'd fallen in love with her.

I'd been so late leaving that Brooks had been downstairs when I snuck back into the house, but I'd dismissed it with a yawn and a confused look.

'Did you know about this?' he snapped at Oz.

I held my breath, I was almost as interested to know the answer as Brooks seemed to be. I was positive Oz suspected something, but as he'd been practically catatonic due to his own love life drama, it had not been brought up since the day I'd made Violet's cupcakes a month ago.

Wow. An entire month with Violet.

It had gone both quickly and infinitely slowly all at once, and I wished I could experience it again for the first time.

Oz shook his head. 'No.'

From the way Brooks' eyes narrowed I wasn't sure he believed him, but his focus turned back to me.

'Okay, so you love my sister, except she doesn't seem that happy about it. So, what's going on?'

'Um . . .' I began, wondering where to start.

Violet snatched her hand back, and crossed her arms over her chest. A move so reminiscent of her brother that I suddenly knew the level of stubbornness I was dealing with.

'Charlie told Evie he'd go on a date with her.'

The water Oz had just sipped sprayed everywhere. There was no one untouched. A fountain of mist caught the light and for ten seconds we were in the midst of a rainbow – maybe I'd be able to summon a lucky charm while Oz coughed up his insides. Eventually, Stella whacked him on the back several times in an attempt to stop him. Brooks was the only one who seemed unaffected, and once Oz had himself under control the pair of them turned to me in sync, identical expressions which demanded an explanation.

'Violet, for the last time I did not agree to go on a date with Evie,' I gritted out.

'It's exactly what you did, Charlie.'

I spun around, shooting a glare at Stella, hoping it would silence her for at least a couple of minutes.

'Well, who's telling the truth?' Brooks snapped.

I held my hand up, 'Okay, I'll start from the beginning. We all know Evie's in my class . . .' I started, to which the boys nodded.

I proceeded to explain the entire situation as I knew it, including the times Evie happened to be waiting wherever I was walking. I was taking it as a good sign that their arms looked less tense the longer I talked. Their fists unclenched, Oz was slowly shaking his head and the disappointment in his face had dropped.

By the time I was finished Brooks appeared less red and angry, at least. Violet had stopped sniffing, Oz and Stella were quietly standing next to each other by the railings.

'Well? Anyone want to say something?'

Brooks' lips pursed and relaxed. Pursed and relaxed until he eventually held them in a straight line. 'You should have never gone out with her in the first place. I said it then, and I'll say it now.'

It wasn't exactly what I'd been expecting, but it was also a typical non-committal Brooks response that didn't help in the slightest. When it became clear no one else was going to add to the conversation I turned to the only person I really wanted to hear from.

'Violet?'

For the first time, she looked up at me, her blue eyes searching my face. I wasn't sure what she was looking for, but when she spoke I really hoped she'd found it.

'Let's go outside.' She turned around to the audience of three, and pointed a finger at each of them individually, 'You lot stay here.'

I followed her to the dry dock, my heart thudding harder with each step as I tried to stop the sinking feeling in my belly.

'I'm going to go home,' she blurted, and I frowned so deeply it felt like my brain was rattling, 'to Somerset.'

'What?'

'I think we need to spend some time apart.'

'I'm sorry, what? This morning –'

'Things have changed since this morning, Charlie. Even if you don't want to acknowledge it, they've changed. For me at least.'

The thudding in my chest was speeding up, hammering so fast I thought my sternum might crack. It was all I could do to swallow down the acid burning my throat.

'Violet, please . . . I'm so sorry.'

'I know,' she smiled softly, and I wished she wouldn't. The smiling made it worse. The smiling made me feel like I really was on the knife's edge of losing her. 'I know you're sorry and I appreciate it. I'm sorry too. But I think we need a break from each other. It's Easter next weekend, and I'm going to go home.'

'When?' I croaked.

'Tonight.'

'Tonight?'

She nodded, 'Stella's called her parents to come and get us.'

Swallowing down the acid had only left room for the tears to clog my throat. 'Violet, come on. Please don't go. You don't have to do this.'

'I do. If this is going to work between us, I want to have a clean slate and start over. We need a total break from each other, no contact so we can reset. Then we can see where we're up to. We can see how we feel in a few weeks.'

'I don't need a few weeks to see how I feel. I love you. I'm not losing you when I've only just found you,' I was almost shouting. 'This is nothing more than our first stupid fight. It's a rite of passage. That's all. You can't just leave.'

Her soft hand cupped my cheek, and as she gazed at me I decided I'd never seen her look more beautiful. It was the one thought that really tipped me over the edge for the tears to start falling.

'I love you. But if I stay I'm nothing more than the girl who helped you out of a bind with your ex. We'd be a relationship of circumstance. An accident. I don't want that.'

'All relationships start because of circumstance,' I snapped. 'Our circumstance is that I love you.'

'Charlie . . .' she sighed.

'You are so much more than that, and you know it,' I sniffed.

'Then prove it.' She dropped her hand and leaned in to kiss my cheek. Like I always did I breathed her in, only this time it came with the terrifying thought I might never have the opportunity to do it again. 'I'll see you in a few weeks.'

'At Chiswick Bridge?' I asked, my question holding as much hope as I could muster, considering I felt absolutely hope*less*. 'I'll win for you.'

She walked away without an answer, only stopping to peer inside the boathouse to collect Stella. I wasn't sure if it was a good sign or not that she gave me a little wave before the two of them disappeared again back up the path.

I slumped down on the dock, dangling my feet over the edge.

What a thoroughly *thoroughly* shit day. The high I'd finished the race with had well and truly popped and as much as I wanted to blame Evie for it, I knew it wasn't entirely her fault.

Mostly, but not all.

Ninety-nine point nine per cent.

'I'm sorry. I'm so sorry,' I mumbled, sensing a movement behind me. It was all I could summon. I was utterly depleted. 'I know I've fucked up but please lecture me tomorrow, I'm not in the mood.'

Brooks and Oz dropped down either side of me.

'I'm so pissed off you didn't tell me, it's not even funny. We've been best friends since we were thirteen.

What the fuck, Charlie?' Brooks started, totally ignoring my 'no lecture' request.

That was fine.

'You said no one was allowed to date her. Even me. That day in the gym when Bitters was being fucking annoying. You said it, "*even Charlie*".' I air quoted, though it didn't lessen the snarl on my lips.

'*Date* her, and fuck her over, exactly like he would have done. Not fall in love.'

'How was I supposed to know?' I grumbled.

'I see you did it anyway.'

'I did it before then actually,' I shot back.

He didn't reply. The three of us stared down at the water as a family of ducks swam past – the dad in front followed by five fluffy ducklings, and mum bringing up the rear. When they reached the bank on the other side of the river, they all jumped out and waddled along the grassy edge to their nest.

'You're really in love with my sister?'

'Yeah. I really am.'

'Well, you can't say I didn't warn you,' he tutted. 'I told you she's a drama queen.'

I wanted to disagree. It was right there on the tip of my tongue, but I was still annoyed enough that she'd left, so I didn't.

'Well, what are you going to do?'

'Fix it, I guess. I'm going to get her back.'

Oz reached out and dropped his arm around my shoulder. 'Join the club. I'll make badges.'

'And then someone needs to tell Bitters that Violet's off the market,' muttered Brooks.

23. Charlie

(At this rate I could put Mary Berry out of a job . . . but not the Poet Laureate)

'So let me get this straight,' Brooks swept his arm around the kitchen, 'all these are for my sister? All of them? All?'

I put the spatula down and wiped my hands on the apron I was wearing, though as it was already covered in three days' worth of icing sugar, chocolate, dried batter and violet frosting, it was hard to find a clean spot.

'No,' I replied, peering over to where Brooks was standing next to the long kitchen table, and nodded to the tray loaded up with the defects of my baking marathon. 'Those ones you can have.'

He bent down until his nose was almost touching the piled-up cupcakes, broken pieces of cookies and the attempts at glazed doughnuts – I don't want to talk about the glazed doughnuts – and took a long deep sniff. 'What's wrong with these?'

I picked up the spatula again, and ran it around the bowl of cookie dough I was mixing. 'They're not perfect.'

'They look pretty perfect to me.' He picked up the tray and moved to the kitchen island – the only surface as yet untouched by any form of baking. 'Come on, Daddy will find you a home.'

'Daddy?'

'Yup,' he replied, smiling down at the piece of cookie in his hand, in a way I hoped I'd never see him smile again, before throwing it into his mouth. He chewed for a second, then stopped.

I wish I hadn't witnessed the way he rolled his tongue around until a lump of chewed-up cookie fell out, but I had.

'What flavour is this?'

I peered over to where he'd picked it up from; an assorted selection of red velvet, double chocolate chip, regular chocolate chip, white chocolate chip, and peanut butter.

'Peanut butter.'

'Ugh. I hate peanut butter.' He grabbed a bottle of sports drink I'd left on the side when we'd returned from training this morning and downed it in one, before picking up a tea towel and aggressively wiping his tongue.

I stood there watching the entire dramatic spectacle, my lips curled in disgust. I'd like to say it was one of the more revolting things I'd ever seen him do, but I couldn't. Brooks, meanwhile, calmly sat back on the stool like nothing had happened, though he was eyeing the rest of the rejects tray with much more suspicion than before.

'Are you done?'

'Yeah, you need to warn a guy when peanut butter is involved. It's worse than liquorice,' he grumbled as he picked up another cookie, sniffed it, licked it, then took the tiniest bite. 'Chocolate chip. Much better.'

I pointed to the tongue-wiped tea towel, 'Go and put that in the laundry.'

The oven timer went off as Brooks got up, and I turned to grab the newest batch of my efforts – the original chocolate chip cupcakes. Violet's favourite. I already had the frosting prepared on the side, and instead of shortbread letters, I'd found some little red heart decorations in a baking shop I'd passed the day before. Shifting up a batch of cookies to make space on the kitchen top, I placed them down and stood back.

There was a small chance I'd lost it.

It had been five days since Violet had gone home and left me here. Five days of not speaking to her. Five days of missing hearing her voice or seeing my phone flash with a message. Five of the longest days of my life. I'd spoken to her every day for the past two months, so to say I missed her would be an understatement.

I'd woken up the morning after she'd gone, and my chest had ached so deeply I thought I was having a heart attack.

For three elite athletes living together, who pushed their bodies to the limit on a near-daily basis, it had taken me far longer than it should have to find a box of painkillers. They hadn't helped. It was only when Oz kept asking me why I was rubbing my chest that he told me the tight, suffocating agony that felt like my ribs were cracking was actually because of Violet.

I thought I'd experienced heartache before, but it was nothing like this constant dull ache in my chest.

That evening, after a full day's water training, the baking started.

It began small – a batch of chocolate chip cookies – but they led to the double chocolate chip cookies, which led to white which led to red velvet, and so forth. Somewhere along the way my brain kicked into gear, while I tried to decide how I could prove my love to Violet.

I'd looked around at my baking exploits and figured as I'd asked her to be my Valentine with cupcakes, therefore I could tell her I loved her with them too. I even tried to create a violet flavour especially for her, but that was soon scrapped when I realized they'd probably end up tasting like soap.

Back to the trusty chocolate chip with violet frosting I went.

But 'Proving My Love' cupcakes were different from Valentine's cupcakes, and they had to be absolutely perfect. The first attempt hadn't turned out quite the way I'd hoped, so I made some more . . . and more . . . and more.

You see where I'm going.

After two trips to the supermarket on my bike, I decided to take Oz's car and load up the boot with ingredients so I wouldn't have to go back again.

The ones I'd just made space for were my thirteenth effort. I was standing in the epicentre of a sugar explosion. I glanced down at the bowl of cookie dough and slumped back against the stove.

Yup. It was official. I'd lost it.

Maybe we could have an impromptu bake sale, because even Brooks couldn't eat all these. Not that he wasn't trying hard. However, he was sniffing everything before he ate it.

'You didn't make any peanut butter cupcakes, did you?'

I shook my head. 'Nope.'

'When is this house no longer going to resemble the inside of Willy Wonka's factory?' asked Oz, walking into the kitchen and sliding onto the stool next to Brooks, only to jump back off and flick the kettle on.

I scrubbed a hand down my face with a deep sigh at the new job I had to add to my list.

'Today. Maybe tomorrow.'

Probably tomorrow as three solid days of baking would take longer than an afternoon to dismantle. I didn't want to count how many cookies there were.

'And explain to us again, why all this?'

'Well,' I began, trying to come up with something that didn't make me sound crazy. 'It was helping me think.'

'About Violet?'

I nodded, 'Yes. I need to prove that I love her for her, and that my feelings aren't because of an accident or because of Evie. I think.' To be honest, I wasn't entirely sure. I'd kind of lost track of everything amidst all the sugar. I was still largely confused at how I'd gotten into this mess. I just heard the 'prove it' part, and that's exactly what I intended to do. Though I'm not sure how close I was.

'How do you fall in love with someone by accident?' asked Oz, which was the question I'd been asking myself.

'I don't know.'

'I mean, you can't control who you love. The entire notion is absurd,' he grumbled, again repeating my

329

exact sentiments. 'Love isn't accidental. It's purposeful. It has meaning.'

I nodded, I was in total agreement.

'Do you want to send any of these to Kate?' I interrupted before we fell down another rabbit hole of Oz's attempts to get Kate back, and while I really *really* wanted to be empathetic and a great friend, I also had my own shit to deal with. Namely how to get rid of/pack up/eat enough baked goods to have McVitie's worried.

'Um . . . no, she'll never believe I made them,' he replied, removing three large mugs from the cupboard and throwing a tea bag into each. 'Have you heard from her?'

I shook my head. 'Nope. She wanted no contact. Have you heard from Kate?'

His response was the same – a long, slow shake of his head. I'd only been dealing with it for a matter of days. Oz was going on six weeks. At least now I understood why he'd nearly killed us in training every day. For the first time I was thankful Oz couldn't cook. There's no way this kitchen could handle baking from both of us.

We turned to Brooks, munching away on another chocolate chip cookie, and I raised my eyebrows at the little pile of peanut butter ones he'd pushed to the side on the counter.

'I haven't heard from her either, if that's why you're looking at me like that. And I'm not getting involved. Consider me the Switzerland of the house.' He threw the rest of the cookie into his mouth. 'She doesn't text me about stuff like that anyway.'

'Wonder why,' Oz mumbled.

'Mate, I think you're going to be fine. Keep baking like this and I'll go out with you, if you're not too fussy about which Brooks you want.'

That had me cracking a real smile, the first one all week. 'Sorry, I kind of have my heart set on the one with the purple hair. Plus, you snore.'

'Fair enough,' he muttered, this time stuffing one of the rejected cupcakes into his mouth, whole. 'I'd end up seriously fat if you fed me like this every day, anyway. You and Violet can be drama queens together.'

I didn't point out that I hadn't actually fed him at all, or that I wasn't a drama queen, and instead picked up the tea Oz had pushed in front of me and slurped in a boiling mouthful.

'So, what's the plan then? And what have we got here?' He peered over the rejects tray which Brooks seemed to be hugging. His hand was slapped away as he reached for a double chocolate chip. 'Oi. You were just complaining about getting fat.'

Brooks lifted his shirt and gave his stomach a hard pat. 'No chance. This six pack's not going anywhere.'

'Give. Me. A. Cupcake.'

Brooks scanned the tray, his eyes slowly moving back and forth before he reached for the smallest one and placed it Oz's open palm.

'I hope you get fat,' Oz grouched, before shoving the entire thing in his mouth.

'Here.' The pile of peanut butter cookies was pushed over to him. 'You can have these ones.'

Oz's frown deepened but he stayed silent as he picked one up. At least this time it wasn't spat out.

'So, what's your plan?' asked Brooks. 'Apart from giving my sister enough cavities to keep every dentist in business forever.'

'My plan?'

'Yeah. You have a plan to get her back, right? To prove your love, or whatever?'

'I mean . . . yeah. I'm working on it. Kind of.'

'Well . . .' Brooks pinned me with a stare, his eyes wide with expectation. 'What is it?'

I was about to answer when Oz bent down and picked up something he'd spotted on the floor by his stool.

'What's this?' he asked, holding a piece of paper in the air.

Shit.

'Give me that.' I reached over, only I was too slow and Brooks snatched it before I could.

'What is it?'

I sighed. I mean, I was already fairly close to rock bottom, and if the current scene was anything to go by, there was no reason why I couldn't make it a little further down.

While I'd definitely gone overboard with the sugar, it had provided me with a little thinking space . . . not enough, but some. Somewhere between the double chocolate chip and the peanut butter flavours a couple of ideas had popped into my head. Though I'm not sure they were any more solid or thought out than the 'Proving my Love' cupcakes.

Last night, in lieu of sleep, I'd spent four hours recording every character Violet's character had dialogue with in *Twelfth Night*. I'd made an MP3 which I planned to send her, so she could still rehearse without me. On a more selfish note, I hoped she'd hear my voice and miss me so much it felt like she was also having a heart attack.

I didn't feel I should be the only one.

The second thing was the piece of paper my two housemates were currently reading with ill-concealed amusement.

'I'm writing Violet a poem,' I said, with all the confidence I could summon. It wasn't much, I tell you.

'Twenty-one chocolate Valentine's cupcakes. I knew my heart would never be the same,' Brooks read aloud, though I wished he wasn't frowning so deeply. 'Hmm. I think you need to work on this, it doesn't rhyme.'

'It's not supposed to. It's a sonnet.'

'A what?'

'A sonnet.'

His eyes flicked back to mine, bulging wide as his finger snapped loudly, 'Hang on a minute, Valentine's cupcakes . . . Those cupcakes you made with the purple frosting weeks ago, were they for Violet too?'

Oz groaned, while I rolled my eyes.

'Yes, why do you think I'm making all these?'

'Honestly, no idea. I just thought you liked baking and decided to send her some.' He looked back down at the paper, 'It says here chocolate, *just* chocolate, but I distinctly remember those ones being chocolate chip. I still think about them.'

He reached across the counter where a lone biro was resting on the side, and I watched him scribble across *my* piece of paper.

'What are you doing?'

'Adding in the chip. You need to get it right even if you're not rhyming.'

'No!' This time I successfully snatched up the paper from his grip. 'Chocolate chip doesn't fit.'

'What?'

'Each line has to be ten syllables.'

'Why?'

My shoulders jerked up, 'I dunno, it's the rules.'

'Of what?'

'Sonnets.'

'Says who?'

'Shakespeare?' I snapped back, wondering what was with the twenty questions. 'Look it up.'

This entire time Oz had been watching the back and forth like he was sitting centre court at Wimbledon, only with an expression of amusement I hadn't seen on him in a long time. His grin widened even further as Brooks pushed out of his stool, rounded the counter and roped me into a big hug.

'Oh mate. Shakespeare?' he cried, holding me in a grip I couldn't escape from. 'Is this what my sister's turned you into? You poor bastard. I'm so sorry. It'll be okay. There, there.'

I eventually managed to push myself free, and the laugh which barrelled up my chest worked to dislodge some of the tension sitting there, especially when he tried to stroke my head. 'It's fine. But thank you for the sympathy.' I put my arm back around him, 'I'm sorry I've fucked up so much.'

'Nah, you won't have done,' he grinned. 'She's just

doing that thing that girls do, you know . . . they like to prove a point. She'll calm down.'

'Not on all this sugar she won't,' Oz laughed, his mouth full of the cookie he'd grabbed after Brooks left the tray unguarded.

I threw down the tea towel I was holding, groaning as I glanced around the kitchen. 'I probably shouldn't send all of this, right?'

Oz's eyebrows raised so high they almost disappeared into his hairline. 'Um . . . there's enough here to last her all year.'

'So . . . no, then?'

'Pick your best twelve and send those,' he suggested.

Yeah. I could do that. Twelve made more sense than several hundred. Thank God I never pressed order on the three dozen cupcake boxes I'd found on Amazon.

'Sure you don't want to send any to Kate? There's plenty,' I laughed.

'No, she's the chef of the two of us,' he replied, and the sadness in his tone was so profound I pulled him into a Brooks-style hug. 'God, we're a mess aren't we?'

'Yeah.'

'Now we've sorted Violet, there's something else we need to discuss.' Brooks downed the remainder of his tea, as Oz and I turned to him. 'What are we doing about Evie?'

I leaned back against the counter.

One thing I'd learned through this mess I'd created, rubbing your fingers against your temples did absolutely nothing to ease the pressure. Or maybe it was that I had too much. Either way, every time I thought of Evie my blood boiled so quickly my brain was on the verge of exploding. My head simply did not have the space to figure out how to prove to Violet I loved her while also coming up with a solution to get Evie out of my life for good. Therefore, as Violet was my priority, I'd concentrated all my remaining brain cells on her.

'I haven't got that far.'

'Well, I'd say as she's trying to ruin your life, you could always ruin hers.'

Oz got up to flick the kettle on again. 'Remind me never to get on your wrong side.'

'I'm serious, you could fuck with her grades or something. What's the point of being able to hack the university servers if you don't use it when you need to?'

'But what would that solve?' I crossed my arms over my chest, 'She's leaving in a few months anyway when she graduates. And now term is over we no longer have class together.'

'To be fair, failing grades isn't going to stop her fucking with Charlie,' Oz replied and looked over at me, 'Why don't you call Olly, he might be able to offer some advice.'

'Why?'

'Because he's reading law. You never know, he might have some words of wisdom.'

I mean, one more brain added to the mix couldn't do any harm.

Oz put three more steaming mugs of tea on the counter and sat back on his stool. Brooks' chin was propped on his fist as I hit dial. Olly answered on the third ring.

'Charles? What's up? How's training going?'

'Yeah, good thanks, mate. Hope you've got the tissues ready, because Cambridge is going down.'

'I'd rather you lost, if I'm honest. I've bet a lot of money on Cambridge winning now we have a new Blue Boat Cox.'

There was a sharp intake of breath to my right, followed by a loud tut. We hadn't talked much about the fact we'd be racing directly against Kate. Outwardly Oz seemed more determined than ever to win this year – his final year as president – but I knew he wasn't happy that winning would mean Kate would lose her first race in Blue Boat.

'How is she?' he asked.

'I haven't seen her for a week or so, but she seemed okay. Always with that hot friend of hers.'

'Imogen,' added Brooks, helpfully, because he may or may not have a huge crush on her.

He definitely did.

'Ol,' I interrupted before we got into a debate about the hotness of Imogen, 'I need some advice about Evie.'

'How someone hasn't strangled that girl yet is beyond me.'

Next to me, Brooks and Oz mumbled their agreement.

'Well, yes, anyway. Long story short, since she moved into my philosophy class and I started dating Violet, she's become even more of a pain in the arse than usual.'

For a second I thought he'd been cut off, 'Hang on . . . Violet? Violet Brooks? You're dating? When did that happen?'

337

Ah. And there was the problem with grand plans and keeping secrets. Because when they all fell apart you had to start from the beginning to explain yourself, again. Which meant you realized how totally and utterly you'd ballsed things up.

I'd just opened my mouth when Brooks jumped in. 'Evie joined Charlie's class. Charlie needed a fake girlfriend to protect him, and asked Violet. Evie's been tormenting them because now Charlie's decided he loves Violet. Something happened with Evie and the race last weekend, Violet's in a mood. Charlie needs to sort his shit out and now our kitchen currently looks like the next season location for *The Great British Bake Off*.' He looked at me and shrugged, 'Did I miss anything?'

I picked up my tea. 'No, think you got it all.'

'Great. Thought it would be quicker if I told it.'

There was silence on the line and the three of us leaned in, waiting to see if Olly was going to speak. Unless he'd stopped listening and disconnected. I wouldn't blame him.

'Well, that's quite a predicament, isn't it?' he said, eventually.

'Yeah. You don't say.'

'You could try a restraining order.'

My eyes flicked left and right. Based on their expressions both Oz and Brooks seemed to think a restraining order was a viable option. It wasn't something I'd ever considered, though probably should have. If it was just me, I'd have left it because a restraining order felt too serious. Too over the top, like I couldn't deal with problems myself.

But now my problem was affecting Violet, I was quickly reconsidering.

'How long does that take?'

'I dunno, d'you want me to ask my mum? She'll be much better at this than me. She might have more ideas too.'

My face screwed tight as a cringe slithered up my spine until my shoulders were practically touching my ears. I wasn't sure which was worse, that Oz and Brooks both snickered either side of me, or that Olly was being deadly serious.

Olly's mum, or Lady Greenwood of St James as she was known professionally, was President of the Supreme Court of the United Kingdom. Therefore, was so far above the pay grade of any problems I was having with my ex-girlfriend, even the thought of her knowing the broad details was mortifying enough for me to stop this conversation dead.

'No, Ol. Absolutely not.'

'Are you sure? She'd probably quite enjoy it,' he replied, which didn't make me feel any better.

'I'm sure. I'll figure it out.'

'Okay. Now what was this about *The Great British Bake Off*?'

'Charlie's been thinking again.'

'That's what I like to hear . . . hang on.' There was a muffled sound down the line, though none of us could make out what was happening. 'Hey, I need to go. Send me some of Charlie's baking thoughts, will you? I need something to get me through the mountain of holiday work I have.'

'Sure, no problem. Thanks, Ol . . .' but the line had already gone dead.

For the first time all week I felt like I'd achieved something. What that achievement was, I didn't know. But at least the hopelessness churning in my stomach had disappeared.

Oz clapped his hands together. 'So, the plan of action is research restraining orders. You'll send your sonnet poem thing to Violet with her purple cupcakes, and Olly can have two dozen of the rest of these.' He turned, pointing to the mountains of trays and cooling racks.

'That will still leave us with approximately four hundred cookies and God knows how many cupcakes.' I rubbed my head, hard. 'What do I do with the rest?'

I hadn't finished my question before Brooks was on the phone calling in the cavalry, loosely translated as the entire crews from Blue Boat and Isis. I just caught my phone before the two dozen message notifications in ten seconds almost buzzed it off the counter.

It flashed up with the last message.

Bitters: *I'll bring the milk.*

24. Violet

(Dogs > boys)

I'd officially eaten all the chocolate.

Definitely all the chocolate in the house anyway, possibly in England.

If the empty bowl I was currently running my hand around wasn't evidence enough, I had two large spots on my chin which confirmed it. I didn't want to calculate exactly how much chocolate I'd eaten but let's just say there'd been ten Easter eggs in the house at the start of the week, and now there were none. I stopped short of licking the crumbs from the bottom of the bowl — or let's face it, tipping the bowl into my mouth — but I couldn't deny how much I wanted to.

At least my misery drew a line somewhere, and for that I should be grateful. I'd been wondering when it would happen, been waiting days for it and now I had the answer. Or I would if I knew what the date was. I'd even settle for the day, because I didn't know that either.

Misery wasn't known for its diary-keeping abilities.

Making a half-hearted attempt to plump up the cushion I was lying on without moving, I hunkered back down under the duvet, taking extra care not to disturb Buddy who was snoring away on my feet at the other end of the sofa. The most faithful boy in my life. I was going to pretend that he hadn't left my side for the past week because of how much he loved me and didn't like me being sad, and not because I was a walking trail of crumbs.

I peered up and looked at him. 'You love me most, don't you?'

He lifted his head and opened one eye, before letting out a loud groan and going back to sleep.

Understandable; I'd probably be exhausted too from all the listening he'd had to do. And unluckily for him, he'd been the only one I'd wanted to talk to, aside from Stella who'd also been witness to my meltdown since we arrived home on Saturday.

Actually, I'd been okay on Saturday. Sad, but okay.

Resigned in my decision that Charlie and I needed to take a break, but okay.

I'd done the right thing.

In what might have been my greatest acting achievement ever, neither of my parents seemed to notice anything was wrong with me at all. But Sunday became Monday, and as the freak heatwave disappeared into more pre-April showers, my mood descended into the black.

While I like to give an outward appearance of having my shit totally together, I do not.

I'd always thought I was a strong, badass, independent woman, whereas in actual fact, it turns out I'm the type of girl who obsessively checks their phone every thirty seconds on the off-chance the boy she loves has messaged her, even when she'd told him not to.

Somewhere around Tuesday it occurred to me that I'd never been dumped before, and therefore everything I was experiencing – the heartbreak, the radio silence, the feelings of despair – was all totally new, and I was therefore completely unequipped to deal with it.

It seemed only right that I became a blubbery, catatonic mess.

I couldn't even blame PMT for the week-long meltdown.

Nope.

This was self-sabotage Violet Brooks style. I had no one to blame but myself. Charlie hadn't even messaged me. He'd followed my 'no contact' order to a tee.

Reaching out, I stroked one of Buddy's silky black ears, 'Shall we watch the rest of *The Holiday*?'

I took his lack of response as an affirmative, and pressed play.

'See,' I sniffed. 'This is the bit where Amanda realizes she loves Graham too, and goes back for him. She goes back for him, Buddy boy.'

Nope. It was no good, I hit pause again while I went in search of one of the many crumpled up, already soggy tissues I'd blown my nose into and/or used to wipe away one of a thousand tears. It was a wonder I had any left to be honest.

I should have known it would happen. I should have prepared myself better. I should have allocated myself a daily cry allowance, then got on with my life for the rest of the time.

But theory and practice are two entirely different beasts.

'Let's spend some time apart, I said. It'll do us good, I said. Let's have a break with no contact. God, you're an idiot, Violet.' I sobbed into the piece of loo roll

I'd found. 'Charlie was right, it was our first fight and nothing more. And . . .' hiccup, 'now . . .' hiccup, 'he's probably . . .' hiccup, 'dumped me.'

Once more Buddy's head lifted, and he looked up at me with his soulful brown eyes.

'Yeah, yeah. I know. I know that if he doesn't come back to me then he was never mine in the first place, blah blah blah,' I wailed, 'but I thought I might have at least had a text message, or something to say he missed me. He doesn't even miss meeeee . . .'

I took another long hard sniff and a deep breath, before dissolving into *another* round of tears. Buddy moved around and sat up.

'Yes, I know I told him not to message, and I haven't texted him either.' This time the sleeve of my jumper was used to wipe my eyes. The tissue had turned to pulp. 'But I'm starting to think it was a stupid thing to do. What if I've lost him?'

Buddy crawled into my lap and took one long lick of my face, mopping up the fresh tears which I'd failed to stop.

'Thank you,' I sobbed, wrapping my arms around his neck, and this time he settled down on my chest waiting for me to stroke his ears. 'Thank you for being the best puppy, and listening to me all week. I love you.'

The steady rise and fall of his breathing, plus the occasional yelp as he began dreaming, was enough to calm me almost into my own sleep. Almost. If my brain wasn't going around and around, I'd definitely be snoring away just like him.

Was it ridiculous I was lying on the sofa, my heavy

winter duvet on top of me, *The Holiday* paused on the TV, while a fire roared in the hearth?

Possibly.

Anyone passing by would assume I'd been stuck in a Christmas time warp. Though maybe if I wished hard enough, I'd be transported back to before December when I could ignore Charlie's text messages the first time they came through.

He'd have to get someone else to help him deal with Evie.

It was lucky Buddy was pinning me down with his dead weight, because even the thought of Evie made me want to get up and smash something. Fortunately, my mum also decided to use the moment to come and find me, peering around the door to the snug with what could only be described as a look of abject horror as she took in the scene.

If I wasn't still on the verge of tears, I'd have burst out laughing.

'Um . . . why are you watching a Christmas film?' she asked, her tone making it clear she was easing me in for what I knew was about to descend into interrogation territory. The arms crossed over her chest confirmed it.

Sadly for her, I wasn't in the mood to talk.

'I'm not. It's *The Holiday*.'

'Do you really need the fire lit? The sun's out.'

'It's nearly night-time.'

'It's four o'clock in the afternoon,' she shot back, and the restraint finally snapped. 'Honestly, Violet, I don't know what's been wrong with you the past few days. Have you got too much coursework? Is that it? You've been in your bedroom most of the week, you've barely spoken, now you're in here . . .' she swept her arm around, before picking up the empty chocolate bowl, along with several screwed-up balls of foil wrappers, 'where you've been watching Christmas films all day long. Yesterday I saw you eating Buddy's Easter egg. That was dog chocolate, Violet. *Dog* chocolate. Not to mention you completely missed Easter lunch.'

Ah, yesterday was Sunday, that made today Monday. Misery calendar, consider yourself updated.

'There's nothing wrong.'

There was.

'I'm fine.'

I wasn't.

'I didn't eat Buddy's Easter egg.'

I did.

She shook her head, marched across the snug, flung open the curtains and cracked the window wide. Jesus. My eyeballs were nearly singed from the brightness of the sun I wasn't expecting. It was low enough on the horizon that it shot right through the gap in the trees, and hit the spot on the sofa where I was lying.

'Okay, well, while you're festering in here for god knows what reason you won't tell me, can you at least let me know about this Saturday?'

Ugh, Saturday. I'd been trying very hard not to think about Saturday. Something made virtually impossible when my mum kept bringing it up every five minutes.

'For the fortieth time, Mum, I don't know if I'm going to go to the Boat Race. I haven't decided. I don't see why we all have to go together.'

346

'Because it's Hugo's last race and we're meeting the Mastersons and Oz's mum for lunch first, and it would be good if you came too. Everyone's going to be there.'

I grunted something indecipherable, but thankfully it did the job and she walked out with an exasperated shake of her head. I knew one thing for sure, and it was that under no circumstances was I going for lunch with Charlie's parents.

Unfortunately, my mum didn't manage to get fully out of the room.

'Knock, knock,' came a familiar voice right before Stella's head appeared around the door, bringing my mum back in with her. Buddy's tail thumped hard, but he clearly decided he'd seen Stella enough this holiday that she didn't require a more excitable greeting. 'Bloody hell, it's like a furnace in here.'

I hid the smirk as my mum's lips pursed. 'Quite.'

Stella put down a parcel she'd carried in and whipped off her jumper. 'Ooh, great, are we watching *The Holiday*?'

I nodded.

'Can we go back to the beginning? Or at least to when Cameron punches Ed Burns, that's my favourite bit.'

She caught the remote I tossed to her. Yeah, I could watch him being punched.

'Stella, you're coming to London on Saturday, aren't you?' began my mother, totally ignoring the fact that Stella was also now under the duvet with me, so we could both watch the only acceptable year-round Christmas film.

'Dunno, why? What's Saturday?' she replied, not

taking her eyes off the screen as she found the spot she was looking for. It was a wonder my mum hadn't stood in front of it.

'The Boat Race,' she tutted, like there couldn't be anything else happening on Saturday. Not sure everyone attending the Grand National would be of the same opinion, but Jane Brooks didn't agree with horse racing. 'It's Hugo's last one.'

Stella's eyes flicked to mine, and then to my mum, 'Oh . . . um. Maybe. Not sure. We might have to be back in Oxford.'

That did it, the annoyance radiating from my mother could no longer be contained.

'You don't have to be back in Oxford, the entire university will be in London,' she snapped, pinning us both with one of those steely glares only mothers could perfect, while she tried to figure out what was going on.

She stood there a good thirty seconds, but it wasn't the first time my mother had attempted to break us with her narrowed glower, she'd been working on it since we were teenagers. We, however, had become experts in standing our ground, therefore would be saying nothing.

I didn't inherit my stubbornness from my dad's side of the family, that's for sure.

'What's that?' I nodded to the large box in Stella's hand, hoping it might distract my mum enough that she'd get bored and leave us alone.

'Oh, nothing exciting,' she replied as she picked up her phone and began tapping away on the screen.

'Honestly, you girls . . .' Mum harrumphed, but didn't add anything else before she walked out none the wiser.

Stella put the box on my knee. 'It's for you, it was at the door. Thought you wouldn't want Janey getting her nose in before you saw it.'

I snorted out a laugh. 'Thanks.'

'Take it you've still not told her about Chuckles?'

'Nope.' I shook my head. 'If I tell her, it makes the whole thing real, and I don't want it to be real if it's over. Because she'll make it a hundred times worse, and I just want to be left alone to be miserable for a little bit. Though frankly I'm surprised my big-mouth brother hasn't told her, since he's the favourite child.'

'You're so dramatic, Vi,' she replied. 'Plus, you don't know he hasn't.'

'He definitely hasn't.' I knew that as well as I knew my own name, which was one saving grace. If my mum knew, there's no way she'd keep it to herself, and I just couldn't handle her level of questioning when I didn't have the answers to give her.

'Anyway, can you open that box please. It smells like sugar.' Stella looked up from her phone and the essay she seemed to be typing. Even with my mum's quick clean-up it was still very obvious I'd spent a lot of time with chocolate this week. 'Not sure you need any more though.'

Ripping open the protective packaging, I pulled out a shoebox-sized parcel wrapped up with a thick violet ribbon, tied in a bow at the top. Tucked underneath were two notes. Or rather a Post-it and an envelope. My heart kicked up a beat as I spotted the envelope with the familiar black handwriting, but instead I picked up the Post-it with the virtually unintelligible scrawl it had taken me years of practice to decipher.

Hi Weirdo,

Not that you want it, but you have my approval to date Charlie. In fact, you couldn't find anyone better. Please get back together, otherwise I won't be able to fit into my clothes much longer.

Love, your favourite brother x
PS. Give Buddy a kiss, tell him it's from the one he loves most.

I could almost feel Buddy rolling his eyes as he looked up at me. *As if I love Hugo more than you.*

'Exactly,' I replied, dropping a kiss onto his face and, screwing up the note, I tossed it into the fire. Enough of that rubbish. 'Now, what do have we here?'

A thick lump was already rolling its way up my throat as my thumb eased open the cream envelope. Drawing in a loud sniff, I pulled out the letter inside and unfolded it.

Dear Violet,

I know you said no contact, but for this purpose I chose not to listen :)

This week without you has been awful. Really truly horrendous.

I always thought I was fine by myself, but the past few months have made me realize just how much better you make everything — going to class, training, even waking up in the morning — because it means I get to see your beautiful face next to me.

I've missed holding your hand and talking to you, I've missed practising lines with you, even when I fumble mine, but most of all I've missed you.

I'm so sorry I made you feel you weren't important enough to me, because you're the most important thing in my life. And

350

I want nothing more than to start over from the beginning with you as my girlfriend for real.

Anyway, you asked me to prove it. So here goes . . .

Violet Brooks walked into the Blue Oar.
I knew my heart would never be the same.
Her blue eyes twinkled like stars in the sky.
Sleep eluded me for weeks, Violet.
Wine. Sandwiches. Tattoos. Kisses. Shakespeare.
Twenty-one chocolate Valentine's cupcakes.
You gave me a night I'll never forget.
I love this girl with violet-dipped hair.
The course of true love never did run smooth.
Now the cupcakes spell out Please Forgive Me.
The first sonnet I have ever written.
Who knew it was possible to miss a . . .
Person like flowers miss water, or the sun?
But I do. Miss you. Very very much.

If you hate this, don't hold it against me. I promise I'll try harder next time.

Please be there waiting on Saturday. I'll be winning for you, and you alone.

I love you,
Charlie xx
PS. Check your email.

It was hard to tell whether I was crying with laughter, or just plain crying.

'Oh my God,' cried Stella, making me jump because I'd been so engrossed with Charlie's letter I'd totally

351

forgotten she was next to me reading over my shoulder. 'That is the worst poem I've ever read. Will Shakespeare can sleep easy.'

'Shut up,' I snapped, trying hard not to laugh too, as I snatched the paper out of her sight and tried to shove her off the sofa. 'It's a sonnet. And as it's the first one anyone has ever written for me, I'm saying it's the best one I've ever read.'

'Let's agree to disagree,' she snorted, propping herself back up on the cushions, before grabbing her phone again.

'Who'd you keep texting?'

'No one.' The phone was slipped under a cushion, and she reached out. 'Now open the box of cupcakes.'

'No, wait. What does he mean about checking my email?' I frowned, snatching up my phone. 'I haven't had any emails.'

I scrolled through the top part of my inbox – once, twice, three times – I might have 17,532 unread emails but none of them was from Charlie.

'Did you look in your junk folder?'

I shook my head right as I clicked into it. Sure enough, eleven emails from the top was one from Charlie sent two days ago. Two days. I'd wasted two days of my life waiting for a message when one was right here under my nose.

Just in case . . .

Charlie x

352

I frowned; if that was all the message, I didn't understand it. But as I opened it up fully, I noticed an attachment of an MP3 file.

The deep timbre of Charlie's voice sounded out so clearly he may as well have been sitting next to me instead of Stella. 'Hi Violet, I thought you might still want to rehearse while you were at home . . .' there was a muffled throat clearing before, '*Twelfth Night*, by William Shakespeare. Rehearsal tape for Violet Brooks. Act one, Scene two.'

I turned to Stella with a gasp, 'Oh my god, he's put the play on audio so I can do my parts.'

'That must have taken him all day,' she replied. 'Wow, that's dedication. I hate to say it, but Charlie Masterson is absolutely Coco-Pops for you.'

'Yeah,' I sniffed, because it seemed the tears weren't done yet.

'Can you open the cupcakes before you start crying again?'

'How d'you know they're cupcakes?'

'It says in the poem, dummy.'

'Oh yeah,' I giggled, which worked miracles to dry up the current flood of tears.

I pulled the box closer and eased the ribbon off the top. Sure enough, inside were a dozen cupcakes with a thick swirl of violet frosting, covered in little red hearts. I was willing to bet a lot of money these were the chocolate chip variety.

'Seriously,' began Stella, easing one out of the box, 'I need Charlie to stop being so swoony, because it's going to make it much harder for any boyfriend I get in the future.'

'Yeah,' I sniffed, because the tears had started up again.

Stella shuffled along the sofa to sit next to me, throwing her arm around my shoulder. 'Come on, Vi. Don't cry again, it's getting a bit boring. Everything you ever wanted has come true.'

'I know,' I wailed, because I didn't seem to be able to stop myself.

'Okay,' she patted my back, 'it's probably better to get it out now. The Boat Race is in five days, which means you can only cry for another three and then we have two to depuff your face, and wean you off all this chocolate. It's really unfortunate he's sent you those cupcakes, because I'll have to eat them for you.'

I sat up and narrowed my eyes. 'Don't you dare!'

She just grinned back at me and bit down into the frosting. 'So, shall we go and tell Janey we're going to the Boat Race on Saturday?'

I nodded, 'Yeah. We're going to the Boat Race.'

25.

(Warning: the Boat Race may
cause heart palpitations)

Violet

'Hey, watch where you're bloody going, will you?' yelled Stella, turning to the guy who'd almost knocked her over as he ran to the bar, but he'd already been swept up in a sea of Boat Race supporters all clamouring to get there before the men's race. 'I'm kind of wishing we went for lunch with your parents. At least we would have got drinks in first.'

I shook my head. 'No way. We'd have to listen to my mum prattle on about Hugo, not to mention Charlie's parents would be there, and I don't know what they know. I'd be too nervous to eat anyway.'

'Yeah, but then we wouldn't HAVE TO DEAL WITH PEOPLE NOT LOOKING WHERE THEY'RE GOING.' This time her anger was aimed directly at the guy who'd hurried past holding four pints, and very narrowly missed spilling one over her.

At least this time she got a mumbled 'sorry' before he ran off to his friends.

Slipping my hand into hers, I tugged her away from the river path we were walking down on our way towards the Ship, the pub directly on the Boat Race finish line. In hindsight, it probably wasn't the best idea in the world to come here. The sun was shining again so ten thousand other people had come up with exactly the same plan.

But the Ship was the place to be if you wanted the best views.

'Come on, we have forty minutes before the race starts, which means we have just less than an hour to get our spot on the balcony. We can definitely wrangle a space before then.'

'I hope so.'

'We will,' I promised as we walked past an enormous guy standing by the door of the pub, who looked like he was supposed to be helping with crowd control. Except, based on the amount of people inside when we entered, he wasn't doing a very good job.

Stella turned to me, which was about all she could do seeing as we'd hit a thick wall of dark and light blues. Moving forward, backward or to either side would pose more of a problem. We were surrounded by Oxford and Cambridge supporters; TV screens bolted to the walls were all tuned into BBC Sport, and the commentators down on the start line by Putney Bridge.

'Sure you don't want to go and find your parents?'

I shook my head again, though I was certainly more tempted than I had been ten minutes ago.

'It'll pass quickly. It's only busy because the women's race just finished, it'll quiet down once the reserves start.'

At least Stella laughed at my attempt to be positive, while making a point to peer up at the back of the guy in front of her. Her only view. 'Violet, sometimes you're truly delulu.'

'I know,' I grinned, 'but you love me for it, and I'm trying to put the positive vibes out for today. We've got a lot riding on it.'

By a lot, I obviously meant Charlie winning. Then seeing him, kissing him and getting back together. In that order.

'Yeah, yeah.' She rolled her eyes, 'Wine? I need wine.'

I jerked forward from the force of someone passing behind me, 'Yes. Wine. Here's my card,' I thrust it at her, 'order a bottle, then we don't have to go back for more. I'll come and find you. I'm desperate for the loo,' I added, hopping up and down to really get the point across before she got annoyed at me.

By the time I'd pushed through the crowds, found the end of the queue and waited for ten minutes while it moved, I was almost bursting. On the plus side, I peed in record time, and there was space at the sinks when I came out. My reflection stared back at me.

Miraculously, following a couple of days cold turkey, along with all the vegetables I'd swapped out and consumed in place of chocolate, my spots had completely vanished. More miraculously, my mum hadn't even had the chance to hunt me down and pop them before they did.

Broccoli and spinach – 1; Jane Brooks – 0.

I smoothed away all my windswept strands of hair. While the sun might have made an appearance, so had the wind, and walking along the riverbank had given me the 'freshly dragged through a hedge' vibe. It wasn't quite the look I was hoping for the first time I'd be seeing Charlie in two weeks. I gathered it all up and fixed a ponytail, because if I played my cards right, Charlie would be tugging on the end to kiss me in a matter of hours.

One last look in the mirror, straightening the neck of the OUBC hoodie Charlie had left for me, a swipe of pink balm over my lips and I headed to find Stella.

Unsurprisingly she'd barely moved through the crowds. 'Still busy, Vi.'

'I see that,' I replied. Easing my phone from my pocket, I opened up the messages where my last one was still unread.

I'd sent it this morning, wishing Charlie good luck and that I'd see him later.

It was the first message I'd sent him since I'd been home. First *text* message.

In hindsight, I wish I hadn't replied to the MP3 email by email, because I had no way of knowing if it had been delivered, and also no way of knowing if he'd read it. But I'd sent it, thanked him for the beautiful poem, cupcakes and play lines, and told him I'd be waiting for him, as requested. I'd broken my own rule of no contact.

However, even with the poem, the cupcakes and the lines, the lack of response to either was enough to stop the anxiety from the past two weeks disappearing completely.

My spiral was halted mid-turn by a voice calling my name. I turned to find Gordon shoving his way through the throng as hard as he could, if his red face was anything to go by. Even his glasses had steamed up.

'Violet, hello.'

'Hey Gordon, how are you? What're you doing here?' I asked, mostly because I wasn't even sure he was old enough to drink. Not that the guys on the door seemed to give a shit who they let in.

'I'm with my sister, but I can't find her anywhere. She was coming to the bar but that was half an hour ago.'

I swept my arms around the crowded space just as Stella moved into a spot by the bar, 'She's probably stuck in this somewhere.'

Gordon jerked forward as someone pushed behind him, and he let out a loud huff, 'Are you watching the race?'

'Yeah, we're going down to the boathouse once we've got drinks.'

'We?'

'Yeah, Stella's in front of this guy.' I thumbed to the person in front of me. 'You want a drink?'

'Oh, um . . . yes please.' He reached into his pocket and pulled out a wad of fifty-pound notes, from which he peeled off the top one. 'Could you get me a lemonade, and my sister a glass of wine?'

I pushed his hand away, trying to stop my eyes from bugging too much. 'Jesus, Gordy, put that back in your pocket. Why have you got so much money on you?'

'Just in case.'

'In case of what? . . . Actually, I don't want to know.' I peered around the guy in front, 'Stel, can you add a lemonade and another glass of wine to the order?'

'Yeah,' she called back. 'Rosé?'

'Rosé.' I nodded, as a space opened up for Gordon and me to move in next to her.

A huge cheer ripped through the pub just as the bottle was placed on the bar, followed by Gordon's lemonade. 'Come on, that must be the reserve crew finished. Let's go find out who won, and get our space on the terrace. You coming, Gordon? We can text your sister and let her know where you are.'

'Oh okay, sure. Thank you. Then lead the way.'

Charlie

I was not someone who listened to drum and bass, yet that's exactly what I was doing.

It all started two days ago when I'd needed to move Oz's car, and reversed it into a different parking spot right before I remembered I'd dropped my bag in the exact place the back wheel happened to be resting.

The last two dozen cupcakes had been eviscerated, along with my phone.

As every waking minute of the days since had been taken up with training and mandatory Boat Race commitments, I hadn't had a chance to get another one. Therefore, I was currently borrowing Bitters' phone to try and zone into the task at hand, and focus on anything but the adrenaline coursing through my body.

Drum and bass had been his only music option.

I'd been racing since before I was a teenager, but in all that time I couldn't remember a single occasion when I'd been this nervous before. Even with my elbows pressing hard on my knees, my feet were still jittering away. I glanced over at Oz, sitting on the bench opposite me. I wasn't sure if it made me feel better that he seemed to be going through the exact same thing, but it didn't make me feel worse.

The rest of the boys were down at the other end of the changing rooms; Brooks was eating his third protein bar in ten minutes, Bitters and Joshi were playing thumb wars, Marshy was talking to Coach, Fellows was on his phone, Drake was playing with a yo-yo and I think Frank was in the loo throwing up for the second time. At least that's the direction he'd run a few minutes ago.

I'd probably be throwing up too if I wasn't concentrating so hard on not thinking about Violet or wondering whether she'd be waiting for me. Because somewhere in the 250,000-strong crowds lining the banks of the River Thames, Violet Brooks was out there. I'd had confirmation.

Her brother might like to think he was on par with the world's most neutral country, but his defence left a lot to be desired. It had only taken a plate of chocolate brownies to crack him enough that I found out Violet would be in attendance today.

But that's all he knew.

To be honest, I think I was faring pretty damn well considering how my nerves were bouncing quicker than Drake's yo-yo. One minute I could picture her waiting by the dry dock for me, the next I had visions of sprinting all over London until I found her, dropping to my knees as I begged for a do-over.

The only saving grace of destroying my phone was that I couldn't obsessively check it to see if she'd messaged, and torment myself if she hadn't. The only thing

I had done was put in a request to Brooks that he let Violet know, and given him a meal of his choosing in return.

Across from me Oz was twisting his hands together. I pulled off the headphones and rested them around my neck.

'Are you okay?' I asked, shifting over to sit next to him.

He nodded, slowly. 'Yeah. Are you?'

'I think so.'

'We never did get those badges made, did we?'

I shook my head, my eyes flicking up to the giant clock on the wall, 'We still have some time.'

At least that raised a smile. 'Only the next hour to get through before we can start fixing all the shit that's gone wrong lately.'

'Yeah. I hope so, mate. I really do,' I said, scratching through my stubble. I really needed to have a shave, I planned to be kissing Violet all night long and I didn't want to damage her skin. 'How are you feeling about racing against Kate?'

'I dunno. I keep thinking about it, and I just don't know.' He dropped his head with a shake, and a heavy sigh that I felt in my chest. 'Part of me hopes she sprints off the start because then I don't have to see her while I'm racing. But the other part has never been more desperate to win a race than this one. But winning means I'm beating her.'

His eyes flicked to the side, his lips curved in a wry smile that I understood well. He was screwed either way. I felt his anguish, and I most definitely didn't envy him. It would be like me on stage in a competing theatre on Violet's opening night.

Not that it would ever happen.

I nudged into his shoulder, 'I don't know Kate very well, but she doesn't strike me as the kind of girl who'd be very happy if you didn't try your absolute hardest to beat her.' I huffed out a quiet chuckle. I knew Violet would likely skin me alive if I let her win by default because she was my girlfriend, and Kate seemed to be cut from the same cloth.

'No. She definitely isn't,' he chuckled.

'Then it doesn't matter how you feel. You need to try your hardest to win. Set the stroke you made us all keep up with for weeks, no one will beat us then. We might all die, but we'll die winners.'

I didn't add that we had to win. I had to win this race for Violet. I *needed* to win this race for Violet. If we won, everything would be okay.

All heads turned to us as Oz let out a roar of laughter, though as nothing interesting seemed to be happening everyone quickly turned back to what they were doing.

'Yeah, sorry about that.'

'It's okay. I get it now.'

'And I get why you swore off love for so long,' he shot back.

I huffed out a dry chuckle. 'Didn't really work though, did it?'

'Nope.' He shook his head, his eyes glancing up to mine, and his tone quietened, 'I hope Violet's waiting.'

I smiled, 'Me too. And if she's not then I'm going to find her. I'm not losing her.'

363

'Yeah. I know how you feel.' He knocked his knee against mine.

'Don't worry, like Shakespeare said, all's well that ends well.'

He side-eyed me, 'Mate, I don't think that means what you think it means.'

'It means it'll all be fine in the end.'

He shook his head, 'No, it doesn't –'

'What? Yes it does.' I held my hand up before he could say otherwise, and this entire conversation could veer further away from the point I was trying to make than it already had, and I was not in the mood for an English lesson. 'Whatever, if Shakespeare's characters can have a happy ending, then so can we.'

'Romeo and Juliet died.'

I didn't get the chance to argue back as an ear-bleedingly loud whistle pierced the air, and once the ringing had stopped in our ears we all turned to Coach standing in the doorway. 'Okay boys. It's time. Get out there and win this race.'

'Seriously?' muttered Oz, as Coach walked away, 'That's it? No big "If you don't feel like you're going to die you're not trying hard enough" motivational speech?'

Removing the headphones from my neck, I tossed them in my bag, pulled on my wellies and stood up. Taking one last look around to make sure I hadn't forgotten anything.

Baseball cap – check.

Sunglasses – check.

Heart pounding like it was about to break a rib – double check.

I threw an arm around Oz, 'Come on, mate, let's get this over with and go get our girls back.'

Violet

'I can't watch. I can't watch this,' I screeched, while making absolutely no attempt to turn away from the giant screen directly below us on the riverside.

It was like the BBC cameraman was deliberately trying to give me an aneurism from the way he was slowly panning over the Oxford boys as they walked out of the boathouse towards Blue Boat. Every time it stopped on Charlie – which IMO was a lot but also nowhere near enough – my heart gave a little excited pitter patter as it recognized its mate but left me wondering if I should seek immediate medical attention.

If only the helicopters overhead weren't making it impossible to hear any of the commentary.

Stella peeled my fingers one by one from the vice-like grip I'd had on her arm. 'Could you please try and contain the screeching at least until the race begins so that you're then drowned out by everyone else?'

'I agree,' added Gordon, unnecessarily.

'Sorry,' I mumbled, peering out to the crowds lining the paths.

It was nothing but light and dark blue stretching left and right as far as the eye could see. Wall-to-wall Oxbridge supporters took up every available space on the banks, only occasionally broken up by the high-vis vests of the Metropolitan Police. A hundred metres away, the stone arches of Chiswick Bridge were holding up thousands of spectators all clamouring for a view of the finish line.

Flags, scarfs and banners flapped in the wind; the giant Boat Race signs attached to all the railings were trying their best to loosen themselves from their restraints. In the last hour the wind had picked up enough that white plumes crested the choppy waters of the Thames. The buoys were bobbing viciously against the river wall, as seagulls swooped down and missed whatever they'd been hunting, only to fly back around and try again.

This was not going to be an easy race.

Taking a much larger than intended gulp of wine, I managed to swallow it without choking and turned back to the big screen. The Oxford and Cambridge Blue Boats were being held in place by the support boats. Oz, Charlie and my brother were in at the front – stroke, seven and six respectively – and I didn't know if it was because they'd rowed together for a decade, or lived together and their lives were intertwined but behind their sunglasses and baseball caps you almost couldn't tell them apart. The three of them moved in sync, gripping their oars, checking their hold, their faces impassive.

'Is that the one Oz broke up with?' whispered Stella as the camera zoomed into the Cambridge cox with her hand up, a tiny girl with dark brown hair, hunkered down in the stern.

I nodded, 'Yeah.'

'Have you met her?'

'No, they broke up when Charlie and I were still faking it.'

God, that felt like so long ago, when it had been so cold the only thing keeping me warm had been thoughts of seeing Charlie every day. Without him, I'd have probably found some excuse to skip lectures so I could stay in bed. It was almost impossible to remember what my life had been like before; when I'd loved him from afar, when I'd only known him as my brother's friend. Not like now, when the thought of missing out on any more of his life produced such a thick lump in my throat I needed to finish my wine just to swallow it down.

'Okay, Gordy, Violet,' Stella grabbed me as both coxes put down their hands and the umpire's flag was raised. 'Get ready to scream your heads off.'

Even though the start of the Boat Race at Putney Bridge was four miles of river away, as the crow flies it was less than two from where we were standing, and when the flag dropped and the race got under way I swear I could hear the thunderous roar of the crowd.

'We've started strong,' cried Stella, her eyes glued to the screen below, like she was privy to insider information, even though she could see exactly what I could see – the flotilla of support boats, umpires, and the two blue boat shells currently neck and neck at the two-hundred-metre mark. The entire course was still ahead of us.

All around us on the terrace, the crowds had gotten over the initial excitement of the start and the volume of chatter had returned to its pre-race levels. But my eyes may as well have been superglued to the screen. Every so often the cameras would switch from the drones flying directly overhead to the ones attached to the end of each Blue Boat, just above where the cox was sitting, and we'd get a close up of Oz, or the Cambridge stroke.

'Oz definitely looks way more chill than Cambridge, that guy's face is bright red,' Stella mumbled.

But I wasn't watching Oz, because every time he appeared my eyes flickered behind him to catch whatever glimpse I could of Charlie. I didn't blink. I didn't want to miss a second, as his jaw popped with every mighty heave of his oar, and the crew powered forward.

But as Oxford sped through the choppy waters, so did Cambridge.

'Shit.'

The boats had passed the mile marker and, reappearing after Hammersmith Bridge and taking the bend, it was clear Cambridge now had the advantage.

'Don't say it,' I muttered to Stella.

She stayed silent. The guy behind me, however, didn't.

'Ooh, Oxford's had it now. Eighty per cent of the crews who go through Hammersmith Bridge and come out first go on to win. Cambridge will be lifting the cup.'

Gordon got there before I could.

'Shut up,' he snapped, as we both spun around only to come face to face with a light-blue shirt. Typical. 'That means nothing.'

'Oh yeah,' the guy grinned, pointing to the screen. 'Doesn't look like it.'

'They're only half a length ahead.' Stella leaned into

me, 'We're lulling Cambridge into a false sense of security. Oz is going to step on it soon. Look at your brother, he's not going to let Cambridge slip past.'

I wish I had Stella's confidence, but the anxiety building in my stomach was becoming too much to ignore, and as the boats reached the Chiswick Eyot, Cambridge's lead increased.

'Shit shit shit shit shit shit. This isn't good.'

Opening my hand, I found tiny crescent moons in a neat line across my palm where my fists had been clasped so tight, my fingernails had almost broken the skin.

I crossed my fingers instead.

'Maybe they'll do what they did with Bath a few weeks ago,' Gordon offered up kindly, sensing my despair.

I could feel a restlessness buzzing through the air. The chatter had quietened down again, only for loud cheers to rip through the crowds with each close-up of the boats on the screen. Flags waved, scarfs were being spun in the air, dark and light blue streamers blew about in the wind. Twelve minutes had gone by, there was just over a mile left, and it was now abundantly clear Charlie wouldn't be standing on the winner's podium at the end of the day.

The last two weeks apart suddenly seemed totally pointless. I wanted to see Charlie, I wanted to be there when he stepped out of the boat. I wanted to hug him and tell him it didn't matter. Nothing mattered.

Why had it not occurred to me to be down by the boathouse?

Because you never thought they'd lose, said a quiet voice. You thought you'd get there in time.

'Oh my fucking god. Cambridge is a whole length in front, they'll never catch up.' Soon, the tears would be pushing up my throat and then there'd be no stopping them. 'Stella, do you think this is my fault? Are we losing because of me?'

'Of course we're bloody not. Don't be stupid,' she snapped, though her words would be more believable if her tone was less panicked.

'Stella, they're nearly at Barnes Bridge, it's only four minutes from there to here, we'll never make it,' I sobbed. 'We need to get over Chiswick Bridge to the boathouse. Why did I think watching it here was a good idea? I'm such an idiot. Stella?' I screeched.

She turned, took one look at my face, and didn't argue. Just grabbed my hand and pulled.

'Let's go. Gordon, you coming?'

Gordon checked his phone, but with no news from his sister, he popped it back into his pocket and took off after us at a laboured jog.

Charlie

Violet wasn't there. She wasn't waiting for me.

I was too slow to stop the plummet of my heart, I was too exhausted to push away the crippling disappointment of Violet not being the first thing I saw when I turned to the riverbanks.

The surrounding cheers were almost deafening as we drifted under Chiswick Bridge, nine of us utterly depleted and dejected. Nine broken hearts. Oz was holding onto Marshy as he sobbed on his shoulder, behind me Brooks was breathing so heavily he sounded like he was about to hyperventilate. Further down someone – probably Frank – was being sick.

I couldn't bring myself to speak. I had no words. Nothing.

I was utterly devoid of anything, and I honestly didn't know whether it was from losing a race we'd spent eight months training for – day in day out, until our hands blistered and our muscles screamed for mercy – or because Violet was nowhere to be seen.

No, I knew.

The Cambridge crew were all messing about in the water, and I barely noticed as our boat was pulled to the dock by the Oxford support staff. Their faces weren't etched in quite as much sorrow and exhaustion as ours were, but it was close.

'Hard fought race, boys. I'm proud of you.'

'Bad luck, guys.'

'Tough loss. Chin up, there's always next year.'

I nodded along, even though there wasn't a next year for me. Not for Brooks or Oz either. We'd lost our final Boat Race.

Oz jumped out first, his focus trained on one thing and one thing only.

'Go and get her. Don't despair,' he muttered to me, nodding to the hordes of spectators swarming by the boathouse as he took off to go and find Kate. At least she'd been at the finish line.

I took my time getting out. I had nothing to rush for except a hot shower and a plan of action.

'Can't fucking believe we lost,' sniffed Brooks next to me, drawing a hand under his nose.

'Yeah. Me neither.'

'I'm going to get blind drunk tonight. You in?' He looked at me hopefully, with big pleading eyes, before something caught his attention. 'Ugh, never mind. Forgot for a second.'

I spun around to where his frown was trained. A flash of violet pushing through the crowds was enough to send my heart rate back to racing speed, and thudding so loudly that even the helicopters overhead couldn't drown out the sound.

Not for one second did she pause in her sprint as her big azure eyes scanned through the Oxford crew and staff, along with another hundred family and friends standing around, until they finally landed on me. I squinted into the crowd ... was that Gordon next to her? Before I could think any more of it, Violet picked up her pace until she ground to a halt in front of me.

'Hang on,' she wheezed, holding up a finger before bending over double to catch her breath, sucking in as much air as Brooks had as we crossed the finish.

'Violet ...'

'Hang. On.'

I bent down and tried again. 'Violet ... if you need to get air in your lungs, stand up and put your arms behind your head.'

She stood up and slowly did as I'd suggested. 'Like this?'

I nodded, biting the inside of my cheek to stop myself from laughing. 'Yeah. Like that.'

Blue eyes locked into mine, her chest rising and falling with each deep breath until it steadied enough that she unlinked her fingers and lowered her arms.

'You okay?'

'Yeah,' she nodded, her cheeks puffing out as a slow smile crept over her face. 'Hi.'

'Hi.'

I wasn't sure what I was waiting for as we stood in silence, the pair of us staring at each other as though we were checking to see if anything had changed. I didn't know if she wanted to speak or if I was supposed to say something first, because the only thing going through my head was that I'd never seen her look more beautiful. A bead of sweat ran down her temple, a thick strand of hair had come loose from the tie and curled around her neck, the pink of her cheeks . . . the pout of her lips . . . all of it. Beautiful.

'Violet –'

'I'm sorry I wasn't here,' she blurted before I could get another word in. 'I'm so sorry. You asked me to be waiting for you and I meant to be, I was over there.' She jabbed her finger over my shoulder in the direction of the Ship, 'I don't know what I was thinking. I'm sorry. I'm sorry you lost. I'm sorry if it was because of me, or anything I'd done. Thank you for the cupcakes and the poem and the recording, it was all so kind of you. I'm sorry.'

There was silence again, and I think she was done. But you never knew with Violet.

'Are you done?'

She nodded.

373

'First, why would you think we lost because of you?' I held my hand up before she could interrupt. 'Wait, let me get to the end. You have nothing to be sorry for. I'm the one who should be sorry. I'm sorry I didn't tell Brooks sooner, I'm sorry about Evie, I'm sorry for the whole mess I created.'

She opened her mouth to speak, but I covered it with my hand. 'Violet Brooks, I love you. I love you more than I've ever loved anyone, and the past two weeks without you have been awful. I never want to be without you again. I should have said this a long time ago, but will you be my real girlfriend for real. One that everyone knows about?'

A smile broke across her face so quickly that even my cheeks ached from it. 'Charlie Masterson, I thought you'd never ask.'

Stepping in, I tugged on her ponytail, tipping her head until her lips were directly below mine.

'Are you ready for our first kiss?'

The tiny crease appeared on her nose, as it always did when she was confused, 'But we already kissed –'

'Not as my girlfriend, not as someone I officially like –'

She cocked her head, 'You didn't like me before? Huh.'

'Shut up,' I laughed, as a future of never getting a word in edgeways flashed before my eyes. A future of fun, so much fun and love. And non-stop talking. A future of Violet. 'You know what I mean. Just shut up and let me kiss you.'

'No,' she shook her head, 'because I'm going to kiss you.'

Unfortunately, neither of us got the chance for a kiss, because that was the exact moment all the parents decided to make an appearance. Mine, Violet's, and Oz's mum. As well as Gordon, who still seemed to be catching his breath.

But then I got a better idea. A much better idea.

Lacing our fingers together, I tugged Violet up to where everyone was standing.

'Oh, darling,' my mum cried, throwing her arms around me, 'I'm so sorry about the race. You all fought brilliantly.'

'Thanks, Mum,' I replied, easing myself from her grip. 'Hang on. I just need to do something.'

'Charlie, what's going on?' Violet hissed, as I tapped her dad on the shoulder.

Timothy Brooks was exactly how Brooks would look in thirty years. Tall, broad, and with the type of smile that said he was up to no good. Except right now, as he glanced down to where I was holding Violet's hand, he looked confused.

My eyes flicked between him and Jane, who was talking to Oz's mum and only stopped when Tim nudged her hard in the ribs. Harder than he needed given the way she nearly fell into Daphne.

I cleared my throat. 'Jane. Tim. I need to tell you something. I love your daughter.'

Violet mumbled something unintelligible next to me.

To be fair to them, after a few seconds of unblinking staring, they recovered surprisingly quickly.

'And does she love you back?' asked Tim, looking at Violet.

Thankfully she nodded. 'Yes, I do. Very much.'

Jane's head cocked, I could almost hear the whirring going on in her brain. Though it wasn't quite figuring out what I thought it was figuring out.

'Oh!' she snapped her fingers, eventually, 'That's why you ate Buddy's Easter Egg.'

'Mum, Jesus!'

'Wait? Wh . . .' I turned to Violet, 'Um, what? You ate dog chocolates?'

Gripping my shoulders she moved me away from our parents, though they'd already lost interest and were back talking among themselves. That was much easier than I'd expected.

'It's a long story. And you already said you loved me, you can't take it back. No matter what.'

'Don't worry, I'm not taking it back. Not now, not ever. But did you really eat dog chocolate?'

'I'm not answering that.' She grinned, so wide I couldn't stop myself from grinning too.

My lips dropped to hers, wishing I didn't have to keep it quite so chaste, but there was no chance of getting carried away in front of three sets of parents, plus the several hundred people standing around by the boat club. Gordon. Or Brooks for that matter.

'Gross,' he grumbled, as he appeared next to us. 'I did not think this through. We're definitely going to have to come up with some kind of agreement that you don't do this,' he swirled a finger in our faces, 'in my presence.'

Violet was on the verge of telling him exactly what

she thought of his idea, but miraculously I got there first.

'A dozen cupcakes of your choice baked every week, and I can kiss Violet whenever I want. . .'

His eyes narrowed, while he pondered on the offer, '. . . and a dozen double chocolate-chip cookies.'

'I can do that.'

'Then we have ourselves a deal.' He slapped me on the back. 'Welcome to the family.'

Epilogue

Charlie

Five weeks later

'Put your phone away,' I hissed.

'Mate, this is so unbelievably boring. I can't believe you dragged me here,' Brooks hissed back. 'I have no idea what's going on.'

'That's because you're on your phone.'

'No, it's because it's boring.'

'Who are you texting anyway?'

'None of your business.'

The man in front of us with the large head and even larger ears turned around. His entire face had turned beetroot red. 'SHHHH. Will you two shut up?'

Brooks nudged me hard, his eyes wide open as he stared at me. Then went back to his phone, though he turned the screen so I couldn't see.

Whatever, I didn't care who he was texting.

I was too engrossed in Violet.

It was the opening night of *Twelfth Night*, and every single seat was filled. It was running for the next seven days, and each performance would be the same. All sold out. I'd bought a ticket for every show, though based on tonight, I'd be attending alone except for the final evening, when her parents would also be joining.

379

Tonight, however, it was the boys. Quickly peering down the row, at least Oz was watching like he was enjoying it. Unlike the idiot next to me who'd now fallen asleep. The second he started snoring I'd be marching him out, if the guy with the large head didn't get there first.

Unfortunately, Brooks had made quite a valid point, it was a *little* boring. The bits without Violet, obviously.

I'd never realized before because I hadn't seen it all the way through, and I'd only ever worked on Violet's scenes when I couldn't take my eyes off her. But the moment she left the stage it was as though the lighting dimmed, and the scenery became a fraction more dull. Not even Stella could save it. As the audience laughed anyway, I figured it was probably just me who held this opinion.

It didn't stop it from being the best play I'd ever seen, however. As far as I was concerned, anything with Violet in would be the best play.

She'd been working so hard on it, I'd barely seen her. Since we'd returned from Easter break, thankfully my training had become a little easier, but with my finals imminent it was virtually impossible to find much time to spend together during the day. As such we'd been limited to the hour before bed to catch up, before we crashed exhausted, only to repeat it all again the next day.

But I wouldn't change a thing.

We also had the luxury of going about our daily business without the worry of bumping into Evie, because luckily – for us, definitely not for Evie – she'd spent the Easter holidays skiing with her family, and broken her leg. I was choosing to view this situation as karma for the simple fact she'd once again lied to me about staying in Oxford over the Easter holidays, and for the time I'd wasted trying to avoid her. As she was laid up in traction for the foreseeable future, there was no chance she'd be turning up to classes. I'd found out that she'd been given special permission to sit her exams in hospital, seeing as she couldn't move.

I'd also spoken to my dad's lawyer, who'd written up a restraining order, currently burning a hole in the top drawer of my desk. As Evie was too busy mending herself to cause any more problems, I'd decided against sending it. But even knowing it was there already made me feel so much better.

We had one more month left until the summer break, and then hopefully she'd be out of our lives for good. A day it felt like I'd been waiting forever for.

As the final curtain fell on the stage, the roar of applause had Brooks jerking awake.

''S it over?' He scrubbed a hand down his face. 'Thank fuck for that. It must be the middle of the night.'

'Not far off,' Oz replied, not bothering to cover a yawn of his own, 'it's ten-thirty.'

The cast returned to the stage one by one. When Violet made her appearance Brooks had woken up enough to jump up next to me, letting out an ear-piercing whistle and an even louder *whoop* of congratulations. We were near enough the front of the stage that Violet could see exactly who was making all the noise.

Brooks leaned in and pointed to the seat in front. 'She turned the same colour as that guy.'

Ten minutes later, as we made our way outside, Brooks was back on his phone, his fingers flying over the screen and not paying the slightest bit of attention to anyone around him including several people who'd moved out of his way.

Oz thumbed behind him, 'Are you coming home?'

'Yeah, but I'll see you there. I'm going to wait for Violet.'

'Cool,' he saluted, and took off after Brooks who still hadn't looked up from his phone.

Five minutes later she bounded out of the theatre doors.

'There she is.' I caught her as she jumped into my arms, her lips landing dead centre on mine. 'You were phenomenal. Oscar winner in the making.'

'Really?' she grinned at me. 'You really liked it?'

'I loved it.'

Easing out of my arms, she looked around, 'Where are the others?'

'They went home already.'

'Did my brother manage to stay awake?'

'Only for the first hour,' I laughed, putting my arm around her, where I intended to keep it as we made our way back.

'I'll take that as a win, it's more than I was expecting.'

A little alley ran down the side of the theatre, and halfway down two people were pressed so close together they could have been mistaken for one larger human, if they hadn't been writhing into the wall while they played the sloppiest game of tonsil hockey. In fact, I'd have passed them by without noticing them at all, but a car across the road switched its headlights on at the very moment we did, and I happened to catch a pair of shoes I recognized.

Only one person wore shoes shiny enough to reflect the lights of a car.

Giving a little chuckle, I nudged Violet, and nodded down the alley.

'Look who it is,' I whispered, 'someone's made a fan.'

Violet gasped. However, it wasn't because she recognized the shiny shoes; she didn't. She did, however, recognize the Nike high tops Leo's companion was wearing.

'Stella?' she shrieked.

I don't think I've ever seen two people jump apart and in the air simultaneously so quickly. I also couldn't contain my amusement. I didn't even bother trying as I doubled over with laughter loud enough that it echoed off the hard brick of the alley.

'Charlie, stop laughing,' Violet snapped, giving me a swift kick on the ankle at the same time. But I barely noticed, the only thing going around in my head was, *'I knew it. I was right.'*

By the time I'd managed to compose myself and stand back up, Stella's head was in her hands while Leo was a little to her right looking more smug than I'd ever thought it was possible to be.

'Charlie, good to see you,' he nodded.

'You too mate, good work tonight.'

'Why, thank you,' he grinned. 'Glad you could make it.'

'Wouldn't have missed it.'

I rocked back on my heels. Violet was staring at Stella with her mouth wide open. I knew this look, it was rare on Violet, and I'd only accomplished it once. But it was, in fact, speechlessness.

'Oh, whatever. Leo and I are . . .' Stella huffed finally, without bothering to finish the sentence. 'Don't make a big deal out of it.'

'No, I'm . . .'

I slapped my hand over Violet's mouth. 'We're just on the way home. Congratulations again for tonight. Great job both of you. See you tomorrow.'

Dragging Violet away, I didn't let go until there was a good fifty metres between us and the love birds.

'Charlie . . . did I really just see that?'

'Yes, babe. You really did.'

'Leo and Stella?'

'Leo and Stella.'

She chewed on her lip, words forming in her brain as she did. But whatever it was she was going to say, she thought better of it. Instead, she smiled, and once again all I could think of was how impossibly lucky I was that I'd finally found her. Even if I didn't want to dwell on how exactly I'd done that.

'Come on,' she said. 'It's Sunday tomorrow. You don't have training and I don't have to get up early for rehearsals. We can sleep in.'

'I'll do you one better. We can stay in bed all morning.'

Her blue eyes flared, catching the reflection of the streetlamps so it looked like little flames were burning in each. 'Ooh, that is better.'

Slipping my hand into hers, I curled my fingers around until they brushed her knuckles. 'Told you. Now lead the way.'

Acknowledgements

It's hard to believe it's nearly a year since *Oar Than Friends* was released, and what a year it's been. Seeing my book in stores was truly a 'pinch me' moment. Standing in Waterstones on release day and watching you pick it up from the tables was the biggest high I could ever imagine. I've travelled to signings, met so many of you in person, or connected with you online, chatting and hearing about your favourite books and characters, and what more you want from the Luluverse. It's been truly wonderful. To all my readers, you've made the last twelve months incredible for me; I'm here because of your love and support. I can't wait to see what the next twelve bring, I know it's going to be exciting to say the least.

To Georgana Grinstead, my wonderful agent, I wouldn't have made it without you. I'm so grateful for the unwavering patience and calm you continue to show every day to my never-ending questions about the processes of publishing a book. The constant 'whys?' I've asked, which you answer seamlessly. The opportunity you gave me has opened up so much, and I'm forever thankful to have you on my side, and can't wait to see what the future holds.

To Valentine, Amy, Jos, Kim, Charlie and everyone at Valentine PR, thank you thank you for the wonderful send-off and support you continue to give to every single one of my books, and Valentine especially for all the advice you dole out on a regular basis. It's such a wonderful network you've created, and I'm so lucky to be part of it.

To Hannah Smith, my editor at Penguin Michael Joseph, it's been so fun to work with you on our second book; one day we'll decide which couple we love more.

To Steph, my favourite thing is that we got to hang out so much this year. I'm so lucky to call you my friend.

To Erin and Amanda, thank you a million times for running The Jupiter Reeves Fan Club so seamlessly. It's no small feat but makes my life so much easier. You ladies are amazing.

To Taylor, my brilliant and creative PA, thank you for sticking with me. My newsletter and social channels would be so boring without you, and I'd be spending all my time trying to figure out reels. Readers, if you're ever in Wilmington, North Carolina, please go and visit her bookstore, Beachreads Books.

I can't write acknowledgements without thanking my puppy, dreaming noisily in his bed while I write. You make this life of mine so much fun even when you steal my peanut butter toast or wreck my shins with bruises because you *had* to have the biggest stick you could find. Writing has allowed me to have you, because if I was still working all hours in an office we would never have met, and that is the best thing ever.

Lastly, if you're new to my books and want to know more, please come and hang out with everyone in The Jupiter Reeves Fan Club on Facebook, or find me on Instagram. I can't wait to connect with you.

Lulu xo

He just wanted a decent book to read ...

Not too much to ask, is it? It was in 1935 when Allen Lane, Managing Director of Bodley Head Publishers, stood on a platform at Exeter railway station looking for something good to read on his journey back to London. His choice was limited to popular magazines and poor-quality paperbacks – the same choice faced every day by the vast majority of readers, few of whom could afford hardbacks. Lane's disappointment and subsequent anger at the range of books generally available led him to found a company – and change the world.

'We believed in the existence in this country of a vast reading public for intelligent books at a low price, and staked everything on it'
Sir Allen Lane, 1902–1970, founder of Penguin Books

The quality paperback had arrived – and not just in bookshops. Lane was adamant that his Penguins should appear in chain stores and tobacconists, and should cost no more than a packet of cigarettes.

Reading habits (and cigarette prices) have changed since 1935, but Penguin still believes in publishing the best books for everybody to enjoy. We still believe that good design costs no more than bad design, and we still believe that quality books published passionately and responsibly make the world a better place.

So wherever you see the little bird – whether it's on a piece of prize-winning literary fiction or a celebrity autobiography, political tour de force or historical masterpiece, a serial-killer thriller, reference book, world classic or a piece of pure escapism – you can bet that it represents the very best that the genre has to offer.

Whatever you like to read – trust Penguin.